D0288909

C.1

Immortal
Hope

WITHDRAWN

Immortal Hope

The Curse of the Templars

Claire Ashgrove

TOR®

A TOM DOHERTY ASSOCIATES BOOK • NEW YORK

LAMBTON COUNTY LIBRARY, WYOMING, ONTARIO

C.1

NOTE: If you purchased this book without a cover, you should be aware that this book is stolen property. It was reported as "unsold and destroyed" to the publisher, and neither the author nor the publisher has received any payment for this "stripped book."

This is a work of fiction. All of the characters, organizations, and events portrayed in this novel are either products of the author's imagination or are used fictitiously.

IMMORTAL HOPE: THE CURSE OF THE TEMPLARS

Copyright © 2011 by Valerie M. Hatfield

All rights reserved.

A Tor Book
Published by Tom Doherty Associates, LLC
175 Fifth Avenue
New York, NY 10010

www.tor-forge.com

Tor® is a registered trademark of Tom Doherty Associates, LLC.

ISBN 978-0-7653-6758-7

First Edition: January 2012

Printed in the United States of America

0 9 8 7 6 5 4 3 2 1

For my father,
whose memory beats within my heart.

Love you.

Acknowledgements

To my mother who has stayed beside me during this journey. Thank you, Mom, for everything. You gave me the wings to soar, and I love you very much.

To my wonderful agent, Jewelann Cone, a constant source of sanity in my insane little world. You have the patience of a saint, and your tolerance for my hop-scotching is a blessing. Even if it does make you a tiny bit crazy at times!

To my editor, Whitney Ross. Thank you for believing in me, for your ever-helpful editorial remarks, and your dedication in making this the best it can be.

To Dr. Jeff Gall and Professor David Miller, were it not for your passion for history, I would have never discovered mine, and this series would have never made it to paper. You are divine educators who know not only how to make lessons entertaining, but also push students to meet expectations in a way that leaves them grateful for the hours spent in the classroom. Every collegiate should have the opportunity to learn from professors like yourselves.

Linda Kage and Jackie Bannon—you were with me when head-hopping was awesome character insight, when commas were like crushed peppers in Thai food, and when heroines could have tantrums because that's what conflict is, right? Thank you for learning with me and teaching me. I'm proud to know you, to work beside you, and will never forget the early days in the trenches. Thank you, Jackie, for standing beside me through everything and being able to say, "Shut up and listen."

Dyann Love Barr, what can I say? You're family, friend, mentor, teacher, and colleague. Your wisdom is invaluable, and it has been such a delight working with you on projects. Together with Dennis, the both of you have given me strength, encouragement, and support. Thank you so very much for the years we've worked together, the late-night plotting sessions, hours-long phone calls, and in general, just being there.

To the other authors who have mentored me, my beta readers, and my critique partners: Melissa Lattin, Goldie Edwards, Alfie Thompson, Marianne Stephens, Carla Cassidy, Elisabeth Burke, Heather Snow, Shannon K. Butcher, Katy Madison, Kiss Carson, Alta Durrant, Diana Coyle, Judy Ridgely, Janet Nuckolls, Nancy O'Berry, Arianna Giorgi, Alicia Dean, Candise Cole, Julie Garwood, and Cathy Morrison—each of you has offered insight and wisdom that helped me achieve a dream, and I will never forget the time you willingly spared or your generosity.

Members of Heartland Romance Authors, Midwest Romance Writers, and Mid-America Romance Authors, the support you've given, the lessons you've taught, and the community you've provided is something I'm sincerely lucky to have.

My friends and family—thanks for dragging me out of the cave when I've been there too long and for simply understanding. Without you, I'd have given up long ago. Matt, you gave me the time and constant encouragement, and I appreciate that a lot. Garrett and Pierce, thank you for being the best little boys in this world. I love you very much!

And to Jason, your patience has been unfaltering and your faith unfailing. The time you've taken to read, to listen to me ramble on, to celebrate and encourage, for simply being a part of my life . . . thank from the bottom of my heart. You are a gift I cherish.

Immortal
Hope

The Curse

In 1119, nine knights rode with Hughes de Payens to the Holy Land, becoming the Knights Templar. All were bound by marriage or by blood. Eight were recorded over time. The ninth vanished into history.

Beneath the legendary Temple Mount, the knights uncovered holy relics, including the Copper Scroll—a document written by Azazel's unholy hand. For their forbidden digging, the archangels exacted a sacrifice. The knights would spend eternity battling the demons of Azazel's creation, but with each vile death they claimed, a portion of darkness would enter their soul. In time, they would transform into knights of Azazel, warriors veined with evil, destined to fight against the Almighty.

Yet an ancient prophecy remained to give them hope. When darkness raped the land, the seraphs would return. Female descendants of the Nephilim would carry the light to heal their dying souls.

Centuries have passed. Azazel's might grows to intolerable limits. With the acquisition of eight holy relics, he will gain the power to overthrow the Almighty.

Six Templars stand above the rest in duty, honor, and loyalty. But each is haunted by a tragic past, and their darkened souls rapidly near the end. As they battle both the overwhelming power of evil and the nightmares of lives they left behind, the seraphs are more than tools to victory.

They are salvation.

Prologue

When darkness rapes the land, the seraphs shall
purify the Templars and lead the sacred swords
to victory.

—ANCIENT PROPHECY OF THE
KNIGHTS TEMPLAR

Atchison, Kansas,
October

Abigail Montfort blew out the solitary candle in her
windowsill and closed her eyes, inhaling the smoke-
laced vanilla. Another Allhallows Eve had passed. Exactly 318 had come and gone since she'd given any real
concern to the night the spirits roamed in droves. As a
girl, she'd hidden in the woods, not knowing which threat
posed the greatest danger—the Salem mob or the real
ghouls who waited in the craggy trees.

The same vengeful spirits who would challenge her—as
they did each Halloween—before she could sleep tonight.

Straightening, she pushed open the window to air out
the musty old Victorian. The breeze rushed in. She rubbed
her arms, shivering. Yet she was not cold.

Danger lingered in the atmosphere. A presence watched
and waited. One far different from the malicious shades or
shape-shifting demons she understood. Something stronger. Deadlier.

Tonight, Azazel's dark knights roamed.

They searched for what they were not meant to find, as they had for centuries. For what she and two others were destined to protect—the relics that would give Azazel the power to overthrow the Almighty. She guarded the crucifixion nail, and the dark lord would stop at nothing to secure this one bit of iron stained with Christ's blood. For with it, the unholy ascension began.

She turned from the window and crossed to the front stairs. One hand on the railing, she paused, remembering the cellar door. She dare not bar the Templars' way. Under these old rafters, the holy knights could rest and heal from the evil they combated. She never knew when they might arrive, but no doubt, tonight they'd seek the adytum's refuge. Gabriel's orders demanded she be prepared.

She hurried down the basement stairs and across the stone floor to a recessed iron door. Producing a set of keys from her jeans, she quickly unfastened the padlock and threw open the hasp, propping the door open. She traced her fingers over the bottom half of a wine-colored cross embedded in the wood. Darkness tainted its once pristine brilliance, as it tainted the Templars. They were threatened, but still protected. As she looked after the adytum and the relic, Gabriel looked after God's warriors. They would persevere. If Azazel turned the tide, the archangels would unveil a vessel far more powerful than even the ruler of darkness could imagine.

"Godspeed, noble ones," she whispered as she turned away.

Front door locked. Holy crucifixion nail safe in its reliquary in the wall. House open to the Templars. All was as it should be. At last, she could rest before the demons came.

She climbed the stairs to her private quarters. In her sitting room, she turned on a lamp and went to the window, opening it to peer at the dormant trees. A shudder rolled down her spine. It was too still, too quiet, even for the midnight hour.

As she crossed to her chair, the hoot of an owl froze her in place. The hair lifted on the back of her neck, stood upright on her arms. Demons she could fight. But *that* was no demon, no simple shade or nytym with a child's wisdom. He who cried an owl's song was a thing of nightmares.

And if he was here, there could only be one reason—the sacred nail Christ bore upon his feet. Two thousand years, and he had finally discovered it. God in heaven, it was happening.

Silence hung thick, the thump of her heart a trumpet to her fear.

She dove for the window and slammed it shut. The urge to run bore down hard. Sweat peppered her brow. She still had time to get away. She could run out the front and be gone from here.

Yet fleeing wasn't an option. Her duty was to protect the relic. It was why Gabriel saved her from Salem's mob, why God gave her longevity.

She hurried to the bookcase to retrieve her book of psalms, prayer already tumbling off her lips. The energy around her altered, became more dense as holy might flooded into the room. Her fingers grazed the ancient tome's scarred surface, and a sense of calm flooded her.

It didn't last long.

Darkness and hatred pressed down on her like a mighty hand, suffocating the candles. For one heartbeat, nothing happened. In the next, the window exploded in a deafening shower of glass that blanketed the wood floor. Abigail cried out as fragments pierced the back of her neck and stung the crown of her head.

Noxious fumes assaulted her nose, heavy with the odor of death. She swallowed down the bitter taste of bile and clutched the book in shaking hands. "Begone. You cannot hurt me." She longed to believe the words, yearned for the confidence that came with each recitation. Yet she didn't need to turn around and face the creature to know the futility.

A wash of hot, fetid air engulfed her. She closed her eyes and trembled, a slave to the fear that emanated off the beast. She felt him push at her mind, great jabs that made her head ache from the effort of keeping him out of her thoughts. She could not reveal the hiding place. He knew the nail was here, but he would not learn where. Not as long as she breathed.

Steeling herself against the certain horror, she turned around to confront Azazel's knight.

But it wasn't the horrendous laughter that drained the color from her face and froze her heart. It was the creature himself. The way his dark form held a touch of beauty. His long limbs bore grace; his face carried the glory of God's creation despite his wicked sneer. Ethereal wings, the fathomless shade of endless night, extended from his back to brush against the tall ceiling.

"Azazel," she breathed.

His laughter echoed hollowly. "And so the witch recognizes her master."

A clawed hand snatched at her. Nails raked across her face, shredded the fabric on her arm. The sharp sting jolted Abigail out of her stupor, and she backed up a step, holding the tome in front of her to ward him away.

He laughed harder, his angelic features twisting viciously. "That will not help you now. Where is the nail, witch?"

Seductively, he reached into her thoughts. His quiet murmur lulled her to confide the holy secrets she possessed. Blocking her mind to the invasion, she raised her voice and recited the words she'd used a thousand times. "By all that is sacred, I command you to leave my presence."

Azazel lunged with a bellow of rage. One viselike hand caught her arm. Giving her a fierce jerk, he dragged her closer. She fought off a panicked scream and chanted louder, pushed her thoughts into a far corner of her mind where all she knew was the protection of the words, the power of the Almighty's divine light.

Fury burned behind his soulless stare. "You will tell me."

"No!"

He thrust her away like a rag doll. The power of his mighty arm flung her into the opposite wall. Searing pain split her head. An unmistakable *crack* knifed agony through her body as her ribs shattered. She crumpled to the ground with the broken whisper, "God, help me."

"If *he* cared, he would not abandon you here. Tell me where I will find the nail, and I shall take away your pain. I care for you, witch. He does not."

She knew better than to believe Azazel's lies. He would remove the pain as he snuffed her life. Defiant, she gritted her teeth and struggled to her knees.

Azazel snatched her into his icy embrace. His face inches from hers, his malevolent gaze scored in to touch her soul. He set his hand over her heart. Gentle strokes aroused her flesh, his touch strangely warm and comforting. Azazel whispered near her ear, "I'll take care of you, witch. Whatever he has promised, I shall grant in double."

His thoughts caressed hers. Tempting. Taunting. Enticing her to yield to his wickedness. To surrender her faith and with it, grant him power. She was captivated by the hypnotic effect, and her fortitude faltered. It would be so easy to succumb. Perhaps he spoke the truth. If she revealed the relic, would he grant an eternity of peace?

"Tell me, and I shall make you young again."

Sudden sense jarred her from Azazel's trance. He spoke lies. Trickery was all Azazel knew. Stiffening against his tender touch, she glared through her fear. "I'd rather die."

Thin lips pulled back in a sneer. Laughter erupted from his throat. The pitiful wails of thousands of trapped souls filled the room. "As you wish."

Abigail screamed as his fingers dug through flesh, snapped through bone. Blood blanketed her body with warmth and poured down the length of his unholy arm. Helpless, she watched his stare spark with delight.

Unconsciousness fingered at her mind. She pushed past it and summoned the last of her strength. On a ragged breath, she cried, "Gabriel, unveil the seraphs!"

CHAPTER I

†

Kansas City, Missouri
November

*T**hings kept secret are revealed.*
    Anne MacPherson held the solitary High Priest-
ess card in both hands. Her brow furrowed as she recited
the tarot card's meaning for the dozenth time. Over the
years, she'd had odd cards crop up for her daily self-
reading, but this one beat them all. And it hadn't just
turned up once. Beyond the solitary draw she began each
morning with, she'd done several readings in between
clients, and the High Priestess showed up in every one.
Always in the position of what lay in the near future.

She was about to learn secrets. With the day half gone,
the chances of that being true rapidly dwindled. A night
of unpacking the boxes in her new house's basement didn't
look too promising for prophecy fulfillment either.

Unless, by some odd chance, she stumbled across some
mystical object the old witch rumored to have lived in the
brick Victorian had stashed away. Again, highly unlikely.
Especially since thieves had ransacked the house after the
woman's death. They'd even knocked in the wall searching
for her spell book, according to Gabe, her boss and much-
adored house finder.

"Anne?" Gabe Anderson called from the shop's front
room. "You about ready to lock up for the night?"

"Yeah." She tossed the card on to the top of her deck and stood up. "Coming." She gave the High Priestess another frown before she gathered her purse and jacket. Secrets. *Right.*

Ducking under the heavy curtain that divided the shop's retail section from the reading room, Anne found Gabe hunched over the counter, fiddling with a small brown box. As she approached, he tucked thick gray dreadlocks over his shoulder and smiled. "How's your sister? Did she get back to California okay? I've been thinking about her a lot."

Anne just bet he'd been thinking about her. With the way he'd fawned over Sophie last week, he probably did a lot more than *thinking* about her fraternal twin. Of course, that was the way things went with Sophie. Anne had yet to meet a man who didn't harbor some fantasy about her drop-dead-gorgeous sister.

She shrugged. "Sophie's fine. She has some charity gala coming up right after Thanksgiving. I guess the emcee canceled at the last minute, and she's been tearing out her hair to replace him."

"Well. Maybe this will cheer her up." Gabe pushed the small box in front of Anne.

She glanced down and squinted. Gabe's elegant hand-writing covered the wrapping with fancy loops and swirls. He'd addressed it to Sophie's Malibu home. Anne groaned inwardly. Just what she needed—her boss fawning over her sister. "What's this?"

"One of these." He reached under the counter and produced a clunky gold bracelet. "I found this when I was in St. Louis yesterday. Since you're doing your doctoral thesis on the Knights Templar, I thought you might like it."

Wrinkling her nose, Anne took a half step back. Gabe had an uncanny way of picking up old objects that had some misplaced spirit attached to them. For a man so in tune with the metaphysical world, he sucked at reading energy. Gingerly, she took the bracelet between thumb and forefinger and held it at arm's length.

When a vision of some previous owner didn't immediately assault her, she closed her fingers around the ornament and brought it closer. What she had mistaken for gold was brass. Veins of black patina etched out a series of intricate scales around the large loop, forming two serpentine heads that joined nose to nose. Two small rubies served as eyes. Atop the smooth heads, two inlaid crimson crosses identically matched the Templar mark in her basement door. Though meticulously crafted, the artistry was crude, and the piece obviously held a tremendous amount of age. "St. Louis?" She held it up to the light, assessing the odd play of color in the snakes' scales. Energy rippled beneath the metallic surface, a pulse Gabe had evidently missed. Yet it laid dormant, content to keep its identity hidden. Not too terribly threatened, she tried the trinket on.

Gabe's weathered features crinkled with a mischievous smile. "Yep. You like it?"

"It's interesting." And too big for her wrist. The heavy piece rested at the base of her thumb. If she tucked her thumb against her palm, she'd bet it would fall off without encouragement. She tested the theory, dismayed when the bracelet tumbled to the floor.

A quiet chuckle made her glance up. Gabe shook his head, amused. "It's not a bracelet, Anne. It's an armband. And it's quite old."

"Armband?" Curious, Anne picked up the adornment and slipped it back on. She pushed it over her elbow and higher, until it came to a neat, snug fit above her bicep. "How old?"

Gabe winked at her. "You study it tonight. Tell me later."

His meaning went unsaid. He knew if she studied it long enough she could identify those who had possessed it before. Doing so would take time and concentration, however. A task better left to late-night entertainment after she unpacked her boxes. And after she caught up on the research she'd neglected for the last two weeks.

"Okay." She tapped the package. "This is the same thing?"

"Black eyed, but yes."

Anne fingered the serpents' tiny gemstones. Fitting. And just like Gabe. Red to match her hair, black to match Sophie's. She dropped the package into her purse.

"By the way." He turned around and punched in the store's security code. "I have to leave town for a while. I'm not sure how long." He slid her a sideways glance that set Anne's instincts on alert. She reflexively stiffened.

"I know things are tight financially right now, Anne. I've arranged for you to receive your usual weekly pay, but I'm closing the shop for a while."

Anne's eyebrows lifted. "What? I can run things here, you know. I don't feel right about taking money I haven't earned." Despair tightened her chest. Though she didn't feel comfortable with the generous offer, she had more important things at stake. Two weeks ago, she'd run into a stranger with a particularly old soul at the library. When the woman discovered Anne read past lives, she begged for Anne's card and promised to come in for a reading. Anne felt certain the woman had some link to early medieval France, and since meeting her, Anne had been unable to think about anything else. If Gabe closed the store, she would miss the opportunity to discover what was essentially a firsthand account of the exact era her thesis depended on.

Gabe shook his head as he took her elbow and guided her toward the front door. "No. Take some time for yourself. I know the semester is in full swing at the college. You've got papers coming in from your students, I'm sure, what with Thanksgiving break next week. You can relax and really move into the new house too."

"But—"

He cut her off with a hard stare. "No arguing. You've let your research slip to make time for this store of mine. You've got an interesting theory, and I won't see you jeopardize your PhD."

Steering her through the exit, he pulled the front shade and locked the door. He leaned down and kissed her cheek. "Go on home. Enjoy a paid vacation. Get that thesis finished. Tell me what you learn about those crosses and how they came to be there when I get back."

Before she could stutter another protest, he shut himself inside his car. With a hearty wave of his hand, he started the ignition.

Anne grumbled as she unlocked her Honda Civic's door. Sometimes Gabe Anderson could be the most frustrating man on earth. She'd worked for him for a year—long enough to learn when he set his mind to something, there was no changing it. With a heavy sigh, she slid behind the steering wheel and tossed her purse onto the passenger's seat.

He was right on several accounts. She *did* have a stack of research papers waiting on her desk. There wasn't much else she could do with the house once she finished her unpacking. Fresh paint and wallpaper adorned all the walls. In her favorite colors too—a surprise Anne had gushed over when Gabe first took her to view the Atchison, Kansas, landmark. He was also right about the financial aspect. She counted herself lucky the house had stigma attached to it. Yet while murder dropped prices, the payments left little bargaining room in her budget.

Then there was the matter of her thesis. When she'd developed the premise that the Knights Templar were deliberately sabotaged by the medieval Catholic Church, it had seemed an easy statement to prove. Using the accepted theory that the Templars found something beneath the Temple Mount, she was able to prove their early rise in power tied directly to the Church and backers within the clergy. She'd even been able to nail out proof that the same rise in power and unique freedoms the Templar Order enjoyed came from hush money. In addition, enough evidence lurked between the lines of recorded fact to prove their last grand master was the Church's pawn. But with most of the documentation about the Order's demise lost to time, her driving theory hinged on discovering *what* the Order had found—something no one in history had ever been able to discover. As such, her paper was at a dead standstill, unless she could find the evidence through the metaphysical.

If she didn't manage to prove the statement by Christmas break, Dr. Phillip Knowles would retire, and she could kiss the position as head of the History Department good-bye. As Dr. Knowles' protégée, and the foremost expert on medieval France despite her relative youth, it had been conditionally promised to her.

She turned the key and backed out of the alley lot. Sometimes she hated the drive back to Atchison. But working at a Catholic college dictated she hide her association with the occult. And she loved guiding people through spiritual journeys. She used the cards as a mask to her true talent, which came with touch. One clasp of the hand with the appropriate focus, and she could see her clients' past, present, and immediate future. More than once, she'd made a *real* difference to people in need.

Then there was the fact that twice she'd found trinkets in Gabe's store that held some attachment to the Middle Ages and the Knights Templar. The possibility she might find a piece that would answer, once and for all, why the Church had eradicated the Order kept her driving back and forth.

Maybe this bracelet would tell her something important. She'd spend some time with it when she got home. If it told her anything, she could justify putting off grading papers for another night.

The miles passed as she envisioned the bracelet's possible originations. Egypt, Rome, China . . . all favored the serpent in some portion of culture. But the Templar cross dated the thing as more modern. Only, by the time the Templar reigned, snakes had lost their divinity, assuming instead the symbol of the devil. Had the bracelet been some sort of alms or payment given to the Order? It wasn't entirely out of the realm of possibility they would have marked it with their insignia to keep something so obviously old within the membership.

She chuckled. What would Gabe say if he knew the tattoo on her ankle bore a striking resemblance to his gift? Two intertwined snakes, both circling her ankle in opposite directions. Although hers were black and lacked the curious crosses on their heads.

Still laughing to herself, she swung past Atchison's post office and dropped Sophie's present into the drive-through box. Her sister would get a kick out of the thing. While she hated to listen to Anne babble about the Templar, Sophie loved anything old. Anne would ask to change bracelets with her later and see if her sister's had anything important to share.

Inside the two-story, brick Victorian, the smell of fresh paint welcomed Anne home. She inhaled deeply, searching for the lingering undertones of vanilla that mingled with the aroma. She'd never been able to identify where the scent came from, but it hung in the air, a comfort each time she walked through the door.

She dropped her purse onto the dining room table, then shoved aside her stack of research materials so she could sit down. Sliding off the armband, she held it between both hands and closed her eyes. The energy attached to the piece buzzed against her fingertips, subtly increasing the more she opened her mind. When it filled her veins and she could identify it as a tangible entity separate from hers, she opened her eyes and stared at the serpents.

An image rose with the force of a fist. Clear, concise, it punched through her subconscious and swamped her with intensity. A clouded sky cast hues of gray on a barren landscape. Trees overhung a narrow lane, their leaves droopy with dew. In the distance, a solitary horse and rider stood atop a grassy hill.

She focused on the figure, expecting features to morph in slowly, to fit together like a puzzle until she could grasp a vague expression, a shrouded picture. But with digital precision, the man's features leapt forth. A mass of unkempt dark hair tumbled against his shoulders. Through a hardened stare, dark eyes fixed on an unseen subject.

Strong jaw, firmly set mouth. Harsh, yet oddly beautiful. Power emanated from his cold expression. He kept a hand on a broadsword's plain hilt. The other held his horse's reins. Her belly fluttered, unaccustomed to the strikingly accurate portrayal.

The image shifted, giving her a broader view. He was dressed in full chain mail, and a white surcoat hung from his shoulders. The cloth was pristine, despite the dreary landscape. Her throat slowly closed as she focused on his attire, the bold crimson cross against his chest unmistakable.

Templar.

Her pulse jumped to life with a buzz of excitement. A real Knight Templar had touched this hunk of brass. But when?

She struggled to identify what he stared at on the horizon. A battle? A building? Was he fleeing or arriving? Where were his companions? For that matter, where was he? Panning backward, she focused on the energy, asked it for more information. Yet the vision vanished, leaving her staring at the armband.

Templar. Her gaze riveted on the crosses in the serpents' heads, and she stepped through the vision once more. He looked so regal sitting on that horse. Intimidating, though he'd been at rest. That long hair gave him a roguish appeal, his chiseled features almost threatening. And his eyes . . . Sudden recognition filtered a chill through her veins. She'd seen him before.

Slowly, she lifted her stare to the closed cellar door. The first day she'd walked through the house, she had touched that cross on the door. Like this bracelet, that emblem refused to grant her the vision after the initial revelation. But she hadn't forgotten the picture—a dark-haired knight digging in soft earth in a torchlit tunnel. He had looked up, as if he'd sensed her, and those onyx eyes stared right back.

Determined to discover more about the handsome knight, Anne closed her eyes and focused once again.

* * *

Merrick crumpled under the weight of a heavy blow. His knees hit the hard cave floor, jarring his spine and forcing the air from his lungs. Evading an onslaught of claws and fangs that tore at his arms and face, he arched his back to assess the enraged nytym, one of Azazel's demi-demons. With skin like cracked leather, it had two hate-filled orange eyes and a gleaming set of razor-sharp teeth protruding from a piggish snout—the word *ugly* did not do it justice. The stench rolling off it was enough to make any man nauseous, but Merrick had long become accustomed to the putrid smell.

He scanned the creature's underbelly and tightened his hands around the hilt of his sword. In one swift upward thrust, he drove the blade deep into the nytym's gut. The cretin let out a horrific scream and toppled forward, its face inches from Merrick's. Foul breath washed across his cheek before its teeth slowly closed. Unholy life drained from its body, and the nytym's eyes went dark.

Merrick drew in a breath, steeling himself against the death. Darkness oozed from the gaping wound. It rolled down his broadsword, disappearing into his sword's un-adorned, leather-wrapped pommel. The vileness seeped into his hand, crawled up his arm, and wormed into his blood.

A slow burn spread through his body as the evil spirit wrapped itself around what remained of Merrick's soul. No longer able to support his own weight, he sank to his heels and bowed his head, struggling to catch his breath. God's teeth, nearly a thousand years of fighting Azazel's minions, and he had yet to become accustomed to the pain.

"Are you all right, brother?" Declan's hand came down upon Merrick's shoulder. The Scot's firm squeeze pulled Merrick from the agony that blurred his vision.

"Aye," Merrick managed through clenched teeth. "'Tis no worse than any other."

Declan gave him a short nod and released his hold. He stepped out of Merrick's line of sight, giving Merrick a clear view of their third companion, Farran, as he sliced off a grotesque head. Farran sheathed his broadsword and joined the pair. The darkness hit him as well, and the younger man dropped to his knees with a groan.

Merrick shuddered as the last of the effects rolled through his body. He sucked in a deep breath and rose on shaky legs. "'Tis the last of them. Declan, move the stone." He inclined his head toward a massive slab of rock against the far side of the cavern. There, in the cold dark depths beyond, the stench intensified. Noxious fumes rolled through a jagged crack and filled the cave with death, warning them if they waited to seal the gate, more creatures would soon arrive.

As Declan gave the stone a mighty heave, Merrick sheathed his sword. He tugged off his gauntlets and tucked them into the thick belt at his waist. The weight of his chain mail felt three times heavier than when he had dressed, and his body ached from head to toe. He would not survive much more of this. The weakness worsened with each vile life he claimed.

Farran struggled to his feet, equally affected by the evil's power. His features pulled tight, grim lines that spoke to the pain none of them could escape. Behind the blond man's eyes, anger burned. Fury that had no outlet. Once they had held laughter. Merrick could recall a time when Farran entertained them all with wit and humor. Now those emotions were as tainted as their souls.

"I am for the truck." Without so much as a faint smile, Farran shouldered past Merrick and strode back the way they had come.

"'Tis sealed, Merrick." Declan's thick brogue echoed in the dimly lit cavern. He picked up their lantern and brought the warm light to Merrick's feet. "What say you to visiting the temple? Many months have passed since we have seen our brethren."

Three, to be exact. Merrick suspected Declan's count was slightly off. Declan had never particularly cared for Fulk to count the days since Azazel claimed him. Yet Merrick knew the precise hour evil overtook his cousin's soul. "I cannot, Declan. I must find Fulk. I gave him my oath."

"Och, one day, Merrick. 'Tis a pity Fulk now fights for Azazel, and well you ken I would expect the same from you, were it me. But one day willna make a difference."

Merrick shook his head. One more day was one more night of killing innocents—a fate Fulk would despise. They had formed a pact hundreds of years ago. The first to convert from a Templar into a knight of Azazel, the other would free with death. Merrick would not rest until he had reclaimed Fulk's soul and sent it home to the Almighty. "You go on. Take Farran with you. I am too full of aches to sit in the truck another two hours. I shall stay at the adytum tonight and meet you here in the morn."

A frown turned the Scot's mouth into a tight line. "Mikhail ordered our return. He bears news he willna relay over the telephone."

Merrick ground his teeth together to temper a rush of annoyance. "You may bring this news to me. I have no need to hear words of hope. I have three, mayhap four, fights left in me. Less, should you consider the toll darkness will take, once I put an end to Fulk. Tell Mikhail to send for me when he has more than words to share."

Merrick unfastened his sword belt and set it on the ground. He jerked off his dingy white surcoat, then bent at the waist to shrug his hauberk over his head. Merrick stuffed the articles into his duffel bag, skipping his cursory damage assessment. If the mail was damaged, he could do naught until he found rest. His eyes would never survive the strain of mending links of steel.

As he fastened his belt around his waist, he felt Declan's heavy gaze settle on his shoulder blades, heard the reproach in his silence. Bollocks! 'Twas not as if he wanted to shirk his duties all together. He simply could not tolerate the camaraderie of temple life until he had fulfilled his oath.

Ignoring Declan, he zipped his duffel bag and slung it over his shoulder. "I shall be glad to see Abigail and remind myself what pleasant company is like. God be with you, brother."

He left the brooding Scot in the middle of the cavern and struck off down a darker, narrower corridor. Whatever Mikhail had to share made no difference. Merrick did not have time to believe in fanciful promises of a day they would turn the tide and forever hold advantage over Azazel. A thousand years had not granted such. A thousand more, Merrick would not live to see.

He trudged down the damp corridor, the fatigue in his limbs weighing him down. Abigail would have food in the cupboards. A bit of bread, mayhap some cheese, and his energy would return enough to take himself up the stairs to bed. In blessed sleep, he would find relief. Let Declan and Farran dine with the men, let them hear the empty words Mikhail offered to rally their dying spirits. He would rest and regain what fragile energy his soul had left.

At the end of the short tunnel, he braced his shoulder against an iron door. It swung open with a *creak*. Darkness greeted him, the familiar light at the top of the stairs shielded by the upper door. The hour must be well toward dawn, for Abigail never barred their way.

He shifted his duffel bag to a more comfortable position and took a step forward.

His foot connected with something large and unmovable. Losing his balance, he stumbled. The armor in his bag gained momentum. It swung forward, taking him with it. He toppled to the ground, barely catching himself on his hands before his nose met the stone floor.

"Saints' blood!"

With another embittered mutter, he heaved himself off the ground. Had it been so long since knights sought the adytum that Abigail became lazy? He would have to speak to her about this. Remind her Gabriel's orders dictated the passage should remain clear.

His arm twitched as he picked up his bag and mounted the stairs. He was spent and exhausted, and each step required sheer determination. Were it not for his abject pride that refused to sleep on stone, he would as soon bed down in the basement than face another flight of stairs. Mayhap he would choose the sofa. Unlike other adytum caretakers, Abigail never minded waking to unexpected guests in her parlor.

He opened the door to the first-floor landing and found a lamp burning at the end of the hall. But 'twas not the distant light that made him frown. The scent of rot hung in the air, making him stiffen. Reflexively, he dropped his hand to the sword at his belt and took a deep breath. Though it was faint, the pungent odor engulfed his senses. A stench he would recognize anywhere.

Demons.

His fingers tightened on the hilt, and he eased his duffel bag to the floor. With a cautious step forward, he braced for confrontation. The house was quiet save for the refrigerator's low hum. Not unearthly still, but full of the comfortable silence that came with a house at rest.

He followed the light, his pulse tapping a rapid cadence as he anticipated a surprise attack. Whatever lurked here waited for something. And for whatever reason, Abigail had not banished it.

Approaching the doorway to the parlor, he watched the light flicker as a shadow moved through the adjoining room. Merrick drew his sword with a wince. Pain rippled through his shoulder. Sword poised at the ready, he stepped into the light. Best to finish this before he collapsed.

His gaze swept the room and came to an abrupt halt on a woman. She stared back with eyes as wide as saucers and as blue as a cloudless English sky. God's teeth! Demons could assume a hundred forms and shapes, but this surpassed all trickery he knew, for he would swear upon his immortal soul, he had never seen a more beautiful creature.

Long auburn hair framed features more delicate than porcelain. Flushed with spots of color, her high cheekbones held a noble air and offset a gently sloped nose. Her parted lips were full and soft, the kind of mouth that begged a man to sample its sweet flavor. His heart kicked against his ribs. With the heavy beat, a sensation he had not experienced in centuries surged through his blood. Desire, as he had never known, rose fast and hard.

By God, Azazel grew bold.

Merrick shoved his shock to the wayside and raised his sword. "Tell me your name, demon. I wish to curse you as you die."

CHAPTER 2

C onvinced the man standing in her doorway was part of the odd dream of Templar knights and Egyptian pharaohs that she'd been enjoying until a thump from the basement woke her, Anne blinked. When he didn't go away, she scrubbed her eyes. Every massive inch of him loomed inside her door frame. Broad shoulders, T-shirt snug across a wide chest, faded jeans that hugged thick thighs—nothing about the rugged stranger was small. He was more than imposing. More than intimidating. He would be magnificent if his features weren't full of silent fury and he didn't have a sword in his hand.

A sword, for God's sake. She was about to be robbed at sword point.

Vaguely, his accusation filtered through her chaotic thoughts. Demon? Had she heard him correctly? At a loss, she gave him an incredulous look. "What?"

"Do not play coy with me. Tell me your name so I may condemn you with it."

Yep. She'd heard him right. What the hell? Who barged into a house with a *sword*?

He took a step forward.

She backed up, her stare glued on the blade. "I, ah." She wet her lips with the tip of her tongue. "Look, I don't know who you are, but if you want money, my purse is to your right." Maybe, if she were lucky, he would take the satchel and disappear.

A sword. She struggled with the absurdity. He looked like he knew how to use it too. The weapon had to be heavy, yet he held it as easily as he might a glass.

"I do not need your money. Tell me your name, demon." He took another step forward, fully entering the light. He thrust the sword at her heart.

Her gaze followed the length of the blade to his face, and Anne sucked in a sharp breath. Dark hair. Eyes like chips of onyx. Strong jaw set in a familiar, grim manner. The same man from her visions with the cross, and the armband, stood in front of her. *Oh God.*

The room took a sharp tilt to her right. She grabbed at the table to keep from wobbling and stared in stunned silence.

"Mayhap I should carve off a limb?" He lowered the blade, bringing the sharp tip against her wrist.

Her heart jumped to her throat. He was serious. He actually meant to hurt her if she didn't tell him her name. Good God! She swallowed hard. "A-Anne."

"Anne?" He let out a disbelieving snort. "'Tis a human's name. Tell me the name Azazel gave you."

Vision from the past or not, he was nuts.

Her gaze slid sideways to the door. If she could draw him deeper into the room, she could make a mad dash for freedom. Pretending to cooperate, she edged away from the table and met the invader's frosty glare. "Anne MacPherson is my name. Who's Azazel?"

Eyes narrowed with suspicion, the man ignored her question. His gaze swept down her body, canvassing her worn blue jeans and loose blouse so thoroughly a strange chill tumbled down her spine. She took another step toward her purse, then stopped as reality sunk in, and with it, despair. As tall as he was, he would catch up to her in three strides.

Which meant she would have to disarm him. Although

how, eluded her. Her self-defense classes had covered knives, not three-foot-long swords. What she would do once she had him disarmed, she didn't know either. He was too large to tackle, too heavy to throw. She fought back a rush of panic, determined to keep her wits. She could outsmart a man who clearly wasn't right in the head.

She extended an arm toward her purse. "I'm going to get my wallet. I'll give you whatever's in it."

The stranger's gaze riveted on her outstretched hand. "How did you come by such?"

She followed his stare, noting she still held the armband. Relief washed through her. Gabe must have given her some black-market artifact. Some trinket that the existing Freemasons didn't want revealed. If this man wanted the armband, she'd surrender it. It didn't seem to want to tell her anything further anyway. "This?" She offered it to him. "Take it."

He crossed the room in two strides, disproving her theory that it would take three to intercept her run for the door. Sword pointed at the ground, he snatched the armband from her hand. Their fingers brushed, and trapped by the unfamiliar jolt of energy that arced up her arm, Anne couldn't move. With the surge, a picture of a man at rest emerged in her mind. Not just any man, she realized. This man. Dressed in chain and the same white surcoat with a crimson cross he'd worn both times before, he clasped his broadsword against his chest.

Not at rest. Dead.

"Stay here," he ordered.

She held back a renegade laugh. Like she was going anywhere. Not as long as he had that sword in hand.

Backing up, the invader kept his gaze fastened on her. He stumbled over a duffel bag she hadn't noticed before, and the oath that hissed through his teeth stirred her amusement once again. She bit down on her lower lip to stifle a giggle. She must be in shock—she couldn't think of any other reason to find anything remotely funny about this situation.

He righted himself, and with the armband dangling from his pinkie, he fumbled inside the bag. When his one-handed search only annoyed him, he set the blade down and shoved both hands inside. His stare left her, his focus on his search.

Instinct took over. Anne grabbed her purse. Using all the strength she could muster, she swung it, clocking him in the temple. He staggered forward, and Anne didn't wait to see if he fell. She raced for the door.

A thick arm wound around her waist, halting her escape. Like an iron band, he fastened her against a chest that felt like steel. A slight lift, and her feet came off the floor. She let out a shriek and clawed at his arm. Kicking with all her might, she sought contact with a shin, a thigh, whatever part of his body she could strike. He grunted with each drive of her heel, but his hold never faltered.

He carried her across the room and tossed her onto the sofa. When she lifted her glare to his face, a storm of fury brewed in his features. Black eyes glinted like brittle glass. His mouth pulled into a grim line. A muscle twitched along his jaw.

"You tempt me sorely," he ground out through clenched teeth. "You will explain how you came by such." He pointed to her arm, and to Anne's horror, she found the armband firmly in place.

She opened her mouth to protest, but words failed her. Just *what* had Gabe brought home? "Look, I don't know anything about this armband."

The stranger cut her off with a glower. "You will wait." He flipped open a cell phone. One eye on her, he dialed. Wisely, she kept her mouth shut, sensing if she did so much as twitch, he would make good on his threat.

He spoke into the phone. "Come to the adytum. I found a demon who possesses the serpents."

Anne blinked several times in rapid succession. He had friends? Coming here? Oh Lord above, if she got out of here alive, she would never, *ever,* accept another of Gabe's strange gifts.

The stranger snapped his phone shut. Sword once again in hand, he pointed it at her throat. "Now speak."

Anne swallowed hard. "My boss gave me the armband."

Again his gaze narrowed, suspicion glinting behind his dark eyes. "What charm did you place on it, demon Anne?"

"I've already said . . ." Anne trailed off as movement behind the stranger caught her attention. A shadowy form spanned the wall from ceiling to floor. It shifted on its own accord, no mere product of the dim light. Two arms took shape, followed by an elongated snout. The faint scent of rotted flesh wafted through the room.

Her words came faster as she glanced back at her invader. "I don't know anything about demons. But I'm not one." She looked over his shoulder, her throat tightening as the shadowy form drifted—no floated—across the floor.

Anne pointed, and her voice took on a higher pitch. "I'm pretty sure that is though."

Merrick realized too late that the rotting smell he had assumed came from Anne in fact came from behind him. As the woman let out a shriek and scrambled over the back of the couch, claws raked down his back. Heat seared through his skin. He bit back the pain with a low growl and wheeled around to confront Azazel's fiend.

His sword thumped into the nytym's side, jostling it off balance. The weight in his arm felt more like a lump of useless steel than any weapon of defense, and Merrick willed his body to cooperate. Widening his stance, he deflected another barrage of claws.

Almost a thousand years of training overpowered the weakness in his limbs. Parry, thrust, parry, slice, he fell into routine. The nytym gave strike for strike, meeting Merrick's advance with speed and accuracy. Pinpricks of pain stung his arms, his hands. He ground his teeth against the annoying stings and pressed forward, forcing the nytym back.

Enraged by his advance, Azazel's minion sought an overhead attack. Massing its grotesque form toward the ceiling, it loomed over him, poised for a deadly assault of fangs. But in so doing, the nytym made a fatal mistake. Its vulnerable underbelly stared Merrick in the face. He arced his sword across his body in a powerful slice that nearly cut the creature in half. It screeched in outrage. Teeth snapped as it writhed and hissed.

Merrick jerked his sword free, assuring a speedy death. Another unholy scream filled the room as a stain of ebony poured down Merrick's sword. With a shudder, the nytym fell still. Its horrendous form waivered in the light, then slowly disappeared, leaving only a pool· of shadows on Anne's carpet.

Fatigue consumed Merrick. Lacking the ability to prepare for the inevitable surge of vileness upon his soul, he dropped to his knees and elbows, panting. As the nytym's vile spirit soaked into him, his shoulders quaked. He fought for a normal breath. A low hum broke out in his ears, warmth filtered through his body, and a frightening feeling of weightlessness settled over him.

"Hey."

Anne's voice pulled him back from the edge of a damning abyss. He could not allow her to see him this way. Though she might not be the demon he once thought her, she had power. Until he knew what it was, he could not risk her escape. He clung to the sound of her voice, its melodic cadence his only foothold on awareness. Trickles of sticky wetness seeped around his ribs, telling him he bled.

"Hey." Closer now, her voice took on strength. The hum in his head faded. His vision slowly returned. Yet he could not find the strength to move. "Are you okay?"

The touch of gentle fingertips upon his shoulder was his undoing. They explored the claw marks he knew shredded his shirt and filleted his flesh. He sank into the carpet with a silent sigh and lay absolutely still, the tenderness of her touch a luxury he had not experienced in hundreds of years. He caught the scent of her perfume, a subtle blend of lavender and warm sugar that stirred some forgotten feeling deep inside his heart.

"Oh God, you're bleeding," she whispered. "Let me get something to clean you up with." Her hand disappeared, taking with it his brief surrender.

As it occurred to him she would leave, he mustered his energy and brought himself to his knees. "Nay. Stay where you are."

Her delicate features pulled with confusion. "I'm just going to the bathroom."

And mayhap out the back door. He pushed himself to his feet with a fierce shake of his head. "Sit down." He pointed at the couch.

The woman let out what could only be a grumble of extreme annoyance and made her way to the couch. As she passed, he took in low-slung jeans that flared over her stylish brown boots. He would never understand why the modern woman felt the need to dress like a man. Yet the loose hem of her blue top gave him a tempting glimpse of a flat abdomen as she tossed aside a throw pillow. His gaze shifted upward to admire the gentle slope of full breasts.

She fastened a glare on him as she flounced into the cushions. Arms crossed beneath her breasts, the soft flesh there pushed against the flimsy material of her short-sleeved blouse. Merrick swallowed. He knew he stared, but he cared not. It had been far too long since a woman had aroused his baser instincts. And this one disturbed them tenfold.

"I appreciate all the macho-guy sword fighting and all. But you're bleeding all over my carpet."

Merrick frowned. Would that her demeanor was as sweet as her body. "'Twill cease." Already he could feel the bleeding lessen. The wounds would scab over, and by the time Declan and Farran arrived, be little more than faint scars. Immortality kept him from bleeding to death. 'Twas the darkness that slayed. Evil, or the power of a Templar sword.

Anne's glower darkened. "Who the hell are you, and what are you doing here? And what, in the name of *God*, was that thing?"

"'Twas not a demon as you thought, but a nytym. A lesser tool of Azazel's. They possess the intelligence of a five- or six-year-old child."

She eyed him warily. The fact she was not screaming and in a full panic as other humans who chanced upon Azazel's minions oft did, impressed him. Nay, not a trace of worry clung to her features. Annoyance set her lush lips into a hard line. Anger turned her eyes to shards of sapphire, but she showed no fear. In fact, if his eyes did not deceive him, behind her glare, her blue eyes held curiosity.

At that moment, the front door burst open. It thumped into the wall, rattling the windows and shaking the lamp on the nearby table. Declan and Farran barged inside, their hands on the swords that hung at their waists.

"Great," Anne muttered.

Merrick shot her a scowl before acknowledging his brothers with a nod.

Farran's gaze fastened on Anne, interest lighting his usually empty eyes. Something about the way he quickly appraised her struck a disharmonious chord in Merrick's soul. He took a defensive step toward Anne, inserting himself between his friends and the unusual woman.

"Och, Merrick, did her beauty blind you? 'Tis no demon here." The concern left Declan's expression as he let out a short laugh.

Merrick clenched his teeth, strangling a string of curses. "She has the serpents," he answered simply. Tossing a sideways glance over his shoulder, he motioned to Anne. "Show them."

Her gaze narrowed, her displeasure evident. But to her credit, she spared him the barrage of her tongue and rose from the couch to approach his companions. She slid the armband off and set it in Declan's hand. "There. Take it. I don't want the thing."

Turning crisply, she started for the hall. Then stopped and stared down at her palm as the armband reappeared in it. "Oh, damn," she muttered.

Farran looked to Merrick. "Mikhail's message mentioned the serpents."

Merrick needed to hear no more. Whatever she was, he would find out before he slept. The serpents had not been seen since the great flood. However she came by this one, it was clearly not something a mortal should possess. Mikhail could explain, and Uriel, master healer of the archangels, could undo whatever charm bound it to her.

He caught Anne around the waist and swung her over his shoulder. The act required little effort as she weighed next to naught. Her softness molded against him in such an intimate manner, he sucked in a sharp breath. Saints' blood, with the way she made heat surge to his loins, she ought to be a demon.

She struggled against him. "What are you doing? Put me down, jerk!"

"Nay. You will come with us."

Her scream of outrage deafened him. She pummeled fists into his back, her concern for his injuries now a thing of the past. A knee connected with his stomach, and he let out a harassed hiss. Securing her in place, he set one hand at the back of her knees, the other he fastened over her thighs. Tempting as they were, he ignored the feel of firm muscles and sloping curves beneath his palm. "Farran, retrieve my bag. I have reconsidered returning to the temple."

CHAPTER 3

✝

A thousand visions slammed into Anne as Merrick carted her out the door. They came so quickly she caught only bits and pieces—a birth, a woman sobbing, a funerary of old, Merrick riding off to war, Merrick approaching some sand-infested, barren place. One by one, they flitted before her eyes, stealing her breath and stilling her limbs.

The last image lingered. Merrick lay unmoving. His eyes were closed. His hands clasped a plain pommel like the one at his waist. Again, it lay atop his chest, the funerary scene crisp and clear. Only this time, she noticed his face bore deep scratches. His lower lip split at the corner, and his left eye swelled with a deep purple bruise.

As the picture faded into nothingness, warmth filtered through her veins and erased the eerie chill. Where he touched her, her skin tingled. The hand beneath her buttocks hadn't moved, yet she was so aware of him she blushed. Like candy set on a counter to tempt her, the brush of his thumb against her bottom made her want to squirm.

Mortified, Anne squeezed her eyes shut. This was insane. The man had broken into her home, threatened her at sword-point, and now carried her off to only God knew where. She ought to be screaming her head off, awakening her neighbors, doing all she could to escape these three barbarians.

But no matter how much she would like to be afraid, she couldn't find a single ounce of fear. Whatever his intention, the energy patterns rolling off him carried no malice. She could sense his underlying anger, read loud and clear his frustration. But danger? Not a bit of it. If anything, his energy patterns hinted at incredible honor.

Besides, she couldn't shake the visions of him she'd seen—in particular the one of him digging in the ground. He held knowledge of the Templar knights. Crazy or not, this man very likely had the answers she needed, and she'd hit such a devastating dead-end with her theory, she was willing to accept a bit of risk in proving it. The High Priestess had warned she would discover secrets—she didn't dare turn away from opportunity.

At a silver SUV, Merrick tossed her roughly into the backseat. The blond man climbed into the driver's seat while the man with the Scottish accent let himself in the passenger's side. Which left her to sit with unpleasant Merrick.

Lovely.

He crawled into the seat beside her, his scowl still firmly fastened on his face. "Lie down. I will not chance Azazel's motives by keeping you in sight."

Anne's lips parted in silent shock. Do what? If she stretched out, she would have to touch him. Another bout with rapid visions and she'd get nauseous. While she yearned for more information, that ceremonial death scene gave her the willies. She'd at least like the opportunity to choose when to open herself to the spirit realm's messages. Further, her pride wouldn't take another minute of his overbearing attitude. Their eyes clashed. "Listen, big guy. I've had it with you telling me what to do. I'm not going to lie down."

Merrick gave her a hard look. "You will do so of your own accord, or I shall arrange you thus."

Anne stared at Merrick. She wanted to tell him he

couldn't order her about like the serving girls he might have known once upon a time. The words, however, forced her to confront a truth she couldn't explain. He *was* a knight. All three of them were men of old. If his talent with a sword or his archaic speech didn't illustrate that, her second sight made his status impossible to ignore. She would stake her life on that impossible fact.

The blond man twisted in the driver's seat to give her a scowl. "Best you do what Merrick says. I care not to hear any more of this argument."

Anne harrumphed. So that one's disposition was no better. At least the other had half a sense of decency. His laughter set him apart from the other two.

She rolled her eyes. "Just drive."

She ignored the flash of fury that glittered in the blond's ale-colored eyes and slunk down in the seat. Let him be mad. She'd had more than enough of this dictatorship.

When he refused to start the engine, Anne grumbled beneath her breath. She caught the twinge of laughter in the third man's smirk. When she looked to Merrick though, her rising humor strangled in her throat. His coal-black eyes glinted with unspoken fury, and the twitch had returned to bounce along the side of his jaw. Evidently she didn't have a choice. Well, she might as well use the situation to her advantage and try to scour through the visions for the information she wanted. If she put a little more effort into controlling her second sight, with luck, it would cooperate.

Carefully, she set her ankle-high boots in Merrick's lap, then reclined against the door, mentally channeling the resulting surge of energy into a narrow band she could manipulate.

Tuning them all out, she shut her eyes.

Merrick's forearm came down upon her shins, and the weight of his hand settled over her ankle. The SUV rolled backward, crunching gravel beneath its tires. As they navigated onto the paved road, Anne chanced another glance at Merrick through lowered lashes. His head was resting on the back of the seat, his eyes closed, and she could see his features were still and smooth. His long, shaggy hair brushed his shoulders and gave him a gentler appearance.

In the early light of dawn, she caught the faint reflection of a scar that ran down his cheek and reached beneath his jaw. Merely a thin vein of white, she'd missed it before. Had one of those nytyms put that mark upon his face? She shuddered as she recalled the shredded nature of Merrick's back. A frown niggled at her brow. Odd, she hadn't seen a drop of blood beneath the tattered fabric of his shirt when he carried her to the SUV.

Though leather separated his hand from her skin, heat radiated from his palm. Comforted by the warm sensation, Anne relaxed and allowed the energy to flow through her mind.

Dressed in homespun wool, a raven-haired woman knelt before a small boy. Her face radiated joy as she pushed a long braid over her shoulder. Her features were kind, full of the adoration a mother would give a child, but they held faint lines of worry around her brow. Her hands were long and elegant. Her dirty apron and the tattered hem at her ankles marked her as a servant, or maybe a peasant woman. The boy turned, his features unmistakable despite his youth. Merrick's onyx eyes gleamed with a bright smile.

Like a shot from an old movie, the vision went dark. With Anne's next heartbeat, another image rose to her mind.

Fully mature, Merrick shook hands with a man about the same age. They shared the same dark hair, but his companion was far fairer. Brothers maybe? They clamped fists over their hearts, a gesture she understood to be a pledge. Maybe an emphasis of some spoken word.

Scene by scene she caught fragments of Merrick's life. She learned snippets, past and present, but never enough to give her a full story. He fought numerous times, claimed both human and demon lives. A glimpse of him addressing a massive army said he led men as well.

Time and again, Anne recognized the legendary crimson cross. Painted on stone walls in an ancient hall, engraved in the shield he carried, stained across his surcoat—it surrounded all the images of him as an adult. Clearly, he had been Templar. Judging from the scenes of him in ropes and suspended from rough-hewn rafters, he had paid the price when the noble order fell from grace too.

But how did a man who had been born in the tenth or eleventh century show up in her living room? *Come on,* she pled to the unseen forces that governed her gift. *Go back to the tunnel.*

Her second sight morphed again, surging a fission of excitement down to her toes. She opened her mind completely, not wanting to thwart any portion of her gift.

She lay naked in a bed, the light of the moon illuminating the dark. Merrick's face loomed before hers, and by the brief glimpse of his bare chest, she assumed he was just as nude. His body lowered into hers with such stunning clarity she could feel the warmth of his skin. His mouth danced over her face, touching her lips, her eyes, her throat. A caress so soft and gentle she shivered.

Shocked to the core, she snapped her eyes open. Her heart tripped into double time. The same enticing heat that her visionary kiss stirred swam through her veins, making the weight of Merrick's hand suddenly unbearable. He was too close, too far away, all at once.

Good Lord, what was the matter with her?

She lifted her gaze to make sure he was still asleep, and her throat closed. His eyes locked with hers. As if he knew her thoughts, heat burned behind his unwavering stare, enough to make their confined space uncomfortable. A spark of nervous anticipation bubbled through her veins, settled in her belly, and turned it upside down.

In the next instant, Merrick reclaimed his mask. His mouth pursed, his gaze narrowed, and suspicion glinted in his eyes.

With effort, Merrick tore his eyes off the woman across from him, wishing he had not tried to steal a moment of sleep. Though a good two feet spanned between them, he felt Anne as keenly as if she were pressed against his side. Her perfume taunted him, reminding him of the all-too-vivid dream that still clouded his thoughts. God's teeth, he could still feel the softness of her mouth, the caress of her breath against his cheek. And his blood still burned with want of her.

He shifted in the seat, attempting to alleviate the discomfort of arousal. If she was no demon, then what curse had she put upon him? He could not recall a time when a dream had felt so very real. The stain of color in her cheeks professed her guilt, but how had this woman managed to invade his head thus?

She tempted his sanity, threatened his oath. They were Templar, each sworn to a vow of chastity. Though they all had broken that minor vow many times, Merrick took care to choose women he could easily forget, ones who would not distract him from his higher purpose. This one held the power to wend herself into his memory, and he could not allow that. Fulk's salvation lay in his hands. He would not put aside their pact to dally beneath Anne's skirts.

Saints' blood, he could not be free of this redheaded witch fast enough.

He took a deep breath to tamp down his rising frustration. This would end upon their arrival. Mikhail would take the serpents from Anne, and Merrick would be free of her. A day at the most, and he would return to searching for his cousin.

To his relief, the SUV stopped in front of a towering early twentieth-century estate in the midst of repair. Three stories of brick spanned across a rolling, isolated hillside, the windows darkened in the daylight. Between the dilapidated shutters, he recognized scaffolding, ladders, and tools that dangled from the tiled roof. Three columns supported a half-moon front porch illuminated by a corroded copper hanging lamp.

Anne sat forward, her feet thumping to the floorboards. "I know this place." She leaned around the passenger's seat, moving entirely too close to Merrick for his comfort. He edged his thigh out of the way.

"The Odd Fellows Home. This used to be an old hospital. Wow. When did they decide to fix it up?"

Declan gave her a smile. "'Tis always been ours."

"Yours?"

"Aye, ours," Merrick interjected. "Let us go inside. I wish to have this over with so I may rest." He kicked open his door and stepped onto the browning grass. Before Anne could open hers, he reached in and grabbed her wrist. With a none-too-gentle tug, he pulled her out his side.

"Let go." She jerked her arm free and scowled at him. "Don't you know how to be nice? Why are we here?"

"To see Mikhail," Farran grumbled.

Merrick shot his companion a look of warning. Until they knew exactly how Anne came to possess the armband, they dared not reveal too much of themselves. Bantering the names of archangels certainly did not work in their favor if the woman possessed some tie to Azazel.

Farran nodded crisply.

Merrick started for the front doors, but Anne dug her heels in, refusing to budge. He turned back in exasperation. "We go inside."

She shook her head. "I'm not going in there. I don't know *you*. I don't know these two, and if you've got a fourth friend around here, he can come outside. I've come this far, it's as good as it gets, big guy."

Gritting his teeth together, Merrick stared at Anne. Exasperating. The woman simply did not know when to hold her tongue. She was in no danger, and this sudden apprehension of hers was unnecessary. "Mikhail will not come outside."

Out of the corner of his eye, he caught Declan cover a grin with his hand. The Scot cleared his voice and gave Farran a nudge toward the door. "We shall meet you anon," he said to Merrick.

"'Tis not wise to stand out here and argue. Though the grounds are protected, they are not always safe. Now come." Merrick tugged on Anne's hand again, but found her just as immobile. He spun around and threw his hands in the air. "Damnation, woman, what is the matter with you? Do you purposefully seek out danger?"

Her eyes widened to twice their normal size, and she spluttered. Then surprise gave way to annoyance, and her blue eyes narrowed to furious slits. She set her hands on her hips. "What's wrong with me? *You* barge into my house. *You* kidnap me. And you think I should *trust* you? You're crazy! I'm all for learning about this armband, but I'm not going inside. Go get your friend."

If there was one thing Merrick could not stand, 'twas a delay in his plans. He wanted answers, he wanted freedom from this woman, and he could not wait a moment longer. His body ached with exhaustion. His eyes were so tired they burned. The short nap on the way here had done naught for his mood either—except torment him further. Knowing only one way to put an end to this maddening argument, he picked her up and tossed her over his shoulder once more.

Tuning out her shriek of protest and the pounding of her fists, he strode inside.

Heads turned as men who gathered in the billiard room overheard her string of curses. Merrick ignored them and descended a wide, stone staircase that led to a maze of caverns modern society had not touched.

Beneath the ground, torchlight illuminated high stone ceilings and cast shadows through the corridors. His boots echoed dully, blending with the distant murmur of prayer. He recognized the chant as one of mourning, and a dull ache settled in his heart as he realized they had lost another brother. The deaths mounted. Brave men who did not ask for this fate gave their souls to a cause that had no hope. Azazel's power grew stronger. Soon there would be too few Templar to defend the crumbling gates between his unholy realm and the mortal world.

Merrick let out a heavy sigh and shoved an iron-studded door open. Inside, he found Declan, Farran, and Mikhail

assembled, along with three other faces he had not seen
in far too long. The ache in his heart lessened as he nodded to Tane, Lucan, and Caradoc. United against the
mighty hand of William, together they had spilled their
first blood and saw a young knight's first victory.

"Merrick, put the lady down." Mikhail's voice held a
touch of censure that matched the creases in his brow.

Merrick guided Anne to her feet, a mistake he realized
too late. Every soft curve of hers slid down the front of
his body. Her knee slipped between his, and she inadvertently glided down his thigh. A sudden, fierce rush of
desire slammed into him as the contact set every nerve
ending afire. His blood warmed. He felt his cock rise. He
clamped his teeth together to silence a gasp and sucked
in a sharp breath through his nose.

Thank the saints Mikhail took charge, for Merrick
could not speak if he tried.

Mikhail bowed over Anne's hand. "Milady. Do forgive
my knights their rudeness. They have been away and evidently forgotten their manners."

Anne flashed Mikhail a smile that made Merrick's
lungs feel small. "Excuse me a minute?" Her dainty eyebrows lifted with the question.

At Mikhail's nod, Anne whirled on Merrick. Wrath
replaced her breathtaking smile, and her glare shot daggers meant to kill. He braced himself for a verbal assault.
Instead, she drove her toe into his shin.

Satisfaction poured through Anne as Merrick grunted.
The sound made the dull throb that worked its way up her
ankle tolerable. "You're an ass!"

In the back of her mind, she knew she ought to be wary
of the sudden fury that filled his features and his stoic silence, but she'd had it with his behavior. "What the hell is
wrong with you? This is America. I get a say in what you
do with me! I thought knights were supposed to be chivalrous."

She cocked her foot again, but Mikhail stepped between

them, thwarting her attack. "Milady, I am certain Merrick is deserving of a beating, but please, put aside your anger. The both of you will need to learn to work together."

In slow motion, both Anne and Merrick's heads swung toward Mikhail. "What?" they cried in unison.

"Indeed," Mikhail confirmed on a nod. His gaze slid to Merrick. "If Merrick had seen fit to return to the temple last month when I summoned him and his men, he would not have made an ass of himself today."

If it were possible, Merrick's features grew even harder. He didn't look at Anne, but kept his stare fixed on Mikhail. At his thigh, one hand clenched into a fist so tight, his knuckles turned white. The muscle along his jaw began to twitch, and the faint scar on his cheek pulled as he clamped his teeth together.

So the mighty knight couldn't handle a bit of criticism. Interesting.

"Have you told her what you are?" Mikhail asked Merrick.

"Nay."

Mikhail's steely silver eyes settled on Anne. She blinked in surprise at his warm smile, at the beauty revealed. He didn't possess the kind of rugged good looks Merrick and the other men did; he was more like a work of fine art. A living, breathing Michelangelo.

Though they weren't touching, his energy poured into her. A strange feeling of peace and contentment soothed her frayed temper, and though she tried, she couldn't remember why she'd been so incensed with Merrick.

"I believe . . ." Mikhail began in a thoughtful tone. He moved behind a massive desk and pushed aside a stack of tattered papers to uncover a thick, leather-bound book. Tapping the cover, he lifted his gaze. "We will begin here. I am Mikhail. You will know me better by words men wrote long ago. Gabriel, or as you call him, Gabe Anderson, sent you to me."

How did he know her boss? She didn't remember telling any of them his name.

Mikhail turned the book around. Etched in gold, two words shone against the darkened binding: *Holy Bible*.

A subtle shift in the lighting gave Mikhail an ethereal appearance. His brown hair assumed a rich brilliance and glinted with shots of red. Against the stone wall immediately behind him, the ever-so-faint outline of a pair of majestic wings stood out like someone had traced them there. Certain the effect came from a trick of lights, Anne glanced around in search of the projector, but there weren't any overhanging lights. In fact, she couldn't see a single lamp—or for that matter a candlestick. For all intents and purposes, she should be standing in a cave as black as pitch.

Impossible, her mind protested.

Real, instinct countered.

Oh God.

Anne's knees went weak. The floor rushed up to meet her, and the room took a drastic spin to the left. Struggling to breathe, she stumbled, but strong hands caught her from behind. Planes of hard steel pressed against her back. Bewildered, she looked over her shoulder to see who'd caught her, and for the first time since she'd met him, Merrick's eyes softened.

"I think I need to sit," she whispered.

CHAPTER 4

✝

Mikhail regarded the young woman thoughtfully. Her face was washed with white, her blue eyes wide. Gabriel had said she possessed spirit, informed them she was strong. But the things she must hear required far more energy than she now possessed.

His gaze shifted briefly to Merrick. Whatever nonsense the weakening knight engaged in, Anne certainly put him in his place. In all of creation, Mikhail would have never believed he would witness a woman take Merrick to task. Or that Merrick would stay his hand and accept the punishment.

Perhaps Gabriel was right. Perhaps Merrick would make a suitable tutor for her.

Mikhail frowned.

Regardless, Merrick had no choice. Gabriel had relayed the Almighty's orders that Merrick would educate Anne on the Templar purpose. He would lead her on the path she had been born to take.

Best to keep this conversation at a minimum. Tell her only the basics and save the rest for Merrick. He would learn when she was ready to understand. Presently, Merrick had things to learn himself.

"Caradoc, Lucan, Tane." Mikhail turned to the three

beside Declan and Farran. "You will inform Declan and Farran what I omit when the five of you leave, as you have already heard what I have to say."

All three nodded in understanding. A surge of pride rushed through Mikhail. These six rarely questioned duty. Of all the knights under his command, Merrick's men embodied Templar honor. Yet a wave of sorrow followed on pride's heels. Whether they would survive these coming trials remained to be seen. Darkness infringed upon them all. Not a day passed when Mikhail did not pray for their tainted souls.

He cleared his wandering thoughts with a brief shake of his head. "Lady Anne." She blushed at his address, and he let out a soft chuckle. "Become accustomed to the title, for my dear, you are the truest lady these men will ever know. Do you know where you are?"

She swallowed. Her gaze shifted to an ancient shield mounted on the wall, and she took in the four legs of the crimson cross emblazoned on its scarred surface. Quietly, she answered, "I believe so. But it seems impossible."

"Rest assured, 'tis not impossible." Mikhail moved around to the front of his desk and leaned against it. Folding his arms over his chest, he offered her a smile. "You sit in the North American Temple, the stronghold of the Knights Templar. The men you see around you have fought Azazel's evil for centuries. But the battle has turned in Azazel's favor, and you, dear lady, are the key to their victory."

He held in a laugh as Merrick, Declan, and Farran all turned to him. Surprise etched into their features, glinted in their eyes. Oh how he loved to catch his knights off guard. So rarely did it happen, he cherished the opportunity.

Anne's frown, however, deepened. "I don't understand. I just want to learn about this armband and go back home."

"Your life is here, Anne. As we speak, your colleagues spread the news that you have eloped with a secret lover."

"A what?" Bless her heart, she laughed. "No one would believe that. I'm not even dating."

"We did not wish to create rumor of your death, in the event there might be someone you wished to visit now and then. Or even if you choose to perform your work—when it becomes safe to do so—from the house in Atchison."

"Mikhail," Merrick interrupted. "Spare us the lengthy prattle. We have not slept, and I wish to rest. Tell us our purpose here."

Mikhail considered drawing out Merrick's wait simply because the knight could not curb his rudeness. He appraised the three returning men, took in the deep lines of weariness in their faces, the dark circles beneath their eyes. They had done more good in the last six weeks than the Order as a whole. Yet for their deeds, they paid a heavy price. Mikhail sensed the growing darkness in their souls, felt the contained hatred that waited for escape. He did not have the heart to make these men wait for rest.

"Very well. Anne, the serpentine you bear is a symbol of the sacred snake, Nehushtan, of healing and salvation. It marks the time when the angels fell from grace, and it was crafted to identify those born from divine power."

Mikhail ignored Merrick's displeased mutter. Focusing instead on soothing the rapid loss of color in Anne's face, he forged on. "You are a descendant of the Nephilim. The blood that runs in your veins has been passed down for centuries. Undiluted, it is the very essence of the Almighty's creation. I will allow Merrick to tell you the remaining theology therein. Right now, all you need to know is that you were put upon this earth for a greater purpose."

A commotion in the corner set Mikhail's smile free. The three who had answered the summons Merrick and his men ignored, and already heard what was to come, had just made the connection. He grinned at Caradoc. "Take the men outside. The rest is for Merrick and Anne alone. Before you go"—he swept an arm toward Anne—"pledge your loyalty."

Angels? A descendant of the Nephilim? Anne's mind whirled with Mikhail's ridiculous claims. Beyond the simple implausibility of them, doctrine stated the flood eradicated the Nephilim. No matter how she looked at it, what Mikhail wanted her to believe just couldn't be true. Then again, a rational person would say her ability to read past lives was impossible. They'd tell her running into a reincarnated knight, who had never really left the Middle Ages, would be ridiculous. Yet she knew the reality first-hand from her visions. While she might doubt Mikhail's claims about her lineage, she was absolutely convinced about Merrick's legitimacy. Angels or no angels, she stood among Templar knights.

And these men had the answers she needed. She would give anything to deny that this was real. Even considering the possibility made her feel as foolish as an adult who still believed in Santa Claus. But in thirty-one years, her visions had never been wrong. Her ability to read energy, when it was strong enough to make its presence known, had never led her astray. Right now, the room buzzed with spiritual strength. A power so indomitable she couldn't hope to ignore it. Every last particle swirling around her reinforced what she wanted to disbelieve. This was real.

Five men lined up in front of her and dropped to one knee, thwarting her ability to consider things further. From their waists, they pulled their swords free and set them on the ground before their flattened feet. The scrape of steel against stone hung in the air.

The man on the far left bowed his head. Shoulders easily twice the size of hers bent, and he leaned one arm on his knee, accenting the thick bulge of his bicep. His sandy-brown hair tumbled forward to cover his face. "Lord Caradoc of Asterleigh."

Asterleigh? She knew that name. It had once been a medieval village, but now was little more than dust and dirt. Good God, he was a noble! The realization sent goose bumps coursing down her arms. She waited for him to say more, expected him to stand.

When Caradoc didn't move, Merrick jabbed an elbow in her side. "Return his blade," he whispered.

Rising, Anne bent to retrieve Caradoc's broadsword. Not expecting the heavy weight, she almost dropped the thing before she managed to hold on tight enough to lift it up. Holding the flat of the blade in both hands, she presented it to Caradoc. With a crisp nod, he accepted his weapon, stood, and sheathed it.

As Caradoc walked away, the next man in line bowed his head. Built with the same incredible strength as the other two, she admired the way his ribs tapered into a trim waist. His hair was dark like Merrick's, but it hung straight and smooth, contrary to Merrick's untamed waves. He was not nearly as handsome as the other two, but she found something about his demeanor pleasing. Maybe he bowed with a bit more grace.

He spoke in a low, smooth voice, "Lucan of Seacourt."

Again, Anne made the connection to a lost medieval village. Although inventoried by the Normans, the tiny town was nothing but rubble by the mid-1400s. Moved by the fact these two had lost even the history of their origin, her heart swelled. She presented him his sword with reverence and managed a hesitant smile.

The third man repeated his companions' actions, but before he bowed his dark head, she caught a flash of deep green eyes behind thick lashes. "Tane du Breuil."

Something about the way he glanced up at her made her uneasy. A flash of envy? Desire? Whatever it was, it made the hair on the back of her neck rise. Moving more quickly, she returned his broadsword with grace.

Blond hair tumbled as the surly driver dropped his gaze to the ground. She noticed for the first time that this man also doubled her in size. Good grief, compared to her petite stature, they were all giants. But man, they were nice to look at. A girl could get used to this.

His voice was brittle, full of underlying anger, as he said, "Farran de Clare."

Anne's eyes widened in recognition of another noble family's name. Why it surprised her, she didn't know. To be Templar, a man had to have descended from nobility.

But seeing these men bow before her, she who didn't have a drop of blue blood and would have been a peasant in that long-ago time, felt somehow wrong. She returned Farran's sword, all too anxious to have this procedure over with.

The Scot's easy smile lessened her discomfort. He bent over his knee with grace and flourish, and dipped his reddish head. "Declan MacNeill." As she bent to retrieve his sword, he tossed her a wink. She smiled as she handed it to him but quickly sobered under Merrick's smoldering stare.

Moving as a collective unit, the five men rose and filed out the door in silence.

The room now empty, save for Merrick and Mikhail, Anne returned to her chair and focused on their leader. His smile had disappeared, his features the same grim mask that Merrick wore. Great. She let out a sigh, pushed her hair out of her face, and looked to Mikhail. "I have students that expect midterm grades. I've got a thesis to finish by Christmas, or I lose a promotion. While I would love nothing more than to stay and learn your histories, I can't stay here indefinitely. How long are you thinking I'll be gone?"

"Eternally. You cannot go back. The things you will learn, the secrets you shall be trusted with—your place is here. I am sorry we do not have the necessary time to prepare you better. But this is more important than any grades, any test, and any promotion you might believe you need."

Her stomach tightened with a knot of apprehension. Throw away her promotion? No way. Who knew when she might get another opportunity at a department chair? Another college would expect her to put in years of teaching that she'd already obtained at Benedictine. She'd thrown herself into medieval France and the Knights Templar since her parents' plane crash, devoted everything she was to fulfilling her father's research and proving the theories he began, and published internationally respected papers on many of them already. She had no intentions of starting over. Not when she was so close. The promotion meant far more than professional success. Her father died while traveling to prove the Church's motives. Her thesis was personal.

Mikhail moved in front of her and caught her hand.

As if to assure she wasn't trapped in some crazy dream, her second sight rose to the surface with a chilling image. Put to death in the Romans' preferred method, an unclothed man suspended from a thick wooden cross. His chin rested against his chest. Long hair tumbled about his face. At his feet thousands wailed as legionaries whipped them, threw stones and rocks. A few even went so far as to kick the mourning in the gut and spit on their prostrated bodies. Her focus narrowed on the dead man's bended head, lingering on a crown of twined thorns.

She closed her eyes when the image faded. Logic and reason combated with her spiritual affinity until her head felt dizzy all over again, but in the wave of nausea, those balmy sensations she'd experienced earlier returned to ground her. The tentacle of fear that reached out for her retreated, and she couldn't fight back the overwhelming feeling of peace.

When she opened her eyes, Mikhail pulled his hand from hers and peered down at her in earnest. "You must listen carefully, Anne. Your fate lies with one of my men. You are bound to him. It was written in the heavens long before any of us touched this earth. There is a mark upon your body, a scar, a birthmark, perhaps even art. Something unique, that in its shape, its creation, or its meaning holds significance. It matches one of the men's, and he who bears the identical symbol is your intended mate."

She shook her head. "You can't be serious."

Mikhail didn't flinch. "Deadly."

"You really mean this nonsense? I'm some descendant of an angel? I'm supposed to give up my life and hide underground with a man I've never met?" She let out a soft snort. "I don't think so."

As if her remark didn't warrant a response, Mikhail turned his attention to Merrick. "By Gabriel's, and thus the Almighty's, order, you will help pair her. Until her intended is found, you will protect her. She is your charge, Merrick. I expect you to devote yourself to her safekeeping. Now give her your oath."

Anne spluttered as Merrick dropped to one knee. He bowed his head and tossed his sword carelessly in front of him, the *clang* as harsh as his expression. If body language said anything, the man was seriously pissed. She couldn't blame him. Stuck with arrogant Merrick? What had she done to deserve misery?

"Merrick du Loire." His tight-lipped response sounded more like a snarl.

She was half tempted to let him retrieve his sword on his own, just to see how long he would sit there on a bended knee. When several seconds passed and she hadn't moved, he tipped his head up. His eyes spoke silent fury. That telltale twitch tugged at the side of his jaw, and he clenched his teeth so hard his lips turned into a tight, cruel line.

"Fine," she muttered. Bending over, she picked up his sword and thrust it toward him. He snatched it out of her hands, jumped to his feet, and stuffed it into the metal scabbard that dangled from his waist.

"What is the meaning of this, Mikhail?" Merrick demanded. "She is a woman. Not strong, not a fighter. How can *she* help us?"

Anne stiffened at Merrick's condescending remark. No wonder he hadn't hesitated to carry her like a sack of potatoes and gave little thought to what she wanted. His brain was still firmly rooted in the twelfth century. Good God. She was supposed to stay with *him* until this supposed predestined husband was found? She wrinkled her nose and opened her mouth to protest, but Mikhail didn't give her the opportunity.

One coppery eyebrow arched, and a rueful smile spread across Mikhail's face. "You cannot mean to tell me you've forgotten the prophecy, Merrick. She carries the light that will balance one knight's tainted soul. She is a seraph."

Anne almost laughed aloud at the absurdity of Mikhail's statement. Ludicrous. *Light* in *her?* Someone evidently neglected to tell Mikhail she'd had a little too much fun in college. So much so, she had almost flunked her freshman year. It had taken five more to graduate. Her parents' death the following year finally pushed her into responsibility, but it had still taken another three years to get her master's, and then another two for her doctoral thesis. By now, she'd settled down. She might *look* light and innocent, but there was far more darkness in her soul than she cared to admit.

The way Merrick's face drained of color and his mouth parted suffocated her humor. Whatever Mikhail meant by those cryptic words, Merrick took seriously. Too seriously for her liking. Fighting down a sickening sense of foreboding, she asked, "Balance?"

Mikhail nodded. "You will keep someone alive, Anne. Now go, and discover who it is."

Keep someone alive? He had to be kidding. She didn't want that kind of responsibility. She killed plants for God's sake. Gabe had made a mistake. A terrible, awful mistake. She wasn't cut out for this kind of thing. Not by any means.

Thwarting her protest, Merrick clamped his hand around her wrist. "Let us get this over with quickly. I have no care to stay here long."

Having had her own desires ripped out of her control, Anne refused to tolerate another moment of his overbearing attitude. She twisted free of his hold. "I'll walk without your help. So help me, if you put one hand on me, I'll kick in your knees."

She stormed through the door, Merrick on her heels. Behind them, she could have sworn she heard laughter.

But before she could peek through the crack and investigate, Merrick swung his arm wide, indicating the dimly lit corridor. "That way," he barked.

Merrick followed Anne down the corridor, all too aware of the commotion her presence caused. A legion of men, once forty-thousand strong, dwindled to less than a thousand scattered throughout the world before the Almighty deigned to reveal those who carried the holy light. Nearly nine hundred years they had waited for the coming of the seraphs. So long, that he had forgotten the very prophecy designed to offer the Templar hope. Even now, he could not recall the entirety of the promise, but the opening passage rang clear in his head. *First comes the teacher.*

Aye, she was a teacher, but her duty would mean more than the lessons she taught. She would guide the seraphs yet to come. Mikhail spoke true—this headstrong maid was the key to Azazel's defeat. Moreover, she would begin their healing.

As Anne stalked on ahead of him, her presence and her purpose sank into him fully. He could not ignore the way men who had not broken from prayer in hundreds of years found themselves silent when she passed by open archways. Heads turned. Murmurs rumbled through the ranks gathered in the barracks' small communal area. He did not need to hear their words to know the question that burned in their minds—Who would she save? Who would she say oaths with, thus forever blocking the darkness from entering his soul and healing the damage already done?

Accusation registered behind more than one face when they looked upon him, as if he somehow had some hand in Anne's fate. Would that he did. He would pair her with Declan and have the whole ordeal over with. Declan possessed the character to deal with this woman's trying nature.

At the end of the hall, Anne stopped. Her back stiff, she did not look at him. Nor did she inquire which way to turn. A smirk tugged at the corner of his mouth. What would the haughty little general do now?

Nothing, he realized, as she remained motionless, her chin held high, tiny fists balled at her sides.

With a grumble, he stalked past her and continued down a private corridor to the left. He could think of naught else that displeased him more than having to guide this woman. His shin still ached from the punishment of her boots. Saints' blood, what had come over her? He minded little that she felt the need to take her frustrations out on him, but he greatly cared she had done so in front of his men. Such disrespect he would not tolerate. Most certainly not from a woman, seraph or not.

He pushed open the heavy door to his small, private chambers and stepped aside, allowing her entry. Dimly, it occurred to him he had not thought to ask where she would reside. But he dismissed the concern as quickly as it rose. In a few moments, she would take up residence with her intended.

As Anne entered, her perfume tickled his nose. He closed his eyes to the smell of sweet lavender as his lungs constricted. He refused to consider the possibility of her meaning, refused to let the question rise in his mind as it had every other knight's. Were she meant for him, it mattered not. One man could not defeat Azazel's poison. Gritting his teeth against a traitorous rise of hope, he opened his eyes to find her seated on the edge of his bed.

The sight of her sitting there sent a whole new rush of sensation surging through his veins. Early morning light poured in through his small window, catching her hair and making it shimmer as if she were some ethereal creation of the Almighty's divine plan. Her features were soft, if not a touch bewildered, and something akin to sympathy tightened his chest. Aye, she was strong. She had yet to give over to a woman's tears, even if her tongue did run away from her. She did not protest her fate, did not demand to return to her home.

The sight of her smile as she had returned Declan's sword lingered before Merrick's eyes, and with it, a foreign spear of envy jabbed him in the gut. Surprised by how strongly that simple gesture affected him, Merrick scowled. Had it been so long since he had spent time in a woman's company that one smile could give him reason to want to strike his brother?

Nay, it must be the darkness in his spirit. He had gone too long on too few hours of sleep. No simple woman was cause for discord between men. He had never allowed one to divide him from his men, nor would he allow this one.

He would find this mark Mikhail claimed she bore and rid himself of her. "Take off your clothes."

Her head snapped up, her eyes wide. "Excuse me?"

"I do not think your hearing fails you. Take off your clothes."

A chuckle stirred her shoulders, and a smirk turned up a corner of her full mouth. "Most men try dinner and a movie first, Merrick. Maybe a little wine. Definitely some pretty words. A kiss usually sets the mood."

He nearly choked on her implication. "You think I wish to bed you?"

She shrugged, but her blue eyes were not nearly as impassive. A storm waged inside them, and they flashed with the deadly brilliance of lightning. "Tell me what else I should think? You've ordered me around, bullied me, insulted me with your *demon Anne*. Do you think I'm thrilled to be here?" She scrunched her features together, cocked her head, and lowered her voice. *"I have no care to stay here long."*

Merrick stared in disbelief. She mocked him. This woman who stood only at his shoulder in her heeled shoes *mocked* him. She even assumed his slight accent. He had slain men for less.

Amusement rolled around in his chest, worked its way up his throat. He gave in and let it escape. With a shake of his head, he laughed.

The look of astonishment that settled into her delicate features only stirred his humor more. For one priceless moment, she sat speechless. But her silence quickly gave way to a punishing frown that stifled his chuckles. He ceased his laughter, but he could not contain his grin. The temptation to tease her was too much. "I do not wish to bed you, *demon Anne*."

Another chortle threatened to break free as her shoulders stiffened. He did not give her time to reply. "'Tis the mark I seek."

Visibly, she relaxed. "I'm not taking off my clothes. I have a tattoo, but I'm in no mood to show it to you."

He took a step closer and glared at her. "You will—"

"No. I won't." Shooting to her feet, she stabbed a finger in his chest. "I will *not* do one more thing you tell me to. You want something, you ask. Got it?"

He caught her hand and brought it gently to her side. "Fine," he grumbled. "Will you show me this mark?"

"No."

God's teeth she was more stubborn than a mule. Conversing with her was like trying to scale a rampart wall—deceptively easy until one encountered the bowmen within. He turned from her and dropped into the only chair in the small room. "You try my patience, woman."

"At least we agree on something then." She flounced back onto the bed. "How do you even know what you're looking for?"

"'Twould be obvious. We all bear marks of meaning. Those we chose, or those that were put upon us. Mayhap we take pride in them, mayhap we wish they did not exist. But we all bear them. Is there naught upon your body that stands out in your mind?"

Understanding flickered behind her frown. She knew what he referenced, despite the objecting shake of her head.

"What guarantee do I have that if I show you, you won't create something that matches?"

At once offended that she would think him capable of

such trickery, he asked through gritted teeth, "You doubt my honor?"

She lifted an eyebrow and let out a soft chuckle. "Is it really necessary to answer that?"

Merrick clenched his fingers around the chair's smooth arm. His word had never been questioned. Even those who despised him for conquering them had never challenged his honor. Not even his uncle, who refused to acknowledge Merrick's birthright, dared such. "I assure you, I speak naught that is false, nor do I tolerate those who do."

"Not going to work, Merrick. You want me to believe this stuff, then you show me my matching mark first."

Clearly, they were at an impasse. He lacked the energy to pursue the battle, however. Raking a hand through his hair, he dropped his head to the back of the chair. "I am weary, Anne." Weak as well, but he would not tell her such. The explanation would only lead to more questions, and he simply lacked the strength to carry on a conversation. "Can we not resolve this so I may rest?"

"I'm not stopping you from sleeping."

"Nay?" He lifted his head to look at her, surprised by the effort it required. "What guarantee do *I* have that you shall not vanish once I shut my eyes?"

"I guess you'll just have to chance it."

The bed creaked as she stood up. Moving to stand in front of him, she gestured at the mattress. "Go sleep."

He did not trust this more agreeable side of her nature. Yet he could no longer hold his eyes open. Exhaustion weighed him down, making the simple effort of sitting upright near impossible. Against his better judgment, he went to the bed, took off his sword, and collapsed into the mattress' welcome softness. Rolling onto his back, he tossed an arm over his forehead and let out a deep sigh. "If you are missing when I wake . . ."

"Oh hell, Merrick. I'm not going anywhere. I'm too damn curious to run."

A smile tugged at his mouth. He peeked out from be-

neath his elbow to look at her and spied her in his chair.
"You speak like a man."

"Get used to it."

He supposed he had little choice.

CHAPTER 5

Declan's gaze strayed down the corridor that led to Merrick's room. For a modern woman, Anne held a simple beauty and charm. She did not accent her eyes with kohl, nor did she paint her cheeks with rouge. And her manner of dress strangely did not hold the tastelessness of so many women of her era, despite her trendy fashion. She resonated with unspoken class.

Yet 'twas not her wholesome good looks that drew his restless stare. The gift she carried inside, the light of angels in her soul, made him want to chase her down and demand she pledge herself to him.

"Abigail is gone then? Azazel has taken the nail?" Farran asked of Caradoc.

Declan forced his attention back to his companions.

Caradoc answered with a nod. He moved across the large prayer chamber, pacing in front of the gathered five. "Aye, 'tis what Mikhail told us last month. We are to anticipate a second attack. Mikhail has reinforced the other two adytum's crucifixion nails. He intends to send the six of us when Azazel's knights draw near."

Declan swallowed down a lump of dread. Another confrontation with one of Azazel's knights, and his time would come to an end. Already he felt the darkness stir each time he confronted one of Azazel's lesser pawns. In the last fight with Merrick, it had become painful to strike the creatures, so close was he to transformation.

"These next few months shall not be easy for us. I fear we will lose those we are closest to." Although he addressed the other men, Caradoc's knowing gaze settled on him, and Declan shifted under the penetrating weight.

The Templar Code dictated Declan inform his brothers that his time neared. Merrick had done so a handful of weeks ago, and yet Merrick's light surpassed Declan's tenfold. But Declan could not bring himself to admit the painful truth. Frankly, he was too weary to care.

Now, with the revelation of the seraphs, he could not tamp down the hope Anne would bring his salvation.

Uncomfortable with the discussion, he rose to his feet. "Excuse me, Caradoc. I canna keep me eyes open."

Farran gave him a curt nod as Declan bid good-bye with a smile. He retreated down the hall, rounded the corner, and let himself inside his small, Spartan chambers. With a heavy sigh, he let down his guise of merriment and pushed the door shut tight.

He took off his sword and tossed it onto his bed. The ache in his chest was a tangible thing, and he rubbed a fist against his sternum. Nine hundred years ago, when he rode south to aid the Christians on the road to Jerusalem, he would have never envisioned his life would come to this. That he would live out centuries having never known a child's love, nor called a piece of land his own. He served the Templar with his heart, and yet what good had it accomplished? He would die at Mikhail's hands, if he were lucky. If he were not, he could only hope they would cut him down when once he wore Azazel's cloth.

A knock at the door startled him. Grumbling, he jerked the door open to find Caradoc standing in the hall. Though the harsh gleam in Caradoc's light eyes and the rigid set of his shoulders warned Declan the visit was not social in nature, he pulled another smile forth and welcomed his brother inside.

Caradoc kicked the door shut with his heel. "Why have you said naught? Does Merrick know?"

Declan sighed from the depths of his soul and shook his head. "Nay."

A long moment of tense silence spanned between them, so oppressive Declan could feel the weight of the stones overhead pushing down on his shoulders. Caradoc moved to the window, looking out at the distant trees. His fingers drummed a steady cadence on the rough-hewn sill, a tell-tale restlessness that heralded his intense disapproval.

Declan waited for the inevitable explosion, sudden shame bowing his head. "I donna want the pity, brother."

"No one wants the pity," Caradoc murmured. He spared Declan a brief glance, then fixed his attention out the window once more.

"How did you ken?"

Caradoc ran a hand through his sandy hair and the tightness in his spine gave way to slumped shoulders. His voice carried the same echo of weariness that haunted Declan's soul. "The maid. The way your eyes looked to Merrick's room once I explained what she is."

Seeking to divert his friend from the truth, Declan said, "She is an entertaining lass." A genuine smile touched his face as he recalled the way Anne had kicked Merrick in the shin. "Her intended will have a handful to tame."

"And if she is not meant for you, Declan? What shall you do then? What if this night we are called to fight and we do not know her mate?"

Declan folded his arms over his chest and scowled. Presented with the selfish nature of his actions was shame enough. He did not need his lapse in judgment berated further.

"Think you not I feel it too, Declan? The pain is unbearable at times, and we all suffer in different ways. Farran is so angry I fear naught shall ever make him laugh again. You grow weary, Merrick has lost hope. Lucan trusts so few he will not fight beside the other men. And Tane . . ." Caradoc dropped his head against the window frame, lowering his voice to a woeful murmur. "Tane has become so covetous that if Anne is not his, I worry for her mate."

Pulling in a deep breath, Caradoc turned to face Declan. Deep lines of worry knotted his forehead. Accusation gleamed in his eyes. "Still we depend on each other to speak the truth. Yet you break the vow and jeopardize those who would give their very lives for you."

Declan closed his eyes against the bitter truth. He stayed silent, for naught he could say would excuse his selfishness. At the scrape of steel, he snapped them open. Sunlight glinted off the tip of Caradoc's blade. Held at the ready, his brother regarded him with such regret, Declan shuddered. So it would come to this. Caradoc would take his life here. Declan ought to praise the Almighty 'twould be swift—for Caradoc would ensure no less. Yet he could not shake off the chill that settled in his veins.

"I will not risk everything for your pride, Declan," Caradoc murmured. "'Tis too much at stake."

Before Declan could take a step backward and assume a defensive stance, Caradoc swept the mighty broadsword across his body. Cold steel dug in deep, searing heat through Declan's arm. He grasped at his bicep in a vain effort to hold the flesh together. Blood trickled through his fingers, ran down the length of his hand. His eyes widened, and he stared, unable to believe he still breathed.

"You will not fight," Caradoc grit out as he wiped his sword on Declan's bed. More quietly, he added, "Not for a while." He snatched a shirt off the floor and tossed it at Declan. "Tie off your wound."

As Declan wound the cloth around his arm and tugged it with his teeth, Caradoc jerked open the door. "Best you pray the girl is yours," he muttered before he slammed the portal shut.

Declan sank to his knees. His brother had spared him in the only way he could. Struck by a Templar blade, Declan would not enjoy immortality's prompt healing. Nay, 'twould take weeks, mayhap longer, before the bone-deep gash would mend enough so he could wield his sword.

He sniffed back his gratitude and struggled to his feet. A wave of light-headedness bowled into him, making him stumble as he reached for the door. He caught himself on the iron handle and sank once again to the floor. Bloody hell, Caradoc meant to see him suffer.

Seated beside the window, Anne watched Merrick sleep. With not even a book present, it was either watch him sleep, take a nap herself, or stare out the window at an empty, sand-filled courtyard and hope someone would come out and work with weapons or something to entertain her. She was bored and restless, and her mind worked overtime. Nothing, absolutely nothing, she could think of could describe what had happened in Mikhail's office. There was only one answer, and Anne's affinity for the spiritual realm embraced the impossible without hesitation. It was the logical side of her nature that kept interfering, arguing that if she accepted what she'd experienced as fact, someone would think she'd lost all her sense.

But did that really matter? No one, except these men here, would ever really know if she'd decided to believe. When she got out of here, she didn't have to tell anyone. She'd be the only one able to snicker behind her hand or ridicule her actions.

In either case, angels or no angels, nothing would convince her that Merrick—and probably the other men— were not Templar. Though she hadn't touched the others, what she learned from Merrick told so many truths it was almost frightening.

Almost.

She found it fascinating, and the part of her desperate for knowledge did a jig so merry inside her head, a strange giddiness swept over her. Somewhere in these halls, she'd likely find everything she needed to finish her thesis. The trick would be discovering it before classes began Monday morning. No one in the school would believe Mikhail's story about her running off with someone, and as long as she showed up for her 9 A.M. lecture on medieval social structure, no harm would come from spending a day researching in some weird temple underneath the old Liberty Odd Fellows Home. When she went back, she'd be more than happy to help Merrick after hours, from within her house.

She just had to figure out how to get Merrick and his friends to go along with her plans before she ran out of time.

A heavy thump in the hall brought Anne to the edge of her chair. At the sound of a hoarse voice calling something that resembled Merrick's name, she rose cautiously to her feet. Did those disgusting things come down here? Surely not. And if they did, they wouldn't last long in a cavern full of men who knew how to kill them.

Again, the voice called out. This time there was no mistaking the distinct sound of Merrick's name.

She glanced at his sleeping form, debating whether to wake him first or investigate herself. Recalling how grumpy he'd been without sleep, she went to the door and poked her head outside. Her gaze swept down the dim corridor. It stopped on a dark form halfway inside a doorway, three doors down. As she squinted at the form, trying to identify it, fingers moved against the stone floor.

Anne rushed to the crumpled body. She skidded to a halt, no more than two feet away as she recognized the man. "Declan?"

"Fetch . . . Merrick . . ." A groan erupted from his throat, and he curled forward, clutching at his arm.

Anne's stare fixed on the scarlet stained rag tied around Declan's arm. When he pulled his hand away, his fingers were drenched with blood. *Oh God above.*

A wave of nausea churned her stomach. Her knees turned to jelly. She clutched at the jagged stone to steady herself against a rush of dizziness and swallowed back the bitter taste of bile. Cuts she could handle, but this . . . She'd never seen so much blood.

With a shake of her head, she cleared away her shock and reclaimed her senses. Running back to Merrick's room, she thrust open the door. "Merrick, get up!" She darted to the bed and gave his shoulder a hard shake. "Merrick!"

Jerking awake with a grunt, he looked at her in confusion. Groggily, he lifted to one elbow, his frown firmly intact.

"Declan's hurt. He's in the hall."

The frown disappeared, giving way to immediate concern. He leapt off the bed and stalked to the door.

She followed as he stormed down the hall. "Get back inside," he instructed on a backward glance.

Ignoring his gruff order, Anne hurried past Merrick and rushed to Declan's side. The blood wasn't so shocking the second time, and she knelt in front of him to take his good hand in hers. "What happened?"

Declan's expression twisted. He answered with a barely discernable shake of his head.

"Damnation!" Merrick's oath cracked through the air as he joined Anne, towering over Declan's injured arm. He bent down and gave the soggy crimson cloth a jerk, tightening it. "Who did this?"

"Caradoc," Declan croaked.

Their eyes met, and something Anne couldn't recognize passed between the two men. Confused by why one of their friends would attack Declan, and by Merrick's impassive reaction, she furrowed her brow and rocked back on her heels.

"Anne." Merrick turned to her, his voice low and clear. "Go down the corridor behind us. Turn left at the end. Four doors on your right, you will find Farran. Fetch him."

Confronted with a wounded man's needs, she ignored the shaking in her hands and jogged away. Her boots clicked against the stone, echoing through the long, dim passage. Caradoc attacked Declan. Why? She'd sensed nothing but camaraderie between the men in Mikhail's office. When Caradoc knelt before her, she'd noticed nothing negative in his energy. Had they argued? Was this how men here solved differences?

At Farran's heavy door, she banged until her fist throbbed. The instinct to shout gripped her tight, but something about the way Merrick and Declan exchanged looks kept her silent. She'd passed a dozen other doors, and for some reason, Merrick sent her here. An oddity that said he didn't want others involved. Also strange.

The door swung open. Farran greeted her with a scowl. "What do you want, wench?"

Wench? She cringed inwardly. Her pride demanded she tell him just exactly what she thought of his crude slang. Reminding herself Declan's needs were more important, she pushed aside her temper and pointed down the hall. "Merrick sent me. Declan's hurt."

Without a word, Farran slammed the door shut and shouldered past her. Though his strides were long and purposeful, he didn't hurry.

Following at a distance, Anne couldn't help but notice Farran's impressive size. Though not as tall as Merrick, his broad shoulders had the same difficulty with the narrow doorways, and he had to turn sideways to pass through. She let her glance skim down his back, noting with appreciation how his dark jeans pulled tight across firm buttocks and thick thighs. She imagined that Webster's definition of *foul tempered* might reference Farran's name, but damn, the man certainly knew how to take care of himself. She had colleagues who went to the gym every day and they wouldn't ever come close to looking like these men.

Good grief, if things were different, she'd be in heaven. This place was a made-to-order catalogue for single women. Pick hair color, eye color, and the rest of the package was waiting and ready. Assuming one could ignore their surly attitudes.

She frowned at the displaced thought. A man was hurt, and she was admiring the view. How insensitive could she be?

And how come, when Farran was put together as nicely as Merrick, she didn't get the same flutters in her belly Merrick stirred? Farran was no more unpleasant than her current guardian.

Farran dropped to a squat near Declan and Merrick. The two men conferred in low voices, but she couldn't make out their words. In unison, they rose and grabbed Declan beneath the arms. As they hefted him up, the Scot struggled to maintain his footing. He leaned against Merrick with a groan.

Merrick gave her a hard look. "Wait in my chambers. 'Tis not safe for you in these halls."

Mikhail hadn't mentioned any danger, but this was the second reference Merrick made to it. She had door after door of big strong man, all completely capable of using a sword, and probably familiar with a few other weapons too. She couldn't think of anyplace more safe.

Then again, several hours ago she wouldn't have believed two friends could come to blows and one would have his arm nearly cut off. Maybe the men weren't quite as noble as their code dictated they ought to be. She'd read accounts about Templar sects that became corrupted by power and ruled in tyranny. If men like that dwelled here, she could understand Merrick's statement. He wasn't exactly the epitome of chivalry either.

Unwilling to test Merrick's warning, she closed herself inside his room and slumped in the chair. The silence settled on her shoulders, thick and imposing. She glanced around, hoping she'd missed a book, a television, or a radio hiding in some corner. But all she found were bare shelves, a tall wardrobe that surely held his clothes, and the sparse furniture—the simple chair she sat in, his large bed, a well-worn trunk, and a small table beneath his window. A closed door on the opposite wall disguised what she assumed was the bathroom.

A sigh tumbled free. No noise, no distraction, nothing to occupy her mind. No wonder he was such a grump. He was missing all the pleasures in life.

The utter lack of modern conveniences only reminded her again that this would never work. She couldn't spend more than a few hours in this . . . prison. Too much silence would make her crazy. For that matter . . . She glanced down at her clothes. She didn't have a thing to wear.

Which didn't really matter, given she'd be gone by the end of the night. Maybe tomorrow evening she'd drive down from Atchison and do whatever it was Merrick expected of her. As far as this intended stuff went—she absolutely didn't buy into that. Besides, even on the off chance it wasn't some fabrication, she couldn't see herself getting attached to one of these antiquated men. It might be fun for a while, but soon enough, all the chauvinism would get stale.

Her stomach growled, reminding her she hadn't eaten since yesterday's lunch. Another reason she had to get home—Dr. Knowles was coming to dinner tomorrow night with his wife.

Thoughtfully, she slid the armband off and examined it. Nehushtan. Ancient Hebrew texts referred to the snake on a pole that could heal. Jesus had compared Moses's raising of the serpent to the raising up of the Holy Son. Eternal life, salvation—this trinket caused all this. One stupid piece of jewelry couldn't be that important.

With a shake of her head, she squeezed her eyes shut. This was so not happening. She couldn't be descended from angels. She *had not* worked for an archangel.

She set the armband on the chair and stood up. Crossing the room, she watched it warily. When she reached the bed, the damn thing disappeared. A weight in her hand told her where it had gone. She glanced down and rolled her eyes.

So if this wasn't happening, just what explained that?

Groaning, she flopped onto the bed. Immortal knights, archangels . . . What did Gabe expect her to do—jump for joy, sing, and dance while she threw away her career? Clearly, he'd picked the wrong woman. This kind of fly-by-the-seat-of-one's-pants stuff was something up Sophie's alley, not hers.

Anne's eyes widened, and she sucked in a sharp breath. Sophie. Unease filtered down her spine as she dropped her gaze to the brass serpents. Good God, he hadn't picked the wrong woman—he'd picked them both.

CHAPTER 6

†

Declan's wound gaped wide, exposing white bone beneath. He groaned as Merrick and Farran eased him onto the fresh linens of a newly made bed within the infirmary. Merrick squeezed the Scot's good shoulder. Though the tear in Declan's flesh was bad, Merrick had seen worse. Declan had survived worse before the fateful day they had stumbled upon the scrolls beneath the Temple Mount. Aye, Declan would recover.

Uriel, with his cart of modern medical supplies and time-honored herbal treatments, quickly assumed command. Muttering a stream of unintelligible words beneath his breath, the angel of healing pulled Declan's arm into the light, ran his thumb up his vein, and gave him an injection of some clear fluid.

In moments, Declan's eyelids lowered, his head lolled sideways, and his breathing leveled.

Merrick turned to Farran, indicating the door with a jerk of his head. Farran pushed through the heavy wooden barrier with Merrick on his heels. In the corridor beyond, the younger man leaned against the wall and flattened one foot on the stone behind him. His piercing gaze was cold, filled with centuries of anger. "'Twas no accident, Merrick."

Merrick kept his voice low so it would not carry down the corridor. "Nay. 'Twas Caradoc."

"Caradoc? But why would—" His furrowed brow smoothed as understanding slowly registered. He looked beyond Merrick, quiet for several drawn-out heartbeats. Then his shoulders slumped with a heavy exhale. "Declan informed me not."

"He said naught to me as well."

Merrick did not want to put the necessary question to Farran, but his vows to the Order, his loyalty—no matter how hopeless their purpose—demanded he inquire after the nature of their souls. "How do you fare, Farran? Are you close enough to Azazel that I must cut off a limb to keep you from fighting?"

Farran's eyes flashed dark. He pushed off the wall and scowled. "I would inform you, as you informed us. You challenge my honor, brother."

"Nay, Farran, I do not," Merrick said. "'Tis my duty to inquire. Declan kept his secret, and I must be certain where the rest of you stand."

His small apology tempered Farran's initial fury, but the anger that brimmed behind his light brown stare dimmed little. "I have a few good battles left in me. Do not worry, Merrick, I shall inform you, should you need to watch me."

Merrick took no offense at the roughness of Farran's voice, for he could well understand the humility of knowing one would soon become useless. He dipped his head in a respectful nod. "Then I shall speak with Caradoc and learn the status of Tane and Lucan. From this point forward, Farran, we stay as one. All five of us—six should Declan heal soon enough—will fight together. No more of this separation."

"That will not be necessary, Merrick. Nor will it be possible."

At the sound of Mikhail's voice, Merrick instantly straightened his back.

"You will continue to advise Caradoc. As second in

command, he shall report to you, and you will learn of the status of the rest of your men. However, those three shall soon depart."

"Depart?" Farran asked.

"I received word from Gabriel just now. Maggie has met the same fate as Abigail."

"And that is?" Merrick asked. He had assumed Gabriel relocated Abigail Montfort. Gradually he was beginning to realize his refusal to answer Mikhail's summons left him grossly uninformed. First the return of the seraphs, now Abigail—he was not sure he wished to discover more surprises.

Mikhail's expression tightened. "Azazel has taken her life, along with the relic she guarded. Azazel now possesses two crucifixion nails. Caradoc, Tane, and Lucan will soon leave for Georgia, to assist with rebuilding the adytum. I am removing them from battle for a time."

'Twas both punishment and reward. Caradoc would resent Mikhail's order to set aside his sword. Yet the reprieve from combat would spare their souls a little longer, a gift to all three men. None would admit gratefulness, but in the secret corners of their minds, and when they believed no one would overhear their prayers, they would give thanks.

Merrick refused to acknowledge the stab of jealousy that tightened his chest. "Very well. I shall inform them."

Mikhail turned to Farran with a warm smile. "Stay with Declan. I must speak to Merrick alone."

Farran gave no indication his dismissal bothered him. In fact, as Merrick watched him stride through the healing chamber's door, he detected a degree of relief in Farran's hurried step. He could not blame him—even after spending nearly a thousand years in his company, Merrick found that Mikhail still had a way of making a man uncomfortable.

As the door swung shut, Mikhail's smile disappeared. "Have you made progress with Anne?"

If arguing could be considered progress, mayhap

Merrick had made headway. He doubted Mikhail would appreciate the sarcasm, however, and shook his head. "She refuses to show me."

Under the power of Mikhail's stare, even Merrick, who feared little, shrunk back. "You *must* find her intended. Look around you, du Loire. Observe the way the knights shrivel each time they confront Azazel's fiends. If we are to overcome his darkness and stop this attack upon the sacred relics, we need Anne. We need the other seraphs. We *will* fail without them. Is this clear?"

"Aye," Merrick gritted out.

"Then I suggest you use that sharp mind for the greater purpose you serve, instead of this oath to Fulk. Fulk will see his salvation when he is meant to."

Giving in to frustration, Merrick tossed his hands in the air. "You know so much, why do you not simply tell us who she belongs with?"

A smile tugged at the corner of Mikhail's mouth, and to Merrick's complete frustration, the archangel began to laugh.

"I find naught to laugh at in your games, Mikhail."

Mikhail ceased his laughter, but mirth glinted in his eyes. "Take your frustration up with Gabriel, Merrick. He alone knows, and quite refuses to speak a word of it."

Merrick bit back an oath. The herald of mysteries was the last archangel he wanted to confront. On more than one occasion, Gabriel's cryptic words and riddles had caused Merrick grief. 'Twas not surprising that the archangel left the Templar knights to decode his cipher.

Having twice now been taken to task by his commander, Merrick left without further word. He stalked toward his chambers and the source of his current problems.

The door gave easily beneath his firm shove. It thumped into the stone and shuddered on thick iron hinges. Striding into his chambers, he stopped short as he caught sight of Anne lying on his bed. His breath lodged in his lungs. Something deep inside his gut wound down like a vise. His blood warmed, and he felt his cock stir against his thigh.

One dainty hand tucked beneath her delicate cheek. Her partly open lips were lush and rosy, as if she had just been thoroughly kissed. She had changed her shirt, exchanging the feminine material for one of his larger, rougher garments. Unbuttoned at the collar, the material gaped in a deep V and gave him the most tempting view of soft flesh beneath a fringe of white lace.

Merrick swallowed hard. God's teeth, the way she had cocked one leg before the other accented a shapely thigh. Her long auburn hair spilled across the pillow, shimmering in the afternoon sunlight like fire-kissed strands of gold. She looked soft and innocent, and for one startling heartbeat, the fierce desire possessed him to scoop her up and drink from her lush mouth until he could no longer breathe.

He scowled at his profoundly physical response. She was but a modern woman, entirely too disagreeable to belong to him. And presently, she was the bane of his existence, the impediment to an oath he had sealed in blood.

"Rise," he ground out harshly.

She mumbled something and sank deeper into the pillow.

A feeling he had thought never to experience again swelled inside him. Dull, almost unrecognizable, hope filtered through his despair. He eased the door shut with his heel. Drawn like a moth to firelight, he moved to the bed.

He gazed down at her sleeping form, took in the youthfulness of her exquisite face. Though he had touched her earlier only out of necessity, the feel of her smooth skin burned against his palm. The memory of her body flush with his stirred the heat in his blood to intolerable limits, and his shaft swelled painfully as he recalled the vivid dream of Anne, naked in this very bed, murmuring his name whilst he plunged himself inside her.

More like a demon than an angel.

He grumbled beneath his breath. In all of his journeys, he had never met a woman with such fierce spirit. She feared him not. Did little more than flinch at the first sight of a nytym. Quite possibly, she did not know the meaning of fear. True, she had nearly fainted in front of Mikhail, yet even then, she did not exhibit fright.

His body moved against his will. He trailed a fingertip across her cheek, marveling at the silken nature of her skin. Unable to stop himself, he moved lower, breaching the shirt's neckline to touch the swell of her breast. Beneath his fascinated gaze, her flesh broke out with goose bumps, and her nipples puckered at the fabric.

Merrick tamped down a groan. He should not take such liberties, but saints' blood, he could not help himself. She called to him like the trumpet of a horn upon a battlefield, and his blood quickened with the same fiercely instinctual response. He knew the darkness in his soul drove him to take liberties he should not, and yet in some twisted, wicked way, he wanted naught more than to tug down her jeans, rouse her from sleep with his mouth, and sheathe himself inside her body.

He closed his eyes to the torment. But when he opened them once again, she had not disappeared as he had hoped she might. Drawn by a force he could not resist, he crawled over her and eased down into the bed. The scent of her perfume assaulted him, stirring the embers of his desire like wind upon a campfire. He draped an arm around her waist and inhaled deeply. So completely feminine. So incredibly intoxicating.

With a mutter, he flopped onto his back and squeezed his eyes shut.

Anne woke in a blanket of warmth. Merrick's bed was more comfortable than she'd imagined, and she snuggled into the soft mattress, unwilling to get up and face the cold, unfriendly stone of his room. As she nestled deeper into the comfort, her back pressed into something firm and unmoving. Awareness seeped through the haze of sleep, and she cracked one eye open.

Merrick lay behind her, holding her as a lover might. The heat that soaked into her came from his body and warmed her all the way down to her toes. Especially where his hand delved beneath the gaping neckline of the shirt she'd borrowed and cupped her breast.

Her eyes widened as she followed the contours of his fingers. Tiny scars marred the back of his knuckles, his olive skin a stark contrast to her pale complexion. A dusting of dark hair shadowed his wrist, traveled sparsely up a corded forearm.

Her mind pulled as another image attempted to rise. She shoved the haziness away, unwilling to see another glimpse of past or future and stared at his hand.

There was something strangely erotic about seeing herself held in such a way. It had been far too long since she'd known a man's touch. So long, that at times she joked with Sophie she'd reclaimed her virginity. Merrick's possessive hold, however, brought all those repressed memories of desire back to the surface in one clang of her heart. Her stomach fluttered, and that incredible warmth fanned through her veins, taking root between her legs.

Shocked by her body's unexpected reaction, she shoved at Merrick's arm to escape his hold. Only the harder she pushed, the tighter his fingers squeezed her breast. A painful pinch shot down her spine, and she let out a soft cry. When the sensation wore off, and his fingers unclenched, she changed her tactic. Bunching her hand into a fist, she beat on his shoulder. "Get off me."

The yell did the trick. Merrick startled awake. He jerked his hand away and sat up, eyes wide, as if he was equally surprised to find himself curled around her.

Anne jumped out of the bed. Whirling around to face him, she fisted her hands on her hips and glared. "What the hell do you think you're doing?"

Merrick's mask of shock gave way to his usual surly frown. He kicked the quilts off his feet and stalked across the room to pound his way through the small bathroom door. A rush of water splashed, then the flush of the toilet gave way to the thump and bump of cabinet doors. Anne flounced down into the chair and rubbed her arms to fight off a sudden chill. She'd liked Merrick touching her. Too much, frankly.

She'd gone five years without a man—not for lack of offers either. Out of devotion to her father's memory, her career had taken priority, and relationships were a distraction she didn't need. She'd avoided the urges, ignored her own desires, and did a reasonable job at convincing herself life without a man was better, less trouble. Why, then, did this one suddenly make her all weak in the knees? This too-big, too-arrogant man who had to be several hundred years old.

Before she could contemplate it further, Merrick stormed back into the room. His glower pinned her to the chair. "We start this now. 'Tis night, the men shall rise soon," he barked from his wardrobe.

"Start what?"

He unfolded a fresh T-shirt with a shake. "Discovering the mark and your intended."

"Oh." That again. She let out a heavy sigh. "I can't do this, Merrick. This place is like a prison. I can't stay here. I need color. Laughter. Television for God's sake. Above all, my work. Allow me to go back home, and I'll work with you every day after I finish my classes."

"Nay. 'Tis impossible. You must remain here until you gain the protection of your intended's immortality."

Immortality? Now that was almost tempting. But the fact remained, she couldn't stay. "I don't think you understand—I'm not really asking. I can work each day at the college. Mikhail mentioned I could chose to aid from my home. You and I can meet each evening, and I'll help with whatever it is you want. But I'm not staying here, Merrick. I have research to finish, classes to teach."

"Nay, damsel."

"But—"

He continued as if he hadn't heard her. "You shall find a television in the common room upstairs. Mayhap your intended shall watch it with you."

The ludicrousness of his suggestion was enough to temporarily sidetrack her from convincing him into seeing things her way. "In the common room?" Her voice rose in indignation. "When I find this . . . this . . . *intended,* I can't even watch television alone with him? What happened to privacy?"

He looked at her with such a quizzical expression she almost laughed. Giving her a shake of his head, his frown deepened. " 'Tis our way. We own very little, as is mandated by the oath we swore centuries ago. Anything of luxury is shared by all."

Anne rolled her eyes. "A TV isn't a luxury. Cable maybe. TV—not hardly. And what about books? I have research to do, reports to write—I can't focus in a room full of people or in one maddeningly silent. And I need my books."

He shrugged. "We have books in the library—far more than you would ever expect. You may read to your heart's content there. I am certain you can find something of merit."

She flopped back against the chair's thick stuffing and grumbled. Obviously, he didn't understand how important key research materials were. She'd spent too long accumulating everything she needed to start over with new references. Under her breath she muttered, "Maybe my intended will be more compassionate."

Merrick must have heard her, for his eyes glittered coal black. He cocked his head and gave her a hard stare. "You think I lack compassion?"

Anne let out a soft snort. "Listen to yourself, and you tell me."

As the twitch started along his jaw, she hurried to end their argument. Enough of this. It wasn't as if she planned on staying permanently. She'd spend some time here, learn the secrets history couldn't record, and get out of this prison. Back to her classroom and her uneventful life. Maybe she could find something new and useful in the library he mentioned. In the meantime, however, humoring him would work to her advantage. If he believed she intended to stay, he'd likely be more apt to tell her things he otherwise wouldn't. Feigning a harassed sigh, she answered, "Fine, let's begin."

He stared down at her, imposing in his size and demeanor. "You will swear to me, if I agree to your terms, you shall admit the truth when you see it."

"Whatever. I'll tell you if I see it. Are you happy?"

His mouth pursed. "Nay. Kneel and swear."

Kneel? Oh hell no. She tightened her hands around the chair's arms. "You'll just have to trust me. I refuse to kneel."

The tightening at his shoulders indicated he didn't care for her refusal, but when she didn't budge, he gave her a shrug. "So be it. Since we are so obviously incompatible, let us get this out of the way first." In a fluid motion, he fisted his hand at the nape of his torn shirt and doffed it.

Anne almost choked. Smooth taut muscles bunched and pulled across his broad chest. Pectorals she'd only seen in magazines confronted her, marred only by a long white scar that ran beneath one, wrapped around his ribs, and disappeared somewhere behind his back. Her gaze dropped to his belly, and she counted four . . . no eight . . . tight cords across the washboard surface. *Oh good Lord.*

She let her stare travel down a thick line of dark hair that led beneath his jeans, and couldn't keep her gaze off his groin no matter how she told herself she wouldn't look. To her complete surprise, the light denim pulled tight. Oh, he wasn't . . . He couldn't be . . . She swallowed. Yes, he was. Hard. A flush crept into her cheeks, and she jerked her gaze to his face.

Merrick's eyes flickered, the only indication he was aware of her appreciative stare. In the next heartbeat, however, the interest in his gaze gave way to the cold impassiveness she'd begun to associate with him.

He turned around and presented her with his left arm. "Does it match this?"

Anne's eyes widened a fraction. There, twining around

his bulging bicep were two tattooed snakes, joined head to head. Where their bodies intersected, they formed the same Templar cross that the pair on her ankle created. Both deep ebony. Both with eyes of gold.

Just like hers.

Oh shit.

She recovered enough to pretend she inspected the design with an eye for details. No way in hell was she about to tell this man who didn't think twice about throwing her over his shoulder to get what he wanted, that she belonged to him. Beyond all the other very logical reasons she couldn't stay, the one repeated vision she'd had of him showed him dead. She would not be party to that—either active participant or passive observer. And she certainly wouldn't give Merrick any more reasons to hawk over her or confine her in someplace even smaller with fewer modern comforts.

"No," she murmured. In a stronger voice she added, "Nice art, but I've never seen it before."

CHAPTER 7

A piece of Merrick's soul crumpled and died with Anne's rejection. He turned away, unable to look at her until he was certain the unexpected ache would not present itself in his expression. He had known better. They were too incompatible. Too ill-suited to possess a preordained fate. And yet, some traitorous portion of his spirit had dared to hope mayhap she would take this darkness from him and allow him to live.

He tugged his shirt over his head and took a deep, fortifying breath. So she was not meant for him—all the more reason to find her mate and rid himself of her quickly. Each passing day her intended took a step closer to damnation, and Merrick would not carry the burden of a brother's fall because, in some secret forbidden place in his heart, he enjoyed the saucy maid.

"I shall return." He reached for his sword and buckled it around his waist.

"Where are you going?"

"To retrieve my men. Mikhail has ordered them away. Before they go, we must see if you belong to one of them." Her harassed sigh as he reached for the door gave him pause. "Something distresses you?"

She worried her fingers through her long hair. "I don't

want to sit in this room any longer. Please, take me with you."

The renegade part of him he had not fully beaten into submission took pity on her. His frown faded, and he gave her a slow nod. "If we do not find your intended in my men, we shall talk, and I shall take you to the dining hall. Until you understand the nature of the temple, however, you must remain here."

"Merrick, take me with you. Please. I can't take another minute more in this room."

The pleading quality behind her bright blue eyes stabbed into him like a red-hot poker. He gave little thought to his chambers; they serviced his need for sleep, naught else. He had never considered how they might appear to someone else—guests were forbidden, and the men shared identical small enclosures. As he glanced around his sleeping quarters, he understood how she would find them bland and boring. It could hurt naught to take her with him. She faced little threat from the less honorable men amongst their ranks as long as she stayed close.

He held out his hand.

Anne stared at it as if he offered her thorns. He anticipated her refusal. But then she slipped her palm into his, her dainty fingers clasping gently, and she stood. The smile she gave him stuttered his heart. He said a silent thankful prayer they met at sword point, for if she had smiled at him thus, he would have done anything to make her his.

Anything.

With a gentle tug, he led her out the door.

They walked in silence down the corridor. Where their palms met, his skin warmed. Caught by the rush of pleasant sensations that worked their way up his arm, he shifted his hold to twine his fingers through hers. A gentleman would release her hand, tuck the delicate digit into the crook of his elbow. But Merrick had never been such, and she seemed uninclined to twist free. In fact, lest his imagination had gotten the better of him, she tightened her grip.

"How is Declan?" she asked at the juncture of three corridors.

Merrick bristled. She liked Declan. She had even given the Scot a gift of her smile. He ought to embrace the possibility Declan and she might share eternity together, but for a reason Merrick could not understand, the idea left a bitter taste in his mouth. He fought it down with effort and kept his gaze fastened straight ahead. "He will survive. Uriel will tend his wound."

From the corner of his eye, he caught Anne's apprehensive glance. "Uriel? I don't think I heard you right."

"You did."

Her brows puckered as she struggled with something internally. "I thought . . ." Her frown deepened, and she pursed her lips.

"You thought what?"

"Doctrine says Raphael heals, not Uriel."

Merrick shook his head. "Through time, much information has been misreported. Raphael holds Mikhail's position in our European temple."

She digested this with a slow nod. Then her confusion fled and her features smoothed. "So tell me, big guy. If there's an archangel tending Declan, why was there ever any worry? Can't he just wave his hands or something, and those wounds will go away?"

Merrick chuckled. "Nay. Uriel will not. He uses only the tools known to mankind to heal."

"But *why*?"

He grinned down at her and gave her hand a squeeze. "Because the archangels are peculiar in their ways. Would that I understood them, I suppose I would be one."

"Well we know you are no angel."

Merrick frowned. Yet as he opened his mouth to return the insult, he caught the gleam of humor behind her gaze and took in the way her eyes crinkled at the corners. Saints' blood, she was teasing him.

The playful banter stirred a lightness in his heart that made him feel much like the young knight he had once been when the world lay before him, ready for his conquest. His mouth quirked. "Aye. You are one to speak, *demon Anne*."

Her throaty laugh stirred something else. His pulse quickened. His lungs felt too tight, and against his thigh, his shaft rose in answer. Bollocks! Could he not spend a moment with her without suffering this accursed desire?

Grinding his teeth together, he banged on Lucan's door.

Anne stifled her laughter as the door cracked open and Lucan stuck his head out. On seeing her, he swung the door wide, grabbed her free hand, and brought the back of it to his lips. "Lady Anne, a pleasure."

She blushed until the tips of her ears burned. "Stop that." She pulled on her hand, but with the friction, her second sight tugged on her mind. Where seconds earlier she'd looked at Lucan's laughing face, she stared now at a man on his knees. Head bowed, his shoulders shook as he mourned. Before him, three bodies lay on a cold stone floor beneath a hanging banner that bore a yellow and blue coat of arms. The eldest of the dead, a gray-bearded man, lay on his back, his sword clutched uselessly in an outstretched arm. At his left, a young boy not much older than ten or eleven, sprawled facedown in a pool of his own blood. The fingers on his right hand stretched over his head to touch a woman's bloodied palm. She lay on her side, her other hand tucked against the deep gash in her midsection.

Lucan rose on shaky legs and drew his sword with a vengeance. Wearing a surcoat of the same blue and yellow, he lifted his chin at the same time he raised his blade. He turned around, the hate and repulsion turning his face into a grotesque mask of rage as he stared at another man who lurked in the doorway to the hall. Blood dripped down the second man's blade, smeared across his chest. The deep crimson stains turned an identically matched surcoat into a fingerprint to patricide.

The horrific vision faded, leaving Anne shuddering in its wake. Tugging her hand free, she tucked it securely in her pocket. His family. All of them murdered save for the man in the door. What Lucan had suffered she couldn't begin to fathom, and yet he still managed to laugh. She didn't think anything could make her forget such a terrible portion of her past.

As she followed Merrick inside, Lucan flashed him a grin, a testament that he had indeed somehow put it behind him. When he slid his smile to her, amusement warmed his gray eyes. "I see Merrick has decided you can walk with only the aid of his hand?"

As if he'd realized they still held hands, Merrick jerked his free. With it went her comfort, and still suffering the chilling effects of her second sight, Anne rubbed her arms. Uncertain what to say, or even whether she should sit or stand, she leaned against a massive bedpost and gave Merrick an expectant look.

As she waited for him to lead the conversation, it occurred to her that not once since she'd awakened with Merrick wrapped around her had her second sight given her any further insight to his past. Nor, thankfully, had it shown her anything else about his future. She furrowed her brows at the oddity. She'd hardly seen all of his past—in fact, what she'd glimpsed could only encompass a handful of years, if even that much. How had she managed to shut him out?

"We are here, Lucan, to see your mark," Merrick stated in a flat, unemotional tone.

Anne flinched inwardly. This all felt suddenly strange and surreal. It had all seemed like some fantastic story—at least the part about a preordained mate. But there was no doubt about it, Merrick matched her, and for that, there simply wasn't explanation. He obviously hadn't staged the events, for if he had, he'd have called her on her lie.

Mark or no mark, she wasn't staying here. Not like Merrick expected. He had answers she needed. He held the key to her career; he could tell her what drove the Church to eradicate the Order. She was only humoring him so she could get out of here faster. Besides, it wasn't

as if he actually needed her help as Mikhail insinuated—
Merrick was more than able to protect himself.

But then, if that were true, just what did the vision of
his death mean?

With a grin, Lucan turned to Anne and bowed with a
flourish, jarring her out of her confusing thoughts. "I
would be honored, milady, to spend eternity at your side."

Uncomfortable by his formal display, Anne shifted her
weight and hugged herself tighter. Definitely not staying
here. She'd never survive that kind of constant flattery.
Maybe someone else would find it pleasant, but she'd rather
have someone with Merrick's rough edges.

Lucan straightened. "However, I cannot show you my
mark. I fear it would be indecent."

Anne's eyebrows lifted at the same time Merrick
smirked. "Indecent?" she echoed.

"Aye. 'Tis on my backside."

Her gaze dropped to Lucan's hip, appraising firm buttocks. An impish thrill jumped up her spine. This could
get interesting. She'd never considered that this mark stuff
might give her a bird's-eye view of prime male flesh.
There was certainly nothing wrong with looking. But as
soon as she caught Merrick's dark expression, she choked
down her amusement. Maybe not. At least *he* didn't look
inclined to let her investigate for herself. Damn.

She summoned a sober, polite smile and asked, "Tell
me what it is?"

"'Tis a mark from birth." He paused to grumble beneath his voice. Averting his eyes, he looked to his boots.
"A spot which takes the form of a damnable heart."

Merrick's guffaw brought the first scowl Anne had
seen to Lucan's handsome face. Gray eyes glinted like
hard bits of charcoal, and as he squared his shoulders, he
gained two inches in height. He stood taller than Merrick, but as Anne looked between the two, a burst of
pride infused her blood. Taller Lucan might be, but more
handsome he was not. Merrick's untamed hair gave him

a roguish quality the more eloquent knight lacked. Never mind how Merrick's grin made Anne's heart tumble upside down.

He should laugh more often. Humor made features that were already handsome, breathtaking.

Their gazes locked, and as Anne's breath hitched, she felt weightless, like she'd fallen down a bottomless chasm. Merrick's smile faded. The light in his eyes took on an intensity that made her shiver. "Does it match?" he asked quietly.

Unable to find words, she shook her head.

"Come then. As I recall you are hungry." His hand closed around her elbow, setting off a wave of tingles that rippled up to her shoulder. Again, she noted, she didn't receive even a buzz in her head that would indicate a coming vision.

She gave him a nod, lifted her hand to wave to Lucan, and allowed Merrick to steer her into the hall. There she took a deep breath. But her guardian didn't give her time to find her composure. With a stride that equaled two of hers, he hurried her to the end of the long corridor where he rapped on another heavy door.

"Enter," a bitter voice called.

Anne wrinkled her nose. By now, she'd gotten used to that harsh voice. Farran. Joy. Exactly what she needed before dinner—a good dose of crankiness.

Merrick pushed the door open. "Farran, we have come to inspect your mark."

Seated at an unadorned desk, Farran didn't bother to look up from a thin book. "Does she have a burn? 'Tis the only mark I bear."

At Merrick's lifted brows, Anne shook her head.

"Nay," he answered for her.

Farran turned a page, still not bothering to take his nose from his reading. "Good, then. I have no desire to be shackled with a woman's petty needs."

Anne gawked. She'd show him petty. She'd show him needs—right after she showed him a woman's slap.

She took a step forward, only to be thwarted by Merrick's backward yank. He set both hands on her shoulders and turned her firmly toward the door. "I think not, little demon," he murmured near her ear.

"Jerk," she muttered under her breath as Merrick propelled her into the hall. When he shut the door, she gave in to a very satisfying stomp of her foot. "Rude, arrogant bastard."

"Bastard he is not. Come, we shall visit Caradoc. Leave Farran to his brooding."

"What's his problem?"

Tucking her hand into the crook of his elbow, Merrick slowed his steps to match her shorter stride. "Would you not be angry if your birthright fell to your enemy, and your bride, your son, as well?"

"How does that happen?"

He fell silent, the tight line of his jaw an indication he found the subject uncomfortable. Anne waited. It would do no good to push. He was too stubborn.

After several long seconds of quiet, he answered, "It happens when nine knights pledged to serve the Almighty wander in tunnels not meant for man, and one digs where he was forbidden to explore."

Anne slowed to a stop. A thrill wafted down her spine as she looked up at him with wide eyes. In less time than it took to catch her breath, the long-ago vision that came with touching the cross in her basement door took root in her mind. Merrick had dug in the dirt there, he had to be referencing himself. She wasn't just with a man who held the knowledge of the past; she stood side by side with one of the original founders of the Knights Templar.

"You founded this," she breathed.

He did nothing more than close his eyes. But before dark lashes dusted chiseled cheekbones, she caught the anguish reflected there.

As her thrill gave way to a burst of uncontainable excitement, she clutched at his forearm. "The Templar knights went to the Temple Mount in 1119. Merrick, you were . . . are . . ." She trailed away unable to voice the thought. *The unknown ninth knight.* All the rest of the original Templar had documented origins. The ninth, however, had disappeared along with the relics they'd uncovered, his birth, his relation to de Payans, his very name, now lost to time.

"Aye," Merrick answered quietly. "Nine of us rode with Hugues de Payens to the Holy Land. The following year, seven more joined with me. The five who swore loyalty to you are all who remain. Hugues, Harold, and my cousin were all lost to Azazel. Tell me how you come to know of such?"

She shook off her stupor and found a faint smile. "I'm a professor of early medieval history, and I'm working on my PhD." She'd tell him the rest when they weren't standing in the hall where anyone might overhear. Alone, she could explain her need for his help and why it was so important she return to Atchison and Benedictine College. Certainly he'd understand.

One dark eyebrow arched. The hint of a grin tugged at one corner of his mouth. "Then mayhap you know more than I." He took hold of her elbow once more. "Come, little demon. We shall speak on this later. To Caradoc we must go."

Anne's mind whirled as he led her through the maze of corridors. The Templar knights had found something beneath the Temple Mount. Sure, she'd accepted that fact, but hearing it now made everything so much more real. Better even, if what he found brought these men to where they were now, it was almost a certainty it carried the power to threaten the Church and instigate eventual sabotage. She couldn't hope to discover anything better than this.

But few artifacts carried that kind of power. Some historians theorized the Templar discovered the Holy Grail and it now lay in the modern order's possession, carefully hidden and cared for. Others swore the knights discovered the ark of the covenant, and now ancestors of Ralph de Sudeley kept it secret. Still others claimed the Order found lesser relics, like pieces of the true cross, shrouds, and articles belonging to saints.

As fanciful as the legends were, none made mention of immortality or archangels or demons. Whatever the Templar found, they'd completely silenced the discovery. So much so, they eradicated the truth. Something powerful scared the Church and she was about to discover what it was. *Dear God in heaven, thank you.*

Unable to keep her tongue silent, she tipped her face up to look at Merrick. "What was down there, Merrick?"

He shook his head. "We shall speak of it later."

Her stomach flip-flopped like she'd just gotten off a roller coaster, the same excitement and rush of the ride running in her veins. Tonight she'd prove her thesis. Tomorrow, when she met with Dr. Knowles, she could tell him he didn't have to be concerned about his retirement, she would have her promotion in the bag.

Drawing up short, Merrick stopped in front of another unadorned, heavy wooden door. He banged his fist on it, but didn't wait for an answer before he tried the handle. The door opened easily, revealing yet another simple chamber. Didn't *anyone* find modern electronics remotely entertaining?

"Ah, Merrick. I wondered when you would come."

Merrick released Anne to take a seat on a heavy wooden chair. "'Twas wisdom that guided your sword today, brother."

Caradoc glanced up at her, his expression curious, but he didn't acknowledge Anne. He focused on Merrick, his voice strong and lacking any trace of shame. "I did what must be done."

Leaning back, Merrick tossed one ankle over his knee. "Mikhail sends you away for your actions."

Again, Caradoc's eyes crept her way. He took her in, in one sweeping glance, leaving her feeling exposed. Seeking to escape the sudden feeling of self-consciousness, she moved to the window and looked out on an enclosed courtyard where two men sparred. Pretending to watch, she tried to hide her impatience at having to wait for the knowledge she yearned to discover.

"Aye. He has told me thus. We shall leave within the week. Tell me, brother, what brings you both here?"

"We come to inspect your mark."

A low chuckle reverberated through the room. Hoarser, harsher, it sounded nothing like Merrick's rich baritone. "I fear Lady Anne looks unenthused."

She turned around to find Caradoc half dressed. His long-sleeved Henley in one hand, he twisted at the waist, presenting her with a view of his back. On his left shoulder blade was the most magnificent tattoo she'd ever seen. With wings that were so detailed they looked lifelike, a beak so sharp it could shred skin, and a long sinewy tail, a regal griffin struck an impressive pose—chest puffed out, its head turned sideways. In tiny eyes, uncanny wisdom glinted. One clawed paw showed off a powerful lion's body.

" 'Tis yours?" Merrick's question held a touch of impatience. Or maybe it was excitement—Anne couldn't decipher his anxious tone. She pulled her gaze off the brilliant symbol for protection and shook her head.

"Yet you recognize it," Merrick pressed.

"No. No." She glanced back, catching a brief view of the beautiful artwork before Caradoc covered it with his shirt. "It's just . . . beautiful."

With a grunt, Merrick pursed his lips. "Do not taunt me so, Anne."

She opened her mouth to protest, but sensed the futility and quickly snapped it shut. Wherever he found his logic, she didn't share it. Arguing her reaction with him would only spoil the temporary truce they'd established, and she needed him in a good mood when she asked him to tell her the history.

"I trust 'tis all you needed?" Caradoc asked.

Merrick eased to his feet. "Indeed. We shall leave you to your privacy and seek out Tane." He reached out an arm, fingers extended toward her.

Apprehension tightened Anne's spine. Tane bothered her more than Farran did—at least Farran's eyes didn't have the same shifting quality Tane's held when he had knelt before her. Grumpy she could deal with. But Tane . . . She'd be perfectly content if she never had to see the man again.

With an impatient wag of his fingers, Merrick beckoned. Reluctantly, she slid her palm into his and told herself she'd misread Tane's expression. It had to have been her imagination—these men wouldn't call an untrustworthy man brother.

"Good luck, milady," Caradoc called as they exited.

Shutting the door, Merrick didn't give her a chance to voice her thanks. He guided her two doors down and thumped his fist against the dark wood.

Silence answered.

"Tane." Merrick banged again. His scowl returned as he pressed one ear to the door. With a mutter she couldn't decipher, he stepped away and started down the corridor. "We shall keep one eye open for him in the dining hall. Mayhap he is eating."

I hope not.

Steering her down another set of corridors that looked identical to every other hall they'd been in, Merrick walked with long, purposeful strides. He led her around a bend, then took a sharp right hand turn and rounded a smooth stone corner illuminated by an antiquated torch. The light flickered across the rough wall and exposed a recessed opening in the stone. Smooth stairs led down into the darkness. From deep within, the muffled sound of masculine voices rose in reverent intonation.

Anne stopped, her abrupt halt bringing Merrick around to give her a quizzical look. She pointed to the doorway. "What's down there?"

"The inner sanctum."

Drawn by the lilting rise and fall of chanted Latin, Anne took a step closer to the stairs. "Show me?"

Merrick grabbed her elbow, his firm hold not painful, but not pleasant either. He dragged her away from the arched doorway and gave her a nudge down the hall. As if a shade had lowered over his face, his features morphed into the firm lines of resolve. "When you have sworn the oaths of loyalty to your intended, you may view the sacred heart of the temple. Not before."

Goose bumps lifted the fine hairs on her arms. Sacred heart—if this temple held secrets, they'd be in those dark depths. Oh God, she was so close to the facts she needed, she could taste it.

Not much longer.

If she'd harbored any doubt at all about staying, that doorway erased it. If she had to wait longer than tomorrow night, she would—Dr. Knowles would forgive being stood up for dinner when she presented him with cited references documenting the Church's malicious designs.

CHAPTER 8

✝

Tane counted to ten, then twenty before he felt certain enough Merrick and Anne could not hear his exhale. He left his place between the bathroom door and his bed, and dropped heavily into his chair. Staring at the armrest, he traced the intricate carvings with his index finger and studied the wear. Centuries of use stained the wood a dark color. In places, the once-precise patterns were worn smooth. Once a regal symbol of his father's status, the chair was all Tane had left of a life he longed to forget.

He ought to burn the thing.

But destroying it meant accepting he had naught. At one time, he would not have hesitated to part with something so sentimental. Yet now he could no more curb the jealousy that raged inside him than he could stop the darkness from overtaking his soul.

And he despised himself for what he could not control.

He thumped a fist against the sturdy arm and shoved out of the chair. Were he not faced with the consequence of becoming Azazel's knight, he would spend himself in battle and leave these disturbing thoughts behind eternally. Yet even death offered no relief. The only difference he would see was the inability to comprehend wrong from right, evil from goodness.

He stalked to his tall wardrobe and flung open the doors. He stared at his clothes, noting their plain colors, the utter lack of anything that symbolized he was naught but a common man. Aggrieved, he closed his eyes to the shameful resentment of his position and shuddered out a sigh.

Anne had turned these thoughts to intolerable levels. One look at that comely wench and envy suffocated him. He could not stand to look at her, for she spiraled him down this dark course faster than lightning could strike. Nor would he consider the possibility she was meant for him—he was a disgrace, a shame upon the Templar knights' principles.

Yet he wanted her like fire craved air.

With the wench's affections, his empty coffers, his tattered clothes would mean little. People would look on him with the respect they once had.

Snarling against the traitorous thoughts, Tane forced the images aside. He would not allow the darkness to pit him against Merrick or his fellow brethren. This was the life he chose, the greater purpose than the wealth he had willingly cast aside. No amount of coin could make the difference the Order did. He did not need respect. What he needed was to be free of this maddening envy.

He jerked an armful of packaged blankets off the topmost shelf and stuffed them into his duffel bag. Only one thing made the war inside him sufferable—spending time with those who had less. Marie and her brother David would be cold beneath the bridge tonight. If he arrived early enough, mayhap he would stop her from selling herself for a scrap of fabric, a bit of bread. A child should never face such a decision.

Hoisting the bag over his shoulder, he stomped through the door and struck off down the corridor. He jogged up the stairs to the temple's first floor and hurried to the recently renovated kitchens. There he pulled two loaves of wheat bread from the refrigerator and grabbed three cans of tuna. 'Twas not much, but 'twould help.

With a glance around to ensure no one witnessed his unauthorized departure, Tane darted outside and jogged across the darkened lawn to a communal truck. He tossed the duffel bag across the seat, then carefully set the bread and cans inside.

The engine rolled over soundlessly. Foregoing headlights, he ambled down the long drive to the street beyond the temple's iron gates. He glanced heavenward, murmuring a simple prayer he would not arrive too late. Then he flipped the lights on and sped out into the night.

Anne sat at a table of twenty or so men in the long dining hall, Merrick across from her. A couple hundred more gathered at the surrounding tables. While he talked with the men flanking him, she tuned out the noise and turned her concentration inward.

The sudden failure of her second sight when it came to Merrick bothered her more than she wanted to admit. She hadn't really realized how much she depended on it, until it refused to tell her anything more about the knight who was assigned as her guardian. It'd be so much easier to discover what she wanted if her vision would cooperate. She could get the answers and never have to explain a thing to Merrick. She could disappear before he ever discovered her tattoo, and this business about having to take some oath wouldn't be an issue.

If she didn't have the sneaking suspicion that taking those vows would tie her up here eternally, she was half tempted to tell him their marks matched just to learn the Templar secrets. Then again, aside from the fact doing so would be completely devious, the memories of his death put an abrupt halt to that line of thought. Being bound to someone who would eventually die couldn't possibly end well for her.

No, it would be best if she stayed just long enough to accomplish her purpose and then leave, having never told a soul about their identical tattoos. Thanksgiving break began this week—as long as she delivered a note

to Dr. Knowles, she had time to explore the secrets here.
Maybe when she was back at home she and Merrick could
work out some sort of agreement—as much as she hated to
admit it, the man was kinda growing on her. Grumpy and
arrogant as he was, she couldn't deny the effect he had on
her system. That damn smile of his turned her world upside down almost as much as the prospect of proving her
thesis did.

"Dine," Merrick insisted as he jabbed at her bowl with
his spoon, the gesture jerking her out of her thoughts.

Anne stared down at the greasiest bowl of . . . glop
she'd ever seen. Merrick said it was stew. But her eyes—
and her stomach—refused to consider this mushy con-
coction as anything but garbage. "Oh. Hell. No."

She pushed the bowl away and fought back the urge to
whimper. She was so hungry her stomach was in knots.
But even starving people had their standards, and that
bowl of crap defied the minimal ones she possessed.

Spoon poised near his mouth, Merrick lifted one re-
proachful eyebrow. The men on each side of him—men
Merrick hadn't wasted time in discovering they weren't
meant for her—stared at her as if she'd just committed
blasphemy. A blush crept up her cheeks, and she offered
Merrick a weak, apologetic smile.

"'Tis food, Anne."

"No it's not." No wonder everyone around here had
massive chips on their shoulders. How long had it been
since they'd had a decent meal? "Is there maybe some
salad somewhere?"

Merrick's other brow shot up. "Salad?"

His companions continued to stare. Behind Merrick,
a stranger with long ash-blond hair turned to looked over
his shoulder. His gaze narrowed. Cold blue eyes flashed.
Dangerous energy assaulted her.

Anne swallowed down unexplainable foreboding and
met Merrick's soothing onyx stare. The uneasy tension in
her belly dissolved. "Yeah, you know—lettuce, celery,
carrots, croutons?"

A chuckle shook his shoulders, but he refrained from smiling. "A man does not eat leaves."

Just like they didn't believe in radios. Somehow that didn't surprise her. She dropped her spoon to the table, folded her arms over the scarred surface, and gave each gawking face a sugary-sweet smile. The two men hastily turned their attention to their meal. Behind Merrick, the nosy stranger abruptly turned back to his meal. Anne gestured at her bowl. "If I'm going to eat greasy crap, I think I'll take McDonald's. Or maybe Pizza Bob's. He delivers, you know."

Merrick indicated her food with his spoon. "What did you tell me earlier? Ah, aye, *get used to it.*"

"Not on your life, big guy. Where's the chef?"

"Our *cook* attends the kitchens in the mornings. Before dawn, he prepares the daily meals."

Well no wonder the stew looked like some Sci-Fi Channel alien slime. Slow cooking was one thing, but twelve to thirteen hours would turn lead to liquid. She pointed at the loaf of bread sitting at Merrick's elbow. "Pass me that, would you?"

He slid the carving board in front of her.

Anne skipped the knife and picked up the whole loaf. Gnawing off one hard end, she chewed and told herself it tasted like fresh-baked bread, not the stale piece of cardboard that it resembled. "You do realize," she said around her food. "If it weren't for this whole immortality thing, you'd all die of heart disease, right?"

Merrick's mouth thinned into an unamused line. Slowly, deliberately, he set his spoon in his bowl and leveled her with a frown. But as the man on his left erupted with laughter, Merrick's tight features relaxed. The dark look in his eyes faded, and once again, she stared into the fathomless coals that sucked her in and left her shivering.

A slow smile tugged at his mouth. Neat, even white teeth broke free, and Merrick gave into a soft chuckle. With a shake of his head, he resumed eating.

"Will you take me to McDonald's?"

"Nay."

She tore off another chunk of bread with her teeth and rolled her eyes. "This is terrible, Merrick. How can you call this food?"

He looked to the man on his right—Nikolas, Anne recalled from her earlier introduction. "She does complain much, does she not?"

Nikolas' green eyes lighted with unspent amusement. He clapped a sympathetic hand on Merrick's shoulder and gave Anne a nod. "'Tis my blessing she is not meant for me."

"Aye," Merrick affirmed. "I would have to gag her, were she mine."

She spluttered. A dozen different curses bubbled to her throat, but she couldn't decide which one to use first. *Screw you,* held the most appeal, but she suspected instead of putting Merrick in his place, the phrase would only make things worse. Either that or he'd take her meaning entirely out of proportion.

Merrick gave her an innocent look, lifted his hands in defense. His dark eyes danced with laughter, and Anne choked on surprise. Teasing. The man was teasing. Just when she thought she'd gotten used to his grumpy side, he changed tactics.

Beyond Merrick's shoulder, the blond knight gave her a sneer seconds before he let loose a derisive snort. The aggressive, daunting energy pummeled into her, skittering apprehension up her spine. She leaned across the table, her hand on Merrick's forearm to capture his attention. He bent forward as she lowered her voice and whispered, "Who's that man behind you?"

At once, Merrick's features turned hard as stone. She felt the rigid nature of his muscles as they tightened beneath her hand. Alarm buzzed in her head.

His voice was nearly inaudible. "'Tis Ranulf of Stotfold. Stay away, he—"

The rest of what Merrick said was lost to the sudden commotion in the room. Spoons clattered into bowls.

Hearty hales of greeting rang out, only to fade to murmurs, then nothing as a thick hush descended. Heads turned toward the massive open arches that opened to the long commons. Straining to see around the sea of oversized men, Anne searched for the cause. Her gaze settled on rich chocolaty hair and sharp aquiline features that were drawn in deep concern.

Mikhail jumped up on a tabletop with a cat's grace. "Knights Templar, some of you know by now that we have suffered another heavy loss. Some of you have already received orders and prepare to leave. For the rest . . ." He dragged his hand down his face and rubbed his chin. His pause carried an ominous threat, and he scanned the faces closest to him. On a deep breath, he projected, "Maggie gave her life for us last night. Azazel holds the second nail."

Murmurs broke through the gathered knights. Heads dipped toward one another, their whispers assuming a frantic cadence. Anne looked to Merrick for an explanation. Yet he remained impassive, only the subtle shake of his head telling her now wasn't the time.

Mikhail waved the rumble down with his hands. As the men fell silent, he continued, "I have sent word to Raphael, requesting he tell us the location of the third. Whilst I await his response, I need all of you at the ready. Do not concern yourself with the gates unless I specifically instruct you to leave."

Merrick's gaze narrowed as he sucked in a sharp breath.

"What's he talking about?" she whispered across the table.

He didn't answer. Instead, he covered her hand with his and gave it a squeeze. Anne instinctively waited for the tugging of her mind, but it stayed silent.

Anne frowned. Nails? What kind of nails? And who was Maggie? Another woman like herself?

The men surrounding her stilled, their expressions grim, their postures rigid.

"Sir Merrick, Lady Anne, a word with you?" Mikhail called before he climbed down off the table.

The way Merrick jumped out of his seat confirmed Anne's suspicion Mikhail hadn't asked. She tossed her bread onto the table. Not like she intended to eat any more of it anyway. She'd rather gnaw on leather. At least it might have some flavor.

As she rose, another commotion broke out. Benches ground against the floor, men hurried to their feet, and the scrape of steel against steel rose above the commotion. To her abject horror, in near-perfect choreography, every last man dropped to one knee and set his sword on the ground in front of him—except for the blond who had glowered, and Merrick, who guided her gently to his side.

Doing her best to ignore the blatant hatred emanating off Ranulf, Anne looked to Merrick, hoping he'd tell her what to do. But the only help he offered was a smile. In fact, he looked almost pleased. What the hell?

"Th-that's really not necessary," she squeaked through a closing throat. "Please, don't."

This had to stop. Now. If another man prostrated himself in front of her, she'd step on his toes to get her point across. No more bowing, no more oaths, no more ceremonial anything. *Pleased to meet you* worked just fine.

No one moved.

"Make them get up," she hissed at Merrick. "I'm not going to return all those swords. I refuse."

He chuckled. "Such is not necessary. Give them your blessing."

Her *what?* She'd never been any good at speeches. Lecturing she could do all day, but say something formal, and she turned into a mouse. "What do I say?"

"Whatever your heart holds."

"What if I don't say anything?"

"You shame them."

Great. Just great. All she needed was a couple of hundred men's shame to weigh her down. Nothing could ever be simple. She cleared her throat. "Please stand. We are equals. And uh . . ." She kicked her toe into the floor. "If you must fight, God be with you?" Gnawing on her lower lip, she waited to see if she'd said enough. Lord, if she hadn't, she'd turn tail and run. To heck with their shame. This was mortifying.

Nikolas rose. Followed by the man on Merrick's left. Then another, and another, until the room hummed with movement.

Merrick tucked her hand atop his forearm. He escorted her out of the dining hall and into the commons where Mikhail waited.

Anne stared at Mikhail, the men's odd behavior forgotten, along with Ranulf and his cruel laugh. In the dim light of torches, the faint outline of Mikhail's wings shadowed the wall behind him. Though they weren't solid, and she couldn't see them if she looked straight at him, in his shadow they were unmistakable, like someone painted them on the stone in a matching shade of gray-black. Her mind struggled with the unimaginable, but the more she fought against what she wanted to deny, the more reality settled in.

Destroying what remained of her doubt, that same powerful sense of peace and tranquillity engulfed her as Mikhail smiled. "Anne, I trust you are finding things to your liking?"

She hesitated. Did she dare tell him what she thought of their food? Of the fact she couldn't watch her favorite late-night sitcom? That she didn't even have a change of underwear? Oh what the hell. They'd brought her here. "You need a new cook. One who knows the value of a salad. And I'd kill for a mindless moment of television along with a hot shower."

Despite Merrick's scowl, Mikhail laughed. "Then you shall be pleased to learn your chambers are completed. I believe you shall find them more to your liking than the simple rooms the men inhabit below." He gestured at the sweeping staircase that led upstairs.

Anne glanced at the decaying staircase warily. Old wood took on a grayish shade, and a well-worn carpet blanketed the treads. Faded paper clung to the walls, a forgotten reminder of what was once a great mansion. On the landing, a cracked and dingy window offered a view of the front lawn. She inhaled deeply. Surely upstairs had to be better. At least it couldn't get much worse than that.

"Merrick will you escort her?"

"Aye."

Anne's stomach rumbled as she set a foot on the first stair. Looking straight ahead, she prayed Merrick wouldn't mention her stubbornness over the stew.

She should have known better.

He dipped his head to her ear. "If you had supped, your stomach would not make such noise."

The wash of his warm breath against her neck sent a shiver rolling down her spine. As he drew away, she caught the lingering scent of his cologne, a blend of sandalwood and something else she couldn't quite define. Something with a touch more spice. The aroma teased her nose, set off butterflies in her belly. Lord, he smelled good.

His body brushed against her arm as he rounded the landing, and she almost tripped. In less time than it took to blink, the grumpy knight who carted her off against his will became a man. One who turned her on with so little effort it was pathetic. The feel of his body curled against hers assaulted her memory, setting nerve endings on edge. Her insides turned to liquid with the surreal sense of intimacy that came with his leading her upstairs, and she issued her body a sharp reminder to behave. He wasn't taking her to bed. To her room, which might have a bed in it, but this wasn't anything but duty.

At the top of the stairs, a warm light peeked from beneath a door at the far end. Through the surrounding darkness, she noted sagging wallpaper, cobwebs dangling in corners, and a crooked chandelier. She'd stake her savings on the fact Mikhail believed she would be impressed with the mansion's former grandiosity. Compared to her own house, however, this all felt sad and gloomy.

Merrick pushed open the door, and the hall filled with light. He gave her a gentle shove, ushering her inside.

Anne came to a standstill two feet into the expansive room. Her jaw dropped, matching the expression of disbelief that widened Merrick's eyes.

Tasteful wall coverings cast a blue-gray comfort against cornflower blue draperies with lace sheers. The ceiling, nearly twelve feet in height, added to the luxurious effect with its painted decals and three-toned molding. Her heart skipped a beat as she took in a crystal chandelier that looked like it belonged in some grand ballroom, not a vast sitting room in a decrepit building that once served as a charitable hospital.

A polished mahogany entertainment system housed a flat-screen television and a stack of colorful CD's. She wandered closer, ran her fingers down the plastic spines, and marveled at her favorite titles. Joy of all joys, a bookcase in the corner held all her prized reference books.

Gabe. No doubt about it, he'd had a hand in this.

She turned slowly, admiring a simple yet plush white couch, two stuffed recliner chairs, and a glass-topped table. Part modern, part a page from Victorian couture, the room made her former residence look small and insignificant.

Merrick inspected the bookcase, then wandered to a pair of French doors. Turning a brass handle, he eased them open, and Anne drew in a breath of awe. Dazed, she stepped inside.

Beyond, her bedroom took up twice as much space as the antechamber. It wasn't nearly as feminine as the adjoining room, but olive-green walls offset thick white carpet and gave the bedroom warmth. A vanity, a dresser, a tall wardrobe—each piece of furniture was a deep mahogany with brass accents. But the bed . . .

The bed was heaven here on earth. Big solid corner posts gave way to intricately carved head- and footboards. Amid a flourish of swirls and other accents, a Templar cross dominated the rich wood. Mountains, simply *mountains,* of pillows invited her to flop down, roll around, and get comfortable on what looked like a mattress made of down.

She pushed on the edge of the mattress and smiled. Yes. Feathers. Oh God, she could sleep here for eternity.

A movement near the doorway caught her attention, and she looked up to find Merrick shifting his weight, a pinched look on his face. So the big guy felt out of place, did he? She chuckled to herself. He better get used to it. According to his claims about matching marks, someday he'd have to share this with her.

She winced as the random thought sent a fresh burst of fantasy through her mind. Images of Merrick and her tangled up in those quilts, his big body sliding against hers, scalded behind her eyes. His kiss, his hands, his simply amazing ass.

A blush crept into her cheeks, and she hurriedly turned away before her imagination took over. She couldn't get caught up in the reality of the unimaginable, nor the incredible effect of her handsome knight. She was leaving in a week, not planning a future here.

Foregoing an inspection of the attached bath, she meandered back to the sitting room and curled up on the couch, her feet tucked beneath her. She gave the cushions a hearty pat. "Come tell me what Mikhail was talking about."

The relief that crept into his expression almost made her laugh aloud. Evidently, knights and finer things didn't go well together. Or maybe knights and big, inviting beds.

He sat down with a heavy sigh. One powerful thigh rested against hers, and as he reclined against the overstuffed cushions, his hand dropped to her knee. Her gaze pulled to where his fingers rested on the denim, her pulse picking up an extra beat. Intentional? Hard to say with the way he frowned at the window across the room, his expression telling her that his mind was far away.

"What do you wish to know?"

"You," the answer popped out before she could stop it. But in that instant, she couldn't think of anything more truthful. She wanted to know about *him,* not archangels and nails. Seeing a thin white scar that spanned across the back of his hand, she traced the mark with her nail. "I want to know about you," she added more quietly. "What caused this?"

Merrick looked down to where she touched him. Using his opposite index finger, he traced the same path her fingernail had taken. Briefly, their fingertips touched. "'Tis a mark from a lance."

"A lance?" Anne struggled with the urge to twine her finger around his.

"Aye. 'Twas a battle that came to us unexpectedly. I was not given time to don my armor before the riders set upon us. The knight struck me there, and here." He touched his ribs beneath his right arm.

Anne's gaze lifted to the vulnerable spot and pictured the battle as it might have occurred: Merrick standing down an armored knight on horseback, the sharp metal spear that punctured his flesh, the way his face might have contorted as he bit back a painful cry. Impulsively, she gathered his hand in both of hers and lifted it, bringing it to her lips to place a gentle kiss over the scar. "I'm sorry."

Merrick said nothing, and in his silence, she began to question maybe she'd taken one too many liberties. They'd hardly begun to get along—what if her unchecked impulse just crossed some invisible boundary? Slowly, cautiously, she lifted her gaze to his. What she found in his fathomless dark eyes, however, said nothing of anger or annoyance. They gleamed with startling intensity, light bright enough to make her catch her breath.

"Do not be sorry," he murmured. His eyes canvassed her face, lingered on her mouth. "'Twas a scar borne from duty. An order I was sworn to obey."

The husky quality of his voice sent shivers coursing up and down her spine. She tried to look away, ordered her eyes to settle anywhere but on the sudden softening of Merrick's expression. But her body refused, leaving her unable to do anything but choke down a dry swallow. When her thoughts cleared enough to form coherent words, she sought to lighten the moment with a bit of humor. "Orders can do that to you, I guess. Like now, you're stuck with me."

"I cannot say I find these orders entirely displeasing." Merrick lifted his free hand to push a length of her hair away from her shoulder.

The back of his hand grazed the side of her neck and goose bumps scattered down her arms. "No?" She closed her eyes a heartbeat too long, time enough for Merrick's thumb to stroke the line of her jaw and heighten her awareness of his touch.

When she looked again, Merrick had moved closer. Or maybe she had, she couldn't say. But his thumb caressed the same sensitive spot a second time, the slow stroke oddly gentle for the strength in his hands. "Nay."

He was going to kiss her, she knew it in the core of her being. Common sense screamed for her to stop him. Longing she'd buried for five years demanded she sit utterly still and wait for the fall of his lips against hers.

Anne chose longing. Afraid the moment would pass before she could fully savor it, she held his gaze, accepting what burned in the dark light of his eyes. One kiss. She'd gone five years without one. She wanted this, wanted *his*.

Time moved slowly as Merrick leaned forward. Her lungs tightened, her pulse bounded so fiercely she thought her heart might leap out of her chest. His long eyelashes lowered, his fingers cupped the side of her face. And then his mouth brushed hers, warm and soft, hesitant and seeking. Anne's breath caught. Her thoughts collided with the devastation of two freight engines in a head-on collision. The vision she'd seen of Merrick and her in bed burst to life, and she parted her lips, inviting him to take her to that heady place of absolute pleasure.

Slowly, his hand crept to the back of her neck, drawing her closer. The tip of his tongue touched hers, and everything inside Anne awakened to his rich flavor. His cologne saturated her senses, luring her into the incredible magic of a man who knew exactly how to kiss a woman until her toes curled.

She didn't bother with restraining herself. Tangling her tongue with his, she took what he offered and curled one hand into his long thick hair. He let out a startled murmur, then settled in deep, returning her eagerness with a kiss so thorough fire sparked in her veins, the warmth spreading through her body.

And then Merrick was gone, the kiss ending as abruptly as it had begun. He cleared his throat and shot to his feet as if she'd burned him. "You requested McDonald's, aye?"

If it weren't for the smoldering look behind his onyx eyes, she'd swear she had imagined that incredible kiss.

"Yes," she answered in a mystified whisper. But Merrick couldn't have heard her—he was already out the door.

CHAPTER 9

✝

Merrick jammed the truck into third with a mutter as another image of Anne in that too-soft bed flashed in his head. God's teeth, he never should have entered her bedroom. Nay, it had been the fool's thing to do. Yet he could not help himself from opening those doors, could not bear the curiosity of where she would sleep and what the archangels had lavished upon her beyond the magnificent outer chamber.

Possessed by the wild imaginings, he had done the unspeakable and kissed her as well. She, another man's seraph. Not only had he kissed her, she had returned his advances with eagerness he had never experienced. It had surprised him, but only for a heartbeat before her sweet flavor intoxicated him so completely he could not hold on to all the reasons he should not indulge.

Now all manner of inappropriate thoughts drifted through his mind. Would she sleep in her jeans, or his shirt alone? Would she curl one of those long pillows around her supple body? Would that silken hair drape them in seclusion as sat atop him while he indulged in the sweetness of her mouth?

He bit back a grumble and rounded a corner. The rear wheels squealed in protest to his speed. Saints' blood, she was not his. He could not allow these thoughts to consume him. She was not his right to claim, and he would not dishonor the brother the archangels intended.

To take further liberties with Anne would break oaths and ties none had tested in nearly a thousand years.

As he punched the overhead button that released the iron gates, Merrick let out a heavy sigh. Gabriel surely meant to test him. No other reason could explain why the archangel forced the two of them together. Though he could not imagine what he had done to spark the messenger's ire enough to warrant such a trial. Unless 'twas still punishment for his transgression so long ago.

He eased into the parking space and shut the engine off. Temptation brought this life upon them, and temptation now plagued him once again. Had he not learned the folly in claiming what was not rightfully his the first time?

Aye, he had. He would resist Anne, no matter how it pained him.

Grabbing her sack of food, he marched up the steps and let himself inside the house. As he headed for the elaborate front stairwell, he felt the weight of several pairs of eyes bore into his back. They all wondered. Half suspected he took liberties already—what man would not? She was but a woman, meant for such pleasures.

The men who regarded her in the dining hall all carried hope behind stares that centuries had turned hollow. Even those who had stood at his side the longest could not hide the flicker of despair when Anne refused their mark.

Her presence would cause unrest. He needed to find her mate before a knight who suffered breached the vows and planted the seed of discord amongst the ranks. With so many close to darkness, the longer Anne remained unclaimed, that risk doubled. By God, a full day had passed, and he had lost sight of his purpose—he had not thought of Fulk all afternoon. If a tie of blood could be so easily forgotten, what would prevent lesser bindings from tearing free? And if he, who put more stock in the oaths of brotherhood than others, could be swayed, little would restrain those who treated the Code as guidelines, not law. She had already drawn Ranulf's attention. Those who shared his same lack of morals would be sorely tempted.

Still, no matter the logic and the sound reasons, Merrick could not forget the gentle glide of her tongue, the pressure in her fingertips as she urged him to become lost in the sudden passion that flared between them. He ached for more. Yearned for Anne to be a simple woman whom he could enjoy as he wished and become lost in the pleasure she awakened.

His steps felt as if he tried to move boulders as he approached her door. The longing to take her in his arms, to lose himself in the softness of her curves, ate at him like salt poured upon a canker. His little demon . . . Aye, indeed she was. For she possessed him like a vile curse.

Merrick let himself inside and found her where he'd left her—curled on the couch. Only now, the flash of light and sounds of sirens filled the room as she watched her television. She looked up with a smile at the same time she picked up the remote and shut off the noise.

"Food!"

Like a child on Christmas morn, she burst to her feet and snatched at the bag. Digging through it as if she had not eaten in days, she stuffed fries into her mouth. Her eyes closed. Her features softened, and she let out a sigh that reached in and fisted around Merrick's heart. Bliss. Would the same expression cross her face when she lay with her intended?

Bollocks! He would *not* think of such.

Tearing his gaze off her, he sank onto the couch. "You wished answers from me. Would you now desire to talk?"

"Yes," she answered around a mouthful of hamburger. "I want to know what you found, what Mikhail meant—everything. Why am I here, Merrick—really?" Taking a seat beside him, she licked her fingers.

He had no idea where to start. At the beginning, in the middle, personal involvement, the effect of the darkness . . . So much ran together. He could not bring himself to tell her of the shame that lurked in his soul, the darkness that tainted him and the rest of the Templar. Whilst she might be more agreeable if she knew they would turn into evil without her oath, he did not want her to look on him with pity. Or worse, with repulsion. Nay, the depth of her purpose would be her intended's responsibility. He could explain the Templar curse when once his soul began to heal, as it would, with the speaking of her vows.

The very likely possibility she would reject the unknown history remained, yet 'twas the most logical place to begin. She understood the time when he was born, and Merrick searched for a place where her knowledge would work to his benefit.

"You know of the Crusades. You know of the Order's origin."

She nodded enthusiastically. "I've studied everything I can get my hands on about the Knights Templar."

A rush of pride lighted in Merrick's blood. Far too many years had passed since he had heard the respect that filled her voice. Too many more brought only disrespect, resentment, and even mockery. He could only hope when he finished speaking that the same would not come from her. Furrowing his brow, he met her gaze. "I assure you, Anne, naught of what you presume to know is true."

Anne's heart tripped a beat. Fascination blended with a touch of apprehension, and she dropped her hands to her lap, her dinner temporarily forgotten. Years of study, countless hours of research, and all the answers were a breath away.

"'Twas 1119, and I was but a young knight desperate to prove himself worthy. I grew up in the shadow of the first victory in Jerusalem and longed for the respect the returning knights received. The cause presented, and I rode to it with Hugues. 'Twas a noble endeavor, a fight worth spilling blood. Protect the pilgrims on the road to the holy places we claimed from the heathens, defend what rightfully belonged to Christians."

Anne nodded, attempting to hurry him along. What he recited was recorded fact—she needed the unrecorded. "Yes, I know the history of the First Crusade. I know how King Baldwin II gave you territory on the Temple Mount and how the Order gained his approval."

As if the story distressed him, Merrick sank into the couch. He rested his head on the back and closed his eyes. Hands fisted at his thighs, he pulled in a deep breath. "We were told to not venture through the tunnels. Yet I was young, foolish . . ." With a shake of his head, he sat upright again and drummed a fist against his leg. "I ignored the order and dug within the tunnels, seeking rumored treasure. I found scrolls. Old things written in a language I did not recognize. I called the others. Together we discovered the words of the ancient Essenes, Hebrew writings never canonized and what the ignorant would call apocryphal. Only there was one we could not reason. Stamped into copper, the language was cryptic. A cipher of some sort."

Anne's mind grabbed at the information like a hungry viper. She resisted the urge to squirm in her seat and folded her hands together tightly. The scrolls needed little explanation—the Dead Sea Scrolls. And the only one that could possibly match his description of cryptic was the legendary Copper Scroll. A known documentation of what many believed to be the lost treasure of Jerusalem. "Archaeologists dig for that treasure now on the Temple Mount," she blurted out.

"They will not find it. All they will discover is an unimaginable hell." He opened his eyes to give her a hard look. "Anne. The scroll does not mark coin, or jewels, or even gold. 'Tis a device of Azazel's, disguised to tempt the foolish."

As everything she'd ever read shredded into pieces of worthless paper, Anne drew back. "To tempt? Why?"

"The sixty-three listings mark the gates of hell. The sixty-fourth marks the final location of Azazel's ascension—should he achieve his desires."

"But." She tried to put into words the screaming protests in her head. "Archaeologists found the Copper Scroll in the caves at Khirbet Qumran in the forties and fifties. It's been translated—scholars have deciphered the listings."

"Nay," he insisted. "There is no preciseness in the language. Sixty-three places, written as if one would be familiar with the locations. 'Tis trickery, Anne, of the greatest kind. As for the deciphering, aye, scholars found and translated the specific words, but not the meaning. When we discovered what it was, we sealed the scroll and reburied it. How would we know that centuries later, the battles of our ancestors would be doubted and the danger of that document would be lost? That Azazel would lead men to the hidden caves as his power grew."

He had a point. But that sounded a bit fantastic. Azazel was just a fallen angel, according to doctrine. A demon. Not a being capable of claiming supreme power.

"'Tis so much to tell you, Anne. I shall try to simplify. Bear with me."

"Of course." Anything to make sense of this. To understand how it tied into the Church's desire to sabotage the Order—if it even did. If it didn't relate, all her father's research, and her thesis, would be blown to bits.

"I, along with my men, was punished for digging where it was forbidden, for unearthing the sacred writings, for they revealed truths the archangels sought to keep from men. For that knowledge, we were punished with immortality." Hesitating, his eyes searched her face.

Anne gazed at him, seeing the pain within his dark eyes. Though he told his story simply, he had suffered. Greatly.

The same compassion his scar had aroused surged through her veins. Instinctively, she reached a hand between them and set it on his thigh. He had been through so much. So many years of fighting, of watching those he knew die. How he managed to drag himself out of bed without surrendering to the heartache that touched his eyes, she couldn't imagine. But he had, and that inner strength did something she couldn't explain to her heart. Made it topsy-turvy, nudged it open more than she'd like.

His larger hand covered hers. Strong fingers squeezed as he took a deep breath. "The nytym you witnessed. Those, and others, we must fight. This is my curse, to guard the gates of hell and keep Azazel's minions from mankind. Your house—our adytum—offers sanctuary for those who battle far from this temple. I had come from such a battle the other night."

His gaze shifted to the bookshelf, and he studied it with sudden interest. His throat worked as he swallowed, and she observed him stiffen ever so slightly. There was something he wasn't telling her. Something he skimmed over.

She didn't press for more. In time, she'd learn the secrets he was reluctant to share. The information he'd given was enough to make her wait for however long that took. Not to mention, she didn't care to consider the implication of what his story did to her thesis. To her career. What he referenced made everything she understood about history into virtual fiction. This was life changing, and she couldn't process it all at once.

"Abigail Montfort guarded the adytum and the sacred crucifixion nail within, until her death. 'Twas the same with Maggie. Gabriel saved both women from a time when witches were burned and he used their knowledge of spirits to guard certain relics the Templar have sworn to protect."

"Relics? You mean like holy relics?" Here it was, the information she'd been waiting for. Possibly, as legend suggested, they harbored the Holy Grail or the ark of the covenant. Those two items alone would be enough to threaten the Church.

"Aye."

Oh this was too good to be true! Unable to disguise her excitement from her voice, she asked, "The shroud of Turin? The Holy Grail? The holy chalice? Do you really guard their hiding places?"

His gaze jerked back to her, his frown firmly intact.

"Anne. I told you we guard the gates of hell and keep Azazel's minions from mankind."

"But you also said you protected relics."

"Protect, not guard. 'Tis the archangels who do the hiding. As for the three you mentioned, one does not exist. 'Twas created as a great fable to distract certain people who came too close to the truth."

She knew she must look like a gaping monkey, but she couldn't help herself. She'd spent too many years tracing dead-end trails. If they'd created a false relic, that would certainly spur the Church's fury, particularly if those clergy members who backed them discovered the duplicity and faced humiliation at the possible discovery. "Which one?"

"I shall allow your intended to tell you that secret . . ." He trailed away, looking out the window.

She resisted the overwhelming urge to cry out in frustration. He couldn't just leave her hanging. Yet if she let him see her desperation, he might get suspicious and draw this out even longer. Hell, he might refuse to tell her anything.

With a heavy exhale, Merrick continued, "All you must know now is that Azazel desires eight relics. Each one he claims gives him power that shall, if they are all acquired, allow him to ascend to the Almighty's throne. He has obtained the sacred nail used in Christ's crucifixion that was ensconced in your house's walls, and now he possesses the one in Maggie's. He will try for the third. Soon."

"Which is where I come in?"

"Aye. You possess the ability to stop him from overtaking the Almighty."

She tried to swallow, but the lump of foreboding that lodged in her throat made the task difficult. Visions of spirits long ago, she could handle. Hell, in some of them she'd seen some horrible things. But she was certainly not equipped to stop a regular demon, much less one powerful enough to overthrow the Almighty. She shuddered. "How is this even possible?"

"Enough tonight. 'Tis plenty for you to consider." Merrick's gloominess evaporated. He slipped his hand around her upper arm, and through the fabric of her shirt, he fingered the armband. "Gabriel told you naught?"

The heat in his touch made her want to squirm. His gentle hold, the stroke of his thumb, so casual, yet so intimate. In less time than it took to draw a breath, she was thrown right back to when he'd decided McDonald's was a better option, when she'd kissed him like she might never kiss another man again. She quickly averted her gaze before the intensity in his eyes made her give in to the urge to touch her lips to his, to discover whether the same all-consuming pleasure could occur twice. With a nervous laugh, she answered, "Not a word. Just that he'd picked two up, one for me and one for—" She stopped, aware she'd said too much. She hadn't intended to involve Sophie until she'd learned all she could.

"For who?" His gaze hardened. When she hesitated, those onyx eyes glittered like glass. His fingers tightened around her arm. "Who, Anne?"

Oh damn. She bit back a disgruntled mutter and let her shoulders sag. "My sister."

Where she'd hoped his expression might relax, it took on more intensity. His mouth pressed into a firm line. For two heartbeats, he remained silent, and then he turned her loose with a contemptuous snort. "'Tis no wonder you stared at Caradoc thus. She bears his mark. You sought to keep this from me."

"No!" The exclamation tumbled off her lips with vehemence. "Sophie doesn't have tattoos."

"You heard Mikhail—the mark may be any kind, not just ink put into skin. 'Tis anything that is unique, significant, not a mere scratch or freckle."

She shook her head violently. "Caradoc showed us the griffin as his mark."

He stared at her, his gaze shifting with suspicion, accusation, and doubt. "If you withhold the truth from me, damsel, Mikhail shall have to cut me down to stop my leaving. I shall withdraw my oath of loyalty to you, no matter the cost."

A sliver of fear needled its way down her spine and froze her heart. She'd already lied and couldn't afford to lose the one person possibly willing to help her. "Um." She shifted position and set her sack of food on the coffee table. Leaning back, she opted to talk about her sister. "Sophie's a former model. She'd never get a tattoo. And you'll certainly never get her out of California."

"Her choice is not her own. You shall contact her tomorrow."

Seraph, light, salvation—whatever these damn armbands meant, she would not sit back and watch Merrick throw himself at Sophie like every other guy did when they realized the other twin was better. Let Farran have her. He'd have an outlet for his anger at least. For if anyone could manage to really piss off these knights, it was her sister. They wouldn't know what to do with a prima donna.

Shocked by the fierce jealousy that rushed through her veins at the thought of Merrick with Sophie, Anne struggled to maintain her cool. "I think Gabe can handle when she's supposed to be here, just fine." Deftly, she changed the subject. "I need a radio—I can't sleep without music. And I need a change of clothes. Underwear. My toothbrush too. My fuzzy socks." Since she'd decided to stay the week out, and Gabe had given her all her research materials, she might as well be comfortable.

Merrick's shoulders shook with his soft chuckle. "Fuzzy socks?"

She sighed in exaggerated pleasure. "Oh, they're the best. It's chilly in here. They'll keep my toes warm. Will you take me back to my house so I can get some things?"

He lifted one dark eyebrow. "You have decided to accept your fate and stay?"

That was a little more complicated. She couldn't accept that her life could be decided by a prophecy, by fate.

Hesitantly, Anne nodded. "I have Thanksgiving break I can spend here." Reaching to her right, she plucked a folded piece of paper off the end table and offered it to Merrick. "I need to get this to Dr. Knowles, the head of the History Department at Benedictine, so he doesn't worry. I'm expecting him and his wife for dinner tomorrow night."

"Nay."

Firm, succinct, he left no room for argument. She gritted her teeth together.

"'Tis not safe for your return. Not until your intended is found. I shall retrieve the things you wish tomorrow night, and I shall speak to Mikhail about seeing your letter delivered." He took the note and shifted position so he could shove it into his back pocket.

The air fled her lungs with a *whoosh*. Anne stared, certain she'd heard him wrong. But the longer she held his gaze, the brighter his eyes shone. He'd offered, and he didn't look a bit put off by having to make an hour-long drive just for her belongings.

Overjoyed, Anne gave in to impulse. She let out a squeal and flung her arms around his neck in a fierce hug. Two days ago, no one could have told her she'd find the prospect of clean underwear so exciting. Now, the simple necessity felt as if Merrick had offered her the world.

His arms came around her hesitantly. But as the stiffness in his posture gave way with his sigh, he held her close. So close, she could feel the beat of his heart against her breast. As one hand rubbed the small of her back, Anne breathed in the spice of his cologne and settled her cheek on his shoulder.

The angled planes of his face, the sharp line of his jaw, fascinated her. Power lurked there, strong lines that spoke of hardship she'd never known and triumph she could only imagine. This man, this *knight,* killed without hesitation. And yet there was a gentleness beneath the surface, one he showed only when he thought she wouldn't notice. Like now. The way he closed his eyes. The way he nudged aside a stray strand of her hair with his cheek and slid his hand up her spine, as if he too enjoyed the stolen moment of comfort.

The way he had revealed a moment of hesitation when he feathered his lips across hers.

She pulled away to study him more closely. Dusky lashes lifted. Confusion passed across his gaze before it morphed into complete stillness. A spattering of freckles lined the tops of his cheeks, so light and faint she'd have never noticed them if she weren't mere inches away. Creases around the corners of his eyes said this man had laughed once, and often. So unlike the rare occasion he let her see his humor.

His gaze dropped to her mouth, and Anne's heart thumped hard. Her thoughts slammed together, her pulse leapt to life. Would he kiss her again? Did she dare kiss him? God above, she wanted to. But a tiny portion of her mind ordered her to wait. He'd been the one who'd run. He should be the one to make the move a second time. She licked her lips and swallowed, suddenly hot in the chilly room.

Merrick's eyes lifted to lock with hers. In those dark depths, desire glowed like hot coals. And just as coals would burn, his gaze seared beneath her skin to warm her blood. To hell with the voice of reason—what could kissing him hurt? He'd already expressed his interest earlier. She'd gone so long without a man's touch that she deserved a little self-indulgence. She was a grown woman, able to take a lover as she wished, and he was hers, after all. *For a little while at least.*

It didn't matter if he knew her tattoo matched his or not. She could keep hers hidden between the combination of darkness and her socks.

Yes—a grown woman. She wanted this. Wanted him. She leaned in and feathered her mouth across his.

CHAPTER 10

M errick did not dare move. He was too afraid to find himself dreaming and too afraid good sense would crash upon him. Anne's breath mingled with his, her seeking touch laden with unspoken questions. Questions he could not begin to answer.

She suckled at his lower lip, and something deep inside his gut ground down so tight he ached. The heat of her tongue, as she trailed the tip of it along the seam of his mouth, warmed his blood. He parted his lips, touched his tongue to hers. A jolt of fire shot through him, and he could not silence a gasp. Though he had already experienced the headiness of her mouth, it affected him with equal power, if not more, the second time.

Releasing her arm, he slid his hand up her shoulder, spread his fingers along the side of her neck. He did not know who moved first, who changed the angle of their body, but as he released a shuddering exhale, the kiss deepened. Her tongue tangled with his, slowly, leisurely. Her sweet flavor soaked into his awareness, erasing all sense of time and place. Aye, indeed she tasted of honey, and something far richer, a heady flavor he could not describe but left him craving more. Unbearably feminine.

He twined his free hand into her hair, becoming lost in

the kiss. It intensified, took on more demand, and Merrick's body responded with frightening ferocity. His cock swelled. His heart thundered against his ribs. The hollow ache in his gut became intolerable. On a low groan, he dragged Anne into his lap, desperate for the feel of her softness.

She straddled his thighs, settled herself atop him with such perfection he nearly spilled himself right there. He sucked several sharp breaths through his nose and fought the rush of ecstasy back. As he trailed light kisses across her cheek, he tugged on her hair, tilting her head to expose her throat. He traced the throbbing vein there with the tip of his tongue and dropped his hand to her breast. Her fullness filled his palm, her nipple puckered beneath the pad of his thumb.

An image of his mouth closed around the hardened nub rose behind his eyelids. Aye, she would have beautiful, creamy skin. Soft with a lingering hint of the fragrance he now associated with her. He swirled his thumb around her nipple as he might do were she in his mouth, and Anne murmured a soft sound of pleasure.

Merrick loosed her hair and caught her other breast. Lifting, kneading, he brought them together until the soft flesh puckered at the open neckline on his shirt. He pressed a kiss there, grazed his teeth across her flesh until the lace of her bra thwarted him. Frustrated, he popped one button free with a flick of his wrist, giving himself room to pull back the scrap of lace. The dusky bud beneath stood erect, begging for attention.

Glancing up at her, he took in her partly open mouth, the way her teeth clamped into her lower lip. She shuddered as he stroked her breast, the motion rolling down her spine and rocking her hips into his. A burst of pleasant pain arced through his veins. God's teeth, he felt as if he might come apart at the seams. Other women had impassioned him, but never such as this. Never had he felt so out of control of his actions, experienced the deep need to seat himself within her and hear her cry out his

name. Truth be told, he could not recall a time he wanted
to hear a woman cry out, as he much preferred the silence, the sound of dampened flesh slipping and sliding.
And yet he wanted to hear Anne's release.

He shut his eyes and closed his mouth around her nipple. His free hand, he fastened at her hip. Her nails dug
into his shoulders as she arched her back, allowing him
more freedom with his mouth. He suckled, he laved, he
teased. Steady pressure of his hand guided her hips until
she moved against his throbbing erection in small, ago-
nizingly faint motions.

His body moved of its own accord, seeking out what it
needed. His hips lifted into hers, grinding against her
sensitive center, the barrier of their clothes a torment he
despised. No doubt, she would be moist and ready, for the
heat that burned between them could not solely come
from his desire.

She trembled in his arms. "Merrick," she whispered,
"make me yours."

He let her flesh slide from his mouth to murmur, " 'Tis
what I—"

Merrick stopped. Like water thrown upon a campfire,
everything inside him turned cold. 'Twas exactly what he
was doing—making her his when she belonged to one of
his brothers. Saints' blood, had he lost so much of his
soul to darkness?

Damnation.

His nerve endings frayed as he eased Anne off his lap.
Tugging at his jeans, he stood. He dared not look at her,
could not bear to see the disappointment certain to lurk in
her expression or the confusion behind her eyes. He ground
his teeth together so hard he thought they might crack and
pulled in a deep breath. "You are not mine to have."

Without giving her a chance to protest, he strode from
the room and pulled the door shut behind him. In the
hall, he sagged against the wall. Leaving her caused unexplainable pain. His body shook with the effort of walking away, of doing what his oath demanded. If 'twere his

mark she bore, naught could stop him from taking all she offered. He would have her until they were both so spent with exhaustion they could do little more than roll into each other's arms and sleep.

Yet that was the crux of the matter. She was not his. Would not ever be his. Going down this path was a road to torture unlike any he had borne before. For her, for him, for the man she would eventually swear herself to. He would rather face the beatings, the stretchings, the carvings he had endured during his imprisonment at Chinon.

Nay, he would not let the darkness convince him he could indulge himself with Anne.

Still dizzy, he shoved away from the wall and descended the stairs to the lower levels of the temple. The halls were dark and quiet, the men's nocturne habits having brought them to the common room, or drawn them to a game of late-night billiards. He marched down the corridor to Mikhail's chambers and let himself inside.

Bent over a thick, leather-bound tome that Merrick knew to be the archangel's record of events, Mikhail did not lift his head as he asked, "What troubles you, Merrick?"

"Anne has agreed to cooperate and stay. I have agreed to retrieve a few of her belongings tomorrow." He withdrew the paper from his pocket and set it on Mikhail's desk. "She asked me to leave that note for someone at the college."

Unfolding the thin slip of paper, Mikhail studied Anne's letter. Gently, he folded it closed and set it back down with a succinct nod. "I shall see 'tis appropriately handled. Thank you. You should rest—you look as if you have not slept in weeks."

'Twas how he felt as well, but he knew his harrowed expression had little to do with lack of sleep and everything to do with an auburn-haired demon whose kiss carried an even greater poison than Azazel's evil. "Aye," he murmured.

Letting himself out, Merrick made his way to his chambers and stripped out of his clothes.

Anne haunted him as he lay down in his bed. Her perfume clung to his pillow and stirred the heat in his loins. Softer, sweeter lips he had not known. Were it not for the whores who pretended interest, he had never heard a maid ask for a bedding. 'Twas his experience women would rather play coy than admit they felt such things as pleasure. Aye, their bodies did not lie, but their tongues omitted much.

Yet Anne left no room for questions. Like a man, she made her wishes known. A trait Merrick found refreshing. Would she speak so freely in his arms? He envisioned her bold, unafraid, her hands guiding his over her body, drawing his fingertips between her legs.

Make me yours.

He groaned aloud as his muscles tensed and his cock stirred against his thigh. He flopped onto his back with a frustrated hiss. Yet she waited for him there as well. He felt the heaviness of her body, the perfect way her hips held him. With an anguished oath, he rolled onto his side. Nay, though he might try, he would not sleep tonight.

Anne dragged herself off the couch after what seemed like hours. In reality, she suspected only twenty or thirty minutes had passed while she sat in stunned stupor, but without a clock or radio, she couldn't be certain.

What the hell had just happened? She hadn't particularly intended for her stolen kiss to lead to making out on her new couch, but when it had, she sure hadn't expected Merrick to withdraw like he flipped a light switch.

Her left breast still tingled, and she absently rubbed at it as she wandered into the bedroom. Full dawning settled over her. She'd asked Merrick to sleep with her. Something had misfired in her brain. While she was more than free to take a lover, getting wrapped up in Merrick complicated things. They lived, literally, in two different worlds. He wouldn't fit into hers, and she had no intentions of getting stuck here. Still, when it came to him, she found herself powerless. He eradicated good sense, made her incapable of thinking of anything beyond the incredible nature of his kiss. The way he made her feel alive.

The way he made her feel, period.

She wanted him. But it was more than physical. It was what he was, what he stood for. The history he possessed. He fascinated her mind as much as he stirred her fantasy. And behind all those grumpy scowls, he hid compassion. A touch of playfulness she'd bet he'd deny in a heartbeat.

She turned down the heavy quilt and stripped off her jeans. With just her black trouser socks and Merrick's shirt still on, she slid into the bed. Wriggling her toes, she bemoaned the necessity to keep her ankle covered. She hated sleeping with socks on, and while she didn't really believe Merrick would walk in on her while she was asleep, she didn't dare risk he might.

His intended.

Trying to deny everything was useless—no amount of logic could explain all she'd witnessed or experienced. She had some purpose here that directly related to Merrick. And she had a week to not only discover, but fulfill that purpose, before her career suffered. One week to gain his trust enough to tell her what she needed to know.

But how to gain his confidence without revealing her tattoo or taking an oath that he claimed was the only way she could learn the secrets of the inner sanctum? How could she crack through a knight's armor when he knew how to shield his weaknesses? She suspected whatever it was he hadn't told her tonight held a key to solving that dilemma. He'd avoided something important.

She carries the light that will balance one knight's tainted soul.

Maybe Mikhail's statement wasn't literal, but rather spiritual. It wasn't as if she had any secret powers—well, maybe her second sight.

Groaning, she dropped her head against the headboard, feeling very much like an idiot. Her gift had to be her purpose. She'd see a vision, and by telling Merrick what she saw, she'd save one of his men.

Now if she could just get her second sight to cooperate with Merrick, she'd be set. In the meantime, she needed to convince him to confide in her and show her the inner sanctum, where surely she'd find the proof that the Order had been sabotaged.

Her eyes widened and she sat up straighter. Good Lord, she should have thought of it right away—Sophie would know what to do. She'd always been able to get men to eat out of her hand. Tomorrow she'd borrow a phone, give her sister a call, and discover exactly how to seduce Merrick into telling her what she needed to know.

Only, what to tell Sophie posed a larger problem.

I've been relocated by immortal Templar knights, and I'm trying to seduce one who's nine hundred years old or so. Oh, by the way, the archangel Mikhail lives in a temple beneath the Odd Fellows Home in Liberty, and you know that present Gabe sent you? Yeah, well, we're both descendants of the Nephilim. That's right, angels.

Right.

Sophie would have her committed.

Anne sank back down into the downy mattress and wriggled around until the feathers cocooned her. The outside air made her nose feel like she stood in front of an open freezer, but beneath the weighty comforter, she was snug and warm.

As long as she could explain without sounding like a nutcase, Sophie would help with effectively seducing him. She didn't need to know about angels and demons anyway. Gabe would eventually take care of that.

Mikhail closed his book and picked up the piece of paper Merrick left him. Leaning back in his chair, he opened it again and scanned the neat handwriting.

Dr. K.,
Working on research. I've discovered a fascinating lead on the Templar theory. I'll be gone a week or so, but

*will return and share my research with you. You'll be
amazed.*
   Anne.

Slowly, he crumpled the note in his hand. Opening his
palm, he narrowed his gaze and concentrated his powers
on the ball of trash. With a soft *pfft,* it burst into blue
flames, then winked out of sight, leaving not even a speck
of ash behind. It would not have mattered what she had
penned—no message would reach her colleagues beyond
the one Gabriel issued. The Almighty's messenger received his instructions from the only one who mattered,
and Mikhail would not intervene with the master's plan.

Anne would come to accept her place in time, as all
seraphs must. He only hoped it would be soon enough.
That she would swear her oath, give her light to her intended knight, and the serpents would form the holy barrier to eternally block Azazel's vile taint from entering
the Templar's soul. If she did not hurry in her acceptance,
the risk ran high she would be too late.

He did not allow the thought that as a mortal, a being
given divine freedom of choice, she could refuse to linger
in his mind.

CHAPTER 11

Sophie shimmied into her new scarlet chemise and shivered at the feel of the fine silk smoothing over her bare skin. She glanced in the mirror and readjusted the spaghetti straps so it fit trimly over her breasts before stepping back to review.

It offset her long dark hair and her coloring perfectly. Short, flattering, tastefully sexy—just the right thing to drive Chandler out of his mind.

She fingered the armband Gabe sent and smiled. After polishing the thing up, it gleamed in the dim light. It was actually almost pretty now. Combined with her nightgown, it reminded her of something Cleopatra might wear. Since she couldn't get the damn thing off, she decided to use it to her advantage.

Gabe and his oddities. Why Anne put up with them, Sophie didn't know. Sure, the man was nice enough, and he was certainly easy on the eyes. She guessed him near fifty, but his smart taste in clothes, and the way he took care of his body, made him look ten years younger. Only his gray hair revealed his age. And that, he kept fashionable too—in long, thick, strangely distinguished dreadlocks that draped to the middle of his back. He smelled good also. His vanilla-spice cologne permeated the paper inside the package.

But he was weird, and everything he gave Anne had some sort of weirdness about it. The bellows for Anne's fireplace came with a two-hundred-year-old ghost. The mirror for Anne's bedroom reflected a heck of a lot more than the mortal world. The chair for her sitting room—Sophie had to do some serious negotiating with a very unhappy, very dead, Revolutionary War general to get him to let her sit there the last time she'd visited.

This trinket, however, took the cake. Standard-issue ghosts didn't attach to it, yet she could feel energy shifting inside the metal. Energy that evidently made the brass swell after time, for the thing was firmly lodged on her arm. Although it didn't hurt, oddly enough.

She didn't dare ask Anne if the matching piece Gabe referenced in his note had the same problems. Sophie kept her ability to see ghosts locked away. When dealing with politicians, producers, and the crème de la crème of Southern California, coming off as slightly crazy could be advantageous. But an affinity for seeing ghosts tipped the scales away from her favor.

Still, it would be nice to know if Gabe stuck them both with armbands she suspected would somehow lead to trouble.

She fingered the cross on the top of one serpent's head and chuckled. Anne was probably having a heyday trying to trace this to her silly Templar theory.

"Sophie, darling, are you staying in there all night?"

Chandler's soft voice disrupted her thoughts. "Be right out." She hastily dragged a brush through her hair and gave the gown one last tug. Three weeks of working together and pretending they didn't want to rip each other's clothes off was about to pay off. Big time. Hence the reason for her new negligee.

She opened the bathroom door to find Chandler lounging on her bed. Bare-chested, he leaned on one elbow and patted the mattress. She took a moment to appreciate him, assessing fantasy against reality. Her gaze skimmed over broad shoulders, a smooth hard chest, and came to rest on his already-tented cotton boxers.

She moved toward him, flipping off the light as she passed the table. Moonlight illuminated the room. "Hey, handsome," she purred as she set a knee on the mattress.

Trailing manicured nails along his thigh, she watched his eyes shift from appreciative to hungry. Teasingly, she traced the length of his erection, listened to him suck in a sharp breath. As she tucked her fingers inside his waistband, the light glinted off her armband.

"What's that, beautiful?" Chandler murmured as she tugged the fabric down.

Flashing him a sultry smile, she twisted to present him with a side view. She batted her eyes. "Don't I look like Cleopatra?"

The light in his heated stare intensified. He sprung upright and caught her arm, his fingers digging in cruelly. "Where did you get this?"

Sophie tried to twist free, but Chandler tightened his grip. He yanked her closer. "Where did you find the serpents?"

Sophie froze, her blood cold. The difference in his voice, a guttural sound so unlike his usual smooth bass, set her senses on red alert. She swallowed and dragged her gaze from his fingers to his face.

His usually warm and inviting brown eyes glittered like pieces of amber. But something wasn't right. It was dark, his pupils should be wide and round. Not tiny slits that opened vertically. She'd seen a ghost like that once. It had terrorized her first apartment in Kansas City. When her butcher's knife had vaulted through the room and lodged in the cabinet above her head, she'd fled to California.

Fighting back a shudder, she tugged on her arm. "You're hurting me, Chandler."

He let out a snarl and flung her onto the bed. He pounced on top of her, pinning her hands above her head as he pried at the armband. When it didn't budge, he lifted his arm and backhanded her. "Who gave you the serpents, bitch?"

Holy shit.

A thousand tiny needles stabbed into her face where his knuckles met her cheekbone, followed by a wash of heat. She struggled against his hold. Kicked her feet. Thrashed. "Get off me!"

Chandler sat on her legs. His fingers attacked the band of brass around her bicep with a vengeance. Nails dug into her skin as he tried to pry the serpents' heads apart. The trinket filled with warmth and tightened like a clamp.

She lunged forward, breaking his hold on her wrists. Her arms free, she flailed and pushed, using surprise to her advantage. God, she'd never realized how strong Chandler was. That so much strength could come from what was otherwise a rather average build.

"You will surrender the serpents one way or another," he growled as he hit her again. Her head snapped sideways, and her other cheek broke out in throbbing pain.

"Get the hell off me!"

With strength she didn't know she possessed, she used the mattress for leverage and bucked him loose. It took less than a second to scramble off the bed and race for the door. She slammed it shut as he bolted after her. To buy a few minutes of time, she propped a chair beneath the knob.

Sophie snatched at the phone and punched in 911.

From behind the bedroom door, an unearthly growl shook the walls.

The phone clattered to the floor as her bedroom door splintered apart. Chandler emerged, her heavy bedside lamp in his hands. He tossed it aside and stalked toward her, the malicious gleam in his eyes unmistakable.

Fuck, fuck, fuck! She had to get out of here.

Her eyes darted around the room as she backed up, searching for something she could use to defend herself.

Chandler moved faster. He caught her unadorned arm and jerked her around to face him. His fingers dug into her shoulders as he stared down at her. "Seraphs die."

Seraphs? What the hell? Didn't matter—*die* was more important. She had no intention of complying. "Get the hell away from me."

She brought her knee up, ramming it into his groin. The unnatural howl he let out sent a fresh new burst of fear surging through her. She struggled to believe it came from the man she'd invited home for what was supposed to be a night of exceptional sex. It held an animalistic quality, a hollowness that mirrored the spiritual voices she'd become accustomed to. But this was no simple ghost.

He dropped to his knees, and the thought briefly occurred that he was at least somewhat vulnerable. Whatever he was, he wasn't all-powerful.

She sidestepped him, reaching for the lamp he'd discarded.

His hand shot out and latched around her ankle. A firm tug snatched her feet out from under her, and she fell. Her elbow smacked against a glass-topped end table, knocking it sideways. Glass shattered.

She ignored the warm wetness that flowed down her arm and scrambled to her knees. Using her free leg, she kicked with all her might, driving several blows of her heel into his head. His fingers loosened, and she lunged for the lamp.

Chandler swayed to his feet, his mutterings now unintelligible.

Panting, she rolled onto her back and clutched the lamp in both hands.

As he reached for her, Sophie swung the heavy brass like a baseball bat. It smashed into his face. Blood poured from where his nose had been, and he covered his face with his hands. She swung again before he could right himself. The lamp hit him in the temple, and Chandler toppled backward.

He swayed on unsteady legs.

Sophie jumped to her feet and threw the lamp away. As she raced for the front door, a heavy thump sounded behind her. She glanced over her shoulder to find Chandler in an unmoving heap. Not willing to see if he would rise again, she jerked her coat off the peg and dashed outside.

She didn't stop running until she rounded the corner two blocks away. There, she sagged against the side of a brick building and sucked in deep lungfuls of air. Hugging herself, her hand grazed the metal beneath her coat, and she closed her fingers around the hidden armband. Good God, what had Gabe sent her?

This couldn't be real. She should go to the police. From the sound of distant sirens, they were already en route anyway. Turning herself in would be the smartest thing.

But as surely as her arm throbbed and her face stung, she knew the police couldn't help her.

Someone, or more correctly *something,* wanted this armband. Until she found a way to get rid of it, this wasn't going to stop.

She lifted her gaze and studied the street. Shadows hugged the walls, footsteps echoed in the darkness.

She couldn't stay here.

She turned toward the streetlamp and hurried down the sidewalk. Her pace quickened and she broke into a jog. Four blocks down, Sophie stopped in front of the welcoming glow of St. Michael's Cathedral and stared up at the white double doors.

It had been a good fifteen years since she'd been inside a church. She wasn't Catholic—they might turn her away. *Screw it.*

Determined, she marched up the stairs and pushed the doors open.

Inside, a man in a long black robe attended to a large arrangement of fresh flowers in front of a massive wooden cross. "I'll be right with you," he called out warmly.

Shoot, how did she address him? Sir? Mister? Reverend . . . *Father.* That's right. Mary Sue had always talked about Father Leopold when they were growing up.

"Father . . ." She began in a shaky voice. "I think . . ." Oh dear God, she couldn't begin to say this, could she? Turning toward an elaborate mosaic on the wall, she pretended interest while her mind worked at the words.

"Yes?" he prompted.

Sophie gulped. If anyone was likely to believe her, it would be the Catholics. They still believed in possessions and exorcisms. She expelled a deep breath and whispered, "I think a demon just attacked me." She winced at the ridiculousness and waited for the priest's certain laughter.

"Sophie MacPherson, I've been waiting on you."

Wide-eyed, she turned around. Her gaze settled on a head of thick, cropped gray hair. Arms outstretched, he beckoned her into his embrace. Familiar blue eyes smiled in warm welcome, and the comforting scent of vanilla spice assuaged her fears.

No freakin' way. Despite his chopped hair, he looked exactly like Anne's boss.

"Gabe?"

"Father Gabriel, for now. Come. We have much to discuss."

CHAPTER 12

✝

Bright sunlight brought Anne out of an erotic dream. As she opened her eyes, she half expected to find Merrick looming over her, his mouth at her breast once more. Her body throbbed, her heart banged hard. Beneath her thong underwear, she was shamefully moist.

Agitated, she kicked the covers aside and sat up. This had to stop. She refused to confront another night of restless sleep because the man she wanted—who seemingly wanted her as well—was too damn hot and cold. But until she could speak to Sophie, she needed to keep her mind on something else.

She slid out of the bed and headed for her bathroom. Beyond the wide arch that separated the sink and wall-length mirror from the bedroom, she surveyed her surroundings, seeing the luxury for the first time. Marble countertops. Brass fixtures. Double sinks. Her eyes fell to the bathtub, and her cheeks heated. It was large enough to make a man Merrick's size comfortable; someone clearly chose the tub with something other than bathing in mind.

Damn Gabe. She didn't need images of Merrick in that tub when she was trying to keep her mind *off* her reluctant knight.

She went to the glass-enclosed shower behind her and

turned the faucets on. As the water ran, she stripped out of her clothes and left them in a heap on the floor. When she stepped inside, she let out a blissful sigh and turned her face into the warm droplets.

Clean at last.

Her mind wandered to her conversation with Merrick while she lathered. She now realized the house Gabe helped her find hadn't been a coincidence. Abigail Montfort wasn't killed by thieves, and the house hadn't been sacked for her spell book. It was all Azazel's doing.

How could crucifixion nails give a demon the power to overtake God? What other relics did he have his eye on? Merrick hadn't elaborated on that. Probably because the relics had something to do with the things in the inner sanctum since he'd shut down with the convenient excuse her intended had to reveal that secret place.

She dismissed the frown that pulled at her brow and focused on the pieces of history that fit into Merrick's puzzling tale.

She already knew the Templar's rise in status came from hush money. Saint Bernard and Pope Innocent II wanted something kept silent, and they'd sacrificed a great deal to see it done. Merrick proved legend true by admitting they had found relics beneath the Temple Mount. Important relics. What held the kind of threat that could bend the only true power to its knees?

Damn it all, she had to get into the inner sanctum. There she suspected she'd find written histories on the Order. Which would serve her needs better than anything—she'd have actual fact to cite.

If not for her death vision, she'd tell Merrick who she was and be done with the whole thing. Yet she couldn't shake the feeling that the oath he wanted her to swear would lead directly to that death. Until she knew exactly what caused that chilling scene, she had to keep her mouth shut. Never mind all the other complications that oath presented, namely her promotion, or lack thereof if she pledged herself to Merrick.

God, she hoped seducing Merrick would do the trick. She needed to figure out that plan fast.

She pressed a hand to her growling stomach. And she really needed to talk to Mikhail about the food. A week here, and she'd lose ten pounds. Not to mention the fact that these men really weren't eating well at all. Who subsisted off of greasy slop and hard-as-nails bread?

Anne turned off the faucets and stepped out of the shower. Wrinkling her nose, she stared at her clothes. Right about now, she'd give anything for her comfortable sweats. With a heavy sigh, she bent over and picked up her jeans. She could live with another day in them. She'd borrow another of Merrick's shirts. The socks were a necessity she could stomach, but she absolutely refused to spend another day in dirty underclothes.

She toed her thong panties aside and shrugged into the rest of the garments. When the denim brushed against her bare bottom, a slightly wicked feeling made her giggle. Surrounded by a hundred knights or so, and she was going commando.

Humming to herself, she stuffed her feet into her ankle boots and pulled open the hallway door. Time for a chat with Mikhail before her stomach turned inside out. Assuming she could find his office in that maze of tunnels below. She hadn't exactly had the best view when Merrick brought her there the first time.

It felt good to be working toward something useful, and in better spirits, she descended into the underground barracks. There she searched her memory for which way Merrick had gone. Left. He'd gone left, then right, and then stopped at the end of the hall.

Oddly, the halls filled with silence as she made her way down their darkened lengths. Identical doors faced the corridor, dark and imposing. Behind a few, snores drifted to her ears. Beyond others, she caught the rustle of movement, a shuffle of feet, the scrape of a chair. It was as if the entire Order obeyed some code for early morning silence.

Then again, Merrick had defended the gate at night. Last night, the halls had been full, filled with laughter and the camaraderie of men.

She stepped over a neatly folded surcoat outside a door and stopped, one eyebrow arched. A grin threatened, amusement rising as she recalled the ancient Templar Code and observed the certain evidence of a broken oath. These men weren't so archaic after all—someone had violated the vow of chastity. His punishment came in the surrendering of his sword and surcoat. Later, when he'd served penance enough, he would have his weapon returned. It was a minor infraction, proof that no matter their purpose, the knights were hardened men. And like the rest of their gender, they didn't take abstinence too well.

Stifling a misplaced laugh, she eyed the imposing barrier at the end of the hall. With a deep breath, she squared her shoulders, stopped in front of it, and knocked.

"Enter."

The heavy wood gave way to her shove with a *creak*. A slow smile filtered across Mikhail's features. "Good morning, Lady Anne. To what do I owe this unexpected pleasure?"

Her cheeks burned at his flattery. "I, ah—" She shifted her weight. "I wanted to talk to you, if you aren't busy?"

Mikhail's chuckle filled the room with tranquillity. "I am always busy, Anne, but I have time. What is on your mind?"

"Um." She wrung her hands together. "The food."

He lifted a coppery eyebrow. "What is wrong with our food?"

Her face flamed as she admitted, "It's terrible. These men deserve better. Healthier menus with more flavor. They've been through too much to suffer through the kind of meal I endured last night on a regular basis."

"The men are rather resistant to change."

"Well, for men who've lived through centuries, their taste buds are still in the Dark Ages." She winced, the shocking truth having popped out before she could stop it.

To Anne's surprise, Mikhail let out a low laugh. His amusement emboldened her, and she met his gaze with a stiffer spine. "I assume I'm not the only woman who's going to come here?"

He shook his head. "Nay, you are not. You are the first, but not the only."

"Then I suggest you let me do something with that menu. I don't know a woman alive who'd eat last night's stew."

Mikhail's muffled amusement shook his shoulders. "Not to your liking?"

"Yuck. And really, I think if you'll let me, your knights will be much happier. It wouldn't take much to make simple meals rewarding. Would you please let me do this for them?"

"Very well then, milady. The men are accustomed to women taking charge of estates. I am sure they will not grumble overmuch at your interference in their diet. I will find another task for the cook to do. Or perhaps you could involve him?"

"Oh." She paused, taken aback by Mikhail's willingness. She'd anticipated a battle over this. Had half expected she'd have to beseech Merrick and get him to step in on her behalf. Recovering with an uneasy smile, she nodded vigorously. "Of course. But I wasn't talking about my taking on the cooking. That's a disaster waiting to happen. I wanted to hire a professional."

His amusement drained from his face. "You want to bring an outsider in, knowing full well there are secrets here?"

"Um. Yes. You see . . ." She pulled in a deep breath. "I read other people's energy. I can see the lives they've lived, feel their disposition by touch. I can choose someone who would be trustworthy."

He considered her for several long moments before slowly nodding. "Gabriel has told me of your ability. I will trust you with this. But give me a day to talk to our cook. He is rather temperamental, and his sword arm is useless."

"I'll see he's involved in my decision. Maybe that will pacify him a little."

"It would be kind of you."

She nodded, uncertain what else to say.

"Anything else?"

Taking the dismissal for what it was, Anne shook her head. "Thank you." At the door, she remembered Dr. Knowles. Turning around, she asked quietly, "Did Merrick speak to you about the letter to my colleague?"

Mikhail folded his arms behind his head and reclined in his chair. "He did. I have handled the matter. You may feel free to enjoy your stay without worry."

"Oh, good! Thank you."

The way he turned his attention back to the book in front of him told her she'd been excused. She ventured back into the hall. As she exited, a knight with reddish hair passed by, conjuring images of Declan lying in a pool of his own blood. He'd been hurt so badly and Merrick had said little about him since. It was early, but maybe he'd be awake and she could check in. Maybe he'd like a little bit of company.

She turned around and stuck her head back inside Mikhail's door. "May I visit Declan?"

"Certainly." An approving smile touched the corner of his eyes.

"Ah . . . How do I get there?"

Mikhail chuckled once more. "Merrick needs to draw you a map. The infirmary is at the end of the hall opposite this one."

"Thanks." She grinned and shut the door.

Her steps felt light as she hurried through the torchlight toward the infirmary. At her light knock, the door opened. Soft brown curls and the brightest pair of blue eyes she'd ever seen greeted her. She didn't need an introduction. Long lashes, a face so pretty it could make women cry, the similar outline of ethereal wings rising from behind stocky shoulders—he must be Uriel.

"Thou hast come as I expected. Enter, if thou would." He stepped back and swung the door wide.

Anne's eyes pulled to the large form lying motionless in a nearby bed. Long reddish hair hung in clumps around Declan's face. His features were pale, lacking the robust quality that she'd seen the day they first met. Hooked up to an IV, he looked small and weak. Nothing like the dominating Scot who laughed freely. Worry slithered down her spine. For a man who was supposedly mending, he had a long way to go. "Is he okay?"

Uriel took a seat in a chair in the corner and folded his hands in his lap. "He sleeps sedated. The wound is stitched, but the sword nicked bone. Were he awake, he would suffer incredible pain. In a few days more, he shall regain enough strength to feel it less."

Sympathy lanced through her, and she turned a sad smile on Declan's bandaged arm. "He's not going to be fighting for a while, is he?"

"Nay. Several more weeks shall pass before he mends."

"Oh." She'd actually thought it would take longer, but didn't feel like admitting her stupidity. "So he won't know I'm here?"

Uriel shook his curly head. "Thou should return when the sun has set. He shall recognize thee then."

She took in the rise and fall of Declan's chest, watched the fluid drip down the tube. She hardly knew him, and yet she worried. He was such a priceless treasure among a world of headstrong, dominating men. If this changed his good humor, he'd become like all the rest. And she'd really had enough of the scowls, the curt words, the cold demeanors that cropped up out of nowhere.

She glanced over her shoulder at Uriel. "You're certain he won't wake sooner?"

"He shall not."

"Why did someone do this to him? Aren't these men supposed to be brothers?"

Uriel's expression remained impassive, but his blue

eyes bore into her as if he sought to read her very soul. One long, slow blink, followed by a string of mumbled words she couldn't decipher, prickled the hair on the back of her neck. Then, that same tranquillity that accompanied Mikhail's presence enveloped her. His words reached her mind, though she couldn't see his lips move.

There is kindness in what thou perceives as cruelty. His fate is unchangeable. And yet, thy companions seek to alter what is already written. Take heed, Lady Anne, for the bond of brotherhood runs deeper than the oceans, and in those fathoms, loyalty can disillusion.

With the riddled message came a poignant vision of Caradoc raising his sword against Declan. The Scot stood in his chambers, unprepared for the attack. But as shock widened his eyes, in the brief moment before his expression yielded to the agony of his wound, Anne read gratitude.

Caradoc had wounded him on purpose. Declan had been grateful. This injury then, this confinement that kept him out of battle, he welcomed. And if what Uriel said was true, Caradoc acted out of kindness.

But what was Declan seeking to avoid? Death? She shook her head, trying to make sense of it all. She looked back to Declan. Maybe she'd get the chance to return later. If not today, then soon. "Will you tell him I stopped by?"

"I shall."

Anne turned for the door, then paused to address Uriel once more. "Could you tell me how to find Merrick's room?"

"Return to the stairs leading to thy room. Turn right, not left. At the juncture of three halls, thou should choose the leftmost. Thou will find Sir Merrick's, four doors upon your right."

Oh-*kay*. Whatever that cryptic speech meant.

Forming a rudimentary map in her head of what she believed Uriel's words created, Anne opened the door. As she pulled it shut, she again caught Uriel's faint muttering—a chain of nonsensical talk that made him seem more like a babbling old man than any sort of supreme being. Chuckling, she started for Merrick's room.

At a bend in the corridor, two hallways opened in front of her. She glanced around. Uriel hadn't mentioned the layout, but she'd followed his instructions—right at the stairs . . . Maybe he meant two instead of three? Or . . .

Frowning, she turned to head back to the stairwell and try again.

But as she twisted, she came face to face with a broad chest.

Startled, she jumped back and craned her neck.

Tane's deep green gaze swept over her with such open appreciation that she hugged her arms to her chest. She could have gone the rest of her life without ever running into this one again.

"Lady Anne," Tane murmured. His eyes settled on her breasts, then drifted up to her face. She fought back a repulsed shudder.

"You look lovely this morn."

"Thank you." She looked around him, hoping someone else lurked near by. Even Farran would be a warm welcome. But the hall was empty, save for another surcoat folded in front of a door. The torchlight shifted, and she caught the gleam of a long steel blade sitting on top of the white fabric.

"Are you lost?"

"Ah . . ." Crap. She absolutely didn't want his help. Unfortunately, it was becoming rather obvious she didn't have any idea where she was, and she couldn't think of any excuse for why she stood in the middle of this hall. "I'm looking for Merrick's room."

Tane's expression clouded over. A movement at his side drew her attention to his hand, and as she watched, he clenched a fist. "Merrick is asleep, I am sure. Mayhap you would wish to see our gardens and the fountains? They are lovely at this early hour."

Not on your life, buddy.

She forced a polite smile to her lips. "Thanks, but I

really need to see Merrick. I'm sure he won't mind if I wake him up." She started around Tane.

He sidestepped, blocking her way. "Come. Walk with me. I shall return you to Merrick's room when we finish. I want but a few moments of your time, milady."

The downy hairs on the back of Anne's neck lifted. She tipped her chin up to meet his hardened stare, and her smile tightened. "I really must see Merrick. Excuse me."

She shouldered past his hulking form, achieving another step. As she let out a breath of relief, all too thankful to have the unpleasant encounter over with, he grabbed her arm.

CHAPTER 13

✝

Merrick drew to a halt at the sound of a feminine squeak. His brows furrowed as he pressed his back to the wall. What in the name of the saints was Anne doing down here alone? He had told her at least twice 'twas not safe to wander in the halls.

"Let me go, Tane. Merrick is expecting me."

Every muscle in Merrick's body tensed. He reflexively reached for his sword. The comfort of well-worn leather rubbed against his palm as he closed his fingers around the pommel. Though part of him hated the immediate assumption that his brother offended Anne, Tane was now a different man.

With a quiet, shuffle-step forward, he moved closer to the open hallway.

"Do I not equally deserve an opportunity to spend some time with you, milady?"

The brittle edge to Tane's voice set Merrick's senses on alert. 'Twas not the voice of reason, nor the compassion Merrick had become so familiar with. The man he knew, the man he would give his life for, thought naught of himself, but for everyone else. Closing his eyes in regret, Merrick dipped his head. He wished not to battle with Tane, but he could not allow harm to come to Anne.

Were luck in his favor, his man would not be foolish. Resolved to his necessary course of action, he tightened his grip on his sword and stepped into the archway.

Anne's relief was obvious. Her eyes glowed bright, her face lit with a smile. "Merrick."

The tremor in her whispered greeting convinced him his concern for her safety was not misplaced. She feared not demon, nor archangel, nor even his own temper. Yet she feared Tane.

Merrick's gaze cut sharply to where the other knight held her. Slowly, reluctantly, Tane released Anne. She jerked farther away and hugged her arms about her chest. When Merrick turned his cold stare to his brother, what he saw in Tane's expression filled him with dread. A look born of malice, it dealt Merrick a heavy blow. More than once, he had witnessed the same defiance of a man who would sacrifice everything to keep what he desired. The same expression a dozen men or more had worn when Merrick stormed their lands, claimed their properties, before he turned his sword to the Almighty. He could recall not a single one who had not met his maker at the end of his blade.

Merrick took a step forward, shielding Anne with his body. Reaching behind his back, he fished for her hand. Slender fingertips slipped into his palm. He directed a warning frown at Tane, telling him without words he was prepared to fight—and die—for Anne. Such was the oath he swore to Mikhail. Yet, to soothe Anne's agitation and to quit the trembling of her hand, he kept the threat from his words. "You are late, damsel. I presume you lost your way."

"Yes. Sorry."

Tane's expression morphed before Merrick's eyes. Where hatred burned only moments earlier, his features twisted with a dying man's anguish. His eyes moistened with grief, and Merrick knew, no matter how Tane might have terrified Anne, he could not fault his brother for the blackness in his soul. Whatever foul he had committed, 'twas just another portion of their curse.

A rush of anger surged through Merrick's veins. Were it not for Anne's foolish presence in these halls, his brother would not suffer this morn. Nor would he himself be faced with shaming a knight whose heart knew naught but loyalty.

Before he could utter a word, Tane pushed past them and shoved open his chamber door. The heavy *thud* as he slammed it shut echoed off the stone.

Merrick turned around and slid his hand to Anne's upper arm. Sparing her no gentleness, he ushered her forward.

She plucked at his fingers. "Ouch. Let go."

"Nay," he ground out through clenched teeth. "You were warned not to walk these halls." He urged her roughly around a corner, then up the stairwell. She struggled as they walked, attempting to twist free. But he was in no mood to give her pardon.

His temper was already black from a sleepless night, and her protests only fueled his anger. God's teeth, she could have been raped, or worse, were it not Tane she ran into. Already her presence disrupted the men—the coats and swords outside doorways evidenced that unsettling fact. If she had encountered Ranulf, who could not escape the long ago betrayal of his wife, she might now lie beaten in some forgotten corner. Or worse, Gottfried, who struggled with the temptation of the flesh and would find no hesitation in taking her without her consent.

'Twas time she realized when he told her to stay put, he meant it.

She stumbled as he mounted the second set of stairs. He hauled her to her feet, ignoring her muffled cry of pain. He forced himself to ignore the tiny squeak, even as his heart twisted against it.

At her doorway, he opened the door and thrust her inside.

She yanked away, rubbing at her arm. When she spun around, her eyes took on a murderous gleam. "What the hell is your problem?"

"My *problem,* damsel?" He slammed his hand down on the back of the chair. "Were you not told to stay out of the corridors? Did I not warn you 'twas not safe for you to wander among the men?"

"I was looking for you!"

A little part of his heart lurched at her words, but he shoved it aside. Nay, she would not soften him. "You put yourself in danger, damsel! You endanger me. For 'tis my oath that binds me to protect you. Should Tane have thought to harm you, 'twould be my sword he faced."

She threw her arms wide. "Listen to yourself! You drag me up here to defend that man when he wouldn't let me leave."

"He would not have detained you, were you where I left you."

Their eyes clashed. Her chest rose and fell quickly, and a touch of color stained her cheeks. Merrick refused to acknowledge the comely way that faint crimson offset her blue eyes, and he clung to his anger.

Anne folded her arms across her chest, the defiant set of her chin marking her unbending position. "This is my prison then? I didn't sign up for that, Merrick. In fact, I didn't sign up for any of this! As I recall, you're the one who barged into my life and thrust it on me."

He dragged a hand down his face and let out a harassed sigh. Nay, she had not asked for this life. None of them had. Anne left a world of comfort, a place where she had freedoms and understood the workings of her companions' minds. Here, she knew naught. He could not expect her to unquestioningly follow his demands. Whilst he wanted naught more than to force her into the world he understood, women left that tradition behind centuries ago.

In a quieter, more controlled voice, he conceded. "You are correct. To expect you to understand is unfair. You are here, Anne. Living amongst men who see you as salvation. Some will do anything to try and change the fates, to see you at their eternal side. Others were never noble to begin with and would give you no more consideration than a serving wench within their great hall."

"Meanwhile I'm to sit on my ass and twiddle my thumbs?"

God's teeth she had a way with words. He straightened and shoved his hand into his jeans pocket. "When your intended is found, you will have more freedom."

She let out a derisive snort. "Somehow, I doubt that." Her anger fled her features, and she sagged into the couch. "He's probably just like you."

He could not help himself—he chuckled. Fighting with her was as unpleasant as any battle of blades, and one he suspected he would not win should he continue. When she shot him a look of false disgruntlement, he let his anger over her wanderings fade away. That blue gaze of hers had a way of making him forget the many worries that plagued his mind.

Moving behind her, he fit his hands on her shoulders and bent near her ear. "I do not recall you found me that displeasing last eve."

He felt her shiver. One delicate hand reached up to slide over his. "No," she whispered. "I don't find you displeasing at all."

The fragile skin along the side of her neck beckoned. At once, he was consumed with the urge to press his mouth to her, to slide his hands down to cover her breasts. The incredible memory of Anne atop him, her eyes closed, her lush lips parted, leapt to life within his mind's eye, and his heart kicked into his ribs. He pulled away, possessed by the same frustrations that kept him awake through the night.

Damnation! He could not spend more than ten minutes with her before his body betrayed him.

Seeking to steer the conversation on a safer course, he asked, "Tell me why you looked for me?"

She scooted around, folded her arms atop the couch's back, and set her chin upon them. "I ran out of things to do. I had a talk with Mikhail about improving your food. I dropped in to see Declan. And I wanted to borrow a shirt of yours."

His mind stopped functioning at the mention of Declan's name. Everything inside him ground to a halt, then twisted. Even after last eve, she thought of the Scot. Such concern for a man she had met but once was abnormal. Mayhap, indeed, they were fated.

The idea felt as if someone drove a knife into Merrick's gut. A handful of days ago, had a woman expressed interest in Declan, he would have celebrated, for Declan required a woman who would not hesitate with her affections. Yet when it came to Anne, Merrick could not stomach the thought of seeing her with his brother. And he hated the uncustomary jealousy that ran like fire in his veins and poisoned his heart.

Feeling much as if someone had shoved a rod down his spine, he stiffened. "I have things to attend to. You will stay here, in this room, whilst I am away. I will see that Lucan brings your meal. If you must stretch your legs and leave your chambers, Lucan shall escort you where you desire."

"Figures," she muttered. With an exaggerated air of submissiveness, she asked, "What else, milord?"

On hearing the title he had abandoned long ago, Merrick's heart swelled. He ignored the pleasant sensation and moved toward the door. "I do not jest, damsel. If you are wise, you will heed my wishes." He glanced over his shoulder and gave her a hard look. "I may be old, but I have not forgotten how to punish a willful maid."

She tossed him a wry smirk. "Will you lock me inside my room?"

"Nay. I vow I will turn you over my knee and take my hand to your backside."

At her wide eyes and colorless face, he stalked out the door.

As he stomped down the stairs, the impact of his promise settled on him fully, and his steps slowed. The idea of Anne squirming in his lap, her heart-shaped bottom bared for his palm, squashed his lungs together. He might punish her, but he would torture himself. He could no more go through with the act than he could indulge in the honey of her mouth. For as certain as he knew his name, he knew he would never survive the deed without abandoning a deeper oath. Before he ever executed the first smack, he would have her in his bed.

Taking the bridge of his nose between his fingers, he pinched the image away. These thoughts would cease once he was free from her. For now, all he needed to consider was keeping her safe. That alone proved a monumental distraction from his pledge to find his cousin. It also required considerable focus, and the only way he could gather his fragmented thoughts into cohesive union was to take a few hours for himself. Away from here. Down by the river where the chill that rolled off the water would erode the ever-present heat in his blood.

He jogged the rest of the way to Lucan's door and roused him with several heavy thumps.

Squinting, Lucan pulled the door open. "Trouble, Merrick?"

Merrick entered with a grunt. "I need you to keep an eye on Anne this eve. She has belongings she desires here."

"You run the lady's errands? I would not have figured you for such, sir *knight*." Lucan's sleepy features shifted into a smirk.

Narrowing his gaze, Merrick skipped over the goading remark. "You will mind your tongue and say naught of this."

"Of course." His wry grin said otherwise.

Merrick muttered beneath his breath. He would have asked Caradoc if he desired teasing.

"What shall I do with your fair maid? Continue your search for the mark? Parade her through the commons? Or mayhap challenge her to a game of chess?"

By Mary, the man was asking for a cuffing. "She is

not my maid," he grumbled. "I am charged with her well-being—as we all are. See that she does not leave her room."

Lucan's teasing ceased with a sigh. He tipped his head in a thoughtful manner and studied Merrick. At length, he asked, "What shall you do, Merrick, when you locate her mate?"

Merrick avoided Lucan's probing stare. The thought of witnessing Anne in her intended's embrace set off an uncomfortable churning in his gut. He shrugged. "I shall bid her good fortune and find my cousin."

"Let us hope that is the case." Lucan flashed him another wide grin. "What shall I do should she leave her room?"

"Tell me immediately." Merrick stepped through the open door. With a slight wave, he bid Lucan farewell. His temper no better than it was when he began the day at dawn's first light, he stormed toward his room where he jerked on a heavy sweatshirt. He unbuckled his sword belt and laid it carefully on his bed. The Templar Code mandated they leave their blades behind if they went out in daylight hours.

Determined to put Anne from his thoughts, he told himself Lucan would keep her from harm. He knew the meaning of the oath, took it every bit as seriously as Merrick did. With a bit of grace, and mayhap a lot of luck, she would learn her lesson from Tane and heed his warning.

God help him if she disobeyed.

CHAPTER 14

✠

U nable to tolerate Merrick's imprisonment a moment longer, Anne pushed her notes aside. She couldn't focus on the intricate timeline of medieval kings anyway. She couldn't shake off Merrick's imperial attitude and his ridiculous threat he'd spank her like a misbehaving child.

She pushed her feet into her boots, pulled her hair into a lose knot at the base of her neck, and went to the door. If she wanted to leave this room, she would. There wasn't a damn thing Merrick could do to stop her.

Anne stuck her head in the hall and reveled in a thrill of satisfaction when she found it empty.

Not a damn thing.

Now to find the inner sanctum. She wasn't a child and she wasn't a prisoner. She wouldn't stay the week out like this, confined to two rooms, waiting for someone to make decisions for her. She hadn't made any progress on her research either, and time was rapidly slipping away. Beyond all that, her snap decision to seduce Merrick was posing more complications than she'd expected. She found herself more affected by him than he appeared to be by her naive attempts.

The best thing she could do was find her answers and

omit herself from the situation before it became any more complicated.

Determined, she struck off down the stairs, rounded the main floor landing, and descended into the lower corridors of stone. With more than a little luck, she found Merrick's room and retraced their path past Lucan's door, past Farran's, past Caradoc's. The hallways ran together, a maze of identical stone interrupted by rough-hewn wood. But a dim light around a distant corner marked the corridor where she'd stumbled over the stairs to the heart of the temple. With a quick glance over her shoulder to ensure no one followed, she approached quickly.

Only, when she stepped around the corner and discovered the dim light came from an open chamber door, not the torch above the inner sanctum stairs, her shoulders slumped. Damn. So close. She had to have gotten turned around somehow.

Glancing around, she searched for something on the wall that might give her an idea of her location. As she scoured the walls, the ceiling, the iron sconces that held unlit torches, a familiar masculine voice drifted through the partly open door.

Edged with heavy frustration, Mikhail's voice rang out. "I cannot guess what lays ahead, Raphael. Without the seraphs, the knights can only hold out for so long."

Anne cocked her head. Mikhail's office—maybe her excursion wouldn't be a failure after all. The conversation certainly sounded interesting enough. On her toes, she edged forward to peer inside the crack. Pacing the narrow expanse of his office, Mikhail held his hands behind his back. A blond man lounged in the chair behind him, one ankle tossed over one knee. His mass of golden curls tumbled carelessly around his shoulders, and he tapped steepled fingertips together in thought.

"Azazel has two nails," Mikhail continued. "The third is almost certain. I do not dare send men out to try and stop him. They will die. Every last one of them will fall."

A chill drifted down Anne's spine. In a heartbeat, the

vision of Merrick's lifeless body leapt behind her eyes. She sucked down a gasp. Surely not. Mikhail had said she would save someone. He couldn't have been wrong.

Raphael lifted his head to respond, but his voice was low and unclear. Anne inched forward to better hear.

"Gabriel alone has been chosen to carry the knowledge. He tells us only what is absolutely necessary."

"Meanwhile we are to watch our men succumb and say naught?"

"As we have since time began. We offer only messages of faith. Strength. When the time is right, Mikhail, we will wield our swords alongside them. You know this."

Mikhail spun on him, his features chiseled with fury. "And what of our men? What of Merrick who is the last of the original nine? What of the five who follow him? I am losing them, Raphael."

"You think I do not suffer the same concerns?" Raphael shot to his feet. His palm slapped the top of Mikhail's desk, the force strong enough to make Anne cringe. "My men are only marginally stronger than yours. Take Gareth—he has watched four brothers turn into unholy things. I am forced to offer you reinforcements, yet I pray each night he fights that he returns. Do you think I do not wish I had the answers for him?"

Mikhail shook his head and his shoulders slumped. "Nay. I know you do. But what of Anne? Can we not press her to disclose her mark? She defies Merrick."

Anne's heart lodged in her throat at the possibility. It was her mark, her tattoo, her body. She alone had control over who saw it. Mikhail's logic bordered too much along the lines of Merrick's attitude for her comfort.

She flattened her back to the wall, knowing she ought to leave. If two archangels found her eavesdropping, nothing good could come of it. Whatever punishment Merrick felt obliged to execute for the simple act of leaving his room would certainly be doubled. Except, her feet refused to move.

"You cannot force the maid to do anything, Mikhail.

'Tis not our way. She was given the freedom of choice. We must rely on Merrick to convince her."

A heavy sigh gave Anne pause. She glanced at the crack to find Mikhail in the chair, his head clutched in his hands. "I suppose I should be grateful she has not said a word. Should she identify her mate, I shall have no choice but to send him to defend the final nail."

"Aye, he must lead the others."

She turned away, her blood cold. Merrick would lead the men to protect the third nail. She didn't need to hear how that would end. She'd seen enough of the vision to understand he wouldn't come home. If her vision wasn't enough, Mikhail had just proclaimed all who went would die.

Oh dear God.

As her stomach pitched, she fumbled against the wall for support. Her oath meant death. Drawing in deep breaths, she summoned her strength and shook off the wave of dizziness.

The vision haunted her as she made her way down the corridor, retreating to the safety of her rooms. Merrick laid out. Merrick's strong hands clutching his simple sword. His handsome face, still in death, never again to light with his incredible smile.

No matter how tempting it was to disclose their matching tattoos, no matter that Merrick might give her the answers to her thesis, she couldn't be the cause of his death. Arrogant jerk or not, he was too special. Too . . . noble.

Her earlier realization that her visions were the key to someone's safety rose to argue with her decision to immediately leave. She couldn't bail on that. Though she'd only been here a short time, she owed it to whoever that person was to discover what her second sight had to share. The noble men here didn't deserve to suffer.

No, she'd stick to her original plan—play along for the week, learn about the Templars. She'd also make damn sure that Merrick stayed out of battle. Then, if her visions hadn't returned and told her something useful, she'd put this whole mess behind her. Nothing and no one would make her reveal the snakes on her ankle and doom Merrick to death.

Dazed, she wandered through the temple, completely lost in the deep maze. The doors all looked the same, the walls identical barriers she didn't have a hope of navigating. Yet as she scoured for the stairs that led upstairs, she stumbled into the alcove she'd wanted originally. Standing less than four foot away, the dark, recessed doorway marked the entrance to the inner sanctum.

It taunted her. As quiet as the halls were, the chances of getting caught were slim. She could sneak down those stairs, look around to her heart's content, and leave before anyone ever suspected. A quick look would be invaluable for her research. Plus she could drop the plan of seducing Merrick and simply revel in the way he made her feel.

She shook her head. No, she couldn't. It sounded good, but felt too devious. If something obscure lurked down there, she'd need Merrick's assistance. Shattering his trust would ruin any chance of that. Seducing him felt sneaky enough, but at least that way he'd *offer* to give her a tour.

Then again, if she found what she needed, she wouldn't have to spend the full week after all. Merrick couldn't crawl any further under her skin, couldn't come anywhere close to her heart, and she'd stop being preoccupied with the well-being of men she barely knew. Her life would return to . . . normal. Boring, routine, normal. But safe. Absolutely safe.

With a surreptitious peek over her shoulder, she checked the hall. Her pulse jumped in excitement as she found it empty. Scarcely able to breathe, Anne approached the descending stairs and stopped at the top, listening for the sound of footsteps below. Heart jackhammering against her ribs, her palms turned clammy, and she wiped them on her thighs. This was it. Centuries of secrets opened up in welcome.

Hearing nothing, Anne took a deep breath and descended.

Careful to keep her steps light enough that her boots

didn't echo, she climbed down ten, fifteen, maybe twenty stairs, and still they went on, a never-ending path into complete darkness. The air changed the farther she went, assuming a cool, heavy moistness.

"Well, well, what have we here? Merrick leaves the comely maid."

From behind her, the harsh masculine voice brought her to an immediate halt. She cringed inwardly, scrambled for a likely excuse, and slowly turned around to face certain punishment. Wearing a sneer, a man she didn't recognize folded brawny arms across his chest and blocked her path. "Ranulf, look what I found."

Ranulf. Anne stiffened, the name prompting an unwanted memory of the man who'd glowered at her during dinner.

He emerged behind the first. His frosty blue gaze fell to her, full of the same malice it had conveyed before.

She backed up, taking another step into the shadows. Her eyes darted past them, a futile search for a means of escape. But the intimidating pair filled up so much of the stairwell she could hardly see the light beyond. "Ah. I—I got turned around."

"Did you now?" Ranulf asked with a smirk. "We can show you where you belong, wench."

"I ah—" Anne stepped down another stair. One more, and she'd turn around and run. Surely there had to be more than one exit out of the inner sanctum. Or maybe so many rooms down there she could get lost in them. "I'll just be going now. I think I can find my way."

"I would not be so certain of that." A deep bass washed over her shoulder, full of dark foreboding.

Whirling around, Anne gasped as a third man, far larger than the others, blocked her only means of escape.

Merrick's voice rose in her memory. *'Tis not safe for you in these halls.* Why, oh why hadn't she listened?

With a lift of her shoulders, she swallowed down a shiver and boldly met Ranulf's jeer. "Let me by."

"I do not believe so. There are three of us, all wondering if we bear your mark. If anything, you will come with us." He reached for her, pudgy fingers clamping around her wrist.

Anne jerked on her arm with a soft cry. She dug at his hands. "Let me go."

A hand settled into her shoulder blades and pushed her forward, forcing her up a stair and closer to Ranulf. Appearing at her side, a fourth giant effectively boxed her in without room to do so much as turn sideways. The anxious beat of her heart turned frantic.

Ranulf spoke again. "Merrick is not here to save his whore. You give him your favors, why should we not take ours?"

"I do no such thing! Let me go!" She drew an arm back and blindly struck out, not caring whom she attacked. Nails raked down the fourth man's face.

He drew back, his oath a violent hiss that came between splayed fingers. "You bitch!"

"Let me go, or I swear to God I'll scream my head off."

For the first time since Merrick stormed into her house, Anne knew fear. It coursed through her veins like big icebergs bent on stilling her heart. She could fight, yes, but it wouldn't take much to overpower her.

A scrape of steel from the shadows behind her made her heart twist. She flinched, anticipating a prodding prick in her back.

The flash of a blade cut through her vision. Slow, precisely timed, the broadsword descended, coming to a harmless stop on top of the hand that held onto her. "Take your hand away, Ranulf, before I remove it for you."

Cold and menacing, Anne recognized the voice long before she looked.

His features tight and dark, Farran held the man's furious stare. Her captor's jaw worked as he chewed on the inside of his cheek, and his fingers clamped down tighter, his intent to refuse crystal clear. When Farran's sword didn't move, the man let out a disgusted snort and flung her arm back at her.

Farran cut through the men, opening a passage for her. The glare he gave her held deadly meaning. "Take your leave. Now."

Anne didn't wait to be told twice. She raced up the stairs, down the corridor. The doorways passed in a blur. Her heels pounded out a frantic rhythm against the stone.

Out of nowhere, a hand wound around her waist, knocking the wind out of her as someone dragged her to a halt. Kicking and clawing at her captor, she tried to escape his suffocating hold.

"Still yourself, milady. 'Tis I, Lucan. On my way to collect you for our evening meal."

Anne collapsed in his arms. Relief coursed through her body, giving way to trembles. She held onto his forearms in search of her faltering courage. Her pride wouldn't let her show him her gratitude, or how terrified she'd been. No, not Lucan, not any of the knights. Not even Merrick. If she wanted these men's respect, she couldn't let them know she felt anything but courage.

As she relaxed, his hold loosened, and her heels touched the floor. Her emotions once again under control, she pushed free of his arm and turned around with a smile. "Thank you, Lucan. I don't think I'm hungry, though."

Not after that encounter. The idea of sitting in a room full of strange men, any one of them capable of the dishonorable actions of the four on the stairs, made her stomach churn. She tried for a smile. It faltered as her chin quivered, but she covered the trembling up by hurrying to add, "I would prefer to return to my room."

Lucan dipped at the waist, a slight gesture but still enough to stir her unease. "Then allow me to escort you, milady."

It took all Anne's self-control not to cringe as he reached for her hand. The sugary words, the chivalrous gestures—the guy was really too good to be true. Compared to the churlish Farran, unyielding Merrick, and the handful of crude men she'd just encountered, Lucan was plain odd. But she'd rather have Lucan nearby than those four jerks.

He settled her hand atop the back of his forearm in a courtly gesture and offered her a stiff smile. Anne braced herself for the rush of energy, anticipated the fuzziness in the back of her mind that came with her second sight. When it didn't come, she furrowed her brow. What was wrong with her gift? For it to fail completely . . . She gnawed on her lower lip as she fell into step beside Lucan, the oddity entirely unsettling.

They made their way to her chambers in silence. As they set foot on the main level of the house, Anne averted her eyes from the men who turned to stare. A blush crept into her cheeks, Ranulf's insinuation about her intimacy with Merrick too fresh to dismiss. Even if she was doing something unethical—not to mention dangerous to her heart—by seducing Merrick, she wasn't a whore, and the fact even one man might think of her that way, left her mortified.

Maybe because she *had* thrown herself at Merrick. Maybe because, in the depths of her heart, she wanted far more than his kisses, or the too-brief touch of his hands. Whatever the case, perception or truth, she felt the sudden need to hide.

How her sister managed to go through life without feeling this kind of humiliation, she'd never understand. Always a flirt, always accustomed to men's attention, Sophie flaunted her affairs without regard. Somehow, she never suffered for it either. In some weird way, it seemed to boost her reputation with the elite.

Anne bit back a self-directed oath. Good grief, she'd almost forgotten she needed to phone her sister. It would be late afternoon in California, and if she didn't get ahold of Sophie now, her sister's ever-demanding nightlife would ruin the opportunity.

"Lucan, do you have a phone?"

He cocked his head with a puzzled crinkle of his dark eyebrows. "Aye, I do."

"May I use it?"

"I see no reason not." He stopped at her door, nodded at the handle.

Anne opened the door and beckoned him inside. "I'll be just a few minutes."

Lucan fished in his jeans pocket and produced a slim, black phone. He handed it to her, the lines of curiosity in his expression deepening.

Dismissing his probing look, Anne snatched the cell phone out of his open palm and wandered into her bedroom. She pulled the French doors shut before she sat on the edge of the bed. He could wonder, but she'd already told one knight about her sister. The rest would wait. No way would she have another man hounding her for information about her beautiful twin.

She punched out the number and waited.

The line rang once . . . twice . . . Four tones later, Sophie's bright and cheerful voice greeted her. "Sophie here! I'm busy right now, but I'll call you back."

Damn. Tamping down a frustrated grunt, Anne willed her voice to remain calm. "It's me. Look I need to talk to you."

On the other side of Anne's door, Lucan leaned against the wall, attempting to show interest in the shelf of books. Scanning the titles out of rote habit, he listened to her one-sided conversation.

"I've ah, gotten myself into a mess. I need to pick your brain for what I should do, and I have limited time to do it in. This is important. I've got to find a way out."

Lucan drew back in shock. As a fissure of suspicion worked its way down his spine, his body tensed. Clearly, Merrick had been displeased with Anne when he left, but Lucan had suspected it came from more of the maid's willfulness than any real bone of contention. So convinced of that theory was he, that he had given Merrick's admonishment to watch her only cursory consideration. Yet her words implied something of more substance came between them.

"I know things I shouldn't. Secrets I've got to tell you. Above all that . . ." Anne let out a heavy sigh. "I think something terrible is about to happen. I don't want to be here when it does."

Nay, of course she would try to flee. Merrick had suspected as much. Christ's toes, Merrick should have been more forthright. Should have made his concern clearer. She had come from the inner sanctum; the Almighty only knew what she may have found or overheard.

"I gotta run. I'll call you when I can."

Lucan moved to the far side of the bookshelf as the mattress creaked. He pretended not to hear the doors open, studied one spine in particular. A copy of their written history stood separate from the other titles, and surreptitiously, he pulled it free. He would not chance further secrets to this woman, no matter what Mikhail claimed she was.

Struggling to keep his expression amicable, he turned to her with lifted brows. "May I borrow this from your library?" He took the risk, hoping she would not inspect the book, and flashed it beneath her nose.

In answer to his silent prayer, she gave the book a brief, dismissive glance. "Sure. Thanks for the phone." Extending her hand, she offered his cell phone.

"Of course, milady." Lucan stuffed the device into his back pocket and tucked his book beneath his arm. "Did you wish anything else of me this eve?"

Distracted, Anne shook her head as she chewed on her bottom lip.

Though he knew it was rude, he did not wait for her to reconsider. With little more than a respectful dip of his chin, he strode to the door and let himself into the hall.

Merrick would be most extremely displeased when he heard the lady had become lost beneath the house. He would rile and rant, curse and swear when he heard Lucan had disregarded the direct order to watch over her. But when he learned the woman he protected intended to spill their secrets to an outsider, Merrick would see red.

They had all sworn loyalty, and a small part of Lucan longed to believe Anne's conversation was innocent. Yet try as he might, he could not convince himself she would not become an unexpected threat. Gabriel relayed that Azazel had heard Abigail's dying command to unveil the seraphs. It would not be beyond the lord of darkness to use the tidbit of knowledge to his advantage and create the perfect lie to fool them all into revealing the sacred hiding places. He had used greater trickery to accomplish lesser victories.

If he succeeded, if the maid was indeed some sort of dark trap, Lucan refused to be the outlet to his brethren's fall. Nay, he had no choice. Despite his vow of loyalty to her, he must inform Merrick of the woman's plans to leave.

CHAPTER 15

✝

As nightfall descended, Merrick eased the truck to a stop in front of the temple and looked up to the window on the second floor. For seven hours, he had sat by the river, contemplating all manner of things. From the futility of the Templar cause, to what sort of belongings Anne might desire; from the hopelessness of his soul, to whom Anne might match, his thoughts continually returned to her.

His solitude served no purpose other than to remind him he wasted time attending to her. Each night Fulk became more dedicated to his evil path, each passing minute he moved farther away. The days of tracking him would be meaningless if Anne did not find her intended soon. Fulk's trail grew cold as the time passed.

Were it not for Mikhail's admonishment that Fulk would find salvation when the time was right, Merrick would beg to be released from Anne. However, Merrick could speak until he ran out of air, and Mikhail would not grant the freedom to pursue his transformed cousin.

Merrick dared not reveal his attraction for the maid either. Should he, Mikhail would confine him in the solitary cell for the inability to curtail his lust. Particularly when such desire involved another Templar's seraph.

A shadow moved beyond the second-story window, and Merrick's pulse bounced. He glanced at the clock radio sitting in his passenger's seat, anxious to present the gift. 'Twas a small thing, a token really, that he hoped might light her face with the same joy McDonald's brought. He could have left it behind—should have, knowing Uriel's distaste for modern music. Yet pleasing Anne soothed the gnawing in Merrick's spirit. Her bright smile eased the ever-lingering sense of despair. And so he had grabbed it as an afterthought, having spent far too long sifting through her clothes.

Which presented a whole new set of frustrations. Rummaging through Anne's closets and drawers exposed him to a far more intimate side of the woman he guarded. Her underclothes created vivid images he felt quite certain the archangels would find sacrilegious. Wispy panties, bras of such fine lace he feared he would ruin the delicate things. All of them carried that same enticing aroma of lavender and sugar. By the time he had stuffed the entire drawer in his bag, he felt awkward and embarrassed, and he had yet to discover the things she slept in.

When he had, he had to leave the drawer in favor of her closet before he could recollect his thoughts enough to dump her lingerie drawer into his duffel.

All told, he packed his bags so full he had trouble zipping them. And now, he could not wait to present them to her.

At the same time, he dreaded the moment. His strength of will would crumble should he witness that ecstatic smile again. The one that made him feel more victorious than any battle won with swords.

As the light upstairs flickered, the television dimming before flashing bright, he realized he could not put off the inevitable. With a muffled mutter, he let himself out of the truck, went around to the other side, and hauled out her belongings.

He would not linger. He would deposit the bag on the floor, bid her good night, and retreat to his chambers. Come morn, he would seek out Lucan, for he did not wish to hear anything that would force him to confront Anne again tonight.

Shouldering his way inside, he nodded to a trio of men gathered around the billiard table. The band of crimson around their left shirtsleeves branded them as members from Europe. They answered with sharp nods, a lift of a hand, a murmured hello.

Odd, he thought as he mounted the stairs. At least fifty years had passed since he had spoken with any of the European knights. The men under Mikhail oft clashed with these—as many claimed rights to properties Mikhail's knights once owned. Men like Caradoc.

Strange they would come so far. Mikhail must have sent for Raphael and reinforcements. Which meant the situation with Azazel worsened.

More things he would consider come morn.

He took a deep fortifying breath at Anne's door. A small portion of his soul demanded he let himself inside and take the liberties he would have enjoyed had she wandered into his life nine hundred years ago. Whilst he shared the residence with many others, the simple fact remained, she resided in his house. Once he had dreamed of such a circumstance. Now the fantasy only created a bitter taste in his mouth.

Resigning himself to reality, he knocked twice upon her door.

She answered as he lifted his hand for the third, concurrent rap. Briefly, she stared, bewildered. Then, her gaze fell to his armload of supplies, and her porcelain features lit with such delight a fist clamped around Merrick's heart.

"My things," she murmured as he moved past her. "Oh, Merrick, you brought my radio."

The whimsical quality of her voice, the gratitude that turned her words into music, swelled his chest. Damnation. She had turned him as soft as butter. This trial of loyalty would surely be the death of him.

He set the bags down, unwilling to look at her for fear

she would see how deeply she affected him. "I brought what I thought you might desire. Should you find something missing, we shall discuss it in the morn."

"Oh. You're leaving again?"

His back to her, he closed his eyes. The touch of disappointment that fringed her question disturbed the accursed hollowness in his gut. "Aye."

Before he could fully shrug off the thick straps digging into his shoulder, her hand settled against the small of his back. "I'd hoped you might stay with me for a while," she murmured.

Her fingertips slid up his back, warming his skin. As he righted himself, she ducked under his elbow and looped her arms around his neck. Stepping in close, Anne pressed her body to his.

Everything inside Merrick coiled tight. Her warmth, the feel of her breath upon his neck, the perfume in her hair, she overwhelmed him in a heartbeat. He battled with the urge to slide his arms around her waist and draw her even closer. The longing to capture her mouth and drink from her honeyed lips assailed his senses with the force of a battering ram. Like a strangled man desperate for one gulp of fresh air, he disentangled himself from her embrace and took a step away.

He knew only one way to combat the fierce desire she awakened. "I must fight tonight."

The air slowly left Anne's lungs as her heart crept to a stop. Fight? Merrick couldn't fight. As he dropped his bulging bags to the floor, her gaze flicked over his body in a frantic sweep. Black long-sleeved shirt, dark jeans— had she seen white or black beneath all his chain in her vision?

Damn, oh damn, he couldn't be going after the nail.

She clutched at his hand and squeezed her eyes shut tight, willing the vision to come back. Her mind refused, her second sight blocked by an unseen barrier.

"You can't fight," she blurted out.

He gave her a look that said she'd be better off locked away in a remote tower. "Why not?"

"I—ah . . ." She what? *Think, Anne, think!* She couldn't tell him she'd seen him in death. Whether he believed her or not, that just wasn't the sort of thing she could relay without the ability to explain how, when, or why. "Because . . ."

With a perturbed grimace, he started for the door. "I will see you on the morrow."

"No!" She ran after him. Grabbing onto his elbow, she set her heels into the rug, trying to drag him to a stop. "You, ah, have to help me put these things away."

Merrick shook his arm free and frowned at her. "Do not be ridiculous. I am not a servant. I shall see you in the morn, Anne."

Darting in front of him, she flattened her back against the door and spread her arms across it. "Merrick, you've got to stay. Please."

"God's teeth, woman, my purpose is to fight. Move yourself."

Anne shook her head. Desperate to find any means of preventing the future she'd foreseen, she swallowed her pride and tried the one thing she felt certain would change his mind. "I disobeyed you. I left and I tried to get into the inner sanctum. Farran had to rescue me."

That did it. His face clouded over with fury, his dark eyes shifted into hard coals. As he set his jaw, the scar along the side of his jaw pulled tight. "You will tell me no more falsehoods. Remove yourself. Now." Low and menacing, the warning in his voice made her shiver.

In defiance, she tipped her chin up and held his gaze. If she had to, she'd antagonize him to the point he forgot all about the demons—or detain him long enough that Mikhail sent someone else. "I swear it's true."

"Nay." He shook his head. "I would have heard. Lucan watched over you this night, and he brought no news of this. I know not what game you play, but it ceases here. Move, Anne."

He reached under her arm and turned the doorknob.

Despite the fact she threw her weight into the door, he opened it with relative ease. When she stumbled sideways, the steady pressure throwing her off balance, he stomped past.

The door slammed in his wake.

Anne scrambled after him. "Merrick, wait!"

He didn't slow down, didn't even glance over his shoulder as he started down the stairs.

Time for a little more honesty. A different kind. The kind that galled her to admit.

Anne sucked in a breath, and in a voice just loud enough he would hear it but it wouldn't carry down the stairs, she called, "I'm scared you'll get hurt."

One foot a step lower than the other, Merrick came to a standstill. Her heart drummed a heavy beat as he looked over his shoulder. Pain, bewilderment, and something else Anne couldn't recognize reflected in his features, before he masked the emotion with the grim set of his jaw. Two slow steps brought him around fully. Another four determined strides, and he stood in front of her.

Her eyes followed his hand as he settled two strong fingers beneath her chin. Tipping her head up, he brought her gaze to his. His eyes searched her face, the crease between his dark eyebrows deepening. "Aye," he murmured. "You do mean it."

Anne nodded on a hard swallow.

Merrick's thumb brushed her cheek, and his expression softened. "'Tis my duty, Anne. You must not worry. I vow I shall see you in the morn. Now go inside before you wound me more deeply."

Wound him? All she'd done was tell him the truth. She didn't want any of these men hurt. Yet as he cupped her face in his palm, and she held her breath wanting nothing more than to feel his mouth against hers, she knew it went deeper than the simple desire to protect someone from harm. It was Merrick. Merrick whom she worried for above all else. Merrick whom she cared for.

He dipped his head and dusted a kiss across her cheek. "Go," he whispered.

Anne caught his shirt in both her hands, curled her fingers, and buried her nose against his chest. For several long moments, they stood unmoving, then Merrick slid his hand through her hair with a heavy sigh. "Anne . . ." His mouth feathered against the top of her head.

She pressed a soft kiss to his heart. "Is it the nail, Merrick?"

"Nay, little demon, 'tis just another hunt for Azazel's minions."

Tipping her chin up, she searched his dark gaze for the truth. "Nothing too dangerous?"

He closed his eyes for a heartbeat. When he opened them again, sadness filled the fathomless dark depths. "I cannot promise you such."

She curled her fingers tighter.

Merrick took her by the wrists and gently pried her loose. With a gentle push backward, he held her at a distance and gazed into her eyes. The same look of longing passed across his face as it had moments before he'd kissed her both times, and Anne inched to her toes, hungry for the feel of his mouth on hers.

Abruptly, Merrick withdrew. He turned crisply and hurried down the stairs.

Anne slunk inside her room and leaned against the door. Maybe he wasn't defending the nail, maybe this fight wasn't as deadly as the one Mikhail referenced, but Merrick couldn't promise he wouldn't be injured. He'd walked into her world, turned it upside down faster than she could blink, and now he faced harm. Because she couldn't stop him from leaving. She sank to the floor defeated. She'd failed with her purpose. She couldn't warn Merrick without the gift of her second sight, and it had seemingly abandoned her. God, Gabe brought her into this, and she'd even let him down.

As tears threatened, she shook her head. *No.* She

wouldn't cry. Merrick promised he would return. The man was obsessive about his word. He'd never dream of making a vow he couldn't keep. Most important, he wasn't defending the third nail. She needed to believe in Mikhail's words.

Easing to her feet, she worried her bottom lip with her teeth. In the meantime, she'd figure out how to get her second sight to cooperate. Her protection was all she could give Merrick, and she desperately needed him to return.

CHAPTER 16

✝

In 924 years, Merrick had never known a woman's worry. When he had reached an age where the frivolous romps with serving maids and whores lost excitement, he had already sworn the Templar oath. He had already discovered the scrolls, and what would have been a short tenure with the Order became eternal. Dreams of a wife and holdings of his own faded. He had cast aside the impossible ideals.

Now, as the gift landed in his lap, the effect was monumental. His insides trembled like a frightened child. Terrifyingly, Anne forced him to confront the reality of his tenacious hold on life. As it was before he came upon his curse, each time he now raised his sword could be his last. Only the price he would pay would be far worse than pain and death. He would serve Azazel, the power of his sword turned upon his brothers.

Whilst Anne's concern gave his heart wings it dared not stretch, he could no longer pretend that he cared not if he returned to walk these halls. Indeed, he cared too much.

Biting back an oath at the unfairness of his situation, he clenched a hand into a fist and lengthened his stride. 'Twas all meaningless. He could care until his heart bled, and 'twould change naught. His fate followed Fulk's. All he could dare to hope for with each sunrise was that he might yet have time to honor their pact. Then, when he claimed his cousin's vile soul, Farran would claim his.

A noble end. He could ask for little else, for Anne offered him naught but frustration.

Frustration Merrick refused to allow to haunt him through another sleepless night. He would chase away this fruitless desire, no matter the cost. Anne had others to offer her protection. She did not need him.

He let himself into his chambers and slung his heavy duffel bag over his shoulder. Aye, he would fight. 'Twas the only thing he knew to expend the anxiousness in his body. Anne had him so tight and tense he feared he might crack in half.

In his doorway, he paused, debating which direction to take. Caradoc would sense his disquiet and prod too deeply. Lucan, he wished not to see, for fear there might be some small degree of truth in Anne's claims she had disobeyed. Tane . . . nay, he did not trust himself to still his hand should Tane broach the subject of her. Which left Farran—he would not plague Merrick with conversation. He fought swiftly, cared little for camaraderie these days. Exactly what Merrick needed to take his mind off the beautiful woman in his charge.

He turned left, his pace determined and swift.

At Farran's door, he gave the rough-hewn wood a sharp rap. Inside, a chair moved over stone, boots drew nearer. The door opened, and Farran ducked his head outside. On seeing Merrick, he swung it wide.

With a curt nod, Farran bid hello. "Merrick."

Merrick shifted the heavy weight dangling from his shoulder. "I need your arm."

He offered no argument, merely stepped inside and picked up bag and sword. "Mikhail sends us to a gate?"

"Nay. 'Tis I who needs the sport."

Shouldering past Merrick, Farran entered the hall. "I shall drive."

Grateful for his brother's lack of words, Merrick fell into step at his side.

* * *

Farran eyed the three shades gathered around Merrick with disgust. Though he longed to drive his blade in deep and snuff out their evil existence, he sensed his brother needed the outlet far more than Farran required victory. 'Twas not as if a shade posed great difficulty, even in a small pack. Unintelligent creatures, they knew only Azazel's simple command to fight. For a man with Merrick's experience, the shadowy beings carried the ease of conquering an angry dog.

Merrick parried a well-aimed strike of claws, then arced his body forward and brought his blade around with the swiftness of a cyclone. One shade let out a bloodcurdling scream as an ethereal arm severed in half.

Nay, Merrick needed no assistance.

Content to keep a watchful eye open for the arrival of a nytym or a demon, Farran sheathed his sword and folded his arms over his chest.

Merrick had said little during the drive to the fifty-eighth gate, forty-five miles south of the temple, in Harrisonville. Nor had he rested, as he was so oft to do prior to a battle. Merrick's stare fixed out the passenger's window, and Farran observed then, as he did now, the war that waged in Merrick's features. Something plagued his brother, and Farran did not need to guess what. Or more precisely, who.

'Twas why he said naught about Anne's encounter with Ranulf and Gottfried. He would tell Merrick of the trouble later, for should he not, someone else would. Common sense said the knowledge would only further agitate Merrick's spirit.

Another powerful arc, timed with the twist of Merrick's torso, and a second shade expired with a ghostly moan.

Farran waited to see if the darkness would affect his brother. His hand on his sword's hilt, he prepared to step in and alleviate the last from life. The only time a shade posed any real danger came when knights succumbed to the infusion of darkness in their veins.

Merrick stood strong, his paces unhindered.

Releasing his grasp on his sword, Farran moved to the cracked portal that filled the tiny cavern with the stench of death. He leaned his shoulder to the tall barrier stone and heaved with his legs. The thick slab inched over the narrow opening, sealing off the gate. Enough of the swordplay. Their souls were too damaged to take the risk.

Behind Merrick, the last shade swept in with a frenzied scream, tentacle-like arms flailing at Merrick's head. Clinks and pings echoed through the cavern as claws made contact with Merrick's mail. The sound of a human bellow, however, told Farran at least one set of talons found his brother's face.

As if the blow strengthened Merrick's resolve, he lunged forward. On a powerful thrust, the tip of his holy blade sank deep into the shade's shadowy gut. With a twist of his arm, Merrick dragged the blade skyward, neatly severing the creature in two.

Farran took a step forward, prepared to clap his brother on the back in unspoken praise.

But as Farran's heel connected with the dampened stone floor, Merrick dropped to his knees. His sword tumbled from his hands, clattered to the floor forgotten. He doubled over with a low moan, bending until his forehead touched the cool rock.

Warily, Farran waited. Such a display, such an anguished effect of the invasion on a soul came in the later days before a knight turned. If Merrick were this close, one shade's paltry darkness could be enough to turn him from holy warrior to evil nightmare.

Another agonized groan tore from Merrick's throat as he collapsed in a heap. His body heaved as he panted, twitched as muscles fought the strain.

"Brother." Farran crossed to him. Squatting at his side, he set a hand on Merrick's shoulder. "You should not be here."

Merrick's breath came in hard gasps. "Aye," he hissed through clenched teeth.

"I will not see you sacrifice yourself over a wench. Come. I know a better recourse."

As Merrick hauled himself to unsteady legs, Farran pulled his cell phone out of his duffel bag. He punched the number he found himself dialing oft and listened to the ring. When a sweet, feminine voice answered, he replied, "Meet me in twenty minutes. I have a friend with me."

He waited only long enough for Leah's agreeing murmur before he tucked the phone back into his bag. Then he bent at the waist and shrugged out of his surcoat, his mail. Helping Merrick to do the same, Farran took in the jagged scratches across his brother's face. They bled at a trickle, the wounds long but not deep. His apprehension over Merrick's soul increased. Marks so benign should have already healed.

Merrick closed his eyes and heaved in a deep breath. He said naught as he dragged his bag over his shoulder and struck off down the corridor. But Farran knew his thoughts. Had battled them too oft of late. Sometimes a man could not help but wish the change would already come upon him. For though his soul would hate, he would lack the capacity to care, and all the wretched feeling would cease.

He followed at a respectful distance, honoring Merrick's silence. At least the women would help. For a time they could both forget. Pretend they were young men again, who knew naught of demons or relics. Men who cared only for the rush of battle and the spoils of victory.

Long blond hair glided across Merrick's chest, soft curls he once would have twined through his fingers and relished. The maid's manicured nails tickled across his abdomen as she let out a husky laugh. A whore. Farran's recourse was a whore. Whilst Merrick would admit the wench was comely enough—he could find no complaint with her body—the heat in his blood had naught to do with her masterful touch.

Nay, where this maid had blond hair, he saw only rich auburn. Her blue eyes were naught like Anne's, and each time she looked at him through a veil of dark lashes, Merrick's gut churned in protest.

Turning his head to the side, he avoided her seeking mouth. He did not want this wench.

Farran brought him to this tiny apartment, intent they should both work off their restlessness. On their arrival, the one Farran called Leah threw herself at him with such exuberance Merrick's thoughts barreled right back to Anne. He had watched, dimly aware of the blonde, as Leah rubbed herself against his brother. Each press of her lips, each caress of her hands took Merrick back to Anne's bedroom, and before he could realize the full effect of witnessing such a display, his body responded with a lion's fury.

When Farran escorted Leah away, the blonde tumbled into Merrick's lap, purring like a cat. She had landed on his erection, and on discovering his arousal, manipulated him to hardened steel. He had shoved Anne aside long enough to slide out of his shirt and allow the blonde to lead him to the bed. But he could not find enjoyment despite her willingness. Her skin was too rough, her perfume distasteful, and the kohl around her eyes too unnatural.

Her hand delved beneath the waistband of his jeans, and Merrick sucked in a sharp breath. Though his loins burned like fire, he gripped his hands around the wench's hips and eased her off him.

Without explanation, he rose from the too-small bed and retrieved his shirt off the floor. The sounds of grunting, of pleasured giggles, drifted from behind the closed door. Like a strong fist clamped around his cock, the noises taunted with fresh images of all he would like to do to Anne.

"Something the matter?" the woman asked.

As he glanced over his shoulder, she sat exposed in the middle of the bed. Her full breasts heaved with her shortened breath, her cheeks glowed with unspent passion.

Merrick shook his head. He pulled a wad of bills from within his wallet and set them on the nearby dresser.

"No skin off my back," the blonde quipped. Her retort came with the squeaking of the bed. She moved behind him, the soft rustle of clothing telling Merrick that she dressed.

He exited the apartment and took a seat on the topmost stair. Below, a solitary car rolled through the parking lot. The November air served to cool him somewhat, and he took in a deep, frosty breath.

Anne.

Not beast, not whore, not duty could keep his mind from her. He could have fought until his soul turned as black as pitch and never expelled her from his system. The early years of his life, where he had fought to overcome his bastard's status, seemed like a carnival ride in comparison to the trial of denying what he most desired.

Dropping his head into his hand, he fingered the tender marks that seared his cheek. Still sticky, they had yet to mend as they should. The whore had tried to soothe them with her mouth. Her touch had only burned.

But the wounds served as a grim reminder to the hopelessness of his fate. He craved what was not his to have, and the irony of it all—even if he should somehow find a way to put Anne from his mind, he would not live to find the seraph meant for him.

He startled as the door behind him opened. Heavy boots approached, stopped at his side. "She did not please you," Farran observed.

Merrick dragged his hand down his face and stood up. "Naught does." Following Farran to the SUV, Merrick let himself inside the passenger's door and punched the lock. He leaned against the door and crossed his arms over his chest. As they drove through the darkened streets, his frustration began to fester. Annoyance flickered through his veins, caught swiftly in his heated blood. He worked his jaw against the rush of undesired emotion and clenched his fingers into tight fists.

He could not exist this way. The darkness pulled, begging him to give in and forsake his oaths. To take what he wanted, enjoy all Anne had to offer until his time arrived. 'Twould only be a few more evenings. Her intended not yet found, he dishonored no one in specific. With his death, she would be free, his sins excused and soon forgotten.

But the dark urges combated fiercely with what remained of his honor. He would be remembered as a betrayer of vows, a man to be scratched from the scrolls of membership. Mayhap even denied entry to eternal salvation should his brothers succeed in extinguishing his transformed soul.

Time passed at a turtle's crawl, his head no more clear than when he left at dawn. If such were possible, he felt even more conflicted.

Farran navigated the SUV to a stop in front of the temple, and Merrick let himself out, all too glad to be free of the stale air inside the vehicle. He ignored the concern that twisted Farran's features into tight lines and jerked open the front door. As Farran turned left, Merrick went right.

He stopped at the stairwell leading upstairs, debating.

CHAPTER 17

A nne drew back from the window, her heart in her throat. When the headlights had flashed against her wall, she'd rushed to catch a glimpse of Merrick, but the SUV's bright light blinded her to who had returned. So fierce was the glare, she couldn't even decipher whether one or two men climbed out of the silver vehicle.

Fingers fisted in the lightweight sheers, she pressed her forehead to the cool windowpane. God, she'd go insane if she had to wait until morning to know if Merrick survived the night.

Closing her eyes, she pushed her energy outward, searching for some fragment of the vision. A fixture, a sliver of his clothing—anything that might tell her of its coming. But as it had done all night, her second sight eluded her. She could feel the power on the fringes of her thoughts, and yet she couldn't gather it in, couldn't open her mind enough to bring the scene to life.

"Merrick," she whispered.

Lifting her shoulders, she turned from the window and stalked to her bedroom. She wouldn't wait. Before she slept, before she *could* sleep, she'd find out if he'd returned.

She tugged her dresser drawer open and fished out a

heavier shirt. After unpacking all the things Merrick brought, she'd donned a pair of lightweight pajama pants and a simple T-shirt. But if she intended to walk through the lower halls, she wanted the biggest, bulkiest object she could find. In case she ran into Tane. Or Ranulf.

As she lifted the sweatshirt to tug it over her head, a fumbling at her door made her pause. Elbows bent, she peeked through the neck as her heart drummed to a stop.

On an uneasy exhale, she watched as the brass doorknob turned, and the door slowly opened.

Merrick stepped inside, his features as hard as they'd ever been. His gaze swept the room, his eyes widening when they came to rest on her.

She dropped the sweatshirt and rushed to him. Unable to stop the tide of emotion that swelled and burst, she threw her arms around his neck. "Oh God, you're okay." He was okay. Alive.

Here.

She clung tighter, nuzzling her face into his shoulder. "You're okay," she repeated on a whisper of disbelief.

"Aye."

The roughness of his voice, combined with the strange rigidity of his body, filtered through her awareness and quelled her surge of elation. Curious, she leaned back and lifted her gaze to his face.

What she saw across his cheek lanced pain through her heart.

Four long claw marks raked their way from Merrick's temple to his chin. Another creased across the bridge of his nose to mar his other cheek. She let out a soft gasp.

As Merrick's arms slowly wound around her waist, Anne let go of his neck to brush her fingertips across his face. "You're hurt," she murmured.

The concern that filled Anne's blue eyes shredded Merrick's heart far deeper than the shade's claws had torn his face. Her delicate eyebrows dipped together, but the rest of her features softened as she gently touched his cheek.

He could not bear the tenderness of her caress. He did not deserve such. For if she knew what drew him here, she would surely think him a monster deserving of such marks. Twisting away, he tried to escape her soft caress.

She forbade him. With a lift of her other hand, she trapped his face between her hands and thwarted his attempt. "Do they hurt?"

He closed his eyes so she could not see the anguish that her worry provoked. "Nay." In truth, they burned like fire. Each time he moved his mouth, the slice across his upper lip stung with the ferocity of an angry hornet. Yet under the soft pressure of her fingertips, the gentle brush of her lips he had not expected to encounter, they soothed.

But he did not want the balmy sensations. The way his heart stuttered unnerved him more than any wrathful foe. He clung desperately to his earlier annoyance, the anger he could more easily understand. Prying her hands away from his face, he turned his head and evaded her feather-light kisses.

What he desired had naught to do with gentleness. Nay, he could not allow feeling. Not tonight. Not ever.

Catching her roughly in his embrace, he slanted his mouth across hers. He nudged her lips apart, thrust his tongue against hers. Hungry for all she had to give, he demanded her full surrender with deep, possessive strokes.

To his complete consternation, she melted in his arms. Her kisses came with matched intensity, the play of her tongue with his, both salvation and damnation. He groaned against the rush of white-hot fire that surged through his blood, and with awkward steps, maneuvered her back to the wall.

Tearing his mouth from hers, Merrick sought the tender flesh near the base of her ear. One hand he slid to her bottom, pulled her hips in tight to his. The other he moved to her breast and cupped the soft flesh there. Heat filled his palms, her flesh as warm for him as his was for her.

Vaguely, the memory of his oath, the reasons why he could not strip her bare and sink himself inside her, rose to the back of his mind. He pushed the accursed thoughts aside and allowed the desire in his soul free rein.

Anne's hands flattened over his chest. Her nails bit into his skin, the pinch a sting so pleasant his head spun. She tipped her head back, allowing him greater access to her throat and the thick vein that pulsed a frantic beat. He pressed his lips to it, trailed the tip of his tongue to the inlet of her shoulder.

"You are truly a demon," he murmured as he gave the delicate skin a nip with his teeth.

She trembled against him, her hips undulating against the hand he held at the base of her buttocks. Through the lightweight cotton of her sleeping pants, he could feel the heat of her sex. He slipped his fingers between her thighs, let them rest upon her sensitive, feminine flesh. The angle of his arm brought her closer to his body, and her nipples stabbed into his chest.

With a stroke meant to further tease, he caressed her central place of pleasure through her clothing, then pulled his hand away to drag her shirt over her head.

She offered no resistance, wriggled her shoulders when the T-shirt became bound. He dropped the garment to the ground and let his gaze feast upon the most glorious breasts he had ever seen. Full and soft, they puckered with her shiver. Captured by the silent call of her body, he trailed a fingertip from her collarbone to the tip of one hard peak. Anne pulled in a ragged breath that ripped through him like a dagger's deadly blade.

He repeated the motion against her other breast, then cupped them both, lifted gently before he covered them with his palms. His thumbs toyed with her nipples as he brought his gaze to hers. What he found in her bright blue eyes, however, was enough to make him tremble.

Behind a blend of things too frightening to consider, boldness shone bright. Not the same brazen wantonness the blonde made no attempt to hide, and yet naught close to the shy, hesitant stare of maid who knew innocence. 'Twas a look of a woman who felt no shame, who knew what she desired. That she might want him with the same ferocity that lived inside him, made Merrick feel like both a valiant warrior and a terrified captive all at once.

She reached between their bodies, gave his waistband a tug to draw him closer. Obeying, he dipped his mouth to her breast.

Anne slid her hands into Merrick's thick hair and curled her fingers against his scalp. The moist heat of his mouth, combined with the chilly air, sent wave after wave of goose bumps rippling down to her toes. His teeth closed around her nipple, and she arched her back to his not-so-gentle nip. God, oh God, her body felt on fire. The urge to cry out, to beg him to release the building ache inside her rode her hard. But after last night, she vowed she wouldn't so much as murmur, and she clamped down on her lower lip to stifle the sound.

All thoughts of deliberate seduction fled her mind as she became caught up in the magic of Merrick, the mystical power of his mouth and hands. This was no longer a coy game. Rather, she couldn't control it if she wanted to. Some part of her that she didn't fully understand needed everything Merrick had to offer. Needed *him*.

While he suckled at one breast, he stroked the other with his hand. Then, when she thought she couldn't stand another moment of the incredible pleasure of his mouth, he alternated his caresses. Every last one of her nerve endings rose to stand on end, the ecstasy of Merrick's caresses overwhelming her thoughts.

Her hips surged forward in a desperate attempt to make

contact with the hard ridge of his erection. He sank into her, the contact fleeting before he drew away and dragged his mouth to hers. His kiss dominated. His hands, his tongue, his body commanded hers. Her legs went weak beneath his feral onslaught. Merrick held her up, refusing to let her fall.

His free hand flattened over her abdomen, the roughened scrape of his calloused palm a pleasant surprise. Withdrawing his hand from her breast, he wound it around her waist and brought her closer. And yet he refused to allow their bodies to meld. As if he sought to keep them deliberately distanced, he held his hips away. Denied her the one touch that would relieve the tightness in her womb.

In an effort to guide him to what she yearned for, she brought her hands between their bodies and freed the button at his waist. As her fingertips delved beneath his jeans and grazed the hot hard length of him, Merrick exhaled on a hiss. His body turned to stone, and for one terrifying moment, his lips clung to hers, unmoving.

She dipped her hand lower and flattened her palm over his erection. With her other hand she pulled at his jeans, giving herself more freedom to move, until she held him fully. His body surged into her palm, and Merrick let out a hoarse groan. A thrill thrummed through her at the sound, and for one crowning instant of glory, she became the victor in their play.

Yet her triumph was short lived, for in one sweeping downward glide, Merrick's fingertips delved into the moistened folds of her aching center, and Anne's world tilted upside down. She bucked into his palm, shuddering.

The tip of his tongue teased her down from a towering height as he traced the inside of her lower lip. She caught his mouth, her kiss far more urgent. With slow finger strokes that matched the firm pump of her hand, Merrick aroused her until she shook with need. The effort of keeping herself silent took its toll as well, and Anne choked back a cry. Lord in heaven, she was going to burst apart if Merrick didn't stop.

One hand supporting her beneath her buttocks, he eased a finger inside her slick opening. Anne could no longer hold back. She whimpered. Dimly aware she still held him in her palm, she squeezed his hardened shaft as her inner muscles clamped down hard. Holding her as close as she could get, his fingers moved in and out of her, each press bringing the base of his palm against her sensitive nub.

She gripped and squeezed, mimicking the way she would hold him were he sheathed inside her, and sought to maintain a hold on her senses.

Yet it was futile. Her body betrayed her will, erupting with intense heat. Wave after wave of sensation rose within her, lifting her to heights she had never known. Had never imagined. And though she longed for Merrick to join her in the dizzying ride, she let go. Release ripped through her, stealing her ability to breathe. She tore her mouth away, sank her teeth into Merrick's shoulder, and bit back a plaintive cry.

He slowed his rhythm, eased his hand from between her thighs, and settled it on her hip. Slowly, deftly, he pushed at the loose waistband on her pajamas, exposing her skin to the room's cool air.

Shaken to the depths of her soul, Anne leaned against the wall, too spent to open her eyes. As the air washed across her legs, telling her he'd bared her completely, her thoughts came together with a cyclone's force. He wasn't finished with her. No, he was merely starting.

She shivered in expectation.

Merrick took a step forward, and Anne boldly guided him home. The tip of his erection slid between her thighs.

Everything inside Merrick throbbed. His cock, his pulse, his blood—nothing was spared the tumult of Anne's release. Seconds away from finding his own ecstasy, the feel of her moistened flesh against his swollen cock blindsided him.

A dozen voices rose within his mind. *Unto your brothers swear your life; from this day forth you shall first be loyal to our purpose, second to those who bear arms at your side; swear your loyalty to her; she will save one man's life.*

The last crashed through all his bliss as if someone plunged a sword into his gut. *Nice art, but I've never seen it before.*

She was not his. This woman who possessed him more deeply than the darkness in his soul belonged to a brother.

At once, he wanted to bellow, scream, cry, and even curse. He could find no salvation, no matter where he turned. He had never known the kind of heaven her arms held, nor the depths of hell they exposed him to. To walk amongst Azazel's realm would surely be a lesser misery.

Dragging in air through clenched teeth, he set his hands on Anne's hips and gently pushed her body away. He covered first himself, then bent down and pulled her pajamas about her waist. His fingers shook with the effort of fastening the button on his jeans, and to his humiliation, his arm trembled as he retrieved her shirt.

When he pressed it to her belly, her eyes searched his face, demanding explanations he could not find the strength to voice. Squeezing his eyes shut to the conflict in his mind, he shook his head and turned away.

"Merrick, wait," she called softly.

"Nay," he answered on a hard swallow. "Nay, Anne. If I stay another moment, I will have you in that bed."

He shoved a hand through his hair and reached for the doorknob.

"But that's where I want you," she whispered.

He nodded once, a sharp dip of his chin. Pulling the door open, he answered, "I know." Another protest, and he would turn right back to her waiting arms, cart her off to that oversized bed. When he finished with her, he would hate himself.

He entered the hall and shut the door.

Determination narrowed his gaze as he descended the stairs. He trained his thoughts to his cousin, focused on the oath he swore to Fulk. The very moment Anne discovered her intended, he vowed to leave. No sacred nail, no protected relic, no other oath would he honor until he fulfilled the promise to his kin. In so doing, he would free himself from this torment and lift his blade in Azazel's name. It was a price he no longer feared to pay.

CHAPTER 18

†

Anne stared at the ceiling, wide-eyed. Though the room was dark, and a ballad drifted from her clock radio, sleep felt like some distant, intangible dream.

Beneath the covers, she rubbed one sock-clad foot against the other and let out a bone-deep sigh. Merrick should be here. She should be curled up in the crook of his strong arm, one hand on his powerful chest, and basking in the sweet afterglow of incredible sex. Yet because of some godforsaken mark, she lay alone.

She supposed she ought to be grateful he had the good sense to stop. Her intended or not, getting further tangled up in Merrick would only make it more difficult to leave. Only for some insane reason, she didn't particularly care about the consequence or the possibility of heartache. She wanted Merrick. Everything about him spoke to her soul. Yet if Mikhail told the truth—and she didn't dare question an archangel's wisdom—staying with Merrick, revealing the tattoo on her ankle, would bring that damning vision into painful reality. As long as she kept herself hidden, she kept Merrick alive.

But in the meantime . . .

She sighed again, the breath stirring a long strand of

her hair. It fell over her nose, and she brushed it aside, annoyed.

In the meantime, she wasn't making any progress on learning the Order's secrets.

Worse, where she'd planned a week-long, strictly physical affair, Merrick was bulldozing his way into someone she deeply cared about. If tonight didn't evidence she had feelings for him, she didn't know what might. If he could have seen the way she'd paced her room for the full hour before his return, he would have laughed.

Or maybe not, given his reaction to her admission that she worried about his safety.

Which made things even more confusing. One minute he acted as if he wanted her affection. The next, he washed so cold he could pass for an iceberg.

What kind of man pulled away from a willing woman, seconds away from burying himself inside her?

The honorable kind.

She groaned at her conscience. Merrick and his honor— how one man could be so loyal to a concept of preordained matches blew her mind. Her body yearned for him. Mark or no mark, consequence be damned, she couldn't walk away from this fierce desire. She wanted Merrick. She'd discover a way to have both him and her career later. There had to be a way to have *him,* without this damning business of fate. A way to work so far under his armor that he'd stop running from the passion that threatened to consume them.

Restless, she flopped over onto her stomach and turned her face to the curtained window. Behind a thick layer of clouds, the moon shone dully. The only thing she could think of that got under Merrick's skin was herself. Her wit annoyed him. When she ventured out alone, he lost his temper. When she visited his injured friend, he turned all grumpy.

Her thoughts ground to a stop. She lifted her head, her eyes wide.

Declan.

When she'd told Merrick she'd visited Declan, he turned all eleventh century on her again. Damn it all—the man was jealous.

Which meant his armor wasn't all that polished after all. At the very least, he had weak spots, and she'd just discovered a potent one.

In all her years, she'd never once manipulated a man with that base emotion. Her sister didn't have the same theories, however, and Anne had learned a great deal about what jealousy could achieve. If Sophie could do it, so could she.

Anne pulled in a deep breath, summoning courage. She was desperate for answers and time was racing past. All she needed to do was voice an appreciative comment, and when a hundred men or more surrounded her, finding compliments would come easy.

Especially when one had a mark and needed to see others to verify a match.

Lucan stopped in front of Merrick's door and lifted his hand to knock. But the string of angry oaths on the other side of the barrier stopped his knuckles before they made contact. Frowning, he leaned closer to the door to listen.

Whilst he could not make out the muffled mumblings, he deciphered Merrick was alone. Any idea he might have had about telling Merrick of Anne's unsettling conversation vanished as something hard thumped into the wall. Clearly, his brother needed no further fuel for his ire.

Another heavy thump, however, brought a frown to Lucan's face. 'Twas not like Merrick to exhibit unrestrained temper. In all the years they had fought together, Lucan could recall only one occasion Merrick had given in to a fit of rage—when the Inquisition strung him up with ropes at Chinon and demanded he confess to sins against the Church. His defiance earned him swifter punishment, and Merrick had lost the use of both arms for several months after his shoulders dislocated so severely the muscles tore.

Concerned, Lucan turned the knob and opened the door with care. From atop a chair poised near his wardrobe, Merrick whipped around. "What do you want?" he barked.

Lucan took in his brother's chambers. Clothes littered the floor. The footlocker normally situated at the foot of Merrick's bed sat upended in a corner. His bed looked a rumpled mess. "You bang about like a blind man on stilts. What plagues you?" Lucan entered and shut the door.

"'Tis none of your concern."

"Nay? Eight centuries of friendship, and I am to turn a blind eye when something is as obvious as blood upon snow?"

Merrick did not deign to answer. He turned his attention back to the wardrobe and pitched another stack of shirts over his shoulder. They tumbled through the air, scattered, and fell in disarray. "Damnation," he muttered.

"Du Loire." Lucan scowled at Merrick's back. "You will tell me what stirs your temper."

"Very well," Merrick grit out, his voice thick with annoyance. "There is a flask here somewhere. Find it."

Drawing back, Lucan's eyes widened to twice their normal size. Merrick du Loire did not drink. Not since he had left the fertile fields near Chinon, where he left his mother's body to float down the river Loire and drowned his grief with a cask of ale. After three days of suffering the ill effects, he rode for the Holy Land. He had not imbibed since then.

Lucan did not have to think hard to discover the reason for Merrick's behavior. 'Twas either Fulk, or the Lady Anne. He reflected on Merrick's arrival at his door this morn and guessed the latter. "When was the last time a woman drove you to spirits?"

Merrick's grumble, accompanied by the malice in his glare, told Lucan his assumption proved correct. Lucan let out a sigh and leaned a shoulder against the door frame. "You would be wise to inform Mikhail and request release from this duty."

As Merrick stormed to the trunk beneath the window

ledge, he growled, "Find the flask." He jerked open the lid and shoved his hands inside. Out came a dagger, a pair of ruined mail gloves, two torn surcoats, and a coif that had seen better days. "Never mind."

Producing a dented silver flask, Merrick held it to the light with a victorious grunt. He waved it in Lucan's direction and twisted off the top. "To sanity." Lucan watched as Merrick tilted his head back, drew deeply, and swallowed.

He jerked forward, spewing the remnants of the mouthful and set his hands on his knees. "Bollocks!" He swiped his mouth across the back of his arm. "'Tis naught but rot."

Lucan's mouth quirked with a smile he dared not loose.

"Have you ale, Lucan? I require several pints."

The question did not warrant answering. Save for those who hid their drink as Merrick had, the Order forbade the use of spirits within the temple except for ceremonial wine.

Merrick dropped onto the edge of his bed. "Leave me to my misery, Lucan. You can do naught."

"'Twould do you good to spend time with the men. You would not wish to hear the rumblings off their tongues about the time you devote to Anne."

The sardonic smirk that played at Merrick's mouth twisted his features cruelly. "If I could rid myself of her, I would."

Indeed, 'twas the maid. Lucan resisted the urge to scold. From the looks of things, Merrick already punished himself enough for the both of them.

"Go with Farran. Oft I see his surcoat outside his door. A wench will cure you of this."

Merrick shook his head and chuckled bitterly. "Go, Lucan. You cannot imagine the trials I have suffered this night."

He knew Merrick well enough to know when words would be wasted breath. Sympathizing with his brother's torment, Lucan set his hand on the door. "She is a pretty maid," he mused as he tugged it open.

"Aye." Merrick's voice dropped, his whisper nearly inaudible. "She is the most beautiful woman I have ever known."

That solitary confession lifted the hairs along Lucan's arms. He needed naught else to confirm his deepest suspicions. Merrick cared for the lady. The pair were as mismatched as oil and water, yet somehow she affected him in ways Lucan would have never imagined. Their fates bound otherwise, this marked trouble for all. For as certainly as he knew his brother would never lay down his sword, he realized Merrick would never surrender Anne.

Merrick flung himself onto his bed. His one remaining salvation—to drink Anne out of his system—held the flavor of hot horse piss.

He was damned. Of that he felt certain. By the Almighty, by the archangels, by the brothers he would inevitably fail. He could still feel her fingers around his cock, still burned with want of her. When he closed his eyes, he saw her face, heard the hitch of her breath. Against the tips of his fingers, her feminine silk still scalded.

A blind man would have better luck navigating this field of bottomless caverns.

Restless and agitated beyond all measure, he rose again and set about righting his belongings. What use was there in attempting to sleep? He would find no quarter there, for she would plague his dreams, and he would wake in a mood far darker than his present temper.

But as he stuffed his things back into his footlocker, an exhaustion greater than a full day of battle beneath the desert sun crept into his bones. He found he cared not about the chaos of his chambers. Whether he ever righted the mess held no purpose. What did it matter? He rose, he supped, he fought. Year after year, century after century. Tomorrow would be no different from today, the only alteration to a routine that never varied, the woman two stories overhead.

He dropped the handful of clothing he held and stared at the clutter, unable to find a single reason why he should pick up the scraps of cloth. 'Twas all meaningless.

His gaze drifted to his bulging duffel bag, and briefly he considered whether he should put away his sword and armor. He dismissed the duty and left them lying in the corner. The sharpest blade, the strongest armor could change naught.

Dragging a hand down his face, he noticed the scrape of whiskers he had neglected. Had they chafed Anne's cheeks?

Harassed, he stepped over his clothes and stalked to the bathroom. A shower he had not tried. Mayhap he could wash her from his blood.

Merrick shucked his clothes outside the small doorway and stepped inside to flip on the faucet. When it ran near scalding, he stepped beneath the spray. The droplets pounded into him, stinging the marks upon his face. He had completely forgotten about the shade's attack. It seemed so long ago, and beneath Anne's lips, the scratches disappeared.

He pulled a small mirror away from the wall and inspected his cheek in the moonlight that seeped in through the small window. Thin and narrow, they no longer bled. His flesh had pulled together enough to scab over, but in portions it had yet to seal. A week ago, he would have found naught but stubble, the thin marks so insignificant they would have healed before he left the cavern.

Twisting, he inspected his back and the nytym's damage two nights past. The marks were nearly invisible, and he could just make out the faint line of new, pink flesh. Those too should not exist.

Confronted by the telltale evidence of his faltering soul, he hung his head and let his shoulders slump. How much longer did he have? One fight? Two? Mayhap a single kill? If he discovered Fulk, did he possess the strength to fulfill his oath, or would he join his cousin as an ally? Did his soul contain enough light that his brothers could drag him back here so Mikhail could grant him peace?

Will Anne grieve for me?

He squeezed his eyes against the selfish query. He should not hope for her tears. Saints' blood, she had turned him soft. Though he had not realized 'twas even possible, she had crawled beneath his skin and burrowed deep. Like the demons crept into his soul. His little demon.

Nay, not his.

He thumped a fist against the wall and shoved her to the back of his mind. Lathering quickly, he washed and shaved, and turned the water off. A few quick swipes of the towel, and he was dry, save for his hair.

Returning to his chambers, he crawled into bed and dragged the covers to his chin. But the faint scent of her perfume that lingered in his pillow brought her to the forefront of his mind. His blood warmed. His cock swelled against his thigh.

Forbidden fruit—Gabriel must enjoy tormenting him.

CHAPTER 19

✦

The halls slumbered as Caradoc wound his way through the maze of corridors, a small plate of eggs and fried ham in one hand. In the other, stiff black coffee, so stout he could stand a spoon in it, sloshed at the lip of a heavy pewter tankard. For a meal, it left much to be desired. For the first breakfast he had enjoyed in a good twenty-five years, it smelled like heaven.

Mikhail's order to remain at the temple proved nowhere near as confining as he had anticipated. Truth be told, he much preferred the reversion to a normal schedule. Of all the knights, he suspected the nocturnal life bothered him most. For when the sun set, especially this time of year, the air cooled, and the chill set into his bones, making the aches in his body unbearable at times. With daylight, he could bask in the warmth of the sun and imagine rolling fields of heather, the sweetness of a maid's summer kiss, the ease of a life long gone by.

"Caradoc, a word with you."

His head snapped up at the gruff bark. His coffee sloshed onto his hand. "Zounds," he muttered as he hastened to juggle his dishes and shake off the scalding drops. "What is your need, Tane?"

"'Tis a sensitive matter."

Caradoc nodded at his chamber door. "Let us go inside."

Tane, in a strange moment of deference, bobbed at the waist before he flung Caradoc's door wide. "Milord."

Unimpressed, Caradoc frowned at the younger knight. "What has come over you?"

"It has been many moons since I have had cause to recall my good manners."

With a harassed sigh, Caradoc slid his plate atop his rickety table and rolled his eyes. "I suppose you would have me simper over your hand and tell you, Sir du Bruiel, 'tis a pleasure to break my fast with you?" He let out a snort. "Enough of this foolishness. Our former status means naught."

Caradoc looked to his food. He grumbled inwardly, accepting the simple pleasure of a hot morning meal 'twas now forfeit. He drank deeply of his coffee and set the mug down. Easing into his chair, he asked, "What is on your mind, brother?"

For several long moments, Tane said naught. He moved to the opposite seat, sat down with one ankle across his knee, and studied Caradoc as if he had something of great import to relay but could not find the words. Then a blankness settled across his features, an expression that made Caradoc question whether his friend had forgotten his intent. But as hope rose, and he began to believe he might yet enjoy his morning meal, Tane gave him a crisp nod. His eyes sparked with interest, an earnest gleam that at once set off warning bells inside Caradoc's head.

His brother was up to no good.

"The maid," Tane began slowly. "She is not Merrick's?"

Caradoc's gut twisted uncomfortably. Something did not sit right in the way Tane's features hardened. "He would not have brought her to us for our marks, were she his."

The churning in his gut became a cyclone as Tane's green eyes lit with fire.

"She belongs to me."

Every fiber in Caradoc's body tightened like a rope

stretched taut. No good could come of this. Were the maid legitimately Tane's, brothers would come to blows, for Merrick's devotion to her defied the simplicity of their shared oath. Should Tane be wrong, the zealot's gleam in his eyes warned Caradoc he would not surrender easily. Choosing his words with care, he asked, "You know this how? Have you seen her mark for yourself?"

"I was shown it in sleep. 'Tis a half-moon scar, to match the mark left on my arm by a scoundrel's blade."

The bells of warning in Caradoc's mind screamed like angry horns. Through the passing of years too many to count, not once had Tane mentioned a gift of foresight or prophecy through dreams. 'Twas highly unlikely such would set upon him now. More plausible, Tane's recent tendency to create excuses for the things he desired, and justify the reasons he should possess them, drove this declaration.

Yet to insinuate such would stain his brother's honor. A taint Tane would seek to amend through blades. And Caradoc had no desire to fight a man who could not control the effect of darkness on his soul. Best to end this discussion quickly. Bring it to Merrick's, if not Mikhail's, immediate attention.

"Mayhap you should disclose this to Lady Anne? Allow her to confirm your . . . knowledge?"

"Aye. 'Tis my intent. I wished to share my news and seek your aid should Merrick refuse to see the undeniable proof."

Ah. Tane sought an ally. A second, should the maid bring brothers to blows. Caradoc shook his head. "I will take neither side, old friend." As Tane's features clouded with anger, Caradoc hurried to add, "I expect Merrick shall honor what is intended."

"You do not think he will deny me what is rightfully mine?"

Caradoc leveled his friend with a dark frown. "You ask that of Merrick? He who was denied his birthright? Do not shame him, Tane."

With a sharp draw of air, Tane rose to his feet, his mouth pinched into a tight line. "Very well. Good day, Caradoc."

Caradoc watched the younger knight leave through a narrowed gaze. Aye, Azazel's darkness worked its vile magic through his brother's blood. 'Twas time to speak to Mikhail.

Inside her closet, Anne stared at her clothes. A woman could learn a lot from what a man picked out for her to wear, and judging from what Merrick brought back from her house, he despised jeans. Not one single pair of denim, dress slacks, or casual pants came home with him. Instead, he chose every one of her long skirts. Floral prints, plaids, and plain, everything she owned that hung at least calf length. The guy evidently liked his women covered below the waist.

Not so much above the waist, however, she observed as she fingered a long-sleeved sweater. Though she'd had dozens of plain tops suitable for the classroom, Merrick chose the softer fabrics, like the lightweight cashmere Sophie gave her last Christmas. He packed nothing with a plain neckline and seemingly went for everything with a V-neck. None of her warm turtlenecks made the cut, none of her cable-knit sweaters. Things she'd call delicate, although she'd never really considered them that way before.

More feminine.

Anne smiled. He'd given her the ammunition. All she needed to do was find the right combination.

She plucked a navy blue sweater off the hanger and sifted through her skirts, settling on white. A thick band of navy wound around the hem, then blended in to a pattern of flowers that spanned the fabric to the tops of her calves, before graduating into plain white that hugged her waist and hips. It matched her more comfortable black boots.

Changing quickly, she ran a brush through her hair and chose to leave it loose. The only nonessential Merrick brought from her bathroom was a tube of lip gloss,

and she smeared some on her lips. With one last look in
the mirror, she headed for her door.

Halfway across the sitting room, her nerves kicked in.
What if she made an ass out of herself? What if this plan
failed miserably, and Merrick laughed at her? Worse, what
if on her way to his room, she ran into those creeps from
yesterday?

Damn, if she were smart, she'd sit here until Merrick
came for her. But no. She'd wasted enough time hoping
Merrick would come around. She had to get to the inner
sanctum with enough time to really study whatever was
down there.

Steeling herself, she swallowed down the rising butterflies and yanked her door open. She'd never been
afraid of her shadow before, and she didn't intend to turn
into a timid mouse because four men didn't know how to
behave. Surely, the rest of them knew self-control, and
Farran couldn't be the only man around who'd answer a
shrill, *help*!

Merrick, on the other hand, wasn't apt to be so agreeable to her logic.

She chuckled. Tough. This was her day to be in control. Not his.

With a deep breath to chase off the last of her jitters,
she descended the stairs.

As she passed the common room, a handful of men
whipped around so fast she had to stifle a giggle. They
stared as if they'd never seen her before, and as she acknowledged them with a gracious smile, Anne noticed
the odd band of crimson on each man's left arm. When
she turned for the stairs that led to the stone works below,
the clatter of steel brought her up short. She glanced over
her shoulder to find all five of them bent on one knee,
their swords on the ground in front of a flattened foot.
Heads bent, they watched through the tops of their eyes.

Shit. Now what?

"Ah—" Her confident smile wavered. "I think I already
said this. That's not necessary." She edged closer to the

stairs. "So. Um. Get up?" When they didn't lift so much as a finger, she wrinkled her nose and took another step toward the stairwell. Trying again, she pulled the words she'd used before from the recesses of her mind. "God bless you, if you must fight."

She waited half a heartbeat before the man on the farthest end reached for his sword. Anne didn't hang around to see if the others followed. She spun and bolted down the stairs. That nonsense had to stop. One way or the other. If she had to send all of them a handwritten message they could carry in their damn pockets, she'd never face another bended knee again.

Though the encounter managed to erase her worries about Merrick. She continued down the hall, lost in thought, jarred only to the present when her ankle smacked into something hard. Glancing down, Anne found another pristine white surcoat folded on the ground. The crimson bars of the Templar insignia reached out along the sides, but otherwise the cross was concealed. Once more, a rather plain broadsword lay atop the stack.

She lifted her gaze and scanned the hall, noting another bundle well beyond Merrick's door. Evidently, Mikhail didn't care about his knights' discretions. She couldn't blame him. The vow was minor to begin with, but after a thousand years, if he'd punished everyone who felt the urge to scratch an itch, his holy army would be rather impotent.

With a lift of her skirt's hem, she stepped over the bundle and continued on to Merrick's door. There, she stood motionless, her hand poised to knock. This was it. Her future lay in her success. She must remember to maintain her cool.

Deciding knocking would take away some of her desired impact, she turned the handle and let herself in. Her eyes widened as she sucked back a squeak of surprise.

Merrick lay sprawled out on the bed, one bare thigh poking from a tangled mess of covers. Thick arms folded over his pillow with his nose tucked against his bicep.

She swallowed hard as her gaze traveled across the broad expanse of his shoulder blades, down to his trim waist, and rested on his covered buttocks. Dear God, he slept in the nude.

Oh, this was such a bad idea.

She'd never considered that he might sleep naked. Her pulse now chaotic, she backed up, intending to return to the hall and knock. Only, she tripped over something on the floor, and stumbled into his table. A wooden candlestick toppled, dropped to the floor, and rolled toward Merrick's bed.

Cringing, Anne stood motionless. Dread rolled around in her belly, tightening it into a hard lump as she realized just how stupid her idea had been. He was going to be seriously pissed. She'd left her room alone, woke him up rudely, and the man wasn't even dressed. Crap, *crap*!

The bed creaked, and she peeked through her lashes. Merrick had turned his face the opposite direction, bent his knee. Otherwise, he hadn't moved. Expelling a long breath of relief, Anne glanced around the room, noticing for the first time the state of disarray. Clothes everywhere. Overturned furniture. His rumpled bed. What in the world?

"God's teeth, what are you doing here?"

Anne flinched at the sound of Merrick's harsh voice. Her gaze jerked back to the bed to find him on lifted elbows, his scowl as dark as night.

Searching for courage she didn't feel, she forced a smile to her face. "Good morning." She paused only long enough to swallow, then continued, determined to ignore the way her insides resembled Jell-O. "We didn't get anything accomplished on this matched mark thing yesterday. I wanted to get an early start."

He arched one eyebrow and eyed her with contempt. "You invade my chambers to tell me 'tis time to play matchmaker?"

Anne's determination surfaced when she was confronted by his usual surly attitude. He would not intimidate her, no matter how he tried. If he really thought a bit of grumpiness would dissuade her, he had a heck of a lot to learn, especially when she had so much at stake. She stepped deeper into his room, bent over, and picked a half-folded shirt off the floor. With a merry smirk, she tossed it in his face. "Get up. We have work to do."

"Nay." He tossed the shirt back on the floor and flopped back onto the bed. "Leave me."

Anne sensed opportunity, and like a falcon diving for its prey, she swept in to goad him into action. "Listen, big guy, it's not my fault you went to bed hard and miserable. Whatever tantrum you had in here, get over it."

His expression darkened as he slowly lifted to one elbow, exposing the glorious expanse of muscle that was his chest. Her belly fluttered, the sudden urge to crawl into that bed tugging at her senses. She glanced away, focusing on the window. If she'd learned one thing, it was that throwing herself at Merrick accomplished nothing.

"Woman, you test my patience."

"And you test mine," she shot back. A wave of satisfaction rolled through her as his glower deepened even more. The other thing she'd learned about this man—when he was angry, he was far more prone to action. "I want to find my intended. Today."

Merrick could not decide which he found more infuriating—the fact Anne rudely awakened him, or that she had done so when she looked more beautiful than ever.

The early morning sunlight set sparks to life within her long auburn tresses. Washed, she must have brushed her hair a thousand strokes or more, for the thick lengths shimmered like spun silk as they cascaded down her back to peek beneath her elbows. A lock tumbled over her shoulder, followed her sweater's deep neckline and curled across the swell of one creamy breast. The sweater itself, although simple, looked as soft as a cloud, and he knew the skin beneath resembled satin. Her simple skirt accentuated the full flare of her hips, then dropped in loose lengths to swirl about her ankles.

His eyes followed the trim lines of her body to her toes, then up to lock with hers, and his mouth went dry. Her cheeks bore a touch of pink that emphasized the fullness of her rosy lips. Her eyes, however, rendered him unable to breathe. Highlighted by the color of her sweater, they were as blue as an ocean, and every bit as fathomless. They sparkled with her smile, danced with her light laugh.

Trapped between his hips and the mattress, his cock stirred. His stomach quivered as something deep inside plummeted into a bottomless abyss. Saints' blood, she was simply stunning.

He could no more rise from the bed than he could pretend he was immune to her. His body felt like hewn stone, his muscles strained so miserably. Grinding his teeth together, he tore his gaze away and studied the sheets.

Her intended. She wanted to finish the search today. He should be joyous. Her pairing freed him to fulfill his duty to Fulk. 'Twas what he wanted, was it not?

If so, why did he feel as if he had just tripped off a high cliff?

"C'mon, get up, big guy." She slapped a shirt across his hip, her chuckle as unnerving as her smile.

"Leave me be, Anne. I am in no mood for your wit."

To his disbelief, she laughed once more and started for the door. Yet where he expected her to pull it open and exit, she instead bent over and swept up a stack of his clothes. She set them on his table, then one by one, folded each article into a neat square.

"What are you doing, damsel?"

"Cleaning up your mess." She smoothed the wrinkles out of his long-sleeved red shirt and flashed him a smile. "I don't think you want this clutter around if you're going to have friends in and out."

"What nonsense do you speak of? 'Tis my chambers. I have no cause for visitors."

Undaunted, she shook out a jumbled heap of black, then tucked the sleeves inside. "I'm going to use your table. I thought it would be a good idea to write down the marks as we find them. That way, if other women come, you can pair them easily."

His table? He grumbled beneath his breath. Not only did she wake him, but she intended to take over his personal effects as well. Damnation if the sight of her tending to his laundry did not set his heart to tripping.

Defeated, Merrick rolled onto his back. "All right, little demon. We shall do things your way. The sooner your curiosity is sated, the sooner I shall find peace."

Light and airy, the musical notes of her laughter washed over him, stirring his already warm blood. "I thought you might agree. Now get dressed." She tossed his jeans into his lap.

Shifting around the edge of the table, she subtly presented her back. Though he felt not the slightest bit of modesty, he recognized the gesture as a symbol of hers and quickly tugged on his jeans. He slid his legs off the side of the bed and bent for a shirt, choosing a long-sleeved gray jersey. Once donned, he stood to tuck it in. The shapely curve of her backside caught his attention as she bent forward to smooth another square of fabric. Merrick choked on a renegade groan.

"Where do these go?" Anne turned around with a stack of shirts between her hands, spoiling Merrick's fantasy of bending her over the table and nuzzling the delicate skin at the back of her neck.

He reached for his clothes, only to have her pull them out of his reach. Their fingers brushed. Her smile faltered in time with the trip of his pulse. Then, her eyes lit and she regained her composure. "I'll do it. You go wake your friends."

Annoyed beyond all measure, he stalked to the wardrobe, pulled open a door, then stomped into the bathroom. Wake his friends. Find her intended. Turn her over to another man's keeping . . .

He pushed his fingers through his hair with a mutter. She asked the impossible. Nay, not her. Gabriel, the archangels, the Almighty, they all expected sainthood.

Merrick took a moment to wash the sands of sleep from his eyes, then returned to the adjoining room where Anne busied herself with making his bed. He deliberately avoided watching her—'twas too tempting to push her into the pillows and resume last night's play. Instead, he stuffed his feet into his boots and swiftly stalked to the door.

Halfway there, he made an about-face and caught her by the arm. She turned, blue eyes wide with surprise. Without thought, Merrick gave in to the longings he had dreamed of and dipped his head to capture her mouth.

Anne flatted a delicate palm against his cheek, the gentle press of her fingertips enough to assuage the fierce heat in his veins. He softened his lips, allowed her perfume to settle into his senses and soothe all the conflict that raged inside his mind. Like this, he felt whole. In her arms naught else mattered, not the pledges of centuries, not the darkness that threatened to consume him. He knew only one thing— the magic of her.

Slowly, thoroughly, he kissed her. If this was to be their last moment together and she would walk out of his chambers with another man, he wanted to remember the sweetness of her mouth until he succumbed to taint of evil. He did not try to delude himself into believing he did not want her to remember this as well. To remember him.

For he could no longer deny he wanted nothing more than to mark her in such a way she would never forget him, though she might give herself to another. 'Twas beyond the measure of rationality, a yearning he should feel shame over. And yet he could not bear the thought that in a few hours she would walk away. That he would look upon her from afar and never again know the simple pleasures of her touch, her concern, her breathtaking smile.

A low guttural murmur rumbled in the back of her throat, awakening the desire that lay dormant in his blood. He eased the kiss to a languorous close before temptation possessed him and he did more than take liberties with her mouth. Cupping the back of her head in one hand, he pressed her forehead to his and took a deep breath. 'Twas time. He must resign himself to the purpose Gabriel chose for him and stand witness as she discovered her mate.

Loathing what he could not control, he released Anne and strode from the room.

CHAPTER 20

Anne traced a nail down the length of a jagged scar embedded in a roughened palm. She took care to keep the caress light, the movement slow. She studied the nondescript mark, her mind automatically comparing the man's hand to Merrick's. This one's fingers were fatter. His palm awkwardly large. And he desperately needed to learn the value of lotion.

Pretending interest in these strangers lost its appeal after she'd witnessed the hope in the second man's eyes dim, then flicker into nothingness. Though maintaining the charade came easily enough, now on the tenth potential knight, she felt more like a betrayer than any preordained savior. Her heart broke a little more with every grim expression, every brusque nod.

But as she snuck a glance at Merrick from the corner of her eye, the agitated way his jaw worked when she took a few moments to delay her verdict, said her efforts were working as she'd hoped. He'd paced all the way through her initial conversation with this man, only stopping to lean against the table's edge when this knight presented his hand. Every once in a while, when she caught him looking, his eyes sparked with the same unmistakable fire of a man who couldn't chain his jealousy.

She lifted her chin enough to look at the man through veiled lashes and found what she hoped was another sultry smile. "You have strong hands," she murmured. She ran her fingers down the length of his as she'd seen Sophie do on more than one occasion when she tried to hold a man's attention. "I am sure they will please your lady, but I'm afraid this scar doesn't match."

With a gentle squeeze, she released his hand.

The man's body sagged ever so slightly as he offered her a deep bow of his head. Wordlessly, he crossed to the door, where Merrick already waited to excuse him. Merrick clapped the knight upon the shoulder, his smile having disappeared after the first go-around, and pulled the door open.

Another knight entered before the first cleared the doorway.

Anne pulled in a deep breath and summoned a bright smile. "Good afternoon."

This one wore the curious band of crimson on his left arm, and instead of taking her hand to bring it to his lips as all the others had, he dropped to a knee. "Milady, I am Gareth of Aletorp and honored to be in your presence." In a fluid movement, he drew his sword and laid it before his foot.

Anne's stomach rolled over, and she held back a groan. "How many times must we do this?"

The knight lifted his head. Soft brown eyes brimmed with confusion. "I beg your pardon? I have yet to swear my oath."

Anne looked to Merrick for an explanation. Head down, he moved back and forth in front of the window, too intent on ignoring her exchange to be of any use. Her brows furrowed as she studied the man in front of her. "I would swear the entire temple was at dinner the other night."

Gareth chuckled low. "Mayhap they were." He shifted, twisting just enough to bring his left arm in front of his body. A band of crimson cloth wound around his bicep. "This brands me as Raphael's. We have only just arrived.

'Twas indeed a delightful surprise to find a seraph in attendance."

"Oh." She felt the rush of heat in her cheeks and sought to cover her embarrassment with another smile. "Well, to tell you the truth I hate this part."

When Gareth laughed, his eyes twinkled. His features held the arrogance of youth, and the roguishness of the devil. Handsome, indeed, Anne didn't need anyone to tell her Gareth knew his way around women. He was just the kind of man they'd fall all over, and she instantly liked him.

"Then let us end it quickly." He dropped his chin to his chest with a dramatic air.

Anne couldn't help but laugh. "If I didn't know better, I'd say you're trying to charm me."

"But of course. Only a fool would not attempt to win the affection of one so very enchanting." A grin set off a solitary dimple.

The movement at her side came to an abrupt halt. As Anne bent down to pick up Gareth's sword, she glanced at Merrick and clamped her teeth down on her lip, silencing another burst of laughter. His glare held the threat of black thunderheads that waited to unleash deadly bolts of lightning, and that baleful look was directed at Gareth. One hand held the pommel of his sword in a death grip. The other worked in agitation at his side, his fingers curling and uncurling, only to repeat the pattern again.

Before he could notice she watched him, she averted her eyes and focused on returning Gareth's sword. "You, sir, are a flirt."

Neat white teeth broke through his broad smile as he leapt to his feet and sheathed his weapon. "The better we shall pair then, milady. For the same runs in your blood, I fear."

Anne giggled again, unable to stop the sound from escaping. Damn. Whoever found him would have a hell of a time keeping him in line. A shame Sophie wasn't here to see this knight. He'd match her beat for beat. She might even learn a new trick or two.

In the far corner of her field of vision, she noticed Merrick fold his arms over his chest. Feet spread apart, his wide stance gave him an intimidating air. A little shiver of delight trickled down Anne's spine. Charming as Gareth might be, he would never embody the meaning of *knight* the way Merrick did. Merrick must have been a formidable foe on the battlefield. One look at the firm set of his jaw, the brittleness of his unyielding stare—she couldn't imagine anyone giving him much of a fight.

His grin still intact, Gareth inclined his head toward Merrick. "Let us move forward so I may whisk you off and away from my churlish brother."

"Indeed."

Merrick grunted.

Gareth pulled his shirt from his black jeans and lifted it up, exposing a hard, flat abdomen covered with a fine shadow of golden hair. What made Anne suck in her breath, however, wasn't the rigid muscles running the length of his torso, but the deep scar that ran from one rib to the opposite hip.

"Aye, 'tis not pretty. But you will notice it bears the distinct form of a cross."

She squinted to get a better look. Sure enough, a faint pink mark, half the length of the first, neatly divided the longer bar. "What happened?" she murmured.

The blond knight chuckled. "'Tis naught but a childhood accident. The result of brothers who chanced upon their father's swords when they were too young for more than wooden toys."

"I see."

Anne picked up her pen and scribbled Gareth's mark in her notebook. When she lifted her head to give him her sweetest smile, she grimaced inwardly at the brightness in his eyes. She would squelch that light in a moment. If she only had a list of matching marks this would be so much easier. She could refuse, then point these men toward their respective women, and she wouldn't feel so damn guilty.

"Well, sir knight, I disagree. That's not an ugly mark. It's quite handsome. I am sure it will earn you some . . ." She paused, dropped her lashes, and lowered her voice. "Entertaining sympathy."

Gareth's shoulders shook with unspent laughter. To Anne's relief, where she expected his bright gaze to dim, those brown eyes lighted even more. "Say no more, milady. 'Twill not be your sympathy I enjoy."

Anne shook her head.

He snapped his heels together, set one hand over his midsection, and offered her a formal bow. Straightening, the adorable dimple puckered his left cheek. "Then allow me to remove myself before Sir Merrick plants his fist into my jaw."

Anne heard, rather than saw, the fury in Merrick's response. A hiss escaped his clenched teeth. He stalked to the door and jerked it open.

In a moment of sheer daring, Anne stood. She caught Gareth's hand, and mimicking what she'd seen in movies a dozen times, she gave him an awkward curtsy. With absolute sincerity, she said, "I do hope your lady arrives soon. It's been lovely meeting you, Gareth. I hope to see you soon." Punctuating her heartfelt wishes, she pressed a chaste kiss to his cheek.

"Indeed." He turned with a one-handed wave, and strode through the door.

As the next man neared the threshold, Merrick kicked the door shut with his heel. "Enough," he barked.

Anne had completely forgotten her intent to make him jealous. Her mouth dropped open. Eyes wide, she stared.

Merrick marched across the room, closing the distance between them. His hands clamped into her shoulders, and he gave her a little shake. "I hope to see you soon?" he mocked.

Wow. She hadn't been acting with Gareth, but whatever she'd done, she'd pushed the *wrong* buttons. Merrick looked mad enough to throttle her. Reflexively, she took a step backward.

He followed. "Do you, Anne? Do you hope to see that fair-haired youth again?"

Anne swallowed hard, the effect of her flirtations hitting her like a tsunami's swell. She'd accomplished jealousy. But at what price? Had she gone too far? She scrambled to hold on to her courage, to shake off the immediate desire to answer no. If she told him the truth, they'd be right back where they were an hour or so ago, he standing guard while she inspected marks. Now wasn't the time to concede. Now she had to somehow land the victor's blow.

She fought for control over her voice and asked, "Does it matter?"

Merrick's jaw worked in a terrible fit to keep his temper in line. His fingers tightened on her shoulders, his grip near painful. She backed up to relieve the pressure of his hands, but Merrick refused to let her go. His body chased hers until her back rammed into the post on his bed, jarring the wind out of her. She let out a startled squeak.

Merrick let go as if she'd burned him. His gaze seared into her, those dark eyes hard and filled with tumult. "Aye," he growled. "It matters." He took another step closer, pinning her between his body and the bedpost. Reaching for a lock of her hair, he twined it around his finger and lowered his voice. "Should you kiss another man in front of me again, I will tear him into pieces."

Anne's heart flip-flopped like a fish out of water. Her lungs squeezed together so tightly she could hardly breathe. She struggled with the cacophony of thoughts that screamed inside her head. What now?

Her tormented knight supplied the answer. "Kiss me, Anne," he murmured. "Let me feel the softness that keeps me awake at night."

Oh God. Her legs threatened to give out, his words powerful enough to make her light-headed. She pushed aside a jumble of untamed ebony waves to touch the side of his face. "I thought you didn't want me."

The groan that rumbled in the back of Merrick's throat shot straight to her heart. He closed his eyes as if anguished by her words, and when he opened them again, they glowed with such intensity she shivered. Gone was the gleam of anger, replaced by the fire of desire. He brought a hand between them, nimble fingers deftly releasing the buttons on her sweater. "Aye, I want you. I want to sink so deep inside you I forget all reason. I want to hear you cry my name as you come, so loudly every man within this temple hears. Make no mistake about it, damsel, this want of you plagues me so I despise myself."

Sweet heaven on earth. She'd never heard anything more honest. Anything so raw. Heat ripped through her veins, flooded over her body, and settled between her thighs. In a heartbeat's passing, she was damp, her body aching to fulfill the promise in his confession.

Merrick didn't give her a chance to find a response. His mouth crashed into hers. One firm nudge of his lips parted hers, and he ravished her mouth with abandon. He brought his other hand between their bodies, doing away with the buttons on her sweater in seconds. A firm tug pulled the garment down her arms, over her wrists. He tossed it aside carelessly. Sliding his hands around her ribs, he freed the fastener at her back and discarded her bra as if it were some despicable thing.

Palms roughened from years of combat scraped pleasantly against her skin as he cupped her breasts. His hands were warm, his fingers gentle despite the feral hunger of his kiss. Her nipples beaded beneath his thumbs, and she arched her back with a murmur of pleasure.

Tearing his mouth away, Merrick gazed down at her, his eyes searching her face. *No,* her mind screamed. He couldn't stop this again. She'd break down and beg if he took his hands away. This would happen. It *had* to, or she'd go crumble into pieces. "Don't stop, Merrick," she managed through her dry throat. She added on a whisper, "Please."

Merrick shook his head slowly, the magic of his hands unfaltering. "Nay. I am not stopping." Hoarse and thick, his voice held torment. "Wrong it may be, but I can no longer fight this. I will choose shame and disgrace if it eases the ache that consumes me." His onyx eyes flashed with something she couldn't recognize. It reached in deep, wound its claws around her heart, and held on tight. Quietly, he murmured, "Touch me, Anne."

When she obeyed by lifting her hands to the center of his chest and exploring the hard planes of his body with her fingertips, he sucked in a sharp breath. She glided downward, pulled the jersey free from his jeans to slide her hands beneath. His skin burned, the muscles in his abdomen jumped beneath her fingers. She watched in fascination as his eyes closed, his hands utterly still against her breasts. His chest rose and fell as his breathing became hard, and as she spanned her fingers over his heart, it thudded against her palm.

"Your hands hold magic," he whispered.

He released her and the incredible warmth disappeared. She opened her mouth to protest, to forbid him to take his hands away. Yet Merrick silenced her words when he tugged his shirt over his head. He opened his fingers, letting it fall to the floor. She reached for him, yearning for the contact of skin to skin. To feel his heartbeat against hers.

Merrick caught her first. His arms wound around her waist, dragged her flush against his body. The moment of tenderness passed as his mouth found hers, and he delved in deep to plunder and master. He dominated Anne. His hands, his kisses, his thighs, his legs trapped her, bent her to his wishes. She surrendered with no more protest than a dandelion offered a crisp breeze.

Strong hands cupped her buttocks, ground her hips into his. The hard ridge of his erection rubbed over her sensitive feminine nub, shooting a streak of fire down her spine. She held on to his shoulders, the tremble that possessed her threatening to topple her over. He steadied her with his body, offering the safety her senses desperately needed. Anne turned her head, breaking their kiss to draw in much needed air.

But Merrick's mouth was unrelenting. His lips scored down her neck, his teeth grazed into her shoulder. Where he nipped, he eased the painful pinch with a swirl of his tongue, each moist caress eroding her ability to think. To comprehend.

In one effortless sweep, he maneuvered her into his arms and laid her on his bed. His body followed, blanketing her in warmth. He fit against her like molten wax. Where he was hard, she was soft. Where her body curved, his narrowed. To think she'd once thought he was too big. Now she couldn't imagine anyone more perfect.

His mouth dusted across her collarbone, the warmth of his breath prickling her skin with goose bumps. He shifted to delve the tip of his tongue between the valley of her breasts, and Anne speared her fingers through his hair. He flicked his tongue over a turgid nipple, provoking her into a whimper that transformed into a low moan when he drew the hardened bud into his mouth and gently suckled.

As he repeated the splendor on her opposite breast, he rolled them onto their sides, his hands coming around to pull the zipper at the back of her skirt. The lightweight material fell apart, cool air washing across the small of her back, then lower when he pushed it past her hips. Shifting them once more, Merrick trailed his mouth downward, grazed her ribs with his teeth. He dipped the tip of his tongue into her belly button and nipped the tender skin beneath.

She didn't know how, but her skirt no longer hindered her legs, and as Merrick's breath washed heat across her inner thigh, he tugged off her boots with one hand. Anne flattened her feet on the mattress, denying him the ability to remove her opaque nylon socks. She lifted her hips, guided his mouth closer to her aching center.

The kiss he pressed to her panties teased her out of her mind. Her womb clamped down tight, moisture flooded between her thighs. He pulled at the thin straps around her hips and eased her thong down her legs. It got caught, the spread of her knees too wide, thwarting Merrick's seeking lips. Before she could flatten her legs to accommodate his desires, he let out a mutter, grabbed the flimsy fabric with both hands, and with a firm tug, snapped both spaghetti straps.

Anne almost giggled, but her humor vanished when he settled himself between her knees, and slid the tip of his tongue between her moistened flesh. On a ragged gasp, she jerked up into him, her fingers fisting against his scalp. He tossed one heavy arm across her abdomen, pinning her to the bed.

Slow, lazy strokes pushed her to the edge of abandon. She squirmed and writhed, the need to feel him deep sheer torment. "Merrick," she rasped. The plaintive whisper turned into a soft cry as he answered by delving his tongue into her opening. Pleasure flooded through her body, carried her high on swells and tides. She bit down on her lower lip until she tasted the coppery tang of blood. With a toss of her head, she tugged on his hair, wanting the length of him, not the ecstasy of his masterful mouth. "Merrick, please."

Her plea was useless. He ignored it. In fact, he devoted himself even more thoroughly and brought his fingertips into play. Caressing her sensitive nub with his thumb, delving in and out of her with his tongue, he commanded her surrender. Rapture built, roared through her veins like fire on a sun-baked field, then consumed her. She cried out, her body trembling.

CHAPTER 21

T he exquisiteness of Anne's features as they turned
soft with her release shook Merrick to the core. She
breathed through lips that were swollen from his kisses.
Her long lashes dusted over cheeks that flushed with
color. But the sound of her voice had unraveled him further than the bliss that crossed her face. He held himself
on shaking arms, his body as rigid as stone, afraid if he
moved one fraction and touched the silken skin beneath
him, he would not be able to control himself any longer.

Sucking in great gulps of air through flared nostrils, he
beat his desire into submission long enough to rid himself
of the rest of his clothing. Freed from the denim constraints,
his cock jutted forth, so swollen with need he ached. It had
been a mistake to bring her to release whilst he watched.
Though he had sought to prolong her pleasure, he had
nearly discovered his own long before he was ready to succumb.

He nudged her knees apart with his shoulders and
eased himself between her dampened thighs. "Forgive
me, Anne," he murmured. In one hard thrust, he slid
within her.

As her swollen flesh gripped him tight, Merrick forgot
how to breathe. He tried to pull in air, but his throat

clamped closed and his chest constricted. His cock pulsed. His head swam. Saints' blood, he had not known such incredible feeling could exist. Closing his eyes against the wealth of sensation that flooded through him, he waited for the spasm to pass. To find his faculties once more.

Anne would have none of it. She lifted her hips and wrapped her legs around his waist. Her hot flesh clenched and released, each grip taking him deeper until he touched the mouth of her womb.

On a hoarse groan, he surrendered. He dove into her mouth and let her honeyed flavor claim his senses. God's teeth, she tasted so heavenly. 'Twas as if he had waited centuries for this moment.

Nay . . . for her.

Their sweat-slicked bodies slipped and rubbed, Anne guiding his hips with the rocking of her body, all thoughts of gentleness things of the past. He could no more seek to draw this joining out than he could attempt to speak, she overwhelmed him so. He had known she would be bold. The moment she had kicked him in the shin, he had realized her spirit. But he had not anticipated she possessed the ability to render him senseless.

She wound her arms around him, clinging tighter. Her nipples stabbed into his chest. Her breath came hard and fast, the sound of her panting an echo of his own. Ecstasy sizzled down Merrick's spine. It built to intolerable heights, and his world ruptured. Pleasure burst free, so intense it threatened to fragment him into a million pieces.

He let out a hoarse cry and gathered Anne tight against him as he spilled himself into her.

"Merrick," she murmured, her body following his bliss. Around his shaft, her sex fluttered. Her nails scored into his shoulders, her legs weakening their hold as she found release.

With the sound of his name came the unraveling of something so deep inside his soul he could not name it. A flicker of bright light, a warmth that had no words. All he knew was that Anne awakened it, and as he lifted his head to gaze at her enraptured features, it spread through him with a wildfire's intensity.

For one precious moment where time stood still, the chains of darkness that bound him in despair released their hold.

Spent and exhausted, he sank into her embrace. Anne dusted her mouth across his shoulder, her fingernails trailing lightly down his spine. He nuzzled the side of her neck. For several long moments, they lay tangled together, heaving in great gasps as they tried to reclaim control over their breathing.

When the shaking in Merrick's limbs receded, he lifted to one elbow and pushed a dampened auburn lock of hair away from Anne's face. "You are more beautiful than any maid should be."

The flush of her cheeks pleased him. Bold though she might be, she was still deeply feminine, and still as vulnerable to praise as any shy maiden. He let out a chuckle, and rolled onto his back, carrying her with him. "Little demon Anne, sent to torment me."

Her lighthearted smile made his heart thump hard. She settled her cheek against his chest, splayed her fingers over his heart. "Merrick, that was incredible."

Aye, it had been.

Nibbling on her lower lip in hesitation, she turned her face up to his. "Is it . . ." Her cheeks assumed a deep crimson color. "I guess I should have asked before. We didn't use any protection."

"I cannot give you any sickness, Anne." He closed his eyes, resentment stabbing into him for all the things he had once desired and could no longer dream of. He dropped his voice, hating the truth he must confess. "Nor can I sire children."

"Oh." A silent heartbeat passed between them. Then, with a smile, she rubbed her cheek against his chest. "Well good. Nothing to regret then."

A sliver of guilt worked its way through his sated comfort. He had taken what did not belong to him, and not once had he considered his oaths. He had no right to feel this happiness that brimmed in his veins.

Anne nestled closer, slipped her leg through his. Molded to his side, she was warm, the exploration of her fingertips across his belly, enticing. His blood stirred in response. God's teeth, he hungered for her again.

Merrick cast aside the shame that threatened to engulf him and drew his fingers through Anne's long hair. He would think on his transgressions later. For the moment, he had more important concerns.

He sucked in a sharp breath as she took his stirring cock into her hand.

Aye, far more important things to put his mind to.

Twilight filled the room with shades of gray when Merrick finally extracted himself from Anne's arms. He sat up with a yawn, rubbed the back of his neck. His gaze fell to her, and he could not stop a smile from lifting the corners of his mouth. Curled on her side, her hair splayed across his pillow, she looked far lovelier snuggled into his bed than he had fantasized she might.

He trailed a fingertip down the length of her slender arm and let out a sigh.

'Twas done. He had betrayed all he knew, shredded oaths, and he could take none of it back. Worse, he had betrayed her as well. Whilst she might not agree presently, when she discovered her intended, she would hate what Merrick must do now.

He eased from the bed and quietly went to his wardrobe. Removing his ceremonial surcoat, he folded it over his arm. From the corner of the bed nearest the door, he picked up his sword. Then he laid them both in the hall.

If he possessed a single ounce of nobility, he would take himself to Mikhail and ask to leave the temple. But beyond the blood of kings that ran in his veins, he had never been a noble man. For the moment, Anne belonged to him. Until the edicts of the heavens forced him to relinquish her, he would not let go so willingly. Mayhap they would never discover her intended—he could very well be with Azazel.

Mayhap it would not matter. Merrick could be blessed with death before he must witness her with another.

Damnation, the woman had weaseled herself so deep he was naught but a weak babe. Soft. Vulnerable in a most embarrassing way.

He eased the door shut and turned back to the bed.

Anne's mesmerizing blue eyes locked with his. She propped herself on one hand and gave him a beguiling smile. "Whatcha doing?"

He pushed a hand through his hair. "We must speak of this, Anne."

Her light strawberry brows puckered. "Why do I have the feeling you're going to show me to the door?"

Easing himself down to sit beside her, he caught her free hand in his. "Nay. But what I have done, I am not proud of. I took what I wanted, with no care to the oaths I have made, and I have offended you."

Anne's expression softened. She lifted to her knees, leaned forward, and pressed the pads of her fingers to his mouth. "Shh. I wanted this. You haven't offended me."

Merrick caught her hand and brought it to his chest. The sincerity reflecting in her eyes made it near impossible to concentrate on the things he wanted to say.

Anne refused to cooperate. She tugged on her wrist. When he did not let go, she leaned in, those amazing breasts brushing against his chest, and pressed her mouth to his. There she stayed, her lips moving softly against his, until he gave in and yielded to the kiss.

Long, velvety slides of her tongue urged away his regret. Where they touched, the warmth of her bare skin soaked into him. He settled his hands on her waist and drank his fill, though he would never get enough.

Anne eased the kiss to a lingering close. Her lashes fluttered up, revealing those incredible sky-blue eyes, and Merrick's heart skipped a beat. He gathered her close.

Held on tight whilst he breathed the sweet lavender perfume in her hair. "Are you hungry?"

Leaning back into his arms, she wrinkled her nose. "Not for the stuff upstairs."

"What if I were to take you to dinner? It has been told to me, I believe, women prefer a meal and wine before they remove their clothes." He tried to stifle his grin, but his mouth twitched.

Laughter turned her smile radiant. "It's a little late for that, don't you think?"

As if she shared the same insatiable desire to touch that forbade him to leave the bed and dress, she kept her hands in constant motion. Fingertips glided over his shoulders, down his arms, up his belly to slide across his chest. Her gaze followed, what he witnessed within those azure depths humbling him. Wonder. Delight. No woman had ever looked at his body in such a fashion, and caught beneath the power of her inquisitive stare, Merrick held his breath, uncertain how to respond.

Her nails traced the long scar that spanned the left side of his body. When she furrowed her brows, he sensed the wound concerned her, but she did not ask. Instead, she pressed her lips to the jagged flesh and rubbed her cheek over his heart. Touched, Merrick settled his hand on the crown of her head and held her in place.

"Mikhail won't care if you leave?" she asked.

"Nay, he has no reason to keep me here."

"But he said . . . What if you have to fight?"

Chuckling, Merrick looked down at her. "Damsel, 'twould be hard to do when presently I have no sword."

Anne jerked out of his grasp. "What?"

Merrick shifted, unwilling to tell her exactly what happened to his sword. Once a serious matter, the custom was little more than formality now that their numbers were so small. Still, setting out his sword and surcoat announced his shame. Certainly she would not appreciate the symbolic habit.

"What did you do with it?"

"'Tis in the hall awaiting Mikhail."

He could tell she did not grasp his meaning by the confusion that clouded her delicate features. She lifted an eyebrow, punctuating her unspoken question with a sideways tip of her head. A sudden rush of embarrassment seized him, and he looked away from Anne's twinkling blue eyes. Bollocks, this should not be so difficult. 'Twas not as if he had not bedded a maid or three in front of his men at arms. Why did this one make the subject so tedious? He averted his gaze so he would not have to see her reproach. "The oath we swore eight centuries ago came with certain punishments for certain misdeeds. Should we break the oath of chastity, we are to surrender our coats and swords. 'Tis impractical these days, but a formality we keep. Mikhail will collect my belongings and do with them as he sees fit."

When she did not immediately respond, he slid his gaze back to her face. To his complete amazement, laughter danced on her lips.

"What amuses you so? You do not mind that the entire Order will know I have taken you to my bed?"

Still chuckling, Anne shook her head. "Did you forget I've studied your Order all my life? I know the Code. I've seen the surcoats in the hall. I just wanted to watch you squirm a bit."

Merrick grumbled. 'Twould figure she would delight in his discomfort. And yet, though he could not fathom why, her amusement soaked into him, making it impossible to contain a smile. Catching her by the hand, he brought her knuckles to his lips. "Do you wish to sup, or do you wish to bask in my humiliation?"

There was something fantastically erotic about having the entire Order know she'd given herself to Merrick. Merrick led these men. He founded something—even if unwittingly—that had transcended time. And he chose Anne. She who had always been second best to Sophie.

Maybe it had something to do with a secret voyeurism.

Like having sex in the open and running the risk of getting caught.

Maybe it just felt damn good to not have to hide her growing affection for this man.

Whatever the reason, Anne's belly fluttered like a horde of bottlenecked butterflies at the light caress of his lips. He could unravel her so easily. She choked down a gasp and pushed aside the growing heat in her veins. Dinner with Merrick meant an opportunity to talk. "I could eat out. But I have a favor to ask."

Merrick's mouth curved with a smirk. "What do you wish, little demon?" He leaned back on the bed, pulling her astride his lap. Mischief danced in his dark eyes as he gripped her waist and rocked her hips against his.

Laughing, Anne wriggled out of his grasp. "Okay, big guy. Tempting, but I'm starving." She ignored his dramatic mutter and picked up her sweater and discarded bra. Choosing her words carefully, so he couldn't hear the anxiousness that roiled inside her, she said, "I want to learn more about Azazel and what these demons are. More about the secrets of your purpose."

"'Tis information you should possess."

A little rivulet of excitement worked its way down to her toes. He would tell her. Holy cow, she'd done it! Seducing him cracked through that polished armor. Not that she'd really seduced him. Making love to Merrick had been completely natural. Spontaneous. Extraordinary.

Still, they'd forged an intimate bridge, and he was at last welcoming her into his world of secrets. Her heart swelled at the realization.

Merrick stood up, giving her a mind-boggling view of firm buttocks. God, she'd made love to him twice, and just looking at him turned her insides to liquid. She'd half hoped that by exhausting herself with him, she'd gain control over the potent effect he had on her.

If he had let her explore, she might have tempered it somewhat. Instead, Merrick had commanded her in the bed, the same way he commanded her out of it. Only, under the power of his kisses, she allowed him to get away with it. No, not just get away. She *liked* his dominant desire. She didn't have to wonder if she pleased him—he let her know exactly what he liked.

While she pulled on her sweater and buttoned it up, she watched him finish dressing. He really was quite spectacular. Incredibly male.

And hers.

She blinked, catching the wayward thought. Hers maybe according to some mystical prophecy, but she couldn't keep him. He belonged to her only for the duration of the week—which was rapidly passing. She had no business getting sappy over this. She couldn't let herself get emotional. Her career was hanging in the balance, she hadn't gained the answers to prove her thesis, and her visions predicted Merrick's death. No matter how tempting he was, she needed to stay focused on her purpose here—discovering the Church's motivation.

Find the answers, keep Merrick from dying, get back home. Deal with the emotional fallout later.

Still, it had been so long since she'd allowed herself to enjoy a man's company, she couldn't bring herself to deny the pleasure Merrick offered. As long as she kept her emotions in check, a bit of fun, coupled with great sex, couldn't harm anything. Besides, she genuinely liked his company.

So she told herself as he stepped into her skirt and smoothed the fabric. A little wrinkled, but she didn't want to waste time with changing. Merrick wanted to take her out in public. It didn't take a genius to recognize the treat for what it was. His archaic speech told her he didn't make a habit of spending time in the modern world.

Glancing up, she caught his heated stare. Onyx eyes followed the movements of her hands, then locked with hers. Heat crawled up her neck and into her cheeks. "Why are you staring at me?"

Bemused, he shook his head. "My hunger for you is insatiable, Anne." He snatched hold of her hand and dragged her close to kiss her thoroughly. When he drew slowly away, she felt his heart thud against her breast. Her resolve to keep him at arm's distance shattered. "Stay with me tonight?" she whispered.

That dark gaze flashed with bright intensity. He cupped her face in his large palm and brushed the tip of his nose across hers. "I would have it no other way."

Anne eased out of his embrace before the thrill that bubbled in her veins got the better of her, and she couldn't. She stepped into her boots, zipped them up, and combed her fingers through her hair. With a shaky smile, a product of the quivering in her belly, she said, "I'm ready."

Merrick threaded his fingers through hers before opening the door. As she stepped over his folded surcoat and polished sword, a giggle bubbled in the back of her throat. His. She was his. Sensible or not, she liked the sound of that.

CHAPTER 22

$\dagger$

Tane moved quietly through the corridors. Thoughts of Marie and her younger brother ran amok in his head. Last night, whilst the wind blew cold and fierce, he had caught her standing beneath the 12th Street Bridge with little more than scarves wrapped around her body. Sixteen years old, and she had all but undressed for the leering middle-aged man by the time Tane had arrived with a paltry offering of canned tuna and bread.

The man put up little fight when Tane insisted he should leave. Were it not for the fact the piece of filth had not yet given Marie coin, Tane would have had to use his fists.

He had arrived just in time. But what would the poor girl attempt tonight to keep her brother from starving? She refused to seek shelter in a home, believing social services would take David. Likely they would. However, Marie could not see how a separation might serve them both well. She would have time to finish her education. Young David would never spend another night with only a trash-barrel fire to keep his skinny frame warm.

Tane refused to bear responsibility for Marie's ruin. And yet he could do naught without the Order's full support. The Templar Knights' coffers overflowed. Their stores of food were an embarrassment to the hunger Tane witnessed on the streets. They could spare what Marie needed. They could provide warmth, shelter, and see the siblings did not suffer.

To accomplish this, however, Tane must sway Merrick. As Merrick was the only living member of the founders, his input carried weight. Tane intended to obtain his approval before the night drew longer.

He rounded a corner and continued down the long, darkened hall that led to Merrick's chambers.

Merrick understood the loss of one's birthright. He would sympathize with Marie's mother's death and her family's disownment. Merrick would understand. If he did not, Tane was prepared to battle for what he wanted. When Caradoc found an old woman wandering the streets, unable to recall her name, Merrick granted Caradoc's request to establish her within a home. When Farran's former whore found herself heavy with another man's bastard, Merrick established her in a small apartment with someone to watch her babe so she could attend the university. Marie deserved no less than those two. Tane spent equal time at Merrick's side, had proven his loyalty along with all the others. His requests deserved equal consideration.

Tane winced against the unwanted rush of emotion. Nay, in his heart he knew Merrick favored no knight. His decisions had naught to do with preferring one man over another. God's teeth, this envy would turn him inside out. A fairer leader, Tane had never known—Merrick would not turn aside one in need.

He would help Marie.

As Tane approached Merrick's door, his steps slowed. His stare riveted on the folded surcoat and offered sword, and he slowly curled his hand into a fist. It could not be. His eyes must deceive him.

Squeezing them shut, he willed the nightmare away. Yet when he looked, the evidence lay at his feet, Merrick's confession announced as plain as day. He had seduced Anne.

White-hot fury arced through Tane. He clamped his

teeth together, silencing a bellow of rage. Anne belonged
to him. Her mark would match if he could but navigate a
few moments alone with her. But Merrick . . .

Tane kicked the sword, sending it clattering across the
narrow corridor. Merrick be damned! He had no right to
touch what did not belong to him. Anne was no spoil of
victory, was not a simpleminded whore. She was a seraph, and Merrick sullied her for his own selfish pleasure.

He pressed his hands against his temples with an anguished groan. Nay, not Merrick. Merrick did not possess
the selfishness required to mislead the lady Anne. 'Twas
not his nature. 'Twas this damnable darkness plaguing
him, convincing Tane to believe his brother would forsake oaths for bawdy pleasure. If Merrick claimed the
maid, something deeper transpired.

Could it be his brother cared for her? Or mayhap she for
him? The idea sent an icy chill rippling through his limbs.
He had waited too long to convince Anne into spending a
few minutes alone with him. He had bided his time, waiting for the right moment, praying the next time she looked
upon his face she did not widen her eyes in fright. In so
doing, he had sent her straight to Merrick's bed.

God's blood, he would not stand for this. The maid belonged to him, she would save him from the darkness so
rapidly overtaking his soul. A truth the entire temple would
learn in proper time. A fact Merrick would soon come to
regret. He would never again touch the fair maid with eyes
like a summer's day. As for Lady Anne, once she left the
temple, whatever feelings she might hold would fade. However long she required, Tane would wait. She would forget
Merrick. But she would not spend another day within his
company.

Fists balled, Tane stormed down the hall. Aye, he would
see his intended at his side, as their fates were written.

Raphael gently set the pristine surcoat and plain broadsword on top of Mikhail's desk. "I thought you might wish
to see this."

Eyeing the offerings of one who had broken his oath, Mikhail frowned. Too many had arrived this week. With Anne's discovery, the vows the Templar knights took centuries ago strained. If Merrick did not quickly find her intended, Mikhail feared what might become of the noble knights.

He let out a sigh and gestured at the corner where several other surcoats lay in a heap, the swords already restored to their rightful owners. "Return it. If I kept all the surcoats and swords I found outside the doors, I would have an armory larger than the sea. Do you still collect them from your men?"

Raphael shook his head. "Nay. But it would not be wise to leave this particular bundle in the hall."

Mikhail slowly lifted his gaze to Raphael's. His usual merriment failed to light his eyes. Where oft a smile laid, his mouth tightened with concern. Though archangels carried the Almighty's words, they lacked the gift of foresight, but in Raphael's serious expression, Mikhail experienced a moment of divinity and heard the certain answer to the question he must ask.

He shifted in his chair, laid his pen atop the ledger of numbers. No mark identified the surcoat, the sword was as plain as every Templar knight's. Yet Mikhail knew without question it belonged to Merrick. Still he must ask. Perhaps he would be incorrect—by all that was sacred, he hoped he was. "Why?"

"'Twas outside du Loire's door. He is away. Anne is not in her rooms. I presume they are together."

Mikhail sank into his high-backed chair and folded his hands across his lap. "You are certain you had the correct room?"

Raphael inclined his head in the positive. "I followed your directions to the letter." A glimmer of his typical good humor reflected in his blue eyes. "I knocked. When no one answered, I looked inside. Her perfume lingers in his chambers."

It took every bit of self-control Mikhail possessed to

keep the agitated hiss behind his teeth. The news Caradoc
brought about Tane concerned him enough. If word reached
Tane about this, only the Creator would know what might
happen. Further, whoever was meant for Anne, should he
learn of Merrick's trespasses against her, would have
grounds to duel the matter. Seraphs were sacred. The edicts
regarding their foretold appearance left no room for misin-
terpretation. No man would come between the intended
pairing. Should one lack the discipline, the wronged man
may, if he so desired, call the other unto arms.

Given the entirely chaotic state of Mikhail's knights,
Merrick could not have made a poorer decision.

"Send Caradoc to the main entry. Instruct him to bring
Merrick here upon his immediate arrival. Anne did not
belong to your Gareth?"

"Nay. Nor to my Tomas. But I daresay my men are in
better health than yours."

A certain fact Mikhail hated to admit. Though it did
not surprise him to find the European members robust.
For a reason the Maker chose not to reveal, the European
knights suffered less. Even the small congregation in
South America, which saw far less of Azazel's vile cre-
ations, did not receive such good health.

"I will push Merrick to locate her intended more quickly.
Though I must admit, Raphael, I have never known Merrick to behave so foolishly. Whatever hold the maid has on
him must be of significance. I may have to assign the duty
to another man."

"Aye. 'Twas my suspicion as well. Although I doubt
the lady will be pleased."

Another time, another place, Mikhail might have argued. But with the modern woman's views, he found it
difficult to believe Anne did not carry equal responsibility for this. If the pair developed feelings for one another,
convincing her to swear her vow to another man would
prove impossible.

He raked a hand through his hair and let out a heavy
sigh. "I will deal with it. Though you cannot imagine how

I wish the Master's plans did not involve a woman. As it was at the dawn of time, she tempts greatly."

"'Tis as it is written, my brother."

Mikhail nodded thoughtfully. It would be far easier to navigate these stormy waters if Gabriel would simply share his knowledge. But that was a hope Mikhail gave up an eternity ago. God's messenger relayed only what the Almighty wished. Naught more, naught less. "What I would do for a bit of peace. Are you aware the gate in Georgia has seen far more activity? I have not sent the men to repair Maggie's house. I dare not risk them."

Raphael moved across the room and seated himself in an overstuffed chair. He tossed an ankle atop a velvet-cushioned footstool, reclining as if he had not a care in the world. "I sense him. Though 'tis far too still in this portion of the country."

Too still indeed. The dark presence Mikhail recognized nightly came in the form of shades, simple creatures that lacked the basic ability to think for themselves. Created only to follow Azazel's commands, even they did not roam in the packs they preferred. One or two slipped through weakened gates. Gone were the more intelligent shifters. The nytyms, and the demons capable of the same intelligence man enjoyed, wandered far from here.

Azazel's knights, men Mikhail had once depended on, were nowhere to be seen.

"He will try for the third nail, Raphael. We dare not move before he does, for we run the risk of revealing its location. In waiting, however, we give Azazel the upper hand. He will have time to prepare."

Raphael ran his hands down his face as he nodded. "Do you believe he knows the location? He has made no attempt to invade the territory."

Mikhail longed to believe they had successfully hidden the third. Centuries ago, when they had brought the crucifixion nails to America, it had seemed sensible. The land bustled with activity, newfound territory, men who cared little for the ways of old. Compared to Europe—where thousands searched for buried treasure, lugged out and sold mummified remains, and created a black market based on falsified artifacts—America was safe. With the loss of the first two nails, however, Mikhail could not hope the third would say untouched.

"He toys with us. 'Tis my fear that in possessing our former knights, he has gleaned information. Whilst we archangels have taken care to keep the secrets among ourselves, bits and pieces have been revealed. Yet our fallen brother is no fool. He will attempt to distract us, spread our men thin, and strike beneath our noses."

Raphael's scowl matched the darkness of an angry sea. "He cannot find that nail. If he succeeds . . ."

He trailed off, but Mikhail needed no conclusion. If Azazel joined the three nails, he would possess the essence necessary to begin the unholy ascension. While he would still need to obtain the remaining five relics, the blood on those bits of iron were the first components necessary. Naught would stop him from pursuing the others that Mikhail and his brothers had hidden. Unless the seraphs like Anne arrived soon, the Templar knights, the Almighty's chosen protectors, would be overrun.

Mikhail sat forward in his chair and rubbed his thumb across the back of his hand. "Once Anne announces her intended, I will send men to guard the nail. Meanwhile, send word to Gabriel that he must return. Perhaps he can speak with her and urge her to reveal her mark. He has her trust."

"I will contact the rest of our brothers and ensure all are aware of the circumstances here. The other relics should be moved."

"Nay. They must stay put. If you do too much, Raphael, Azazel will notice. We must move with stealth. If our numbers were larger, it would not be a problem, but we cannot afford to be careless."

Raphael's blue eyes sharpened like glass. "The time is upon us, Mikhail. Since the dawn of time we have prepared for war. 'Tis here. Now. We must—"

Mikhail cut off his brother with a crisp lift of his hand. "We must bide our time. We must be careful. As you said, 'tis written. Our hands are bound. Go and find Gabriel. The seraphs control our destiny." He leaned back once more, closed his eyes, and recited the Almighty's ancient prophecy that no archangel dared forget, though many of their knights had.

"Whence comes the teacher, she who is blind shall follow. The one who digs in dust precedes the finding of the jewel. And she who understands the sword precludes the greatest loyalty. When darkness—"

"—rapes the land, the seraphs shall purify the Templar and lead the sacred swords to victory," Raphael finished in a hushed voice.

With a sagely nod, Mikhail opened his eyes. "Aye. We wait. Fight only as necessary. 'Tis our only option."

CHAPTER 23

☩

Wearing a smile she couldn't contain, Anne reclined in the silver SUV's passenger's seat. Almond-encrusted salmon and wild rice had never tasted as good as it had with Merrick for company. They'd talked, mainly about her, throughout dinner. She didn't dare ask much about him, or his life, or even his former life, for fear someone might overhear their conversation. Now, though, in the quiet of the car, as he held her hand atop the center console, her mind ran amok with questions. There was so much she didn't know about this man. So much he kept hidden that she yearned to understand. Curiosity that went beyond simple craving of the Templar secret history and the Church's eradication.

Sitting forward, she turned to study his profile. His strong jaw spoke to the power of his body and of his spirit. A slightly offset nose told a tale of a long ago battle where surely he'd broken it. Rugged features carried a distinct mark of pride and grace. Handsome. Every time she looked at him, her breath hitched and her heart stuttered. He was all man. Down to the annoying arrogance that strangely pleased some buried, all-too-feminine part of her soul.

He glanced at her, those hard features softening with his smile. "You have grown silent."

"Yeah. There's so many things I want to ask you."

"Ask, damsel. My secrets are yours."

Though she knew he spoke of her tie to the Order, his remark sent a thrill sliding through her veins. While he would only share what he felt she needed to know, she couldn't help but hear something more intimate. As if he'd just given her a cherished freedom.

"The nails Mikhail mentioned—why does a lesser demon want them?"

Merrick chuckled long and low. He gave her hand a gentle squeeze and shook his head. "Azazel is no lesser demon, and the nails are not any kind of nail. They are the three spikes that held Christ to the cross. Driven through his body, they carry his blood and the last of his living essence. There is power in those bits of iron."

"But why would he want them?"

"You will not believe the truth if you should hear it, Anne."

She scrunched her eyebrows together and gave him a frown. "Try me."

"Azazel rules all darkness. He alone—"

"Wait," Anne interrupted. "That's not what I was taught in church. Satan has that job, last I checked."

Shaking his head, Merrick explained, "Nay. Again an error of man's. The scribes misinterpreted doctrine. Such can be expected when languages differ, when words are not common for others, and when time passes. Satan is a thinker. He plots. He plans. He wishes ill and guards the depths of hell. But Azazel holds the power. He acts. He solicits souls to work his evil."

"Merrick, you can't expect me to believe that. All the major religions in the world reference the devil as the greatest evil."

"Let me illustrate the linguistic issues, as most of this occurred in the years following my birth. The name differs in Hebrew. 'Tis not a proper name, but rather a description of an adversary. In Judaism, the prince of all evil points such evil out to God. He does not create, nor act on it, and is powerless."

Anne considered with a short nod. Truthfully, she didn't know Scripture well enough to make much of an argument. Merrick continued before she could comment.

"In English, the word Satan descends from the Greeks, which translates loosely as one who slanders. Again, 'tis a nondescript word, not a proper name. The word devil appeared in the thirteenth century. This too began with actions, not as a proper name. 'Tis only in modern understandings of the original Hebrew that all three have become the same and have transformed into one being."

"Okay," she replied hesitantly. "I'm not sure where you're going with this."

"Beelzebub is used as a synonym. He was in fact an ancient Philistine god. Leviathan, Metatron—all names used to signify the same. Each, however, are different entities. Leviathan was correctly described as a sea monster. He sits now in the depths of the waters, waiting to sink ships. Metatron is the highest of the angels according to some Scripture."

Anne furrowed her brows, his circular references difficult to follow. She held her tongue, waiting for him to make his point, though the urge to interject and argue made her want to squirm in her seat.

"Is it not possible that in translating acts, in describing deeds, names were used interchangeably and some of the accuracy has become lost?"

"Well . . ." She paused, glanced out the window in thought. "I suppose it isn't impossible."

"Then consider, for this I can personally attest to. Morning Star—would you agree 'tis a reference to the prince of darkness?"

"Of course."

"In my family's era, the bright light in the heavens we

believed as such was proven in your family's era to be Venus."

In the silence that followed, Anne tipped her head to the side and watched Merrick's features. Through the light of streetlamps, his expression filled with animation, a testament to his convictions.

"If this could be proven false, can it not also be possible the rest of what is *written* today is the result of different cultures attempting to understand, and relate, the *basis* of a truth?" He glanced at her briefly, lifting his eyebrows before he returned his stare to the road.

She shrugged her shoulders. "I guess."

"Regardless, Anne—is the name particularly relevant? The principle is the same. A great evil bent on destroying man. One who covets the kingdom on high. 'Tis Azazel who has the power. 'Tis he who has the ability and fortitude to ascend. Satan is but his counselor."

He had a point—they were arguing semantics. Who did what, who held what name, was insignificant.

"Ask Mikhail. He will tell you the same. They are brothers, after all."

"Okay, okay." She held her free hand up in a gesture of surrender. "Go back to this ascending."

Merrick flashed her a grin as bright as the moonlight outside. He nodded toward the windshield, and Anne's gaze drifted where he indicated. They'd parked, sat now in front of the temple's exterior house.

"Let us go in, and we shall talk some more. I will tell you more of the relics that so fascinate you, when you are seated at my side where I may kiss and touch you as I desire."

Her cheeks flushed with color, and she dipped her head. This new side of Merrick would take some getting used to. She'd become accustomed to his distance, but now he didn't hesitate in voicing his wishes. All night long, he'd sneaked in a comment or two that had her remembering their afternoon together, along with a few that made it clear he intended to pick up where they'd left off before dinner.

He got out of the vehicle before she did, and as she reached for the handle, her door opened. Taking her elbow, he helped her out of the SUV, then threaded his fingers through hers and shut the door. He caught her chin with his other hand and tipped her face to his. Slowly, he took her mouth. The tip of his tongue traced the seam of her lips, nudged them apart. When it danced against hers, the heady flavor of Merrick soaked into her soul. Masculine richness, fringed with the spice of desire, stirred warmth through her veins. She gave in to a murmur of delight and settled her free hand on his shoulder to keep her weak knees from giving out.

Merrick drew back, breaking the kiss. "I have waited all night for that," he whispered. "I hunger for you, damsel."

She stood up on tiptoe and pressed a gentle kiss to his lips. "Take me inside."

Grinning like he'd just brought home the spoils of a great battle, Merrick escorted her to the door. He opened it, ushered her inside first, then turned toward the stairs.

"Merrick."

The curt, masculine call brought him to an immediate halt. Not particularly in the frame of mind to share him with his buddies, Anne groaned inwardly as Merrick turned them around. Her gaze settled on a very serious-looking Caradoc who leaned against the entryway to the large common room.

"Caradoc," Merrick acknowledged.

His friend didn't smile as he folded his arms across his chest. "Mikhail sent me to retrieve you upon your immediate return."

At once, Merrick stiffened. The same tense line Anne had become so familiar with settled into his jaw, and he turned to her. Yet instead of annoyance flickering in his dark eyes, they shone with warmth. He took a step closer, bent his head near her ear. "Go on upstairs. I will join you soon."

With little room to argue, she nodded. "Can I use your phone? I'd like to call my sister while you're gone."

Merrick brushed his lips across the top of her head and fished his cell phone out of his back pocket. "Stay in your chambers, damsel."

Anne didn't bother to respond. Twisting free of his embrace, she jogged up the stairs. Though she no longer needed Sophie's advice, her twin was probably worried sick. She'd understand, however, when Anne explained she'd been studying the Templar legends. She wouldn't mention a word about the chain of recent events, but Anne intended to find out if Sophie's armband had brought her any surprises.

Inside her room, she dialed her sister's number. The line rang four times before her voice mail picked up.

Anne hung up. No sense in leaving messages when her sister hadn't bothered to return the others. Instead, she dialed her own phone, certain Sophie would have left a dozen messages or more. But as she pressed the button to transfer into her system, her empty mailbox greeted her.

Frowning, Anne pressed the disconnect button. Strange. Damned strange. They talked every night. Under any other circumstance, Sophie would be worried sick. Her voice mail should be full of hysterical questions.

Where in the world was her sister?

A feeling of unease churned around in Anne's stomach. Desperate to settle a rise of nausea, she dialed Sophie again.

As Caradoc eased Mikhail's office door closed, Merrick stood in front of the archangel's massive wooden desk. Hands clasped behind his back, he stared at the ornate sword above Mikhail's head. Fashioned similarly to the Templar blades, the broadsword bore the same golden cross in the pommel. But in stark contrast to Merrick's plain blade and unguarded hilt, Mikhail's sword had a golden guard, and intricate etching adorned the flattened length of steel. Beautiful, yet deadly.

"I am glad you are both here. I needed to speak to Caradoc about Maggie's adytum in Georgia."

Merrick slid his gaze down to Mikhail's face. The archangel looked between them both, his gaze resting on Merrick a fraction longer than necessary before he turned his focus to Caradoc.

"I had intended for you to take the men to Georgia, Caradoc."

"We are ready for your command, Mikhail."

Mikhail shook his head. "You will not be going. Raphael's men will tend to the repairs."

"Sir," Caradoc cut in. "We are more than capable of—"

"'Tis not a matter of capability." Standing, Mikhail moved across the room to a large, comfortable chair and sat down on an overstuffed arm. The formality in his voice vanished as he continued. "There is increased activity at gate twelve. Too much for our men here. Raphael's visiting knights shall handle the repairs. I require my strongest men present, as I anticipate Azazel shall strike again."

Caradoc's affronted pride relented with a respectful dip of his head.

Merrick shifted his weight, the meaning in Mikhail's words unmistakable. Should Azazel attack, Merrick would be called upon to fight. Whilst he would offer no complaint and would honor his eternal oath, the difficulty the shades had given him made the condition of his soul unavoidable. Another battle would surely claim the last of his remaining light.

"I want the both of you to gather Nikolas and Gareth of Aletorp. Use Nikolas' knowledge of his archers and formulate a strategy to defend Elspeth's adytum along the Bayou Bourbeaux, should the need arise. Gareth shall prepare the remaining men from Europe to reinforce our knights."

Bristling at the mention of the young knight Anne had so shamelessly bestowed her favor on, the same one who had pushed him beyond all reason and driven him to obliterate his oaths, Merrick watched Mikhail through narrowed eyes. He would rather run the man through than work at his side.

"You two are to act as each other's second. Should one of you fall unto Azazel's power, the other will be informed of our plans. Merrick, you will lead the men. Caradoc you shall assume his place, if such becomes necessary. Whilst you arrange this, have Gareth tend to the weapons stores and report to Raphael what we lack."

"Do you anticipate an attack?" Merrick asked.

Mikhail lifted a solitary dark eyebrow. "Do you not?"

Nodding, Merrick stayed silent. After the recent events, to expect anything less would only be wishful thinking. Azazel would strike. 'Twas only a matter of when, and with how many former Templar knights.

"That is all, Caradoc. I will speak with Merrick alone now."

Merrick lifted his chin a fraction, his stance at once rigid. There could only be one reason Mikhail abruptly dismissed his second most-trusted knight. The reason Merrick believed he had been summoned to begin with—Anne.

Caradoc shot him a brief, supportive glance before he exited the spacious chamber and pulled the door firmly shut.

Returning to his desk, Mikhail pushed a surcoat and sword across the scarred surface toward Merrick. "I believe these belong to you."

Merrick allowed his gaze to fall to the folded surcoat and the broadsword as he slowly let out a deep breath. "Aye."

"I shall spare you the tediousness of reminding you of your oath. Of all the men in this temple, you understand the gravity of your actions."

A wash of shame rolled through Merrick, and he gritted his teeth against it. All evening, he had fought back the rising guilt, focused only on the way Anne lightened his spirit. But now, he could no longer pretend an afternoon of pleasure broke only the ritualistic vow of chastity. He had claimed what did not belong to him. Sullied another man's honor. He had cared naught for the vows of brotherhood and cast them aside as he might toss away a scrap of rubbish.

His shoulders bent under the weight of full realization. "Aye," he murmured.

Mikhail leaned back into his chair and studied Merrick for several long moments. As he did, the commander's sober expression gave way to compassion, and his brows crinkled with the hint of a frown. "Do not look upon me as your general, Merrick. I am your friend. Speak to me as such. I know your heart. You would not do this out of simple lust. What is it about the maid?"

Merrick turned away from Mikhail and stood before the well-worn kite shield that bore the marks of time. Deep scars gouged into the painted planks, paired with smaller punctures, remnants of long-ago arrows that sought flesh beneath. He studied the emblazoned crimson cross and searched for the words that would answer Mikhail's question. At length, he bowed his head and stared at his feet. "She gives me hope."

The creaking of wood signaled Mikhail had risen. Heavy feet moved across the stone floor, and a hand settled on Merrick's shoulder. "You are certain she is not meant for you?"

Shaking his head, Merrick closed his eyes. He had looked. God in heaven, he had searched every part of her body the second time he had made love to her, in hopes she would bear a mark in some place he bore a scar, a freckle, anything he might recognize. She had refused to remove her socks, swearing the room was far too cold. But even if she had, he knew it would be futile. He had naught of significance on his.

"She is not mine," Merrick answered on a sigh.

Mikhail's grip tightened on Merrick's shoulder. "I will not attempt to order you away from her, Merrick. You would not listen should I try. Yet know this." He turned away, Merrick's gaze following as Mikhail resumed his place behind his desk. "The men who witnessed your surcoat already grumble. You must be careful. I cannot afford to lose your skill on the field, should her intended seek to avenge the wrong you have done to him."

Merrick returned to the desk and scooped up his belongings. "It will not matter, Mikhail. I am not long for this world. When I am gone, Caradoc may see to her keeping. He will not fail as I have."

A dark frown engulfed Mikhail's features. "Are you so close, brother?"

"Aye. I have but a few more battles left in me." He pulled the door open and paused in the entryway. "Mayhap you should give her to Caradoc's keeping now."

"Nay, Merrick." Mikhail's low voice filled with unspoken emotion. "Know love before you know Azazel's hate."

Love. Merrick had not given such consideration to his attraction to Anne. Once, he had yearned for naught else. Yet those dreams died the day he took his oath and pledged himself to the Templar way. He had cast aside what seemed frivolous for a greater cause. But at the mention of the word now, the icy fingers around his soul released their hold. 'Twould be useless to avow he felt naught for Anne. He cared. If he did not, her flirtations with the men this afternoon would not have driven him to madness. But love he did not know. The woman's emotion made men weak.

Unwilling to further examine the uncomfortable quivering in his belly, he strode into the hall. He buckled his sword around his waist, stuffed his surcoat beneath his arm, and made his way to his chambers to collect a change of clothes. As he rounded the corner, he found Farran leaning against his door. Arms folded across his chest, he wore a scowl as dark as a starless sky.

CHAPTER 24

✝

Farran's stare flicked to the surcoat beneath Merrick's arm before brown eyes locked with his. "We must have words."

The subtle underlying venom beneath Farran's command had Merrick's senses on immediate alert. Whilst he had become accustomed to his brother's continual anger, this went deeper. Far more serious. Whatever plagued him was not the result of Azazel's taint. Merrick inclined his head to his door. "Let us take this matter inside."

Farran reached behind his back and opened the heavy barrier. He backed inside to lean one hip against Merrick's table. Following, Merrick went to his wardrobe to restore his surcoat to its place on the top shelf. He dragged out a handful of fresh clothes, set them on the table, then fixed Farran with an expectant look. "Do you wait for an invitation to speak?"

"Nay. I wait to see if your temper is better than last eve."

Merrick leaned both hands on the table, the horns of warning in his head a deafening racket. "For the moment, 'tis improved."

An unexpected glimpse of Farran's previous good humor slipped out in the quirking of his mouth. "As I suspected when I discovered your surcoat on the ground this afternoon. You have chased away your demons."

With a perturbed frown, Merrick grunted. In no mood to make light of the seriousness of his actions, he grumbled, "Speak your words, then leave me be."

Farran's smile vanished. He braced a hand on the table and leaned down, bringing the hard light of his eyes even with Merrick's. "Do not leave your sword, Merrick. The men talk amongst themselves. I have twice this afternoon been the recipient of threats against you. Though both recanted when I reminded them I well know how to wield a blade and would not hesitate to do so on your behalf, they are not the only ones who gabble like hens."

Merrick ground his teeth together as a burst of rage rushed through him. "Who cannot control their tongues? I will be happy to let them say such to my face."

Shaking his head, Farran stood up straight. "'Tis not worth repeating their names. But I fear for Anne more than I concern myself with you."

Anne? Merrick turned a look of confusion on his friend.

"I should have informed you yesterday, but you were in no mind to hear it."

The unsettling awareness that Farran brought news Merrick would not care to hear turned his gut into a ball of lead. He pulled in a steadying breath and remained silent, feeling much like he faced a deadly opponent whilst he stood holding a broken sword.

"Yesterday, I found Anne near the stairs to the inner sanctum. She was—"

A loud buzz set off in Merrick's head, the product of a dozen angry curses. Not only had she disobeyed his order to stay in her room, but she had also sought out the secret chambers. He thumped a fist against the tabletop and bit back the sting of betrayal.

On the heels of the ache that throbbed up his arm, he choked down an inward groan. Nay, she *had* told him. She had confessed Farran intervened. He, on the other hand, had believed she made up stories to keep him at her side. God's teeth, he could be no more foolish.

"Merrick?"

He snapped his gaze to Farran's. "What?"

"She did not tell you."

"Aye, she did. I did not believe her."

As if he addressed an inattentive child, Farran let out a harassed sigh. "I do not mean the secrets of our lower quarters. I speak of Ranulf."

Ranulf? Realizing he had missed the rest of Farran's tale, Merrick frowned. "The Fearless?"

"Aye Ranulf of Stotfold. When I stumbled upon her, he and his faithful, including Gottfried, had her in a fright. He turned her loose only when I drew my blade."

A whole new course of rage surged through Merrick. He shoved past Farran out into the hall, intent on putting an end, once and for all, to Anne's unescorted wanderings. Saints' blood, the Almighty only knew what would have happened to her had Farran not happened along. A man of questionable morals, Ranulf had, on more than one occasion, faced eviction from the Order. Shortly after taking his oath, Merrick had stumbled on him behind a barn, the maid beneath him crying through her panicked protests. Were it not for the fact Mikhail feared Ranulf would speak of their dark secrets, Ranulf would have been dismissed that very afternoon. And in truth, when it came to an ally on the battlefield, Ranulf earned his merit. But the man's personal endeavors elevated him to slightly more than Azazel's vile ways.

Gottfried was marginally better. To Merrick's knowledge, he had never broken a significant oath. Still, he was a Norman, a man who knew only to take what he desired through brute force. As a scholar of history, Anne should understand the Norman ways.

Why had Lucan said naught? He was to look out for her. Instead, 'twas Farran who came to her aid.

Pivoting, Merrick turned for Lucan's chambers. His inattentiveness could not be excused. He had sworn to watch over Anne, and he had left her open to harm at a Norman's hands. Yet halfway down the hallway that led to Lucan's chambers, Merrick came to an abrupt stop. 'Twould do no good to confront Lucan now—Merrick's temper would only cloud his ability to listen to Lucan's explanation. 'Twas Anne who needed to be dealt with. Her and her refusal to honor his requests.

He spun around and marched to the stairs. She would learn that behind these walls, her modern theories meant naught. He sought not to limit her freedoms, but issued instructions to keep her from harm. In disobeying him, she exposed herself to unacceptable danger.

At her door, he did not bother to knock. He stormed inside, unconcerned by the banging of the door. From her perch within a too-large chair, she looked up in surprise.

"Did you think I would not learn of Ranulf and Gottfried? That Farran would stay silent about aiding you?" Merrick crossed to her. "You attempted to enter the inner sanctum whilst I was away."

If he had expected her chagrin, he was sorely mistaken. As she lifted her gaze to his, those sky-blue eyes glinted like shards of glass. She sat up straight, her fingers clenched into the chair's arms. "I told you. Maybe not all of it, but you were hell-bent on leaving. Don't you *dare* turn twelfth century on me because your buddy filled in the gaps."

Merrick clamped his teeth against a string of obscenities. Blast the damnable woman. He was in a fury, and she did not possess the good sense to hold her tongue. Nay, she spoke as freely as any man ever had, and she quite refused to give quarter when such was deserved. "Anne, do not try my patience this night."

"Why not?" she retorted hotly. Pushing out of her chair, she made to pass him.

He halted her retreat by latching onto her elbow and spinning her around. Hands on her shoulders, he leaned down, close enough she could not hope to misjudge his anger, despite the levelness of his voice. "You put yourself in danger, damsel."

Anne jerked free. Her hair whipped across his chest as she stalked past him toward the bedroom. "As I said, I tried to tell you. It's not my fault you didn't listen."

Merrick followed on her heels. This would not end so quickly, no matter what she might wish. But as he barged into her bedroom, she spoiled his argument by speaking first.

"If you lay one hand on me, Merrick, I will scream my head off."

He stopped in midstep. Saints' teeth what did she speak of? He was angry, aye, but he had never raised his hand to a woman. "What is your meaning, Anne?"

"My meaning? If you can't remember, I'm certainly not going to remind you." She glanced over her shoulder as she jerked her dresser drawer open.

Turning back to the dresser, she rummaged through bright scraps of fabric Merrick distinctly remembered as belonging to her intimate things. He tore his eyes away, determined to keep his focus. Distantly, the exchange they had shared that eve filtered to his memory, and slowly, he became aware of her meaning. He had threatened to turn her over his knee. At the time, he had quite meant the vow. But 'twas naught else but a product of his frustration.

Though he had half a mind to make good on the idle threat, he shoved a hand through his hair and expelled a heavy sigh. "You will tell me why you disobeyed."

A handful of black silk in her hand, Anne marched into the adjoining bathroom. "Merrick, I'm a prisoner here. I can do nothing. I can speak to no one. I can't even reach my sister on the phone. I want my freedom, and I can't believe you'd have so much trouble believing this. Didn't you fight the Normans for the same reasons?"

He paused, his lips parted, and his eyes widened. Quickly, he recovered his surprise and furrowed his brow. "How did you know? I have told you naught of my past before the Order."

From behind the open doorway, she answered, "I'm not

stupid. Du Loire—from Loire. The river that runs through France. It's recorded fact the majority of noble families were Saxon around the time you were born."

His frown deepened as she returned to the room dressed in a long satin robe she had belted tightly around her waist. She yanked a brush through her hair, tossed it onto the dresser, and flounced onto the edge of her bed. "Are you going to yell at me all night?"

"I have not yet begun to yell."

"Then you understand why sitting in these rooms, no matter how pretty they are, drives me crazy?"

Merrick eased onto the mattress next to her. He bent over, elbows on his knees, and covered his face with his hands. He did not want to understand. By all rights, he had reason to be furious with her. Yet though he snatched at the remnants of his anger, hopelessly trying to hang on, he could not deny she had kept no great secret from him. 'Twas not as if she tried to hide her actions. She had told him the very day she defied his orders. His anger would have been warranted then. Now it felt insignificant, as if he were the one in error, not she.

Then again, 'twas not the first time Anne had swayed his temper by doing naught. Though he could not begin to explain why, he could not stay angry with her no matter how he tried.

Lifting his head, he cast his frown her way. "If I give you the means to move freely through the temple, will you vow to me you will let your intended take you to the inner sanctum?"

He could see the wheels turning in her head, took in her hesitation as she considered the full measure of his question. After several long moments of silence, she answered with a vigorous nod.

"Do you swear it, Anne?"

"Yes."

Reaching between them, he covered the back of her hand with his palm. "I do not wish to fight with you."

"Nor do I," she whispered. Hesitantly, she nibbled on

her lower lip. "You aren't going to try to put me over your knee are you?"

With a chuckle he could not hold back, Merrick pulled her into his lap. He wound his arms around her waist, the feel of satin heavenly beneath his hands. "Nay. I will teach you how to defend yourself, to use a sword."

She dropped her hand to the pommel at his waist. Reverently, she traced the contours, inspected the leather sinews around the shaft of steel. "Like this one?"

"Aye. We will begin tomorrow."

Her hands drifted between their bodies, and she tugged at the silver buckle that kept his sword belt in place. Merrick sucked in a deep breath, the play of her fingers against his abdomen an unbearable taunt. His blood warmed at the intimacy, for no other woman had removed his belt before—he had let no one close enough to trust with the task. 'Twas a thing only allowed to pages . . . or to wives.

Her hands splayed upward, taking his shirt with them. The chill air washed across his midsection, arousing his body further. His cock swelled. In a damning moment, Mikhail's lecture rose to the forefront of his mind, and though Merrick wanted naught more than to allow Anne to undress him, he covered her hands with his and stilled them against his chest.

It took every last fragment of his willpower to meet her curious gaze and confess what honor demanded. "Anne, we cannot continue this," he murmured. "'Twas wrong of me to take what is not mine. You are another man's intended. One of my brothers."

She rose to her knees, straddling him, and plucked her hands free. Twining them around his shoulders, her fingers toyed with the lengths of hair at the back of his neck. "No." She leaned in close, brushed her lips against the side of his throat. "I'm yours." Her teeth raked against his neck, a brief pinch of pain she eased with the velvety caress of her tongue. "Believe with me."

Lowering herself fully onto his lap, she ground herself against his hardened shaft. Merrick let out a groan, and his resolve crumbled. He shoved the ties of honor to a far corner of his mind where they could not threaten the amazing fantasy of her request. Another woman he would set aside. But no more with Anne. Mikhail, the Order, the Almighty himself could damn him. Merrick no longer cared.

Fisting his hand into Anne's long hair, he dragged her mouth to his and claimed her in a savage kiss.

CHAPTER 25

✝

Merrick's mouth was harsh and unrelenting, his hold upon Anne's hair almost cruel. And yet the feral nature of his kiss held a strangely erotic appeal. Behind it, Anne felt his turmoil, the struggle between what honor dictated and his body craved. She answered the plunder of his tongue with her own hungry thrusts as pleasure oozed down her spine.

She let her hands wander, slid them beneath the roughened fabric of his jersey. There, his skin was hot to the touch. His heart drummed fierce beneath her palm, and the intoxicating scent of aroused male engulfed her. She squirmed closer, craving the feel of his body flush with hers.

He broke the kiss long enough to jerk his shirt over his head and give the belt of satin around her waist a harassed tug. It pulled free, and Merrick shoved the satin aside, exposing the delicate fabric of her spaghetti-strapped black negligee. A tiny thrill bubbled around in her belly as Merrick's dark eyes glinted across the lace neckline. He traced a thick fingertip over the deep V, then stroked the soft flesh of her breast where it rose above the lace.

He lifted his gaze, and what she read there shook her to the core. His eyes burned bright, dark onyx chips lit with

stark arousal. To realize a man could want her the way
Merrick did left her shaken. She didn't quite know how to
embrace the way her heart clanged into her ribs, or her
sudden inability to breathe. She tried to suck in a steadying breath, but it lodged in her throat and strangled on a
gasp. The need to feel him deep inside rose hard and fast.

As if he shared the same ache, Merrick's mouth crashed
into hers. His hands gripped her waist, rolling her hips
over the hard ridge of his erection. She shuddered as a
wave of ecstasy ripped through her. Clinging to his shoulders, Anne held on, afraid the tingles that jetted through
her body might sweep her into some unreachable place.

God and heaven above, nothing about him was gentle.
Not this time, as the warrior who ravaged long-ago bat-
tlefields took rapid command of her. He nudged her into
the mountain of pillows, dominating her with his hands,
his lips, the weight of his body. His thighs trapped her
against the mattress. With one hand, he gathered her
arms above her head and scored a trail of kisses down the
length of her neck. The other gathered in the neckline of
her nightgown and ripped it open.

His breath scalded against her breasts, and she arched
her back, lifting into him. He flicked his tongue against a
puckered nipple, reducing her to putty in his hands. When
his mouth closed over her flesh and he suckled, she let out
a mewl of pleasure. Tugging to free her hands, she sought
to capture his head, to hold him in place as she squirmed
beneath him, but he forbade her the freedom and tightened his hold on her wrists.

Anne tossed her head to the side, clamping down on
her lower lip to silence a cry of frustration. Her entire
body trembled, the pleasure of his loving a torment too
great. She lifted her hips, rubbed against the straining
fabric of his jeans, and gave in to a whimper.

When Merrick moved to her other breast, treating it to
the same exquisite torture, she twisted against the heady
bliss. Captured so she could do no more than experience
every prolonged stroke, each perfect nip of his teeth, heat

swamped her body, gushed between her legs. Lord above, Merrick would kill her this way if he didn't let her touch him soon.

But contrary to his seemingly determined purpose, Anne caught the measure of his faltering control in the hardness of his breath, the shudder that rolled down his spine and vibrated into her. He tore his mouth away and pressed his hips hard into hers. Stilling, he closed his eyes and sucked in short ragged gasps. Opening them, his gaze locked with hers.

"Let me go," she whispered.

Merrick let go of her hands and rocked back to his heels. As he reached for the button at his waist, Anne pushed his hands aside and freed him from the confines of his jeans. He wasted no time in shrugging out of them, then reached for her sock-clad foot. A moment of panic stormed through her at the possibility he would realize the truth behind her confession she was his, and she jerked her foot beneath her, rising up to meld her body against his.

Hardened planes of muscle warmed her naked flesh, a heady sensation that momentarily rendered Anne unable to think. Slowly, her senses returned, and she tilted her head in search of his mouth. He gave it to her freely, his large palms wrapping around to cup her buttocks. Pulling her closer, his erection pressed against her sensitive feminine nub and sent another arc of pleasure rolling through her body.

Consumed by need, Anne pushed against his shoulders, urging him to his back. As Merrick tumbled into the thick quilts, he took her with him. She straddled his hips, bent forward to brush her breasts against his chest.

Yet Merrick would have none of her attempts at loving him. He turned his head, breaking their kiss and fastened his hands at her waist. Holding her gaze, he lifted her up, and in one swift thrust, impaled her. Shock rolled through her body, the sudden invasion more pleasant than she'd ever imagined. She moaned against the flood of sensation. Her nails curled into his forearms, as release pounded through her. Trembling, she gave into ecstasy, and held herself upright on his arms.

Around his throbbing shaft, Anne's flesh gripped and squeezed, edging Merrick closer to his own release. But though he had claimed her quickly, though he had heedlessly sought his own fulfillment, he had no intentions of making this joining quick and insignificant. He rolled his hips backward, withdrawing from her silken folds, then sank into Anne again, marveling at the feel of her tight flesh.

Saints' blood, the woman was too perfect to be real. It would be too easy to become lost in her, to yield to the demands of his body. Yet he wanted naught more than to share her splendor and surrender in unison.

As the last of her climax pulsed around his cock, she found strength enough to lean closer. He caught her mouth, tangled his tongue with hers. Her flavor soaked into him, honeyed and rich, a taste far more exotic than any foreign ale. When she settled her hands over his chest and her fingers burned into his skin, he dropped his thumb to the juncture of her legs and pressed against the sensitive nub there.

She keened, a strangled noise that got lost in his throat. His body moved of its own accord, thrusting into hers, and he shook with the effort of holding himself in check. Impatient need demanded he slam into her, toss away the vain intent to see to her pleasure once more. He cast it aside with a vengeance and willed his body into a slow, even tempo. Nay, he would wait for her, no matter how it pained him.

Anne moved against him, each roll of her hips scalding pleasure through his veins. He glided in and out of her body, focusing on the sweetness of her mouth. God's teeth he was so ready he thought he might snap in half.

His belly quivered against chained desire, his cock swelled near painful limits.

When he felt the moistened folds of her flesh flutter around his shaft, he eased their kiss to a close and captured one hand in his. Threading his fingers through hers, he allowed her to guide him, to take him at the pace she required. The undulation of her hips, the jagged gasps that tumbled from her lips spiraled him so far into her, he could no longer decipher where she began and where he started. She consumed him, and Merrick closed his eyes to the ecstasy she alone created.

"Merrick . . ."

Her quiet cry was all he needed. In one hard thrust, he plunged deep inside her. His body jerked upward, curling toward hers, and he wound one arm around her waist, holding her close. Pleasure burst forth, so bright and burning he felt dizzy. It stormed past centuries of darkness, lighting that distant part of his soul she somehow managed to touch. He sank his teeth into her shoulder, choking back his own hoarse cry, and spilled his seed.

Long moments passed as Merrick held her, the velocity of their ragged breaths a shared intensity. Though his body slowed, and the pounding behind his ribs eased, his limbs quaked with the fierce effect of their loving. He lifted his head, pressed a light kiss against the side of her neck. There he tasted the faint flavor of salt that accompanied the fine sheen of perspiration.

He found her mouth, drew her into a slow, sensual kiss. Her fingers twined into his hair, and he allowed his body to relax. Spent and boneless, he tumbled into the pillows, bringing her with him and reveled in the feel of her soft curves. No other woman had ever rendered him so utterly powerless, and yet this tiny scrap of one somehow weaseled her way beneath his skin far enough he could not even think. She commanded him as easily as any man of arms. His little general. His beautiful little demon.

Throat so dry he dared not speak, Merrick tucked her head against his shoulder and closed his eyes. He recognized the evenness of her breathing, felt the limpness in her limbs. Long auburn tresses cascaded over his chest like fine strands of silk that beckoned to his hands. He stroked her hair, traced the delicate bones of her spine, content to bathe in all she was.

CHAPTER 26

Bright sunlight streaming through her window roused Anne to morning. She cracked one eye open, admiring the way Merrick filled up the bed. In sleep, he was even more handsome. His features softened as they did when he smiled at her. She let out a contented sigh and snuggled deeper into the covers, twining an ankle through his legs.

On the heels of her contentment, despair bubbled through her veins. Last night she had confessed. Though she'd masked the slip with convincing words, in that moment, had he pressed her, she would have shown him the tattoo on her ankle. She wanted to—God knew she longed to spend eternity with this incredible man. But she could not sacrifice a career she'd devoted the majority of her life to, or risk Merrick's inevitable death. Beyond her professional losses, pledging herself to him, revealing he was her intended, would see him to the grave. She couldn't face that responsibility, even if the Almighty had written it in the stars.

Add in her concern over Sophie, and she faced only one option—she had to leave. If it meant saving Merrick's life, she'd leave before she learned the Church's motivation. Though walking away from the knowledge in these halls would haunt her for eternity, she dared not stay. She frowned at the quandary. There had to be another way she could learn the Templar secrets, discover the truth among much rumor, without either breaking her promise to Merrick or revealing her tattoo.

Maybe Gareth would tell her. He'd seemed amicable enough. Heck, of all the men she'd met here, he remained the only one who treated her with any decency—with the exception of Merrick. Declan was friendly, but he was still in the infirmary. Lucan had been civil, but his loyalty ran deep. Like Farran, he'd tell Merrick if she did anything that threatened the Order's code of ethics.

Yes, that's exactly what she'd do. The next time Merrick left the temple for any length of time, she'd seek out Gareth and convince him into showing her the inner sanctum. Not exactly the most honorable thing she could contrive, but the only plausible option. When she left, Merrick would be angry, but at least he'd be alive. For that, eventually he'd thank her.

An angry banging on her door brought her upright.

Merrick rolled over and tossed a heavy arm around her waist.

"Merrick!"

Through the heavy pounding, Anne recognized Mikhail's bellow. She shoved at Merrick's shoulder, and he groggily opened his eyes. At the continuous thumping, he too sat upright, the sheet falling to his waist.

Unabashed, Merrick kicked the covers aside and strode through the bedroom door to answer Mikhail's unfriendly awakening. Anne gawked after him, stunned to see him so comfortable in his nakedness, so absolutely unashamed. Her cheeks heated, and she scrambled to cover herself.

Thankfully, she righted the sheet just as Mikhail barged into the sitting room. His gaze flicked briefly to her, before he turned his back and folded his arms over his chest.

Mortified, Anne wanted to vanish into the bed. With Merrick standing there in all his naked glory, and she clutching at the sheets like a frightened mouse, there could be no confusion about how they'd spent the night. To have an archangel witness what could only be sinful in his eyes, was a greater humiliation than Anne had ever considered.

When Merrick beckoned to her, she almost died of shame. But she managed to find the courage to yank the sheet out of the bed, wrap it around herself, and stumble to the door. Halfway across the room, he gestured at his discarded jeans, and Anne salvaged the last of her pride to pick them up, enter the sitting room, and hand them to him. Without daring to look at Mikhail, she scurried back to her room and pulled the French doors shut. Leaning against them, she listened to their anxious exchange.

"You, Caradoc, Lucan, and Farran shall go to St. Louis, along with Nikolas, Geoffrey, and William the Strong."

"Aye. 'Tis the disturbance significant?"

"Enough I need the seven of you present. Again, Caradoc shall act as your second. I will instruct the others. You must leave at once, Merrick."

Anne covered a gasp with her hand. Leave? Mikhail was sending him to battle? Fear coursed through her veins, turning her blood to ice. Not to fight. Please, God, not to fight. In a moment of fleeting insanity, she considered hiding Merrick's sword.

"You do not send Tane?"

"I cannot locate Tane. Another thing, Merrick," Mikhail continued, his voice lower, less agitated.

"Aye?"

"Raphael's scout mentioned he caught sight of Fulk."

Merrick fell strangely silent. The closing of the outer door was all that echoed through the room. For several never-ending seconds, she waited, debating whether she should go to him, or wait for him to return to the bedroom. Yet as she reached for the handle, opting to inquire on her own, Merrick's footfalls approached the door. She stepped away, giving him room to enter.

His expression was hard, the same grim lines she'd witnessed the first night they'd met. He moved at a slower gait, picking up his shirt as he approached the bed. There, however, he sat down, the garment dangling between his knees while he stared at the bathroom entryway.

"Merrick?" Anne asked softly. She trudged to his side and peered down at him curiously.

As if she drew him from some trance, his gaze snapped to her face. "I must take my leave. My men are needed in St. Louis. It will take us all day to prepare, travel, and seek the rest we must have before we approach the faltering gate."

Anne closed her eyes on a wince. Reaching for him, she found his shoulder and steadied herself against the sudden spinning of the room. Battle. She hadn't heard wrong. Though no one had mentioned the nail, he'd been injured the last time he fought. What if this time was worse? "Why you?" she blurted out. "Can't he send someone else?"

Merrick covered her hand with his and gave it a gentle squeeze. "Your concern touches me, Anne. Yet 'tis my duty to command. I am the eldest. I am sent on every mission, unless I am away." Though he offered her a smile, the light in his eyes didn't match the gesture. He would never confess it, but he worried.

"Don't go," she whispered.

Chuckling, he released her hand to pull his shirt over his head. "I must. Hand me my sword, please."

Snatching what little courage she could from the knowledge that he was guarding a gate, not a sacred nail, Anne bent down and wrapped her fingers around the cool metal sheath. Standing, she hesitated, her gaze searching Merrick's grim expression. He wasn't telling her something—she could sense it in the depths of her soul. The last time he'd left, he hadn't looked so preoccupied. True, he'd been angry then. But this was different. This hinted at danger Merrick didn't feel the last time he went to fight.

Desperate for answers, she set the sword on the bed and grabbed for his hand. Opening her mind, she reached for her second sight like a drowning man might reach for a floating log.

Please, God.

Merrick pulled at his hand, but she clung tighter. With a sigh of resignation, he wound his free arm around her waist and dragged her into his lap. She barely had time to realize his intention before he settled his mouth over hers and drew her into a leisurely kiss. The rapid beating of her heart subsided as his tongue glided against hers. Slowly, tenderly, he took her back to the night before, the way he'd loved her so thoroughly she'd fallen asleep in his arms.

As he eased the kiss to a lingering close, he cupped the side of her face in his hand. "Do not worry for me, damsel. I shall return to you tonight, and we will resume this kiss." His thumb brushed against her cheek, his eyes full of warmth. "Should you need anything whilst I am away, ask Gareth to attend to you."

That sealed it. Something wasn't right. Anne didn't know everything about Merrick, but the fact he would pair her with the man who inadvertently brought them together said more than Merrick's words. A fresh burst of fear slid through her veins, restoring her heart to its same, erratic beat. What wasn't he telling her?

"Now dress yourself, damsel, so you may see me to the door."

Merrick didn't give her opportunity to argue. Gently, he set her feet on the floor and gave her a push, dislodging her from his lap. With little other option, Anne snatched up her robe and quickly stuffed her arms inside. She belted it tight as Merrick shoved his feet into his boots.

She followed him into the sitting room. "Who's Fulk?"

One hand on the door, Merrick's shoulders stiffened. He glanced behind him, his mouth set in a grim line. With a shake of his head, he answered, "We will speak of it tonight."

Anne hurried across the few feet that separated them and flung her arms around Merrick's neck. "I don't want you to go," she murmured into his shoulder. "Stay, Merrick. You can choose to stay."

With the patience one might give an obstinate child,

Merrick unwound her hands and held them between their bodies. "I do not wish to leave, but 'tis my duty." He bent down to press a chaste kiss to her lips.

Before she could say anything more, Merrick stepped through the door.

It wouldn't have mattered if he'd waited. Anne couldn't speak. She stared, her heart plummeting to her feet. In his last embrace, her second sight had returned with a vengeance. Though she caught only two fleeting glimpses, what she saw chilled her to her soul. A knight, clad similarly as Merrick, brandished an identically plain broadsword. But where Merrick wore white, and his broadsword shone like a well-cared-for blade, this knight dressed in black from mail to surcoat to boots. His sword held the same dark hue.

The chilling vision gave way to what haunted her most—a fleeting glimpse of Merrick dressed for the grave.

She stumbled against a rush of dizziness and clutched at the back of a nearby chair. As certainly as she knew her name, she knew that vile knight waited for Merrick.

Four hours later, Anne left her room long enough to send for Gareth. Knowledge had nothing to do with her summons either—the inner sanctum hadn't crossed her mind since Merrick's departure. Preoccupied with worry, she couldn't tolerate another idle moment of watching the television and pretending Merrick wasn't in danger. She needed something to do, something to take her mind off the horrible images of Merrick's funerary. Arguing with the cook presented the perfect outlet. And it gave her the ability to focus on a positive. Something she could do for Merrick, who'd done so much for her, and the rest of his men.

Gareth arrived with a jaunty knock on her door.

Anne leapt off the couch, flipped off the television with a press to the remote, and hurried to the door. Swinging it wide, she nearly threw herself at Gareth, his bright smile had such a profound effect on her taxed nerves.

"Milady." Gareth caught her hand and brought her knuckles to his mouth. "You called for me?"

"Yes," she answered with a light laugh. Tugging her hand free before any more damning visions could assault her, she tucked it into her skirt pocket. "I can't stay here a minute longer. Merrick told me if I needed anything I should send someone for you."

"Aye, Mikhail informed me of such."

She backed up a step and opened the door a bit more. "You don't mind baby-sitting then?"

Gareth's soft brown eyes lit with humor. "Nay, I do not mind. 'Tis a pleasure to spend time in your company. Du Loire is a very lucky man."

Anne felt the heat climb into her cheeks and dipped her head to hide her embarrassment. "Yes, well, let's get one thing clear. No more of this formality. Deal? You are Gareth, and I'm Anne. Not Lady Anne, not milady, just plain old Anne."

His mouth curved into a boyish grin, setting off that charming dimple again. "If you shall admit you are not plain, nor old, I shall concede to call you Anne."

"Whatever," Anne grumbled beneath her breath. "Let's go. I need to speak to the cook, and I need you there in case he gets angry with me." Ushering him out of the door, she pulled it tight behind her. With a wave of an impatient hand, she indicated he should descend the stairs.

"Why would Simon become angry with you?"

It was Anne's turn to grin. With a mischievous wrinkle of her nose, she answered, "Because I'm changing his menu and hiring a new cook. The men here are being tortured with their meals."

Gareth stopped on the stairs, his loud laugh echoing through the tall-ceilinged enclosure. He fished at his belt for something, then produced a small dagger. Flipping it so he held the point, he passed her the polished bone hilt. "Mayhap you best carry this. Simon is difficult, to say the least."

Anne pushed aside the blade and shook her head. "That's why I have you. Now let's get this over with."

For a fraction of a minute, the teasing light left Gareth's eyes and his stare became serious. He pushed the dagger at her once again. "If Merrick feels you must be escorted through these halls, 'twould be wise for you to keep this close."

She stared at the long thin blade, trying to ignore the unease that filtered into her veins. Carrying a weapon felt out of place. Wholly against her character. But two men now expressed concern over her safety—Merrick in word, Gareth in deed. She gave him a hesitant nod. "Keep it for me, for now. I have no place to put it."

He sheathed the dagger, and his smile returned. "Very well. To Master Simon's chambers then."

Following on Gareth's heels, Anne wound her way through the large commons. As they passed, a group of men gathered around the communal television turned to stare, and Anne edged closer to Gareth. After her encounter with Ranulf, she had no intentions of giving any of the strangers a chance to separate her from her guard. Once was enough. Maybe the dagger wasn't such a bad idea after all.

He set his hand in the small of her back and nudged her in front of him. "They are good men. When your intended is announced, you will be surprised by their loyalty."

"Shouldn't they be loyal now?"

"They are, in their hearts." He indicated a set of double doors with a nod of his head. "But you cannot comprehend how long we have awaited the seraphs' arrival. Until your oaths are sworn, the hope lives on that mayhap they contain the mark needed. Mayhap you overlooked something."

Backwards logic as far as Anne was concerned. But his next statement made far more sense.

"We were born of a time when all was free for the

taking if we worked hard enough to attain it. Loyalty to man outweighed loyalty to woman. She could be had, as long as the ties of brotherhood were not strained. Once a man set claim, the noble distanced himself. Aye, those of lesser hearts paid little heed to spoken vows, but the men within these walls, Anne, are not of that cloth."

Once again, she was reminded she'd walked into a world straight out of the twelfth century. Gareth's logic was the truest statement of the rule and laws that bound medieval society she had ever heard. All her studies, all the research did nothing to drive the reality home. She nodded slowly, comprehending far more than Gareth's simple statement.

He stopped in front of a wooden door beside a set of surprisingly modern chrome swinging doors, through which she glimpsed an even more surprising modern kitchen.

"Master Simon," Gareth called as he banged on the door. "You have a visitor."

The man who answered looked nothing like the rest of the knights. Long gray hair tumbled past his shoulders. Watery gray eyes glinted bright above a neatly trimmed salt-and-pepper beard. Stockier than the knights, he dressed in a long black robe marked with a red cross that he had tied beneath his right shoulder, concealing the remnants of his arm.

"What do you want?" he grumbled.

Anne bristled at the gruffness of his gravelly voice and braced herself for inevitable confrontation. Summoning courage, she offered him a smile. "I'd like to talk to you about the menu, Master Simon."

The old man's eyes narrowed to suspicious slits. "There is nothing amiss with my menu. I will not have a woman dictating how my kitchens should operate."

Gareth's reminder of the men's mindsets fresh in her memory, Anne recognized pride behind Simon's rebuke. Suggesting his meals weren't fitting for the knights would only insult him. Refusing to let his gruffness intimidate her, she strengthened her smile, caught his hand in hers, and changed tactics. "I would never presume to insult your talent or ability. You've worked hard, and your skills are notable. But it's come to my attention that there will be more women here in short order. I thought I might consult with you before they arrived, so you wouldn't have them in your hair."

He cocked a wiry eyebrow. "Aye?"

"Oh yes." From the corner of her eye, she caught Gareth's amused smirk. He turned sideways, as if he surveyed the hall, and she noticed the way he covered his mouth with a false cough.

Encouraged, Anne continued, "I thought we could discuss giving you a staff as well. Trusted cooks—men of course—who would be willing to learn from you. It would give you some time to enjoy your hours off as well. A man with your success shouldn't have to slave over the oven. He should be able to sit back and admire his accomplishments when he wants to."

Simon rubbed a gnarled hand over his beard, his expression thoughtful. Anne held her breath, silently praying her attempt at flattery would work. When he nodded at first slowly, then bobbed his head with more enthusiasm, the tension fled her shoulders, and she exhaled deeply.

Simon opened the door wide, revealing a long row of books on the far wall. Colorful titles that stood out against the dark wood shelves and gave the room a cozy feel. "Come inside, Lady Anne. I am of a mind to hear your thoughts."

CHAPTER 27

✝

As twilight descended on the temple, Anne finished off what could reasonably be called a bowl of soup in a private dining area beside the kitchen. She ate the last of a hunk of dried bread, then pushed the empty bowl aside. Across from her, Gareth folded his hands beneath his chin and fixed her with an amused grin. "You possess the skills to manage vast holdings, Anne. I have never seen Simon more agreeable to change. Are you certain you have not negotiated with servants before?"

Anne returned his grin. "Nope. Just students, professors, and the usual politics associated with higher education." She stretched and gave into an expansive yawn. "Though it certainly isn't easy."

"Are you tired?"

"Yes. That took a lot more work than I expected. I think I'll go curl up with the TV for a while." *And wait for Merrick to come home,* she added silently. Lord knew she wouldn't sleep until he walked through her door. If he didn't . . . She shook off the thought along with the chill that filtered through her blood. He'd promised he would come back. As much stock as he put in vows, he wouldn't break his word. And he hadn't gone to protect the nail, hadn't said oaths with her—she needed to remember that. Without the combination, her vision couldn't come true.

Rising to his feet, Gareth extended his arm. "The men will be dining in the great hall. Allow me to escort you properly."

"Of course." Anne pushed her chair away from the table, rose, and fitted her hand in the crook of his elbow. Grateful for the comfortable companionship he provided, she gave him a smile and patted the hand that covered hers. "Thank you, Gareth. I'm sure you had other things you would've rather done than sit while I talked about recipes and chefs."

"And miss the decisions that shall affect my stomach for the rest of my stay in America? Surely, you jest. I would not have spent my afternoon any other way."

His wink belied his sarcasm, and Anne couldn't help but chuckle. With a shake of her head, she followed him down the darkened hallway toward the great hall and the common area.

At the doorway, the all-too-familiar tugging at the back of her mind brought her up short. Her second sight. Twice in one day—it hadn't fled her after all. She tamped down a rush of excitement and closed her eyes, opening her mind to what the supernatural realm wanted her to see.

Like a portrait of a long-ago battle, several men gathered on a hill, blades in hand, bows at the ready. They wore the white surcoats of the Templars and beneath, hauberks of chain. Opposing them, a terrifying legion of men in ebony blended with the fiendish creature she'd witnessed in her living room, and others she'd never seen before. Foul beasts whose mere presence turned her pulse into a staccato tap dance.

What made the picture far more chilling, however, was the eerie light that played across the ground. Where men would have once held standards, both sides brandished crude torches, the combination of smoke and orangish light creating wispy shadows that reached between the opposing armies like a ghoulish hand. Waiting to reach in and steal souls.

The vision shifted as quickly as it formed. The armies clashed, sounds of clanging steel rang in her ears. Bellows and cheers drowned out anguished cries, and where boots tread, they tromped through blood. In a small cluster of three, separated from the massive sea of knights, Gareth fought against a nytym and a hellish knight. The black visage lifted an ebony blade, let out an unholy howl. It slashed across his body, driving deep into Gareth's side. He doubled over, one hand clamped beneath his ribs as his sword faltered.

Horrified, Anne pushed at the images. She could not witness his death. Not here. Not like this. She struggled through the chaos in her mind, shoved beyond the cacophony of noise, desperate to surface and rejoin the present.

But the vision refused to let go. Shifting once more, the sounds of battle disintegrated into terrifying silence. Torchlight flickered on a long stone wall, giving life to thick shadows. Beneath the play of yellow light, her sight centered in on the same damnable vision of Merrick laid out in death. His sword clasped in his hands, it lay atop his chest. Battered and bruised, his face was pale, and the spatter of bloodstains on his surcoat left no question as to where he'd been.

Anne's knees threatened to buckle. Unable to stifle her heartbreak, she let out a sob as she clutched at Gareth's arm to hold herself upright.

"Anne." Gareth wound a thick arm around her waist. "Are you all right?" His warm brown eyes searched her face, concern shuttering his normally vibrant humor.

She expelled a shaky breath. "No."

"Here, sit down." He ushered her across the hall to a rickety bench fastened into the stone.

Anne shook her head, her legs feeling far more steady. "No. Take me to my rooms."

He hesitated, looking very much as if he intended to

forbid her request. His features pulled tight with a frown. "You possess the wisdom of the heavens."

With a sigh of regret, Anne nodded. "I have visions. Please keep this between us, Merrick doesn't know. Would you take me to my room, Gareth? I feel sick to my stomach." She pressed a hand to her midsection to stop the churning in her belly. Merrick and Gareth. What more did God want from her? Wasn't one man enough?

Taking a tighter hold on her arm, Gareth ushered her through the common area. Dimly aware of the heads that turned, Anne focused on the far stairwell, anticipating the salvation that would come with being locked inside her room. There she could crumble. Give in to the tears that welled in her eyes. For the first time in her life, she found herself wishing she'd never been given her psychic gift. But then, if she hadn't, nothing would have stopped her from telling Merrick about their matching tattoos. This way, with the foresight, she could alter the present course and keep him off that damnable battlefield. She still had control, and she'd do whatever it took to keep Merrick safe.

She'd leave tonight. Once she knew Merrick was safe, she'd steal out of the house, borrow a car until she reached the nearby town of Liberty. There she'd call a cab and go straight to the airport. No more visions. No more promises of death.

No more Merrick.

To hell with her career, she wouldn't lead him to the grave. And the longer she stayed, the more she risked he would discover her tattoo and demand her oath.

Her heart twisted.

Then again, maybe he would leave with her. If she could convince him to return to Atchison with her, there was still some hope she could achieve both of her heart's desires—a life with Merrick, and professional success. He cared about her, she could feel that in his kiss, let alone the way he made love to her. If he knew they were fated, and understood they'd be separated if she took the oath, surely he wouldn't insist on maintaining archaic vows when they could have a real future together.

As she stepped on the stairs, the hair on the back of her neck bristled. She turned her head toward the billiard room and swallowed hard. There, standing against the doorframe, Tane watched. His unblinking gaze locked with hers. His energy hit her like a square of bricks—cold, detached. Dangerous.

Anne moved closer to Gareth and hurried up the remaining stairs.

Several paces ahead of the rest of the men, Merrick moved through the twisting cavern tunnel silently. Behind him, his friends joked, they chuckled, they told tales of previous hunts and victories they had achieved. They had discovered early on he was in no mood to join in their banter and did not attempt to involve him.

Leaving Merrick to listen to the *plip-plip* of distant water and the *ching-ching* of his mail.

And wallow through his thoughts.

A Templar did not leave the field of battle. He did not allow himself to be taken captive. He fought until death claimed him, but for the first time since Merrick had touched a childhood wooden sword, he combated the fierce desire to retreat.

He had promised Anne he would return. How he would accomplish such, he did not know. He could not command his men to fight whilst he stood and watched. He could not dismiss the threat upon the gate and order them to return to the temple. Yet somehow he must find a way to hold on to the last of his soul and honor his oath to Anne.

"Merrick." Caradoc's low voice reverberated near his ear.

Merrick turned, acknowledging his companion.

"We are twenty paces away. 'Tis too quiet."

Cocking his head, Merrick observed the silence he had not recognized before. This close to the gate, they should hear the ghostly scratchings, should have encountered at least one escaping fiend. He lifted his hand, signaling the men who followed to halt. For several long moments, no one moved. Their breaths came in shallow draws. Their fingers curled around steady swords.

Merrick beckoned with his fingers. On silent steps, they inched forward toward a large, jutting slab of stone. The sound of water grew louder as it plunked into a hidden reservoir. The lantern Nikolas carried illuminated the narrow passage, filling the distant enclosure with a warm beacon of light. Enough brilliance to enrage a waiting foe.

Strangely, no beastly howl filled the cavern. No screech of rage erupted through the stillness.

Exchanging guarded glances, the men converged into a tighter group. Swords at the ready, they moved forward as one collective unit, rounding the protruding stone into a large, towering grotto.

The light bounced off stalagmites, glinted against watery stalactites. Against the far wall, a gaping maw expulsed a fetid stench, and from deep within, the moans of souls lost unto time spewed forth. Merrick's gaze riveted on the open gate, searching through the dense dark for a sign of glowing eyes, a shadow's ripple.

A *pop* from the lantern echoed like a warning horn, and all seven men froze. If Azazel's minions had not been aware of their presence, they certainly would know now. In a handful of heartbeats, the vile creatures would spill forth, claws and fangs ready to shred them to pieces. If they were lucky, no fallen knight would defend their unholy ranks this night.

Nikolas eased the lantern to the floor and slid his bow from his shoulder. Nocking an arrow, he pulled the bowstring tight and motioned for the men to spread out. William the Strong joined Nikolas. Behind them, Geoffrey aimed a crossbow above their coif-covered heads.

In unison, they loosed their arrows. Three broadheads soared through the cavern, plunged into the gate, and disappeared into the vile fog. When naught happened, they repeated the attack, this time firing two arrows per each man.

Stillness reigned.

"Naught is here," Farran observed.

"Yet the gate stands wide open." Lucan moved closer, his sword extended in front of his body. "They should be present. We have seen naught leave or enter."

Unusual to say the least. Merrick turned his gaze to the cavern's ceiling, searching for another means of escape. Mayhap Azazel's evil beasts had chosen a different route. However, naught but solid stone and a cluster of sleeping bats lurked overhead.

"Close the gate," he instructed. "Azazel has never left an open portal unattended—we must take this to Mikhail at once."

As Farran, Caradoc, and Geoffrey moved to shove the massive boulder back into place, Merrick shared a knowing look with Lucan. Neither would dare to speak their thoughts, but both realized something far darker had occurred tonight. What it was, they could not guess. Yet an open, unattended portal could only be a harbinger to something deadly. Something had come out. Or worse, someone had been invited in.

Merrick sheathed his sword and pushed his coif off his head. Stuffing it under his arm, he shook out his hair and let the cold air cool his scalp.

"Farran, you will drive. Return us to the temple immediately," Merrick barked.

He picked up the lantern, waited for the slab to settle into its deep groove, then took off at a brisk walk, retreating from whence they had come.

"What do you make of that, Merrick?" Nikolas asked as he jogged up beside him.

"I do not know, but it cannot be good. 'Twas not even a being inside." He did not voice the suspicion that turned his stomach into a mass of knots. 'Twas the certain kind of diversion Fulk would attempt, should he seek to draw his enemy away from his real target. He would be the most skilled of Azazel's knights, and he would understand his threat lay with his cousin, Merrick. Should he wish to avoid Merrick's sword, he would send them elsewhere.

A tactic Merrick shared with his cousin. Particularly when faced with limited numbers.

Convinced of the theory, Merrick quickened his pace and jogged down the rest of the corridor, forcing his men to assume the same tempo or be faced with the cavern's dark.

CHAPTER 28

The hollow sound of tires skidding to a stop against gravel brought Anne to her feet. She leapt out of her chair and rushed to the window, flinging aside the curtains to look down at the parking lot. Dust rose beneath two silver SUVs. In unison, eight doors sprung open and seven men filed out. All seven walked, unaided, to the front door at a purposeful stride.

Her heart flipped against her ribs as joy soared through her. "Merrick," she whispered as her fingers curled into the thin sheers. Home at last. *Safe.*

She breathed a sigh of relief, and the tension that had coiled in her shoulders relaxed. She bowed her head, pressing it to the cool glass as a smile broke across her face. Any minute now, he would walk through the door. He'd take her in his arms, kiss her until she couldn't see straight, and she'd let him know in every way she could contrive, how very glad she was to see him.

Then she'd do what his safety demanded and drag him into a conversation where she revealed their fated pairing and begged him to abandon all this. If he refused, when he slept, she would leave.

Frowning against the unpleasantness that clamped her belly down tight, she dismissed the thoughts of her possible departure. Heaven above, she'd miss this man. For as long as she breathed, she'd never again find this kind of bliss. He'd gotten under her skin, dug down so deep she didn't stand a chance at forgetting him. She had to explain tonight. No matter how he protested, no matter how angry he became at her suggestion he leave all this—and he would most assuredly—she must find the courage to convince him to walk away. If he did, the mark would never threaten him again. They could live their lives together, without the worry of his duty to protect the nail and the death it would bring.

If he refused, she would leave to prevent the destructive fate from occurring. Without her oath, Merrick would stay alive. Maybe not safe from harm, but alive.

Anne turned from the window and went to her bedroom where she pulled on a long, hunter green nightgown. Belting her robe around her waist, she sat down on the bed and picked up a book off her nightstand. As she stretched out her feet, something heavy hit the floor. She glanced down to see the dagger Gareth had left her with, its long blade glinting in the lamplight. Bending over the edge of the mattress, she plucked it off the floor.

A rustle at her door brought her smile back in full force. She snapped upright, her pulse a rapid tap-dance in her veins. Holding her breath, she willed herself to wait, to resist the urge to leap out of the bed and meet Merrick at the door.

It opened slowly, as if he expected her to be asleep. Anne silenced a giggle by chewing on her lower lip.

When he stepped inside, Anne's smile vanished. Instead of Merrick, she stared at Tane. His expression was anything but joyous. He stalked toward her, determined.

A scream rose in the back of her throat, and she scrambled backward. The headboard thwarted her retreat. Tightening one hand around the dagger, she stuffed it behind her and slid off the opposite side of the bed, keeping her distance.

"Lady Anne, stop," he commanded in a low voice.

From the doorway, he held up one hand, palm out. "I will not hurt you."

Anne swallowed hard, mistrusting the glint in his green eyes. Though perspiration turned her palms clammy, she wound her fingers around the bone hilt more securely. "Merrick will be here any minute, Tane. You better leave."

He shook his head, a wry smile curling one corner of his mouth. "Nay. Merrick and the others speak with Mikhail."

Panic pressed down on her hard. Her lungs constricted, together with her throat, and she fought for the ability to breathe. His eyes held a far different light than any other time she'd encountered him. Somehow darker. More brittle. She glanced at the narrow space between him and the doorway. Could she make it to the doorway before he caught up with her?

As if he sensed her intention, he widened his stance and blocked her escape.

Anne's mind worked in triple time. She couldn't go out the window—the drop to the ground would break her legs. She didn't dare scream. He'd reach her long before anyone made it up the stairs. And unless he was so close she couldn't hope to miss, the dagger in her hand was useless. If he got that close, he'd overpower her.

Yet contrary to the signs of imminent violence, his voice wasn't clipped, his features weren't tight. A strange surge of peace wafted off him, conflicting with the dangerous energy he'd radiated earlier tonight.

She willed the panic from her mind. The only possible way out of this would be to keep Tane talking. If she could stall long enough, cooperate just enough to make him believe she'd go along with him, Merrick would be here to diffuse the situation. Though Lord help him—she feared Tane wouldn't come out unscathed.

"What do you want, Tane?"

He pointed at the bed. "Sit."

She glanced at the fluffy comforter, then looked to him once more. Hesitantly, she set a knee on the mattress, then another, all the while her gaze glued to his body, looking for some sign he intended to pursue her. In the middle of the bed, she knelt, the hand that held the dagger still planted in the middle of her lower back.

"You will come with me, Anne. You will say naught until I grant you leave to speak. I have no desire to harm you."

"I don't want to go—"

Against his thigh, he clenched a hand into a tight fist. "I have not given you leave to speak."

Anne gulped down a sob, nearly choking. Oh God, she should have locked the door. But never in a million years would she have thought someone would be stupid enough to break in. These were her rooms. Her safe haven, given to her by Gabriel.

Approaching the edge of the bed, he reached for her.

She flinched, anticipating the pain of his fingers. But to her surprise, he did nothing more than stroke her hair.

"So pretty. I had wondered if it was soft."

As his strong fingers brushed against her shoulder, her vision blurred. At once, her second sight kicked in, and images of Tane flashed rapid fire within her mind. Tane amid a great hall, sitting in a chair of velvet, a beautiful woman at his side. The woman gazed at him in adoration, a look he returned tenfold. Then Tane at the head of a mighty army, and at his side, another knight bore a standard she didn't recognize. They led a long chain of prisoners alongside the parading horses. A man stumbled, and a knight slammed the flat side of his sword into his back. Tane rode over, stuffed his blade beneath his man's chin, his glower fierce.

The third scene brought her to the present, showing Tane confined within what she presumed to be his room. He knelt before a small altar, made the sign of the cross across his chest. It shifted once more, painting a picture that stole her breath. Beneath a graffiti-covered bridge, he squatted beside a raggedy teenage girl and a younger boy. From within his duffel bag, Tane produced several cans of food and a loaf of bread that resembled the hardened loaves Anne had dined on. The young girl wept, threw her arms around his neck, and held on tight. Tane embraced her as a brother might, then let her go to rumple her hair.

As her senses returned, the visions fading to black then slowly restoring her sight, Anne gazed up in wonder at the man who touched her shoulder. What kind of man fed homeless children then kidnapped women?

He ran his hand across her hair once more, and Anne concentrated on his energy. Beneath a hardened layer of what she could only describe as hate, waves of compassion oozed forth. It tangled with something she couldn't recognize, a foreign matter she'd never encountered. There, that generosity got lost, unable to rise to the surface.

"Put out your hands," he instructed.

Determined she could somehow reach in to his buried goodness, Anne thrust her hands in front of her. He didn't want to hurt her, she sensed that innately. Whether he would, if she resisted, was a variable she didn't care to chance. Besides, no matter how she might like to consider otherwise, in the depths of her heart, she knew she couldn't use the dagger to hurt him. She didn't have it in her to physically harm a human being—particularly when she recognized no immediate threat.

His gaze fell to the dagger in her open palm. Approval sparked in his eyes. "Good. You keep yourself protected. 'Tis wise until your oaths are said." Holding her wrists in one hand, he plucked the dagger from her palm with the other and tossed it aside.

Before she could react, he wound a thick scrap of cotton around her wrists, then looped a sturdy rope in place. With a snug yank, he cinched her wrists together. "I do not wish to gag you, Anne. Will you stay silent?"

Wide-eyed she looked up at him. His expression twisted, as if he anguished over his actions. It lit hope within her, encouraged the confidence her behavior was the right approach. Nodding, she agreed.

Tane stepped back from the bed. "You will come with me now." He hauled her into his arms. With Anne's knees

dangling over his elbow, he carted her out of the room
and pulled the French doors shut. In the hall, he flipped
off her light switch, shut the exterior door, and bounded
down the stairs.

The cold November air penetrated her flimsy nightclothes, and Anne shivered as he carried her to a truck.
Though her hands were tied, they shook with fear. Safety
lay with Merrick. Trusting her second sight got her bound,
and though the instinctual need to scream her head off
pounded at her senses, she couldn't shake the suspicion
that if she did, whatever decency Tane possessed would
shatter.

He set her in the passenger's seat, locked the door, and
shut her in before he climbed behind the wheel. The engine purred to life, the dash lights filled the cab with a
neon blue glow.

Anne whimpered.

At the sound, Tane turned up the heater. "You may not
speak yet," he murmured.

Merrick shifted his weight as he stood before Mikhail.
Every instinct he possessed demanded he rush to Anne,
inform her he had returned. Yet duty instructed him to suffer through the necessary delay. No matter how he craved
her, he could not cast aside the more important matters.

"You say you found naught?" Mikhail looked between
the seven gathered knights.

"Aye. 'Twas barren," Nikolas answered. "We fired nine
arrows into the maw, and naught came forth."

Mikhail rose from his desk to pace before them. Head
bowed, hands clasped behind his back, his steps were
slow and thoughtful.

"I suspect 'tis a diversion."

Merrick's interjection brought Mikhail to a stop. Pivoting, he stared at Merrick. "A diversion?"

Merrick nodded. "Have you heard any other reports?"

The grimace that crossed Mikhail's features served as
answer enough. He dragged a hand down his face and

closed his eyes. "There was much disturbance at the third gate. So far, it has held, according to Raphael. He is there now, watching. But I fear you are correct, Merrick. Louisiana calls to Azazel. I had hoped I was wrong, but he plans to move on the third nail."

"Then we are to leave?" Caradoc asked.

Mikhail shook his head. "We wait for Raphael's word. 'Tis possible the gate will hold. Until we know Azazel's true strength, we dare not anticipate an attack, for if we leave en masse, we will certainly reveal our hand. He will track our movements. Have you all formed a strategy?"

Merrick expelled a breath he had not realized he held. "We have. Gareth will require the details, but they are simple enough we can inform him should the need arise."

"Good. You will meet with me tomorrow to discuss it. For now, go and rest."

As the men relaxed their rigid stances and filed toward the door, Mikhail called out, "A moment, Merrick."

Tempering a groan, Merrick hung back and waited for the door to close. When it latched in place, Mikhail surprised him with a smile. "I thought you might wish to know of Anne's endeavors today."

He could not help but wince. If the last time he had left proved anything, he could only imagine what kind of trouble Anne had created for herself today. Had she finally sated her curiosity and breeched the inner sanctum?

Low and warm, Mikhail's chuckle bounced off the walls. "'Tis not as you think. She has tamed Simon."

Merrick's eyebrows shot up his forehead. "You jest."

"Nay. Gareth relayed to me she spoke with Simon at length. In stroking the old man's pride, she has convinced him to hire on three chefs and reevaluate the menu to accommodate a woman's taste."

A laugh rumbled in Merrick's chest, then rose up his throat to break free in a hearty burst. "'Tis a tactic of a lady—to know her servants' needs and negotiate their tempers. She will do well within these halls."

"You need to find her intended. She cannot accomplish

anything with the men on edge. Her oath must be sworn, and my knights need to free themselves from the distraction."

Dutifully Merrick nodded. Though he would rather walk over hot coals than locate her intended, he knew he had delayed long enough. She should already be paired. But his selfishness had gotten in the way. "I will commence the hunt again tomorrow. If I may have your leave, I would like to attend to her."

"Of course. Gareth said she was quite distressed over your absence. Go. Tell her you have arrived in one piece."

Anne distressed. Merrick suspected he would never get over the way her worry warmed his blood. Unable to hold back his smile, he gave Mikhail a crisp nod and pulled open the door. A few more minutes and he would hold her. Taste the sweet honey of her kiss. His cock stirred at the thought, swelling against his thigh as he anticipated the warmth of Anne's body against his.

"Merrick, a word with you?"

Pivoting, Merrick checked a frustrated mutter. His gaze settled on Lucan, who leaned against the wall. Recalling he had wanted to speak to his friend about his lapse in duty, he beckoned Lucan to join him as he marched down the hall.

"You did not tell me Ranulf accosted Anne."

Lucan choked on whatever he had intended to say. "I was not aware such had happened."

A fission of annoyance slid down Merrick's spine. As he had suspected, Lucan had not taken his duty seriously enough. He ground his teeth together, biting off sharp reprimand. When he felt in control of his reaction enough to chance words, he said simply, "If you had been near her, not only would you have known, but she would have also not experienced Ranulf and Gottfried's threat."

Lucan had the grace to be chagrined. He ducked his head in deference. "Apologies, Merrick. But 'tis Anne I wanted to speak of."

Anticipating another lecture on the folly of his ways, Merrick asked through clenched teeth, "What of her?"

"I did see her that afternoon. I have not had the chance to speak with you about what I observed. She asked to use my phone."

To contact her sister, most likely. Merrick continued down the hall, unconcerned by the notion Anne had made a call.

"I cared little for her conversation, Merrick. The things I heard . . ."

He hesitated long enough that Merrick stopped and had to turn around. The way his brother's features contorted spoke to his discomfort with his news and set off horns of warning inside Merrick's head.

"I fear she plans to leave with our secrets."

Merrick blinked. Once. Twice. Three times before he could find his tongue. "What do you mean?"

"Exactly as I said—I believe she intends to leave with the Templar secrets. I cannot recall her precise words, but what I heard made her intentions clear."

Merrick's heart did a slow roll, and the breath he attempted hitched in his throat. Anne leave? She could not. She had a duty to fulfill. He furrowed his brows. She could not think to leave. Mikhail just informed him she had negotiated the kitchens. If she did not intend to stay, she would not go to such trouble . . . Would she?

Nay, she would not. Lucan's mistrust clouded his reason.

Anne was upstairs, waiting. He had seen the light in her room, glimpsed her silhouette against the window. She worried for him. She *would not* leave.

"Have you found her intended?"

Merrick bristled at the second insinuation in less than ten minutes' passing that he neglected his duties. He needed no one to point out he delayed her discovery for his own means. The knowledge plagued him as it were. "Nay," he snapped.

Taking the hint that Merrick did not want to discuss

Anne further, Lucan gratefully fell back. "I shall see you on the morrow, Merrick."

Merrick did not bother with an answer—his thoughts had spiraled too far into guilt to try. Selfish. He was naught but a selfish bastard bent on gratifying his own desires. She would not leave, yet Anne could no longer stay with him. Saints' blood, he had denied two of his closest friends the ability to learn whether she belonged to him. He had no cause to deny the salvation of those who had never once broken loyalty with him.

Grinding his teeth, he abruptly changed direction.

Tane he would not find—he rarely spent the night within the temple. But Declan . . . Declan Merrick could locate with little effort. He would learn Declan's mark, and then speak to Anne.

CHAPTER 29

†

Merrick pushed open the infirmary's door and let himself inside. From a bed across the spacious room, Declan turned his head. On seeing Merrick, he attempted to sit, but the effort required was too much, and he collapsed back into the bed.

Merrick approached the bed. "How do you fare, brother?"

The big Scot answered with a weak grin. "My arm feels afire, and my belly protests the broth Uriel feeds me. How do you ken I fare?"

"Aye, you are well enough." Merrick laughed low. "Your lazy arse has slept through much."

The humor slipped from Declan's expression as he raised himself on his good arm. "How fares the Lady Anne? Have you located her intended?"

"She is well and still without a mate."

Hope lit behind Declan's eyes, so bright and desperate Merrick could not stand to look upon it. He turned away, casting his gaze to the window. His gut cinched tight against a wash of guilt. A better man he did not know. Anne would do well to have Declan as her intended. "Tell me, brother, what is the mark you bear?"

Declan eased into the bed and shook his head. "Nay. 'Tis meant for her eyes alone."

Merrick pulled in a long breath. He had been so consumed with his own attraction for Anne, he had ignored the desperation of his friends. All looked to her as their salvation, and only one man would know the light she carried within her. The others, including himself, would look on, outwardly happy for their brother, while inwardly they would die a little more. If all had acted as he had, the Order would break to pieces.

Casting his gaze to his boots, he let his shoulders slump in defeat. He must surrender her. "I will bring her to you. 'Tis my hope you match."

Declan squeezed Merrick's forearm, a silent gesture of thanks. He closed his eyes, the smile once again pulling faint across his face. "She enjoys my company. 'Tis all I have ever asked for."

Indeed, and exactly what Declan needed. He would never accept a woman on the simple basis their marks paired. Not after surviving the horror of his first wife.

Merrick clamped his hand over the Scot's burly knuckles. "Rest, Declan. I will bring Anne here."

At Declan's acquiescent nod, Merrick turned toward the door. From the darkened corner behind the wooden portal, Uriel's gaze settled on him, silent judgment written in his stare. He ignored the archangel's reproach and let himself out, knowing there was but one thing he could do to right the wrongs he had indulged in.

On heavy steps, he made his way through the stone corridors to Anne's stairwell. There, he braced himself to tell her their time had come to an end. He would resume his chambers, take his leave of her tonight. For in his heart he knew, should he spend one more night lost in her heavenly embrace, he would never leave.

Silence greeted him at her door. He eased it open, let himself into the darkened rooms. When she did not call out to him, disappointment he had no right to feel tightened his chest. He had not realized how he looked forward to her greeting, how he had become accustomed to her hello.

Ah well, 'twas better this way. He could crawl beside her in the bed and hold her close. Tell her in the morning.

He opened the French doors and looked to the bed.

Rumpled covers greeted him.

Fear, as Merrick had never known, surged through his veins. His insides turned to a quivering mass. "Anne?" The tremble in his voice shamed him, and he swallowed to restore its strength. "Anne?"

When she did not answer, he charged to the bathroom, convinced he would find her in the tub.

The empty bathroom sent his heart clanging into his rib cage.

Merrick rushed to the window, pulled the drapes aside and stared down at the line of vehicles the Order used. In the far corner, one empty spot stood out like a gaping chasm.

Lucan's words rang in his ears. *She intends to leave.*

Merrick closed his eyes to the noise. Nay, she could not have left the grounds. Someone would have seen her, would have alerted Mikhail. Would have alerted him. Likely, she had wandered off, used his absence to her advantage, and ventured into the inner sanctum. When he found her there, he would follow through on his punishment no matter how she protested.

Only something did not feel right.

His gaze swept across her room. Shoes near the door, her clothes in a pile beside the bed. On her nightstand lay the book she had been reading, and her bed looked slept in. Whilst Anne was not a particularly neat person, she would not leave her bed rumpled if she intended to . . .

Everything inside Merrick ground to a standstill as his eyes skimmed across a dagger lying on the mattress. Polished steel peeked from beneath the thick down quilt.

He lunged toward the bed and snatched the blade into his hands. As he held it, inspecting the tiny scars embedded into the polished steel scabbard, footsteps sounded behind him. He spun around to find Gareth in the open doorway. Merrick whirled on him. "You were with Anne today. Did she speak of leaving?"

Gareth's eyebrows lifted into his hair. "Leaving? Nay. She was anxious for your return." He nodded to the blade Merrick held. "I gave her the dagger so she would feel safe until you arrived. She was quite worried about the men."

"*You* gave her this?"

"Aye, Merrick."

The bitter taste of bile rose in the back of his throat. If Anne had been genuinely worried about the knights within these halls, she would not leave her only means of defense behind. He glanced once more at the bed, the twisted covers, the askew pillows. 'Twas then he noticed the barren post at the foot of her side of the bed. Where she usually hung her robe, the thick wood column stood empty.

His gaze darted to the narrow bookshelf, full of her precious research materials and reference books. He knew then, she had not left. Not of her own accord.

Merrick palmed the blade and bolted from the room. He barreled down the stairs, rounded the corner, and descended into the stone corridors. Racing through the twists and turns, he blindly drove forward, oblivious to those he passed and the curious stares that followed. He did not stop until he reached Mikhail's chamber.

Barging in without so much as a knock, Merrick slammed a fist down on Mikhail's desk. "Someone has taken Anne."

As Tane navigated southbound down the highway, a war waged in his head. He could not tolerate Anne's voice, for every time she spoke, the protests of his heart made it impossible to concentrate. He had sought only to speak with her. To engage her in a conversation safe inside her chambers. When she had looked at him in fright, however, the darkness forbade him decency. Azazel's taint declared he had a right to her and refused to let him walk away.

He hated the fact he had scared her. Despised his inability to remain noble.

Yet he could not conquer the black stains within his heart.

The last fragments of his once-noble soul demanded he explain, and he sucked in a fortifying breath. Tightening his fingers on the wheel, he stole a glance at her, grimacing inwardly at the stark terror that turned her delicate features white.

"Do not be afraid, milady. You are safe with me. You will always be safe at my side. We shall talk in a few moments, and you will learn 'tis I you are intended for."

She shook her head violently, opened her mouth to speak. Thinking better of it, she clamped it shut and pursed her lips so tight he caught the gleam of bloodless white.

"I know you care little for me now, but in time, you will learn I am quite generous. I would lay down my life for you, Anne."

Silence came easier than words. Her protests only added to the doubt that plagued his thoughts. Mayhap he had been wrong. *Nay,* he argued vehemently. He could not be wrong. She had not discovered her intended. The fact they had yet to speak marked the truth for what it was. She was his eternal light, he her immortal blade.

The high-rises of Kansas City grew skyward around the truck, and he steered through a maze of one-way streets into the heart of the old warehouses, the crumbling fixtures near the old stockades. Beneath a tangle of bridges, the warm glow of fires illuminated the painted concrete. He nosed into a shadowy corner, his agitation lessening as he joined the dregs of the city. They embraced him here. Never questioned why he came, never asked about the long blade he wore at his side. To the homeless of Kansas City, he was their strange equal, and their acceptance soothed his darkened soul.

Shutting off the engine, Tane twisted to face Anne. "I will carry you to the fire. 'Tis too cold for you to walk, and you already shiver. There you will warm yourself, and I shall prove myself to you."

To everyone.

He jumped out of the cab and hurried around to her door. Opening it, he scooped her into his arms and carried her toward the distantly gathered homeless. As he trekked beneath the overpass, a breeze gushed around the cement pillars. On it rode the rotting stench of death.

Tane slowed to a standstill, his senses on alert, his gaze scanning the thick surrounding shadows. Stillness settled around him. Ominous silence. He eased Anne to her feet, and his hand crept over the pommel of his sword. Jerking his head toward the SUV, he whispered the insistent order, "Go back. Run."

Anne's chin lifted in defiance. Sharp refusal made her eyes glitter. But as the breeze once again brushed by, stirring her long hair, her eyes inched wider, and apprehension morphed her expression into stone. She glanced at him, seeking confirmation of the stench she could not have missed.

"Go!" Tane demanded.

Anne had barely turned her back when the shadows surrounding them came to life. Pulling free from the natural darkness, vile forms took shape, elongating into creatures of nightmares. A low hiss echoed off the concrete retainers. Deathly claws scraped down the hardened stone.

Tane drew his sword with lightning speed. He scrambled to place himself between Anne and danger, feet braced apart, broadsword at the ready. Azazel's minions would not have her. If fending them off claimed the faltering bit of light he harbored in his soul, Anne would reach safety.

Flanked on one side by three demons, and on the other by four nytyms, Tane drew in a deep breath. He shifted his grip on the leather-wrapped pommel, holding it tighter, letting nearly a thousand years of reflexes take command of his body.

Behind him, Anne let out a shrill scream.

He looked only long enough to discover his error before he swore beneath his breath. From the opposite side of the SUV, two demons loped toward her, their gangly humanoid forms caught in midtransition from a body of shadows into false replicas of man. Yellowed fangs snapped as one taloned hand snatched at Anne. As one passed the silver vehicle, a strong fist slammed into the windshield, shattering it. It clutched a jagged shard of glass and advanced on Anne.

An angry battle cry broke from Tane's throat. Charging blindly, he reached her side a heartbeat before those deadly claws connected with her slender arm. In one arcing sweep of his sword, he cleaved the offensive arm from the creature's body. It dropped to the ground, writhing, before folding in on itself and dissolving into a pool of shadows.

Anne flashed him a brief look of gratitude. Then her long hair whipped into her face as she swiveled and ran toward the SUV. He heard the slam of the door, but did not have time to confirm she made it inside. A heavy chunk of wood thumped him in the gut, doubling him over, stealing the very air from his lungs.

Stumbling, Tane struggled to remain upright. He lifted his head, forced his arm to move before his body and defend the next strike. The demon swung again. Wood met polished steel, and the sturdy collision vibrated all the way to Tane's shoulder. His clamped lungs let go at the same time, granting him the ability to breathe. He sucked in air like a drowning man. Throwing his weight forward, he thrust the long blade deep into the demon's gut, not stopping until bone met the razor-sharp tip.

With a fierce backward yank, Tane freed his broadsword. An agonized scream filled the night. As it died into a high-pitched whine, the demon collapsed in a useless heap.

Yet total victory would not come so easily. The creature's death blanketed Tane in darkness that dealt his soul a heavy blow. His vision faltered, and he stumbled. God's teeth, it had been too long since he had fought so many on his own. Once he would have disposed of these nuisances in minutes. Now, he could only pray he would survive.

Forcing back the encroaching darkness, Tane blinked several times to clear the black spots from his vision and gritted his teeth. He had only just lifted his head to assess his opponents when two pairs of claws raked down his unarmored back. A groan tore free, the sound giving him much-needed strength. He sidestepped, ignoring the sticky feel of blood that ran beneath his shredded shirt.

Through the windshield, his gaze connected with Anne's. Before him, Azazel's creatures converged, now recognizing they must remove him if they were to have the seraph. In that moment, Tane knew he could not risk the possibility of his damaged soul. She was too priceless, too worthy to the Order, too much a weapon for Azazel to ever claim. Mayhap he would never know the salvation she offered as his mate, but he would risk eternal damnation to fulfill his vow to protect her.

He thrust his arm across his body at the empty street behind the SUV. "Go! Take yourself from here!"

Freedom.

Bound hands hovering over the keys, Anne stared at the shattered windshield. Escape from Tane, from those horrifying creatures rested beneath her fingertips. All she had to do was turn the key, back out of here. Return to Merrick . . . go home.

She wasn't a prisoner anymore, didn't have to confront the damning circumstances of her fate. Of Merrick's fate. Heck, she could bypass Atchison and keep going, assuring Merrick could never find her, force her into an oath, and doom himself.

She could go all the way to California and check on Sophie. She would miss Merrick beyond belief, and she'd sacrifice every professional opportunity she'd worked so hard to build. But she could prevent him from discovering their pairing and being sent to protect the third nail.

Anne keyed the engine.

As it purred to life, polished steel glinted beyond the windshield. Her gaze focused on the bright gleam, her body recoiling as Tane arced his sword from shoulder to thigh and sliced deep into a fiendish chest cavity. The disgusting smell of decaying flesh poured through the SUV's vents. Her measly dinner churned violently.

Farther down the dark back alley, figures gathered near a glowing trash can, the noises outside drawing their attention. Instinctively, she knew the archangels would be furious if news of this attack spread. They might be homeless, people not often given much credit, but wagging tongues could still damage, no matter the source.

Tane evaded a blow aimed at his head, then lunged forward, spearing the smaller, less coordinated thing. Coalesced shadows spewed forth, rolling down his deadly blade, pooling against his hand. He faltered again, the effort of combating so many taking a significant toll on his body.

Come on. Stand up straight.

Catching herself praying for Tane's safety, Anne closed her eyes on the scene, acknowledging why she hadn't yet moved the SUV out of gear. He'd taken her. Sworn he wouldn't hurt her, but kidnapped her all the same. Now he was fighting to protect her.

Urging her to run away.

He dropped to his knees, his sword dangling uselessly at his side. Blood turned his white shirt into a patchwork crimson cloth. Rivulets ran down his back, trickled across his weakened shoulder.

Anne's heart lurched in her throat. He was immortal . . . but Mikhail said they could die.

Damn it, she couldn't leave him here like this. Even if he was a bit crazy, a bit frightening, she couldn't abandon him to die alone. Not when he'd set her free and set himself in the heart of danger.

She shut off the engine and glanced around the SUV, searching for something that would cut the rope around her wrists. Her gaze instead settled on a sharp object in the backseat, partially hidden in shadow. Shuffling sideways, she contorted her body until she could reach both hands into the space between the seats and kicked with her feet to tip her farther over. Her fingertips grasped cold metal. Encouraged, she wriggled back into her seat and brought her hands in front of her face.

Similar to the dagger Gareth gave her earlier, a small blade protruded from a bone hilt. The designs in the grip were different, save for one—both daggers brandished the Templar cross.

A quick glance out the window revealed Tane had moved, but not by much. He held his sword feebly above his head, struggling for the ability to rise.

Awkwardly, Anne worked at the door handle until it gave, then kicked the door open. Her bare feet hit the pavement running straight for the closest of the two remaining creatures. Three feet away, she lifted her hands over her head, and with the last stride forward, threw all her weight into the strike. Flesh gave beneath her hands, the dagger sinking deep into a shadowy back that had more substance than she'd imagined.

Her stomach heaved again. She ignored the taste of bile at the back of her throat and yanked with all her might. The dagger pulled free.

Again she stabbed, and again, until the creature gave up the notion of attacking Tane and turned to face her. Fear wedged between her lungs as unholy eyes gleamed a bright red-orange. She backed up, her courage vanishing beneath the demon's foul stare.

At her side, Tane let out a muffled curse. She glanced his way long enough to see him rise on one knee, before a rush of air drew her attention back to her opponent. Claws sliced in front of her face, a breath away from her nose.

"Damnation!" Tane wheezed as he pushed to his feet. "Get in the truck and leave this place!"

Anne shook her head, backing up another step, her gaze glued on him. He stepped in front of her, finishing off the beast she'd wounded with one neat slice across the belly. He barely had time to swivel before the remaining creature set upon him.

Jaw tight, expression hardened against the pain, Tane stepped forward and fended off the blow meant for Anne's head. She backpedaled closer to the SUV's front bumper. He wheezed with the effort of maintaining the fight, and for several terrifying heartbeats, Anne thought he'd fall to his knees again. But with a vigorous shake of his head, he reclaimed his balance and ran the lesser creature through.

One hollow, ghostly moan filled the air around them before the beast melted in a puddle of fathomless black.

Tane doubled over, hands on his knees, panting.

She watched the gathered people, surprised when they slowly turned away, their interest fading, as if seeing unholy creatures from the grave was a nightly occurrence.

When Tane's breathing leveled out, he lifted his head and caught her gaze. Mixed emotion flickered behind his green eyes, combining gratitude with appreciation with regret. He shook his head. "'Twas foolishness, Anne, to do such."

To her surprise, a slight smile tugged at her lips. "I couldn't leave you behind."

The fierceness returned to his gaze with her simple remark, his look once more that of a man on a mission. A man possessed by a convoluted mistruth.

He took her by the elbow. "Come. We must finish our discussion. 'Twill take time for Azazel to learn of his failure. He shall not come again this night. 'Twould be folly."

Denying her opportunity to protest, he steered her in a semicircle and guided her toward the glowing lights at the far end of the alley. His limp slowed their progress, the blood on his palm wetted hers. Streetwise stragglers parted, allowing them access to the fire. A few offered smiles. One lone man greeted Tane with a hearty wave.

With a pained grimace, he balanced her as she sat beside a lighted barrel, then helped her pull her robe around her body. Someone offered him a blanket, which he accepted without word. Tucking it about Anne's shoulders, he covered her from the wintry breeze. He rocked back on his heels and set his hand beneath her chin. As he lifted her face, he offered a weak smile. In his gaze, apology burned, along with a smattering of regret. She struggled to hold on to her earlier anger, but the way he'd unhesitatingly defended her made fury hard to find. She wanted to hate him for the danger he exposed her to, for taking her against her will. Instead, all she felt was a strange stirring of pity for this noble, misguided knight.

Anne's sad eyes cut Tane to the quick, and before the heartfelt stare could penetrate his will, he jerked his hand away. He stared at the flames in a desperate attempt to sift through his conflicting emotions and locate the truth that lay within his heart. Already he wronged her. He had abused her person by binding her hands and had risked not just her safety but her status as well. 'Twas only one thing he could do to right his actions—prove they were paired. Once she realized this, she would have no choice but to forgive, and he could begin to make amends for his unacceptable wrongs.

He rolled up his right sleeve, exposing his forearm. In the flickering light, a long half-moon scar glinted white as it wound from elbow to wrist. Unable to confront the silent accusations in her gaze, he looked at the fire and turned his arm up in front of her lap. "I was twenty-four. 'Twas my first battle to defend my father's lands from a neighboring lord. We won the day and brought back many prisoners. On the return trip home, however, one of my men flogged a man too wounded to match our hurried pace. I sought to stop him, and he challenged my command. In the fight that followed, his blade shredded through my leather gauntlet. 'Twas deep, but the knight soon learned his error."

His gaze narrowed, the scene as fresh in his memory as if it had happened the day before. The fight, the pain, the shattering of brothers' love. His oldest sibling he had never seen again. "I sent him on his way. A year later, the man lost his life to a border skirmish."

Chancing a glance at her, he took in the way her eyes followed the narrow white line. She studied it so thoroughly, 'twas as if she recognized the flaw, and Tane's heart leapt to his throat. He pivoted to face her fully. "You recognize it," he breathed. "Show me the one that matches."

Anne's eyes widened again, large saucers that made her blue eyes stand out like bright beads. She shook her head in rapid time. "I can't."

He gathered her bound hands and pressed his lips to the backs of her knuckles. "Anne, do not fear me. I beg you. I meant naught of what befell you tonight. Once I was honorable, and I shall spend the rest of my days proving what lies buried in my heart. I cannot control the darkness that guides me now. In time, 'twill subside." His voice caught, and he cleared the emotion away with a short cough. "I swear this on my life."

Her throat worked as she swallowed. She closed her eyes as she shook her head once more. When she looked at him again, Tane could not mistake the fine mist of tears that gathered in the corners of those lovely blue orbs.

"I'm not yours, Tane," she whispered.

He drew back, whipped by the fierce lash of disbelief. "You are. How else would you recognize my scar?"

She opened her mouth, then shut it, only to repeat the motion once again. He watched the indecision pass across her face, each flicker of her expression turning his gut into a chain of tight knots. He gave her hands a gentle shake of encouragement. "You may tell me anything. I will carry your words to my grave, should you ask me to."

"I see things," she murmured as she pulled her hands free from his. "I saw the scene you described when you touched my hair earlier. But I'm not your intended, Tane. My mark isn't the same."

Stung, Tane scowled. She must be wrong. She had fought for him. Risked her own life to aid his. It could not be possible they did not share a predetermined bond. "Show me!" he thundered.

She shrunk away from him, wincing. "I can't."

"You can, and you will. Else I will assume your fear of me stays your tongue. If you speak the truth, lady, best you prove your words."

In her hesitation, he sensed her fear. Of what, he could not be certain. Him mayhap. The way he had forced his will upon her. Did she think he would so force her, once their oath was shared? "Anne, though I doubt your claim, I have no right to hold you if we are not paired. I am not like Merrick. I will not keep you chained if you are not mine."

She shifted position, rocking onto one hip. Slowly, she extended her slender left leg and set a sock-clad foot in his lap. Had she the use of her hand, the gesture would have been elegant, yet with her balance threatened, she toppled sideways, catching herself on her elbow. Her muffled mewl as her skin ground into the pavement cut him deep. He reached for her, intending to help her upright.

Twisting, she refused his help. "No. Look for yourself."

Tane stared at her foot, anxiety thrumming through his veins. His pulse jumped chaotically, and to his horror, the overwhelming understanding that he had somehow erred settled into his spine. Not wanting to see the evidence of his mistake, but unable to accept her words, he tugged the sock down her foot to expose her ankle.

Twined around her creamy skin, twin serpents wound together, their bodies crossing midway in an eerie depiction of the Templar cross. The very same art that wound around Merrick's arm.

He let go, her skin scorching his fingers. Christ's blood, he was a dead man.

"He does not know."

Anne shook her head. "No. Telling him will kill him. My visions, and Mikhail's words, say it's so."

A thousand emotions crashed down upon his shoulders. Grief, pain, guilt and shame flooded through him.

His lungs felt tight, his chest a band of iron that refused to expand. Righting her sock, he set her foot from his lap and sank his head into his hands. He had accused Merrick wrongly, had escorted a seraph into formidable danger. Worse, he had disobeyed every oath and vow by taking Anne, and in so doing, betrayed the one man he most admired. Merrick, who had trusted him with the secrets of the Templar. Merrick, who gave a man who had lost everything something to believe in.

By all that was sacred, he deserved to die.

CHAPTER 30

Anne huddled into the scratchy wool blanket. The smell of mildew assaulted her nose, threatening to send her into a sneezing fit. A miserable prospect, given she lacked the use of her hands. Her fingers felt numb, Tane had bound them so tight.

Beside her, Tane stared into the firelight. The conflict that warred behind his eyes made the battle Merrick fought over his attraction to her seem small and insignificant in comparison. Though she couldn't quite decide whether Tane was just plain crazy, or if something deeper caused his grief, he mourned his actions, that much was evident. Still, while she longed to despise him, she couldn't shake the remembrance of how he'd defended her, and in that act, he earned her respect. He might have kidnapped her, but he'd sworn an oath of loyalty and he hadn't hesitated to uphold it.

"Tane." She broke the strained silence. "Unbind my hands."

He lifted his head, her voice drawing him from his thoughts. He reached for his sword, then as if he thought better of drawing it in public, dropped his hand from the leather-wrapped pommel and picked up her bound wrists. He pried at the knot, the task more difficult without the use of a blade. At last, the rope slid free and tumbled away. Blood rushed into her fingers, turning annoying tingles into needlelike pulses of pain. Gasping, Anne rubbed at her wrists, alternately shaking them to aid the blood flow.

"I am sorry, milady," he murmured.

She couldn't bring herself to tell him it was okay. It wasn't, and if he hadn't shown such obvious remorse, she'd run like the wind. She'd been taken without consent, forced into a ride across town, and nearly attacked. Nothing about that was okay.

Despite it all, she couldn't bring herself to get up and walk to the SUV. He was in no condition to drive, and her overtaxed nerves wouldn't allow her to take the wheel.

Moreover, beyond the burning trash bin, a cluster of three dark figures huddled near a concrete pillar. Every once in a while, Anne caught the flash of something silver. She couldn't make out what it was, but the suspicious way they kept leering at her was enough to make her decide Tane was the lesser threat. He at least had no intention of harming her, despite his kidnapping. And he'd said no more demons would come tonight.

She fixed him with a hard stare. "Call Merrick, and hand me your phone. I want to return now."

He hesitated, acceptance passing behind his deep green eyes. He knew as well as she, Merrick would be furious. Her sympathetic heart got the better of her, and she offered, "I'll tell him I came willingly."

Tane shook his head. "Nay. I deserve whatever punishment Merrick chooses."

"Don't be stupid, Tane. The two of you are friends. Don't let me ruin that. Go, if you must, I'll wait here for him." She understood too well what would happen if Merrick learned the truth of Tane's errors tonight. His body already bore payment enough for those mistakes. If the SUV's windshield didn't resemble confetti, she'd drive them both back to the temple and make excuses for her absence. Tane hadn't harmed her directly. He didn't deserve Merrick's inevitable wrath.

Inclining his head toward the gathered figures, Tane made his awareness of further possible danger evident. "I vowed to protect you. I will not dishonor that oath. I will stay." He pulled the phone from his hip pocket and flipped it open to punch a solitary button before he passed it to her.

Anne lifted it to her ear in time to hear the first ring. It rang no further.

"What have you done with her?" Merrick's voice boomed through the receiver, full of the fury of a thousand men.

She cringed, even as emotion filled her to capacity and she whispered, "It's me."

"Anne?" The relief that flooded through the line turned her heart over. A heartbeat passed, a long moment that hung between them as he exhaled. God, if only she could reach through the line and touch him. She closed her eyes, imagining his face.

In a hoarse voice he asked, "Are you all right? Did he hurt you?"

"I'm fine."

"Where are you?"

"In the city. Down by the haunted houses." She glanced around, searching for a street sign. Finding a green marker, she added, "Near Twelfth Street."

"Are you safe?"

Her glance settled on Tane, the vision of how he'd fought to keep her safe rising once more. Slowly, she nodded. "I am."

"Stay there, damsel. I will arrive in a few minutes." With that, the line went dead.

Anne passed the phone back to Tane and pulled the mildewed blanket tighter around her shoulders. "Don't tell him, Tane. I care too much to see him hurt."

He bowed his head, but not before she noticed the fine

sheen of tears glimmering in his eyes. "I told you I would carry your secrets to my grave."

Merrick yanked a sweatshirt over his head and hastily unfastened his sword, exchanging it for a less noticeable dagger. "She is in Kansas City."

Behind him, Farran and Caradoc sheathed their swords. For an hour, they had turned the temple upside down, rousting men from beds, demanding to inspect their chambers. Each failure had twisted Merrick's insides so tight, he felt as if he had been turned inside out. Now the relief that flooded through him left him light-headed, a staggering effect he had not imagined could be possible.

Caradoc backed through the doorway. "I will tell the others they may cease their searching and inform Mikhail."

"I will go with you, Merrick." Farran did not ask. He grabbed at the jacket hanging on Merrick's wall and stuffed his arms in.

Mayhap a good thing, for Merrick did not trust himself should Tane still be with her. He had known, when Mikhail demanded the men step forth and present their blades, that the sword belonged to the missing man—his trusted brother. Only he had no idea where Tane might have imprisoned her. Had she not phoned, they could have searched for days before any one of them thought to scour the city.

Reason contradicted his fierce desire to gut his brother. In his heart, Merrick knew Tane would never steal away a seraph if the darkness did not drive him to insanity. Yet he could not excuse the action. Not when others suffered equally and still maintained control somewhat.

He rushed through the door without a word, Farran on his heels. At the SUV, Farran nudged him out of the way to claim the driver's side. "You are of no mind to drive."

Nay, he was not. He shook as if he had walked through a yard of ghosts. His thoughts were so jumbled he could not begin to speak, not the least of which was the realization he loved Anne. Loved her so deeply the idea of losing her left him weak. Powerless.

Lost.

He climbed into the passenger's seat and slammed the door. Farran gunned the truck in reverse, and as they sped down the side streets, Merrick could only stare at the landscape's passing blur.

The miles passed in anguished minutes, each feeling more like hours. It seemed they would never reach her, and he could not shake the deeper fear that when they arrived she would be gone again. That Tane would whisk her away, and Merrick would never again see her beautiful face, or feel the tenderness of her touch.

When the orange glow of homeless fires lit the overhanging bridges, Merrick grabbed at the door handle. He scanned the sparsely gathered people, his heart lodged firmly in his throat. Everything inside him lit up bright and burning as his eyes found long auburn hair.

Anne.

He flung the door open before the SUV stopped, his boots hitting the pavement as Farran slammed the gear into park. Merrick willed himself to walk, not run, but as he approached, and Anne looked up at him, he struck a jog. Her eyes glistened with unshed tears, the glimmer tugging fierce on his heart.

Halfway across the pavement, he spied Tane. 'Twas all it took to bring out the centuries-old warrior within him. As time ground to a halt, he was twenty-three and stood before the vile earl who dared to force himself on Merrick's mother as a payment for rents she could ill afford.

Logic fled. In one mighty blow, he drove a fist into Tane's jaw. The thick bone gave with an unmistakable *crack*. Another fist doubled the younger knight over, and Merrick wasted no time in crushing his nose.

Dimly, he heard Anne's cry, "Merrick, stop!"

Yet he could no more stop the force of his rage than he could reverse the damage Azazel had done to his soul. He grabbed Tane by the shirt, mindless of the blood that poured from his nose, and shoved him back against a crumbling warehouse wall to slam another fist into his face.

Strong arms caught Merrick from behind. He twisted, struggling to break free, but the more he fought, the more crushing the embrace became.

"Enough!"

Farran's bellow cut through Merrick's blind fury. With a fierce jerk, Farran hauled him away from Tane. Merrick watched the traitor knight crumple to the ground where he made no attempt to rise.

Farran spun Merrick around and gave him a shove in Anne's direction. "See to the lady. I will deal with Tane."

Tears trickled down Anne's face, each salty drop piercing through Merrick like a knife. For a moment, he knew not what to do. The sight of her unexpected sorrow left him speechless. Her sniffle, however, turned his heart with such force, he winced. God's teeth, he had seen countless women mourn, yet not one had ever reached in and wound such a fierce fist around his core.

His fury dissipated as he dropped to his knees before her. With a sob, Anne flung herself into his embrace. Her fingers dug into his shoulders, her dampened cheek pressed to his chest. Merrick gathered her close. "Anne," he murmured against her hair.

She turned dampened eyes to him, and he became lost in her watery gaze, wondering how this bossy little woman had ever worked her way into his heart. He dipped his head, touched his lips to hers. Soft and warm, her mouth parted beneath his, and she melted into his arms. The salty flavor of her tears reminded him she was not always brave, that behind the grand facade and stubborn will she was feminine and vulnerable. Mayhap as vulnerable as he.

When she kissed him back, his blood warmed. The chill of November night disappeared, the gathered homeless faded from his awareness. Slow, languid strokes of her tongue erased all sense of time and place, and he tangled a hand through her long hair. Her perfume infused his thoughts, awakening a storm of desire. His shaft stirred against his thigh.

On a shaky breath, Merrick eased the kiss to a lingering close. He loosed her hair, framed her face between his hands. His gaze searched hers. "Did he hurt you?"

Anne shook her head. She wound her arms around his waist and burrowed deep against his chest. Her tremble shook through his limbs, and he realized for the first time that she wore naught but her nightclothes beneath the raggedy blanket. Leaning out of her embrace, he tugged his sweatshirt over his head and pressed it into her hands.

She pulled the heavy garment on. "Take me home?"

"Aye." He could think of naught he wanted more.

At his side, Farran ushered Tane to the rear of the SUV. A cloth pressed to his nose, Tane walked with his head bowed. His posture lacked resistance, and Merrick choked down another rush of anger. It would do no good to pound him with his fists now—to give in to the urge would only stain Merrick's honor. Tane had suffered at his hands. What remained of his future would be price enough to pay.

Merrick swept Anne into his arms and carried her to the vehicle. He crawled in the middle seat beside her, ignoring Tane. With Anne tucked against his side, he fell into silence and the twenty-minute trip to the temple passed quickly.

There, however, Merrick's simple plans of disappearing with Anne crumbled around him. Caradoc and Lucan waited on the doorstep. They swamped the SUV, determined to drag Tane inside and force Merrick to join them in front of Mikhail.

"Merrick, you must make your wishes known," Lucan insisted. "He should be removed from the Order, immediately."

"Mikhail will want your explanation of what happened," Caradoc echoed.

It took all of Merrick's patience, and then some, to help Anne out of the SUV without flogging them. Farran, however, came to his rescue as Merrick collected Anne into his arms.

"Cease," he ground out evenly. "Tane can be dealt with

on the morrow. 'Tis late. Too late for words. Take our brother to Mikhail and see that he is confined for the night." He nudged Tane into Caradoc's grasp and shoved through the gathering crowd to the door.

Merrick followed in his wake, carrying a dozing Anne up the stairs into her rooms where he deposited her gently on her bed. She snuggled into the pillows and gifted him with her first smile of the evening. Though it trembled at the corners of her mouth, he could think of naught more beautiful.

"Sleep, my sweet," he murmured as he bent to kiss her good night.

She shook her head and flattened her hand against his chest. "I was so scared when you left. Then you came back, and you were okay. I wanted to talk to you . . . Then Tane . . ." She trailed off, shuddering. "Make love to me. My heart craves you so."

A feeling of tenderness unlike any he had ever known overcame Merrick. It went beyond the pleasantry of knowing she worried for him, surpassed the rise of desire that accompanied her simple words. It swamped through his veins, thickened his tongue, and closed his throat. He stepped back from the bed to shed his clothes. At the same time, she shimmied out of her robe and gown. She leaned over and clicked off the lamp.

The light of the moon shone through her window, bathing her skin with silver. Slender fingers beckoned him into the bed, and Merrick's entire body trembled with emotion. Love her. Saints' toes, he loved her beyond all reason. If she were but his, he would tell her until he exhausted all the words. But admitting such would only make things more difficult when she met her intended, and so he choked down the rising confession and buried it deep within his heart.

He lowered himself into the bed, kneeling between her parted legs. Bending forward, he kissed her with all the pent-up feeling he felt for her, and slowly sank into her silken embrace. Her arms came around his neck, her fingers teased through his hair. In a slow, unhurried manner, he kissed her lips, her eyes, her throat. His hands explored her curves, traced the soft contours of her body, and though he knew them all by heart, he etched them into his mind with the thoroughness of a blind man's touch. The whisper of her breath against his skin seared into his memory, her kisses more sweet, more tantalizing, than any sugar treat.

Anne luxuriated in Merrick's mesmerizing warmth. The power of his hands amazed her. Moments earlier, she'd watched him shatter a man's face. Now he caressed her body with such tenderness she had difficulty believing the two men were the same. Gentle fingers massaged her breasts, stirred the warmth that flowed in her veins down into her belly where it spread and fanned lower. They cupped and lifted, kneaded and stroked, until every nerve ending above her waist stood at attention and begged for the feel of his mouth.

Something was different tonight. Between her legs, the hard evidence of his desire pressed into her moistened flesh, but Merrick showed no signs of impatience. Unlike the other times they'd loved, he seemed content to draw their joining out indefinitely. This was somehow richer, more sonorous. As if each kiss, each touch, each brush of his skin against hers spilled a part of him into her.

And she responded with the same deep feeling he aroused, opening herself completely to the man who had broken oaths to keep her at his side.

When at last he dusted his mouth down her neck and closed his lips around her nipple, she sucked in a sharp breath and arched into his arms. Closing her eyes, she tipped her head to the side. Her fingers found his hair, and she hung on while sensations thrummed through her. Oh the idea of being his eternally—how tempting it was to tell him. To swear this oath the knights referred to and never have to leave his side.

But in the back of her mind, she knew it was only a dream. While this pleasure defied her darkest fantasies, it wouldn't last. She would pledge herself to Merrick, and he would forfeit his life. The only future they had would be if he'd leave the temple and come with her. Yet she was too weary to broach the subject of leaving with him tonight, too tangled up in bliss to instigate a fight. Later . . . Tomorrow when he—

Merrick took her nipple between his teeth and nipped hard. A burst of pleasure chased away the disparaging thoughts of their polarized circumstances. She cried out, her fingers tightening against his scalp. But the swirl of his tongue soothed the painful pinch and heat washed across her skin.

His hand slipped between their bodies, swept across her abdomen then lower. He cupped her sensitive feminine flesh, pressing fingertips to her moistened folds. She lifted her hips into his palm as need burned. Obliging her silent demand, Merrick slid a finger inside until the base of his palm pressed against her sensitive nub. Anne gasped at the taunting friction. She wriggled her hips, chasing the surge of ecstasy.

Abruptly, Merrick withdrew his hand and his mouth. Lifting to his elbows, he caught her face between his palms and gazed down at her. His dark eyes filled with intensity. When he spoke, his hoarse whisper filled her to overflowing. "I have no right to ask, but swear to me you will never forget me."

She closed her eyes to the tears that swelled and swallowed hard. "Never," she whispered.

He nudged her thighs apart and entered her slowly. Pushing deep, she felt every thick inch of him fill her up and stretch her perfectly.

His body glided in and out of hers, steady, unhurried thrusts that awakened far more than physical pleasure. The familiar tide of sensation built with the pleasant friction, but it was different too. Not so much a quest for ultimate pleasure, but a rising storm of feeling Anne couldn't comprehend. It flowed from him, into her, and caught her on a crest so high she trembled at its ferocity.

Love, she realized. He loved her. She recognized it in his kiss, tasted it on the velvety stroke of his tongue. Felt it in the reverent slide of his skin against hers. The discovery stole the breath from her lungs.

Ecstasy slammed into her, and the building tide of emotion crested. "Merrick, I—"

He silenced her with a possessive kiss as he thrust in deep and hard. Her body arced, and Anne surrendered to a staggering release. She hung suspended in his embrace, shaking as layer after layer of sensation slammed into her.

Merrick's body stiffened. Deep within her, she felt him shudder, a tremor that rolled up his spine and coursed into his arms. He lifted his mouth from hers on a ragged gasp, then went utterly still.

Slowly, dark lashes lifted. His onyx eyes burned fierce. He lowered himself against her, his weight a welcome comfort. Unable to form words, they lay together in silence, the jagged sound of their breathing blending in the quiet.

When their shared gasps leveled into a somewhat normal rhythm, Merrick gathered her into the shelter of his strong arms. His mouth dusted across her shoulder, settled at the side of her neck. He ran a roughened palm down one arm, found her hand, and twined his fingers through hers, whispering, "If such were possible, I would wish my seed to sprout tonight."

Anne shivered. She could think of nothing that could complete their loving more than a child. If he refused to leave with her, she would always have a piece of Merrick to remind her of these stolen nights together. But immortal knights couldn't father children, and the wish was strictly fancy.

CHAPTER 31

✦

Anne rolled over, seeking Merrick's warmth. The gray light of morning seeped through the curtains, announcing the winter chill carried rain. She ran a hand down the hardened planes of his chest and traced the long scar that ran around his side with a nail. His skin jumped beneath the light touch, his belly tightened.

Tipping her chin up, Anne found him watching her. Beneath the heavy pile of quilts, one large hand found her bottom, and he pulled her against his side. "Good morn," he murmured.

"Mm. Good morning." She ran her fingertip over the crease in his smooth skin again. "What happened to you, Merrick?"

His torso turned rigid beneath her palm, and he turned his head to the window. The all-too-familiar tick crawled along the side of his jaw.

"Hey." She gave him a gentle nudge. "I'm not trying to bring up bad memories. I want to know more about you."

Merrick let out a long, heavy sigh. "'Tis too long a story."

Determined, Anne lifted to an elbow and planted a kiss on the large vein that ran the length of his throat. "I have all morning." She dragged her teeth down his neck to give his shoulder a playful nip. With a provocative wriggle of her hips, she promised, "I'll make it worth the telling." Besides, she could think of no better way to soften him to the discussion that would likely bring them to blows.

Merrick turned to her with a tight frown. But when she draped her body across his, and slipped a hand beneath the covers to take his cock into her hand, his mouth quirked, and a chuckle broke free. She felt him swell and quickly dislodged her hand.

"Little demon, cease your games," he threatened.

Anne rained kisses across his chest. "Tell me what I want to know."

Laughing freely now, Merrick rolled her over, pinned her to the mattress, and kissed her thoroughly. "How is it you take the ache away?" he asked quietly. Before she could answer, he propped himself up on an elbow. "Very well. 'Tis only fair, I do suppose."

"Tell me how you became a Templar knight."

He arched a dark eyebrow. "You ask for much."

"So did you when you dragged me out of my house."

His grunt made her giggle.

"All right, demon Anne. Tell me what you know of Geoffrey Martel."

Anne scoured her brain, digging for names she had little cause to remember. The French territories were so vast, had changed hands so many times and shared a dozen different ties that crossed and recrossed between families, it was like one big jigsaw puzzle. "He was the count of Anjou, allied with King Henry I against William of Normandy and had a bunch of wives. Right?"

Merrick nodded. "Only he sired no heirs. He bequeathed his holdings to his oldest nephew, Geoffrey the Bearded."

Anne propped herself up with a pillow, her interest piqued. "The Bearded fought with his brother, right?"

"Aye. Fulk le Rechin coveted the inheritance, and seven

years later, he imprisoned his brother at Sable. Pope
Gregory II demanded Geoffrey's release, and all seemed
quiet in the country for a short time."

"Forgive me, Merrick, but I've forgotten the details.
I'm sorry." Anne ducked her head with a blush.

"'Tis understood. Fulk imprisoned my father again, a
year later at Chinon. There he stayed for twenty-eight
years. He died shortly after his release."

It took a moment for Anne to realize what Merrick had
said. As the dawning settled on her, her lips parted in
surprise. "Your father?" she gasped.

"Aye. My uncle imprisoned all who swore loyalty to
my father. According to law, my mother, the blooded heir
of two formerly royal families, was naught but a peasant.
She cared for my father whilst he was in prison. They
would have wed, had my father lived long enough. When
I was conceived, he sent her from Chinon to keep my
uncle from discovering me."

Anne stared, dumbfounded. A noble bastard. His blood
gave him the right to join the Templars, his birth con-
demned him. Her heart twisted, envisioning the young life
he must have suffered. She reached between them and
took his hand. "Merrick, I'm so sorry."

Bristling, he withdrew his hand. "Nay. I will finish before you give me pity. 'Tis unnecessary." He ran his fingers
through his mussed hair and heaved a sigh. "We lived in a
small village near the Loire. I could see Chinon from my
doorstep. There were several men in my village who once
bore arms for my father. They took me in their tutelage,
taught me the ways of swords and horses. Though 'twas
forbidden to own weapons, we hid them beneath the floors,
and my lessons were oft at night."

Unable to offer comfort she sensed he needed despite
his staunch pride, Anne snuggled into his embrace and
linked her leg through his. Merrick dropped his arm
around her waist and held her close.

"I joined with those who opposed my uncle. It mattered
not what fight, so long as I could hold the hope of taking

his life. There were victories, there were losses, but my mother's health demanded my return. I was thirty-two, and some ten years earlier a baron of Fulk's had forced himself on my mother for rents she owed. She never recovered. She died that year. After I sent her body down the Loire, I sought her distant family, de Payans."

"And rode to Jerusalem."

"Aye."

Anne lay quiet, absorbing his tale. Treachery, betrayal, the severed bonds of family, vows thrown to the wind—no wonder the man put so much weight in oaths. He'd known nothing but deceit. The full weight of his birthright wasn't lost on her either. Almost two hundred years later, the mighty fortress at Chinon would hold his sworn brethren on charges of treason and heresy.

She'd deceived him too. Was deceiving him still, albeit in a rather benign way compared to his past.

Swallowing rising guilt, she ran her fingertip down the length of his scar. "And this?" she whispered.

He covered her hand, stilling it. "The price I would pay for defending the Almighty. King Philip's eternal brand."

"But your wounds heal. How did you scar?"

Merrick wrapped her fingers tightly in his. "A Templar blade will wound and leave behind the evidence. The holy steel, and Azazel's demons, are the only weaknesses we have." His mouth curled in a cruel smirk. "What better way to torture the devoted than to turn his sword upon him."

Anne couldn't stop a shocked cry from tumbling free. She bolted upright. "But the Inquisition could not draw blood."

He shook his head with a snort. "They did. They hung me from the rafters with weights on my legs in my own property and carved on me to contrive a confession."

Anne's throat closed. Imprisoned at Chinon. *Oh God.* Impulsively, she leaned forward and pressed her lips to the timeless reminder of what his loyalty cost. Working her way up his body, she showered him with light kisses until she found his mouth. There, she settled in deep, telling him the only way she knew how that she shared his pain, his grief . . . That she understood.

A rumble of pleasure rose to the back of his throat, and clasping her body to his, he eased her into the pillows. One roughened hand covered her breast as he claimed her mouth with greedy hunger. Against her thigh, she felt the hard length of his arousal, sure evidence of his intentions. Resigning herself to a morning of absolute bliss, Anne looped her arms around his neck and made room for him between her legs.

The loud peal of a horn crashed through the pitter of rainfall against her windowpane.

Merrick leapt from the bed so quickly she almost believed he'd never been beside her. In seconds, he had his jeans on and was shaking out his shirt.

Anne sat up, her brows furrowed in confusion. "What is it?"

"Azazel has found the third nail."

Her heart drummed to a stop. Not the nail. Shaking her head, she refused to believe his implication.

But as he reached for his sword and buckled it around his waist, she couldn't pretend ignorance. The time for silence was over. They must discuss her vision now. She swallowed hard and asked quietly, "You're going to fight?"

He paused only a moment, the look he gave her full of dark foreboding. With a short nod, he murmured, "Aye." Merrick turned away to stuff his feet into his laceless boots. "Wait here. I will attend you before I leave."

As he straightened, Anne clutched at his hand. He was leaving without their binding oath. Mikhail sent him regardless, and Mikhail swore none would return. This wasn't happening. She had to stop it. Words rushed out, discombobulated and nowhere near as eloquent as she'd planned. "Don't go, Merrick. You don't have to fight. Stay with me. We can leave, we can go wherever, but don't go to this battle."

His stern expression squashed all the hope she'd harbored. "Never ask such of me again, Anne. I gave my word. I am sworn to the sword."

With that, he stormed from her room.

Merrick descended into the lower chambers, then deeper, entering the inner sanctum. There, every man filed into place and stood at rigid attention, turning the spacious, circular nave into a sea of expectant faces. From atop the far dais, Mikhail and Raphael looked out amongst the gathered knights, patiently waiting for the slower members to arrive. Beside them, Caradoc, Nikolas, and Gareth stood silently.

Merrick joined them, his heart heavy. Hours from now, he would inevitably meet his cousin to fulfill their oath. But Merrick found the vow no longer mattered. The only thing he cared for lay upstairs in that great bed, and all he desired was the means to spend a life with Anne. But her proposition that they leave was unacceptable.

He stared out at his brothers, feeling the futility of their plight. No other seraph had arrived, and Anne knew not her intended. Without one strong enough, without the moral compass to lead the faltering knights, they were certain to fail. 'Twould be a better fate to surrender the third nail and rally for Azazel's subsequent strike.

Looking to the three who gathered with him on the dais, he read the same futility in their vacant stares.

"Brothers in arms," Mikhail's voice rose above the hushed murmurs. The room fell silent. "Raphael has returned from Louisiana only a few moments ago. Gate three is strained to its limits. By nightfall it will fail. We have reason to believe all manner of darkness will converge upon the adytum along the Bayou Bourbeaux and the nail hidden in her stairs. Elspeth has been relocated to safeguard her life."

Merrick eyed Mikhail as he mentally processed the grounds, the coordinated plans, and where the knights would have the largest advantage. If Elspeth no longer resided in the antebellum home, then he would need to assign several men to guard the front doors. He would take that position as well—for most assuredly Fulk would strike for the nail ensconced beneath the sweeping stairwell. Meanwhile, Uriel would lead a handful of the European knights in rebuilding the time-decayed gate between Azazel's realm and man's.

"The cars are ready. You will depart in groups of ten, close quarters, I know. Fill the vehicles and depart immediately. Your placements will be given in cipher over your phones. I am sorry I cannot better prepare you with our strategy. Our time is too short, the travel too long."

A low rumble broke through the ranks as the men grasped the urgency. Even Merrick felt the thrum of anxiety. After centuries of fighting, the call of battle ran so deep in their blood they could not help but anticipate the conflict. Too long their skills lay idle, tested only in brief skirmishes at ruptured gates with creatures who offered no severe threat.

"Begin your personal preparations. Attend to your prayers, your armor, your thoughts. Gabriel shall return to look after the temple in my stead, and I will fight, as will Raphael, beside you. Go now. I shall see you all along the banks."

The men filed up the stairs in pairs, their voices somber, if they spoke at all.

In no mood for conversation, Merrick evaded Mikhail's expectant look and fell into step beside Gareth, following Caradoc and Nikolas. At the top of the stairwell, Gareth clamped a firm hand on Merrick's shoulder. His usual jovial smile missing, he gave Merrick a hard look. "She loves you."

Like a blade slicing through his flesh, Merrick's heart bled. He grimaced, the truth too powerful to confront. "Mayhap," he allowed in quiet murmur.

"Go from this, Merrick. What proof have you that her intended still lives? Take her away. Take yourself from this madness."

Stiffening, Merrick set his jaw. "I cannot. I swore my oath, the same as you. Another as well. Whilst I might accept the condemnation of the Order, I pledged salvation to my cousin. Until he rests eternal . . ." Merrick shook his head. "Nay. I cannot break my vows."

"Then pray well, and I shall stay at your side."

Merrick turned away from Gareth's earnest stare. Grief poured down upon him in great buckets. He had but found her. He cared not about her intended, she had rooted herself so deep into his heart, and that disregard bore down on him like a vise. That he could turn from his brothers so easily spoke to the stain upon his soul. 'Twould be a better fate for all, should he not return. Whilst Anne would mourn, she would not bind herself to one who possessed no honor.

Aye, he would welcome his fate, take comfort in the knowledge Gareth would send him unto the Almighty when the felling blow forever claimed his soul. Anne would rise above her sorrow, become a great lady among the men. She would suffer no more of his selfishness, of his dishonorable acts.

Accepting what he could not change, Merrick shoved his way into his chambers. He looked to the bed, pictured her sleeping there. She lived in the table, still positioned where they had recorded marks. Her perfume clung in the air, a scent he longed to capture and take with him.

Closing his eyes, he stifled tears that had not risen since his mother's death. God's teeth, he would never forget his demon Anne.

CHAPTER 32

An hour of ghostly silence had Anne jumping at every sound. Below, the house was as still as death, the only interruption in the deafening silence, the occasional slam of car doors and a departing silver vehicle.

Merrick had been annoyed with her plea, might very well have left without saying good-bye. Her chest heaved in unison with her empty stomach. She'd never forgive him if he had. This wasn't happening. Couldn't be. It didn't make sense either. Mikhail had mentioned the vow. Had specifically said with it, Merrick would be forced to lead. Yet he was leading anyway. There had to be a way to make him see reason and choose her, their love, over all the deaths, the risks.

Another set of footsteps preceded the slamming of the front door, and Anne darted for the window once more. Ten more men piled into a silver SUV, swords in one hand, duffel bags in the other. The vehicle's lights cut through the heavy rain as it reversed. Barreling through the open iron gates, it disappeared down the narrow street.

She'd had enough waiting. Oath or no oath, she'd convince Merrick to leave with her. If she could have just ten

minutes alone with him, she'd tell him everything. Somehow, she'd make him agree.

Foregoing shoes, she ran from her room, down the
stairs, and skidded to a stop in the vast commons area.
The television sat dark and silent. The chairs were empty.
Anne rubbed her arms as a chill crept down her spine.
She'd never seen the house so desolate.

Following the sound of hushed voices, she made her
way to the stairwell that led to the private rooms beneath
the house and descended into the stone depths. As she
walked the halls, she passed small gatherings of knights,
all absorbed in conversation. For the first time since her
arrival, no one turned to look. Not a single man noticed
her presence.

She stood in the centermost corridor, debating whether
to try Merrick's room first or whether he would be with
Mikhail. Deciding to try the closer destination—his
room—she pivoted around, only to collide into a wide
chest. Startled, she backed up, an apology ready on her
tongue.

Farran's grim features silenced her words. He caught
her by the shoulders, steadying her, all the while studying
her with his usual dark frown. Anne flinched beneath his
scrutiny, certain he'd send her back upstairs, tell her she
had no business down here.

Instead, Farran turned her around and pointed toward
the narrow doorway that led to the inner sanctum.

Anne looked at him in wide-eyed disbelief. The man
who didn't know the meaning of a smile wanted her to
enter?

"Be quiet, milady. Stay out of the way." With the hushed
warning, Farran gave her a nudge toward the stairwell.

Her heart skipped a beat over the prospect of finally
discovering the Templar secrets. She checked a threatening squeal of delight and forced her demeanor to look
calm, disinterested. The history would wait a little longer. Merrick's life wouldn't.

Still, her curiosity refused to step aside as she slowly descended and studied the time-honored symbols etched into the walls. A bright sun, a quarter moon depicted with a face, the star of David, a horse bearing two riders—all carried meanings she and her colleagues had only guessed at through the years. Would she learn their true purpose? Was there, somewhere down here, a key to the pictorial cipher?

At the bottom of the never-ending, crude stone steps, Anne came to a standstill, and a soft gasp tumbled loose. The air was cooler, tinged with dampness. But where the stonework above was simple and crude, this was nothing less than breathtaking. A page ripped straight from ancient Europe reached out all around her.

Towering vaulted arches, nearly fifty feet tall, supported a mosaic ceiling painted in bright color. Fleurs-de-lis, crosses, knights and a dozen other mystical symbols were carved into the massive stone blocks that created the base of the arches. In the joints, the areas designed to give cushion to the shifting of the earth, intricately detailed gargoyle heads merged with floral patterns and ornate scrollwork.

She took a tentative step into the candlelit nave and spun in a slow circle, amazed by the exquisite hand-tooled art. As she turned, her eyes followed the designs, and another piece of history clicked into place. Like the Temple Church in London, this too mimicked the layout of Jerusalem's Church of the Holy Sepulchre. Only, where the others opened into a larger, rectangular area, the nave here branched in two opposite directions, two short halls, both lit with torches that illuminated a series of wooden doors.

Moving to her right, Anne rounded a thick column. Her gaze followed the bright play of lights and the glitter of gold filigree along the walls to a stone-topped altar draped in crimson cloth. Head bowed, Merrick bent on one knee before an ornate golden cross.

He wore the regalia recorded by scholars—pristine white surcoat over a hauberk of chain. His sword extended beyond his left thigh, and his long dark hair dusted across his shoulders. Anne's heart tripped at the sound of his low voice, the deep baritone murmur echoing off the massive walls. He spoke in Latin, a melodic language she hadn't heard beyond the classroom.

One hand braced on the column of stone, Anne stared speechless. The reverence of the temple soaked into her. Men lived and died here. They had been doing so for centuries. Each swore his life to the cause, and had done so willingly, even knowing the threat he faced. No one forced their hands. No one pressed them into service.

The low melodic cadence of Merrick's prayer mingled with her awe, each hypnotic syllable unveiling secrets that had been beneath her nose the entire time. The threat the Church feared had nothing to do with symbols, or relics, or even battles. What cowed the mighty clergy was faith. Faith in brothers, in mankind, and above all, in the Almighty. The symbols meant nothing if no one believed. An ark was a box, a grail a basic cup.

The vows these men took, the noble purpose they truly lived by, generated thousands of followers, numbers so high and property so vast they could have easily formed their own nation. In a time where clergy could be bought, where power came from purchased loyalty, the Templar jeopardized the Church's reign of fear. Tied so tightly to the corrupt vassals of religion, one word contradicting the Church's position on anything, and the Templar possessed the ability to turn religion upside down.

Sabotaging them became a necessity.

Goose bumps lifted the hairs on her arms. Merrick couldn't leave with her. She didn't dare even ask. This wasn't just something he participated in, something he could turn away from. It *made* him. Men counted on him, angels depended on him. Like this simple stonework that picks and chisels turned into art, the simple man born a noble bastard transformed into beauty with purpose. In every sense of the meaning, every fiber of his being, Merrick was Templar.

As he rose and crossed himself, he turned toward her. His stormy eyes locked with hers, and Anne's heart swelled. She loved him. More than the knowledge she'd craved, more than the career she'd worked for. Merrick du Loire meant everything to her, and just as she couldn't ask him to abandon what he was, she couldn't walk away. Somehow, she had to find the courage to stay. She could art over her tattoo, fill her role—whatever it was—without ever taking the damning oath that would claim Merrick's life.

Anne rushed across the floor. "Merrick . . ."

He grabbed her to him. In the fierceness of his kiss she felt his love, heard the silent words her heart longed for. When he released her, the hitch in his breathing made her belly flutter. He touched his forehead to hers and gathered her hands between them to press a kiss against her knuckles.

"Come back to me, Merrick," she whispered.

He withdrew, closing his eyes to pain she couldn't understand. When he looked at her again, those onyx portals filled with sorrow that clawed at her soul. His throat worked as he swallowed, and he pulled in a deep breath. "I cannot come back to you, Anne. You belong to another man."

The claws raked deeper, shredding her into pieces. "No," she protested.

Firm resolution turned his features hard. "You will write down your mark and leave it with Gabriel. You shall be safe whilst I am away—Tane will fight with us, then shall be removed from the Order."

"Merrick." She tugged at her hands, desperate to touch him, to draw him back into her arms and convince him out of this insanity. He loved her. She loved him. This business of her stupid tattoo was all red tape. She'd tell him. He couldn't make her swear an oath that would kill him. But he'd know who she belonged with, and he'd have to return.

He held her wrists fast. "No, little demon," he murmured. Leaning forward, he pressed his lips to hers in a lingering, chaste kiss. "You will always have my heart, but you are not mine to love."

"But Merrick, I—"

A firm bellow she knew all too well cut her off. "Anne!" *I love you.*

Merrick whipped around. Over his shoulder, Anne glimpsed Gabe's unmistakable gray dreadlocks. Ignoring her former boss, and God's messenger, Anne pulled on Merrick's shoulder. "Merrick, I belong with—"

Gabe caught up to them and clasped her elbow. "Anne, let Merrick go. You have plenty of time to kiss him later. Come with me—I must teach you your role in this battle."

Merrick kissed her cheek then released her hands. "Always my heart," he whispered as he turned away.

Torn, Anne took a step toward him, intending to stop his retreat. But Gabe held her fast, the pressure on her arm forcing her to follow him. "Oh, for God's sake, let me go, Gabe. He's leaving."

"Yes. As is every knight."

"But you don't understand." She plied at his fingers. "I have to tell him I love him, or he'll leave *me*!"

With a shake of his head, Gabe led her into one of the connecting rooms and laughed. "Don't be silly. The oath you took won't let him leave you. If you're fighting, it will work out. You two are bound for eternity. Or did Merrick neglect to tell you that?"

The hair on the back of Anne's neck lifted. Something wasn't right. Gabe was entirely too jovial in the face of death. If they were bound for eternity, that implied Merrick couldn't die. She stared at Gabe, afraid to even breathe.

His smile vanished. His eyes dropped to her arm, as if he could see the armband beneath her sleeve. "You *did* take the oath didn't you?"

With a gulp, Anne shook her head.

Gabe closed his eyes and slowly presented his back. Looking skyward, he mumbled, "Why must your humans be so infinitely stupid?"

That was enough to jerk Anne back to her senses. Her

pride reared, and she folded her arms across her chest. "I'm not stupid."

"No?" Gabe whirled on her. His usually warm blue eyes burned with bright anger. "Of all the seraphs, Anne, you were chosen as the first because of your knowledge of the Templar. I didn't have to explain as much. I expected you'd have no trouble accepting the ways; that you'd be delighted at the prospect of living among the men you've studied for so long. Yet you stand there and tell me you haven't taken the oath that makes you a part of the Templar world?"

She pursed her lips, refusing to react. She didn't intend to stand here and be scolded like a child.

"Was Merrick's explanation unclear? You love him—why would you condemn him to death?"

Anne's jaw dropped open. "Stop." She held out a hand. "Just stop. Mikhail said I would save someone. Merrick explained very little about this oath, only that I had to take it. What *he* doesn't know is that damned oath is going to kill him. I saw it, and I heard it from Mikhail."

Gabe's gray eyebrows furrowed deeply. He eased a hip onto a worn tabletop and folded his hands in his lap. "What do you mean you saw it?"

"My visions. Since the day I met Merrick, I've seen him laid out in death. Face beaten. Sword on his chest. Blood on his surcoat. Dead, Gabe."

His frown deepened, and he scratched the top of his head the way he always did when he was in thought. A few silent seconds later, he asked, "And what did Mikhail say?"

"He was talking with Raphael." A chill possessed Anne as she recited the phrase that had haunted her dreams. *"I suppose I should be grateful she has not said a word. Should she identify her mate, I shall have no choice but to send him to defend the final nail."*

Gabe's gaze pierced her like a spear. "Think clearly. In your vision, Merrick held his sword?"

Anne nodded.

"What did it look like?"

She shrugged. "Plain, like always."

"Oh, Anne." Gabe sighed. He rubbed the back of his neck. "Need I remind you the nature of visions? That a glimpse into the future is only how things are, *given the present circumstances*? Have you forgotten a person has the ability to change the outcome of his future if he is given the proper means?"

Anne's heart slowed to a stop. Her lungs contracted, and her palms turned suddenly sweaty. Whatever Gabe was about to say, she didn't want to hear it. Not in this lifetime, nor the next.

"Your oath is a holy vow, more powerful than any marital pledge. With it, you gain Merrick's immortality. And he . . ." He lifted his head to turn sorrowful eyes on her. "He gains the light that combats the darkness in his soul. Each vile beast Azazel creates claims part of him when he kills it. In time, he will turn into a thing of nightmares."

She closed her eyes, willing Gabe to stop. At once, the image of the dark knight that had wounded Gareth leapt forth. She shuddered involuntarily.

"Your light heals him. Without it, Anne, your vision will come true."

"No," she wailed. "Why didn't my second sight show me more?"

Gabe let out a heavy sigh. "It was a test, Anne. Of your faith. Of your ability to trust the hand that guides us all. To trust in the things you cannot see and believe in the preordained." He lowered his voice to add, "One you failed."

Failed.

The word pounded through her head. She hadn't just failed, she'd killed Merrick. In an attempt to keep him safe, she'd done the opposite. Oh God, she had to tell him. Before he left, they had to say their oaths. Racing for the door, she jerked it open.

"You don't know what to say," Gabe called after her.

Not slowing down, she called over her shoulder, "I'll bring him back to you."

She barreled up the steps, nearly falling several times

when her socks slipped on the time-smoothed stone surface. At the top of the long flight of stairs, she grabbed a passing knight and demanded, "Where's Merrick?"

The man pointed a nubby arm at the stairs. "He leaves now."

Anne shoved away from the face she didn't recognize and ran as fast as her legs would carry her up the second flight of stairs to the front door. As she reached for the handle, tires crunched against gravel. Anne's stomach rolled over. She yanked the door open, bolted out into the rain.

The last silver SUV rolled down the drive and turned onto the lane. Running after it, she chased until she reached the heavy iron gates. There, she stopped, staring down the empty street as distant taillights crested a hill and disappeared.

Anne's legs gave out. With a choked cry, she sank to the ground, one hand twined around a thick iron post, the other clawing at the dirt. He was gone. Off to battle and doomed to death, and there wasn't a damned thing she could do to stop this nightmare.

CHAPTER 33

✝

Merrick leaned his shoulder against one of the plantation home's tall white columns and stared out into the darkness. He watched. And waited.

Beyond the artfully maintained gardens and several yards of cropped grass, tall pines canopied a dense growth of brush. Out there, Azazel's fiends crawled among the scrub. Rising shadows announced their presence, accompanied by the occasional snap of a branch, rustle of leaves. They slunk through the surrounding countryside, gathered their forces, and like the Templar, they waited.

He shifted his helmet to his other arm and surveyed the knights between the adytum and Azazel's evil. Squatting behind evergreen bushes, kneeling beside tree trunks and laying against low mounds of earth, they too watched the trees. How many would lift their blades for the last time this night? How many would take their last breath at the end of their brothers' swords when their souls succumbed to Azazel's hate?

The gentle breeze stirred his hair, and he closed his eyes to his thoughts. Fulk was there somewhere. A mighty foe far more dangerous than any other fallen knight. He possessed the strength of three men and the skill of several more. In light, he had been a formidable ally. Now he was the threat Merrick must slay.

A task made more difficult by the vile being inhabiting his cousin's shell. His face would hold the same charisma, his eyes the same familiar light. But the spirit Merrick once laughed with, he must remember had vanished.

Restless, Merrick pushed away from the towering support and crossed through the bright porch light to the opposite side of the entry stairs. His boots scraped across painted wood, the echo ominous in the unusual quiet. Another column down, Gareth acknowledged him with a nod. Further still, Merrick observed Caradoc's long shadow. Behind him, he would find Farran and Tane. He had yet to speak a word to his traitorous brother, but now, as the hour approached, he said a silent prayer for Tane's presence.

Inside, Lucan, Tomas, and William the Strong guarded the stairwell and the hidden ark that held the nail. Overhead, lining the second-story balcony, Nikolas assigned four men. The legendary archer assumed a frontal position behind the immediate row of juniper. Mikhail and Raphael joined forces with the men in the open, strong arms much needed.

Well fortified, the strongest and most skilled protected the relic. Yet they were such a tattered bunch, Merrick could not help but question how long they could hold out. He could not shake the feeling of futility. In all the battles against Saladin's terrific Muslim forces, only the march from Hattin left Merrick with the same unease. There too they had outnumbered Saladin's men, but like tonight, their health weakened their swords. At least Azazel's creatures could not pelt them with arrows—in that, the Templar held advantage.

The clink of chain pulled him from his memories. He looked to the open field. Swords at the ready, helms now donned, the knights prepared. A long, low whistle broke through the quiet, and Merrick set his own upon his head.

"To arms," a voice hidden in the dark called.

The front lines broke. A sea of shadows descended on

the grassy plain, met by the fury of the noble knights. Hoarse cries joined the enraged howls as nytym, shade, demon, and man clashed beneath the starless sky. Above, ahead, the twang of bowstrings punctuated the battle calls, and Merrick watched as holy arrows rained down upon their foe.

"God be with us," he murmured as he drew his sword.

Anne didn't know how long she'd huddled on the wet pavement, sobbing, until Gabe hauled her back inside. She distinctly remembered the warmth of his hands as he hefted her up and dragged her through the door. However, she couldn't remember returning to her rooms, and she certainly didn't recall changing her clothes.

But as she opened her eyes to the dim lamplight in her sitting room, she was warm and dry. An empty bowl on the coffee table told her she'd eaten something too, and the matching one on her end table hinted someone had eaten with her. Probably Gabe. She didn't have the faintest idea when, though.

Her face felt swollen and stiff, her eyes as scratchy as if she'd been through a sandstorm. She ached all the way down to her toes, and though she'd slept hours judging by the dark outside her window, the hollow feeling inside hadn't gone away.

She'd failed Merrick.

Out of the hundreds of readings she'd done, she'd forgotten the one thing she tried to pound into her clients' minds—never take a glimpse of the future as unchangeable fact. They were guides, markers on a path. Change an aspect of the present, and the future would adjust.

Nothing was ever permanent except the past.

She'd gotten caught up in her emotions, and Merrick would pay the price.

Tears welled again, and Anne covered her face with her hands. The whole Order would condemn her when they realized she'd deliberately kept Merrick in the dark about her tattoo. If he died, they'd lose their leader. Tane would suffer for no reason. She had inadvertently divided ties. For that, she'd never forgive herself.

God, please let there still be hope. Let Merrick come back alive.

Swiping at her eyes, she forced herself to sit up. Why couldn't Gabe have come back a day earlier? If he had, this nonsense would be over, and Merrick wouldn't be in some battle for his life.

She should have told Merrick from the start. Even if he did return, he'd be furious. She'd looked him in the eye, lied, and thrown him right in the path of danger. If he survived, he would hate her.

With a heavy sigh, Anne glanced around her room. Memories swamped her—Merrick exploring the room for the first time, Merrick on this couch kissing her, Merrick in her bed . . . Why hadn't he told her about his soul?

Her gaze caught on a white envelope taped to her door. Curious, she rose on weary legs and shuffled across the carpet. Pulling it free, she studied the handwriting across the front. The fancy loops and swirls marked it distinctly as Gabe's.

She tore open the flap and withdrew a folded square of paper covered on front and back with his writing. Frowning, Anne scanned the first line.

I have to meet a scientist in D.C. I'll return when I can. Heed the words within.

The angry sound of steel against steel engulfed the adytum's grounds. Men and beast alike grappled and clashed, each matched in determination, if not might. Merrick had never seen so many of Azazel's creatures in one spot, and worse, he had never witnessed so many evil knights. They had poured out of the trees, numbers he had forgotten, and clearly so had the other Templar knights, for the ensuing moment of hesitation gave their attackers immediate advantage.

They stormed the grounds, cutting through the first line of Templars as if they sliced through butter. The charge forced the archers to their swords and brought them from the balcony down into the field.

"Behind you!" Gareth bellowed.

Merrick spun. Arcing his blade from his hip to his shoulder, his momentum gave him extra power, and he neatly lobbed off a demon's arm. The thing screamed in rage as its vile life force oozed onto the ground.

Charging in for the felling blow, Gareth sank his blade deep within the demon's heart. As he had done since the fiends had reached the wide porch, he used his healthier spirit to Merrick's advantage and prevented Merrick from assuming the taint. There was no need for thanks, Merrick's gratitude went unsaid. He needed his strength for Fulk.

Gareth shuddered as the darkness rolled down his sword and into his veins. When he looked up, his brown eyes flashed to black before shifting once again to dark toffee. 'Twas the only sign he suffered from the stain of evil.

Merrick whirled back around to parry off a nytym's razor-sharp claws. As his sword deflected blows intended for his neck, Merrick scanned the grounds for the face he had known since boyhood. Sweat soaked his brow, rolled down into his eyes. He squinted against the sting and blinked the droplets away. As his vision cleared, he spied his target. Fulk stood tall and imposing in his ebony armor, his uncovered face unmistakable.

Nudging Merrick aside, Gareth stepped in to finish off the nytym, and Merrick moved behind him to attack a shade. He dealt with it quickly, removing its foul head with a backward slice.

As the vile shadows seeped into his veins, Merrick grimaced. The darkness that already consumed him rose with a dragon's fury, embracing the invading evil. His spirit roiled, his blood burned.

Taking advantage of his weakness, a nytym slammed a shadowy hand into his face. As if he had been hit with an iron club, pain erupted and tiny pinpricks of light burst behind his eyes. He grabbed for the railing to keep himself from dropping to his knees. As he panted, Caradoc stepped up to send the creature back to hell.

When the tremors in Merrick's limbs subsided, and the spinning in his head ceased, he felt the fire in his tired muscles. He could not take much more of this. If his spirit did not fail him, his body soon would.

Yet as he sucked in a deep, fortifying breath, determined to fight until he could no longer move, he looked once more to the battlefield. When he took in the scene that played before him, his gut coiled, and his chest collapsed. "No," he whispered.

Several feet away, Fulk advanced on Nikolas. The knight could not see him, his focus riveted on a pair of demons to his left. They pushed him backward, their skilled attack too fierce and fast for Nikolas' lesser-trained arm. He set one foot behind him, widening his stance as any trained soldier would. Sword extended, he thrust and ran the first demon through.

The felling blow exposed him, and Fulk closed in like a hungry lion. Mirroring Nikolas' strike, he plunged his onyx blade into Nikolas' back. Nikolas' body convulsed. His head jerked backward, he sank to his knees. His weight dragged the blade through his flesh, until he hung suspended by his ribs.

"Nikolas!" Merrick bellowed.

Enraged, Merrick vaulted over the railing. He cut through the sea of despicable shadows, ignorant of their wretched screams. Possessed by the need for retribution, Merrick advanced like a blind man. He swung wildly, landing a heavy blow to Fulk's left shoulder.

The strike forced Fulk to acknowledge his attacker. He settled his hate-filled gaze on Merrick.

Years of fighting side by side gave Merrick the benefit of knowing Fulk's weaknesses. He knew his cousin's strongest attack, understood his vulnerabilities. Merrick took full advantage. He thrust and retreated, parried and struck, landing several damaging but otherwise insignificant blows.

Yet the same advantage applied to the thing that possessed Fulk's mind and heart. In less time that it would have taken the former man, the demoniacal knight gauged Merrick's tactics. He countered his blade, evaded his lunges. They danced together in unison, a perfect pairing of mirrored counterparts.

The weight of his sword settled deep into Merrick's shoulder. His muscles burned in protest. He assumed a defensive stance, aware the same weariness would hinder Fulk in time. Fending off the deadly onyx blade, he waited for the moment when he could counterstrike.

From the corner of his eye, he caught Gareth's presence at his side and sucked in another lungful of air. But before the younger Templar could engage Fulk, a second dark knight descended upon him, leaving Merrick to finish his battle alone.

Distracted by the momentary clang of swords, Fulk glanced over his shoulder at Gareth.

Merrick sensed opportunity. Summoning his strength, he advanced. Strike after strike, he pushed Fulk backward, deeper into the fray of shades and nytyms. Claws raked across Merrick's face, but he did not feel their sting. Determined to satisfy their oath, Merrick pressed in hard. Taking his broadsword in both hands, he arced it across his body with such power it scored past Fulk's mail and cut deep into his side.

Yet victory would not so easily be had.

As Fulk twisted away from Merrick's blade, he lunged in a sideways manner, entering the unprotected area beneath Merrick's left arm. His sword sank into Merrick's thigh, so deep it scraped against the bone.

Stunned, Merrick's eyes widened in horror. Nay. Fulk could not win. He had sworn to release his cousin from Azazel's hell. Heat seared through his leg, spread up into his abdomen. Merrick glanced down, took in the blood that poured onto his boot.

A wash of dizziness engulfed him. He forced it down and shook his head. Shifting his grip on his hilt, he set his weight on his good leg and trained his thoughts on survival. One blow. 'Twas all he needed. Deep in the chest where his sword would still that foul heart. His oath would be fulfilled, he would not fail the only family left to him.

But Merrick's body could not match the strength of his will. His leg gave out, and Merrick sank to his knees. He fought back the stars that lit behind his eyes . . . he fought to drag in a normal breath. The warm sticky wetness of his blood seeped down his leg to pool in the grass beneath his knee.

The wicked smile that twisted Fulk's features turned Merrick's stomach. His cousin's eyes gleamed with the thirst for blood, and the unearthly cry of victory that spilled from his throat turned Merrick's heart to stone. His shoulders sagged, and he let his chin drop to his chest. As unconsciousness pulled at his mind, a low hum broke out inside his head.

"Du Loire!"

Dimly he recognized the distant call of his name. The voice grew closer, the bellow louder, and Merrick clung to the sound. Each syllable pulled him back from unconsciousness, slowly restored his vision. He sucked in a deep breath, and lifted his chin, setting his jaw against the pain and willing his body to cooperate.

He would not die this way. 'Twas not the death he desired.

Staring into the face of his attacker, Merrick eyed the way Fulk lifted his sword above his head. The strike was predictable—a quick cut meant to sever heads. 'Twas a favored move of his cousin's and Merrick waited. He had one chance to emerge victorious, and he would not waste his energy.

Time moved in slow motion as the blade descended toward his neck.

At the last moment, Merrick threw his weight into his good leg and propelled himself to his feet. Fulk's sword connected harmlessly with Merrick's left shoulder. But Merrick's blade sank deep into his cousin's gut.

Agony ripped down Merrick's spine. He used the last of his strength to jerk his broadsword up, elongating the wound. Fulk's eyes rounded in disbelief, and the angry beast inside let loose a deafening bellow. As the horrendous noise tapered into a whine, recognition flashed within Fulk's features. His expression softened. His dark eyes returned to the familiar shade of olive.

His whisper washed across Merrick's face. "Cousin."

Merrick did not have time to consider the oddity of what had just happened. In the next moment, a wispy film of white spiraled heavenward. On its heels, however, the darkness spilled forth.

It flooded into Merrick, consuming him with insatiable rage. As if some beast clawed at his insides in a desperate attempt to escape, his body lit with fire. The need to wretch bore down on him with a hammer's fury, and he instinctively reached for his sword.

Through the bleary haze, he saw only shadows, the ability to decipher between friend and foe an impossible task.

"Merrick." A hand clamped down on his shoulder.

He knew the voice, and yet he could not place the face. Confused, disoriented, Merrick whirled with a ferocious sweep of his blade.

He did not know whether his attack struck true. Whilst he struggled to make sense of his surroundings, something heavy slammed into his temple.

Darkness blanketed his mind.

CHAPTER 34

✝

A nne turned off the water faucets and stepped out of the shower. She bathed to wash away her shame. As she bent over and took a towel to her hair, the lavender light of dawn spilled through the bathroom's entryway. Morning. Somehow, she'd made it through the entire night without crumbling into pieces.

A door slammed outside her window, and the towel tumbled from her hands. She stared at the sheers, unmoving, caught between the terrifying fear Merrick had met a terrible fate and the joyous realization the men were home.

The sound of a second closing door pulled her out of her stupor. She bolted to the window. Outside, an entire line of parked vehicles framed the house's porch, telling her she'd spent far longer in the shower than she'd imagined.

She grabbed yesterday's clothes off the floor, dressing as she ran for the door. She dashed into the hall and darted down the stairs, her singular thought to find Merrick. Dead or alive, she had to see him. Had to apologize. Oblivious to the cold stone beneath her bare feet, she jogged through the common room, following a pair of men she didn't know. "Wait," she called as they stepped into the stairwell.

The pair looked back at her, their somber expressions making her heart skip a beat.

"Where's Merrick?"

The two knights exchanged wary glances, then wordlessly continued down the stairs.

Sirens screamed in Anne's head, angry peals that warned her something terrible had happened. Fighting back a wail of despair, she pushed past the two knights and sped down the steps. At the bottom, she took a sharp turn to her right and hurried toward Merrick's room. Why he would have gone there, instead of to her, she didn't know. Unless Tane had told him, and he was so angry he didn't want to see her.

The alternative was too terrible to consider, and she blindly made her way down the hall until she reached his open door. There, Lucan and another man she didn't recognize stripped Merrick's bed.

Her world tilted dangerously on its axis. Digging her fingers into the wooden door frame, she hung on tight. *No. No!* She swallowed hard, willed her voice to cooperate. "Where's Merrick?"

Lucan turned slowly, the sheet slipping from his hands. "Milady," he murmured. "I did not expect to see you here."

Anne ground her teeth together to quell a rush of panic. Her stomach flipped wildly at the way Lucan's eyes didn't quite meet hers. He turned away, sidetracked by the shirt Merrick had left on the ground when he'd lost his self-control to jealousy. Picking it up, Lucan continued in a low voice, "We lost the nail. Nikolas perished. Gareth is with Uriel. So many others . . ." Straightening suddenly, Lucan looked at her as if he hadn't seen her there before. "You should not be here, Lady Anne."

A wave of sorrow washed through her as she pictured Nikolas' face. Dead. And Gareth injured—just as her second sight had portrayed. Oh God, did that mean . . .

"Lucan, where's Merrick?"

He stared at her, his eyes vacant and unseeing. Then he shook his head. "Merrick injured Caradoc."

Oh for God's sake, this was going nowhere. While his strange behavior could be attributed to shock, it did nothing to soothe Anne's rapidly rising panic. He was evading her question. Through a closing throat she choked out, "Damn it, Lucan, where's Merrick?"

His brows furrowed faintly, and he looked beyond her into the hall. In a voice so low she had to strain to hear him, he answered, "He is with Farran. But milady—"

Anne didn't wait for him to finish. Following the directions Merrick had given her the first day she'd arrived, she raced to Farran's door. For fear he'd refuse to answer if she knocked, she barged inside.

The room was empty. Only the duffel bag on Farran's bed hinted to the fact he'd been here.

Where the hell were they?

Hurrying through the long corridors, Anne made her way to the infirmary and pushed open the wide double doors. Where the room had been empty, save for Declan, the last time she'd entered, occupied beds lined both walls. Uriel bustled between them, checking IVs, carting bandages, all the while muttering to himself. But Farran was nowhere in sight, and no one matched Merrick's size.

Distraught, she closed the doors and leaned against them. Tears welled in her eyes, her frustration at impossible limits. The vision that had haunted her plagued her memory, filling her head with all kinds of nightmares. She covered her eyes with her hands, not only to stop the flow of tears but to ground her thoughts.

Downstairs. There were too many vehicles outside to account for the few men she'd encountered so far. They had to be downstairs doing something important. Something she'd probably get in trouble for interrupting. Anne no longer cared. If she didn't find Merrick, she'd break down in the hall right here.

Striking off at a purposeful pace, she marched to the

stairwell that led to the inner sanctum. At the top, she peered down into the dim depths below and watched as several men in black Templar robes hurried back and forth. They were down there all right. And she'd be damned if they stopped her from entering.

She started down the stairs slowly, half expecting someone would yell at her to stop. Footsteps followed behind her, slow, steady beats that matched her own. After about ten steps, she realized the man could have stopped her at any time. Instead, he waited for her. As if she had every right to be in their sacred place.

Encouraged, Anne picked up her pace and took the narrow steps two at a time. When she reached the bottom, she scanned a group of men gathered near the altar and muttered a curse. The only way she'd find out if Merrick or Farran was with them would involve interrupting their prayers. Damn. She pulled in a deep breath, resolved to the only option she could find. If Merrick prayed with them, she'd suffer through a thousand years of his temper. As long as he was okay. Nothing else mattered.

Mikhail nodded at her as he hurried past, sword in hand. At the sight of blood drops on the stone behind him, Anne's eyes widened. She turned her head, following the direction he took, and gasped as he entered the same off-shooting hall Gabe had dragged her down.

Her gaze settled on an imposing figure standing before a closed door. Arms crossed over his chest, feet spread wide, Farran stood at rigid attention, his stare glued straight ahead. The grimace on his face was unmistakable, and her heart tap-danced as she recognized his features. She'd never been gladder to see the surly knight. He might be unpleasant, but she'd come to realize he was honest. If anyone would tell her about Merrick, Farran would—and he wouldn't mince words.

Her skirt tangled around her legs as she ran down the corridor. He looked up as she entered the hall, and Anne didn't need anyone to tell her he wasn't happy to see her. His jaw tightened even more, and his brows drew together so severely they threatened to become one. Refusing to be intimidated by his unfriendly demeanor, Anne slowed her pace and walked up to him. "Where is he?"

"He does not wish to see you."

Anne blinked. Did Merrick know? Was he that angry with her? As the questions pummeled her mind, she gradually heard a deeper meaning to Farran's response. If Merrick didn't want to see her, he was still alive. Her pulse jumped, a wave of fierce emotion surging through her.

"Is he in there?"

"Aye."

Anne reached for the door handle, but Farran moved to block her. Positioning himself firmly in front of the opening, he barred her from entry.

"Let me in, Farran," she demanded evenly.

Farran set his hands on her shoulders and bent down to bring his gaze level with hers. "Anne, he is not himself. He waits for Mikhail to bless his soul and send him from this earth. He told me very precisely he did not wish you to see him like this."

Like hell. If Merrick was alive, she had an oath to swear. Farran could talk until he was blue in the face, and it wouldn't matter. She was going inside. No matter what it took. "I don't give a damn about what he said. Let me in."

He shook his head. "I cannot. I gave my word." His fingers tightened on her shoulders, and he turned her away from the door.

Frustration welled. The man she loved was injured. Quite possibly dying. Oaths, vows, honor . . . She'd had enough. More than enough.

In a moment of sheer insanity, Anne did the only thing she could think of. She spun on her toes and decked Farran in the jaw.

While she doubted her punch had done any real damage, he was so shocked by it, he let her go. Which freed her to do the only other thing her self-defense classes taught her—drive her knee into his groin. A low blow, yes. But desperate times called for desperate measures.

When Farran doubled over, Anne bolted through the doors. The sight that lay before her eyes, however, stilled the frantic beat of her heart. Atop a long table, Merrick still wore his surcoat and mail. His helm sat on the floor, his sword rested on his body. Just as in her vision. But her second sight had never shown her the large crimson stain around his thigh.

She closed her eyes, unable to tolerate the sight of his blood. Her stomach protested with a violent lurch, and for a moment she thought she might faint. But the low, anguished moan that drifted from his makeshift bed jerked her from the dizzying sensations.

She steeled herself with a deep breath. This was Merrick. She had the power to heal his wounds. Save his life.

Reaching behind her, she pulled the door shut and lifted her chin. Quick, determined steps brought her to Merrick's side where she set her hand on his shoulder and pressed a kiss to his battered cheek. "You came back to me," she whispered.

Merrick's lashes fluttered up. His gaze locked with hers. A flicker of confusion passed over his eyes before they welled with emotion. He closed them, licked his lips, then tried to lift his hand. The effort provoked a grimace that tore at Anne's heart. He dropped his arm back to his side. "Aye," he answered on a hiss.

His fingers free from the pommel of his sword, Anne fitted her hand in his. Though she didn't want him to see her tears, she felt them slip down her face and laid her cheek against his shoulder. His fingers tightened around hers.

The gesture spilled her heart to overflowing, and Anne cried harder. "You can't leave me. I won't let you. You already ran away once before I could tell you I love you."

Merrick's grip turned into a vise. Beneath her cheek, his shoulder shook.

* * *

To Merrick's shame, he could not order the wetness from his cheeks. Hours now, he had lain here, wanting naught more than to leave this world before Anne discovered they had lugged him home. When he learned he had turned on Caradoc, Merrick had fought Farran about his return, insisting they put an end to him on the field. Weak as he was, however, he had no means to enforce his words. Against his wishes, they brought him home to die by Mikhail's sword so his soul would know purity, and he could join those who found salvation at the Almighty's feet.

Now Anne had found him. The words he had longed to hear but could never accept tumbled off her lips. She loved him. He whom she could not have. Bitterness filled his throat, the impossibility of their circumstances too much to bear. He did not want her to remember him this way. Could not tolerate the idea of knowing she grieved.

"Anne, stop," he ordered thickly. "Let me remember you as hopeful."

She rubbed her cheek against his shoulder. The feel of his armor could not be comfortable, but the gesture had him wishing she would never stop. What he would give to find the strength to wrap his arm around her, hold her close one last time. Yet even as he imagined the feel of her soft body against his, the darkness rose to torment him. A sliver of rage needled through his veins. 'Twould not be so difficult to take her with him in death. If he dug deep enough, he could find the strength to choke off her air. Then she would never leave his side.

Merrick snatched at the remaining shards of light in his heart. Nay. He would never hurt this woman. He had to make her leave before Azazel's poison touched her. "Anne, you must go."

With a sniffle, she lifted her head and shook it in defiance. "I'm not leaving you."

He grimaced at her resolve. 'Twas the thing he loved the most about her—her courage. Yet now he wished she would be meek. "Mikhail will be here soon."

"Then let him come." She let go of his hand and slid her armband off.

Through a wary stare, he watched as she reached for his sword and pried it from his hands. "What are you doing?"

She lifted the pommel away from his body and dropped the armband around it. Then she leaned across him, gathered both his hands, and looked into his eyes. *"Meus vita, meus diligo, meus eternus lux lucis, fio vestry."*

Merrick's heart drummed to a stop. *My life, my love, my eternal light becomes yours*—the oath of seraphs. What in the name of the saints was she doing?

With the last of his strength, he lifted his head and frowned at her. "'Twill not work, Anne."

She gave his hands a shake. The tears trickled harder down her cheeks. "Just say it. Say it, damn it."

Too weary to fight, he let out a sigh. It could hurt naught, and if it made her happy, he would do it. If 'twould make her smile, make her *leave,* he would say whatever she desired. He closed his eyes, wishing with all his might the words were not just a meaningless recitation.

"Meus vires, meus mucro, meus immortalis animus, fio vestry." My strength, my sword, my immortal soul, becomes yours.

A warmth unlike any he had ever experienced slid through his veins. Through his closed eyelids, a white light burned, and Merrick opened them in disbelief. His sword shone bright, the light coming from the armband. Before his eyes, it morphed, elongated. Then moved.

The double-headed serpent wound around the pommel of his sword, forming warped quillons. One golden head opened to reveal tiny teeth that latched on to the golden cross in the center of the pommel. The other affixed itself to the inlaid dagger at the broadsword's point of balance. With one undulation of its body, the serpent shook the blackened patina between its scales free, then moved no more. A perfect barrier against Azazel's evil.

The light extinguished like a snuffed candle.

As the heat spread through Merrick's body, all but the ache within his thigh disappeared, and new strength flowed. On a gasp, he lifted to his elbows. His gaze searched Anne's face, his vision blurred at the sight of her radiant smile. "How?" he asked in wonder. "I have seen your body, Anne. Where is your mark? Why did you hide it from me?"

She pulled her hands free and wiped at her face then stepped back to set her bare foot high upon the table, beside his thigh. With a lift of her skirt, she revealed her ankle for the first time. "When I touched you, I saw a vision of you like this and overheard something Mikhail said that made me believe if I told you, you'd die." Her gaze filled with anguished remorse. "I didn't know how wrong I was, Merrick. Forgive me, please."

Merrick traced the outline of the tattoo that matched his own with a shaking finger. Forgive her? When she had sought to protect him? Nay, 'twas naught to forgive. Overcome, he dropped back on the table. "Come here so I may hold you."

Gently, she laid herself against him, and Merrick gathered her into his arms. His mouth found hers, his kiss full of all the emotion that welled in his heart. *His*—'twas too incredible for words. He lost himself to her sweet taste, unashamed of the tears that crept from the corners of his eyes to blend with hers.

The door crashed open, jarring them apart. Anne's eyes widened, and she whispered, "Uh-oh."

Lifting his head once more, Merrick found a very furious Farran standing in the doorway. His face filled with color, his eyes burned dark. Merrick needed no one to tell him the anger that clouded his brother's expression had everything to do with Anne, but for some reason he cared not. "Leave us," he ordered.

A look of such surprise filled Farran's features that Merrick could not stop a laugh. As the doors pulled shut once more, he set it free, and looked to Anne. "What have you done, little demon?"

Her cheeks stained with bright color and she dropped

her eyes from his. "I, uh. Well. He wouldn't let me in. So I made it impossible to keep me out."

He did not want to know. In truth, he did not care. He had everything he needed right here in his arms. Whilst he could not lose himself in her supple body the way he longed to, he could enjoy the pleasures of her mouth before exhaustion snuffed out his newfound strength. He dusted light kisses across her cheeks, over the bridge of her nose, then lower, in search of her honeyed lips.

Unfortunately, the Almighty seemed determined to make him wait for the privacy he craved. As the doors opened once more, Merrick pulled away from Anne with a groan. His little demon muttered beneath her breath, expressing the same displeasure, before she twisted around to investigate the cause of their interruption.

With a squeak, she slid back to her feet, exposing Merrick to Mikhail's look of consternation.

"Merrick, you are not to have visitors."

He opened his mouth to explain, but Anne stepped forward and spoke first. "Mikhail, we'll need men to move Merrick to the rooms upstairs."

The archangel studied first her, then Merrick, then Merrick's sword. Understanding crept into his stiffened features, and Mikhail clapped a hand on Merrick's shoulder. "You may have begun the healing, but 'twill be many more days before you are well enough to walk. The wound upon your thigh will require Uriel's attendance."

"I can look after his leg," Anne declared.

"Milady, I have no doubt of your talents, but 'tis to the infirmary he must go. 'Twill not be for long."

Anne squeezed Merrick's hand and lifted her chin. "Then put a cot beside his bed. I will stay with him."

Unable to take another moment of his helplessness, and possessed by the deep need to hide Anne away from the rest of the world until he was quite finished telling her just how much he cared for her, Merrick found the strength to sit upright. Slowly, he swung his legs over the edge of the table, ignoring the flames that surged up his injured thigh.

His back to Mikhail, he pulled Anne between his knees and set his smile free.

Sliding one hand through her silken hair, he murmured, "I will stay with the Lady du Loire."

"Merrick, 'tis not possible."

With a distracted shake of his head, Merrick continued, "Send my men to take me up the stairs. Uriel may tend me there." His eyes never left Anne's. Their bright blue depths drew him in, sucked him down until he drowned. She gazed back up at him, and in her softened features, Merrick read her love. It burned fierce, and strong, a holy flame that naught could extinguish. Their vows were said, no one could ever tear them apart. For the rest of time, she would stand at his side . . . and he beside her.

His heart swelled to painful limits, and he pulled her closer. In the back of his mind, he recognized the closing of the door, yet it mattered little. He had words he needed to say, regardless of who watched, or who waited.

Framing her face between his hands, he stared into her mesmerizing blue eyes. His thumbs brushed against her cheeks, and for a heartbeat, Merrick did not know the words. Yet as her lashes lowered in a slow blink, they came back in a rush.

"I love you, Anne," he whispered hoarsely.

She offered him a soft smile. "I love you."

He took her then, claimed her mouth, and kissed her thoroughly. He had lost friends, brothers he loved, and the battle had been a complete defeat. Yet here, in this tiny scrap of a woman, he found life. In time, the darkness would leave him completely. Their union would give the Order hope. He would be required to share her attention now and then, but for the moment, he selfishly let the world fade and basked in the infinite glory of her love.

Epilogue

Sophie kicked a dusty wooden crate in front of a grime-covered arched window and sat down heavily. The wide pane of glass would have overlooked the cathedral's manicured rear courtyard, but with the layers of neglect, all she could see was a thin white film that turned the world beyond into a dreary landscape.

She sighed as her sister's worry filtered through the bond that only twins could claim. It wasn't often she could sense Anne, but the more time Sophie spent locked away from the world, the once-faint bond strengthened. Not really a surprise given all the suffocating quiet Gabe forced her to accept. If she could talk to Anne, explain what had happened with Chandler, why she hadn't called in days . . .

Sophie sighed again. Wishing would get her nowhere. Gabe made his expectations clear. In exchange for the archangels' protection, Sophie was bound to this dreary attic until she mastered her metaphysical gifts. Gifts that evidently had very little to do with her affinity for ghosts, and focused on auras—something Sophie had never once witnessed before. Not only that, she had to learn to use a sword. *A sword.*

The idea was ludicrous.

Then again, everything else Gabe said bordered on insane. Demons overtaking the world, Templar Knights born centuries ago, her *sister* the reigning lady of the North American Templar stronghold? Little Anne, who loved her books, her research, and threw-up at the sight of blood, bound forever to a man who lived by the sword. Who *killed* things. Creatures like what Chandler morphed into.

Creatures like the man Sophie was fated to join.

A shudder gripped her. Rubbing her arms to ward off goose bumps, she rose from the crate. Pacing helped. With Gabriel on the other side of the country in D.C., doing whatever it was he did and unable to keep her occupied, the endless treks across the cathedral's attic eased Sophie's nerves. But when the silence set in, all she could hear was his warning words: *Prepare yourself, Sophie. You must* survive *your mate's need to kill.*

Sophie stopped in the middle of the wide-open expanse and slid the bronze serpents from her arm. Since she'd been here, she could remove the armband at will, and she turned it in the dim light, watching the tiny onyx eyes sparkle. A handful of days ago, her biggest concern was finding an emcee for the charity auction this coming weekend. Now, the fate of the world rested in her hands. Gabe hadn't exactly said *that*, but everything else he explained implied the meaning.

If only this little trinket had been a regular old antique with one of the usual ghostly presences attached to it. Life would be a hell of a lot easier then.

As she pushed the armband back over her elbow, the other emotion she regularly sensed from her sister seeped into Sophie's subconscious. Contentment. Happiness that Sophie had never felt from Anne. She knew, innately, that peacefulness came from Merrick, that this commander of the Templar knights healed all the empty places inside her sister's soul. And knowing her twin was happier than any woman had a right to be made it easier for Sophie to accept her own waiting fate.

She walked to the weapons rack on the far side of the room and withdrew the heavy broadsword Gabe had introduced before he left. It weighed down her shoulder uncomfortably. The leather-wrapped pommel chafed her palm. Yet this awkward weapon was her salvation, the only hope she would have of avoiding death.

If Anne can do this, so can I.

Lifting her shoulders in determination, Sophie set her feet apart the way Gabe had shown her and tested the broadsword by gently guiding it across her body. Somehow, someway, she'd master the art. If she didn't, she'd lose her life.

And damn it, she just wasn't in the mood to die.

TOR
ROMANCE

Believe that love is magic

Please join us at the Web site below
for more information about this
author and other great romance
selections, and to sign up for our
monthly newsletter!

www.tor-forge.com